HAMMOND INNES

Solomons Seal

FONTANA/Collins

First published in 1980 by William Collins Sons & Co Ltd
This continental edition first issued in Fontana Books 1981

Made and printed in Great Britain by
William Collins Sons & Co. Ltd., Glasgow

SOLOMONS SEAL

HAMMOND INNES's highly individual and successful
novels are the result of travel in outback parts of the
world. Many of them follow the central character to
strange countries where the forces of nature, as much
as people, provide the conflict. He has also written two
books of travel and one of history. His international
reputation as a story-teller keeps his books in print;
they have been translated into over thirty foreign
languages.

This story of a unique ship stamp, and of the family
that required it for their schooner trading in the South
West Pacific, was the result of a journey Hammond
Innes made to Bougainville and Papua New Guinea in
1975, just before Independence. From his earliest
days, he always wanted to write a novel about the
Pacific; not the Pacific of coral islands and blue
lagoons, but the real Pacific where the Western World
breaks in upon old cultures. Sorcery, the Cargo Cult
and a copper-rich island on the brink of revolution –
hardly was the writing complete before rebellion broke
out in the neighbouring New Hebrides group.

CONTENTS

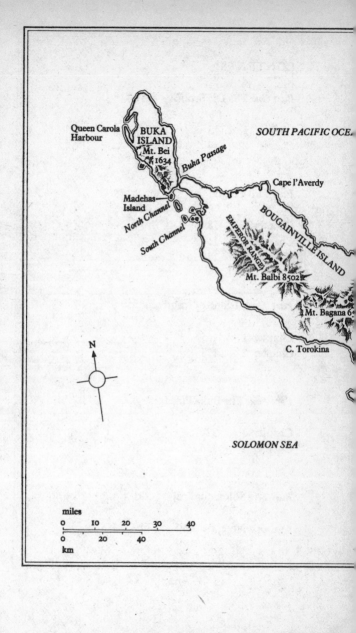

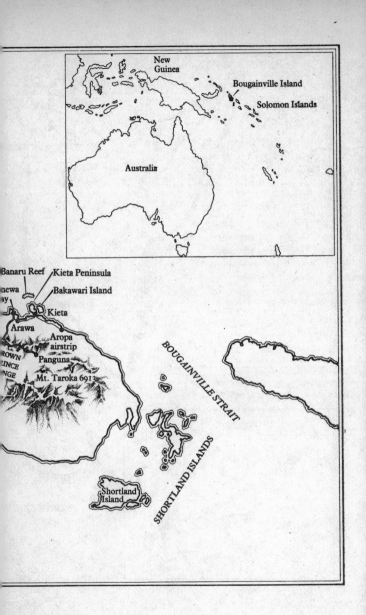

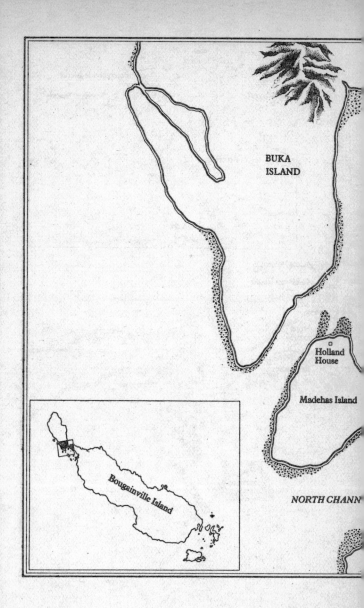

BUKA
ISLAND

Holland
House

Madehas Island

Bougainville Island

NORTH CHANN

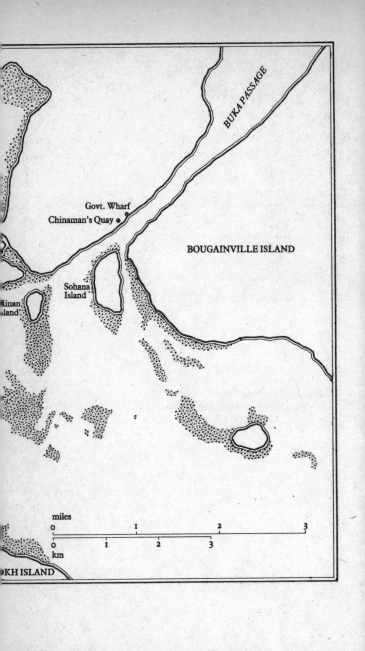

BUKA PASSAGE

Govt. Wharf
Chinaman's Quay ●

BOUGAINVILLE ISLAND

Sohana
Island

Minan
sland

miles
0   1   2   3

km
0   1   2   3

KH ISLAND

PART ONE

THE DIE PROOFS

===

1

It all began so quietly, so very ordinarily – a routine job, something any junior in an estate agent's office could have handled. The only difference that morning was that my mood did not match the brightness of the day. I was, in fact, in an odd frame of mind when I arrived at the house, the girl I had been living with married to a farmer, myself turned forty, and now the very real prospect of being out of a job.

The instructions to sell the contents of The Passage, River Road, Aldeburgh, had come from Rose, Walker & Chandler, a London firm of solicitors based on Chelmsford. They also wanted an indication of the market value of the house itself. I had glanced at their letter briefly, lying on the beach after a swim. The contents of the house were the property of a Mr Timothy Holland, whose family they had acted for over many years. He was now seriously ill and had been moved into a nursing home. During his illness he had apparently been looked after by an unmarried sister, so that I was expecting to be greeted by a faded spinster as I stood there on the doorstep in the blazing sun.

It was four years since I had started working for Browne, Baker & Browne, always with a partnership in mind, and now that one of them had died suddenly the vacancy had gone to Sam Baker's nephew. Maybe he did have a better education and London auction room experience, but it was still plain bloody nepotism, and that's what I had told the senior partner when I had stormed in to see him the night before. It hadn't exactly helped, my temper getting the better of me and the old man sitting there like a half-poisoned owl, peering at me over his glasses and informing me, very coldly, that a partnership was out of the question, I hadn't the right temperament.

Half my life gone and nothing to show for it – just an old car, an older boat, a few nice pieces of furniture and some stamps. No education, no qualifications, no bloody future, and now this piddling little contents sale thrust on me because Packer was in hospital, a listing and valuation job any junior clerk in the office could have done. I jabbed my finger on the bell, feeling hot and sticky with salt after my bathe. There was no passage anywhere to explain the name on the brick porch, and the house itself was little more than a glorified bungalow, much like its neighbours except that the paint was peeling from the window frames and there was a general air of neglect. This did not extend to the front garden, however, which was full of roses and carefully tended.

The door opened and a woman's voice said, 'Mr Packer?'

'No, my name's Roy Slingsby.' And when I explained that Packer was in hospital and I had come in his place, she thanked me for keeping the appointment. 'Come in, please.' I couldn't see her very clearly, the hallway dark after the glare of the sun. In any case, it was the contents I had come to catalogue and my eyes went immediately to a wooden carving on a rather ornate mahogany side table. I couldn't place the design of it, which annoyed me, for I was certain I had seen something like it quite recently on a commemorative issue.

'Where would you like to begin?'

'Oh, here will do,' I said, putting my briefcase down on the table. 'This figure – ' I bent forward to examine it. 'African?'

'No. South West Pacific.' She had one of those gentle, implacable voices, a slight huskiness in it, and I thought I detected a certain hostility, as though she hadn't yet come to terms with her brother's absence, the protective instinct still strong. 'I think it's from the Mortlocks, or maybe New Britain –

I can't remember. Does it say on the bottom?'

I picked it up and turned it over. A small square of paper had been gummed to the base and in tiny, spidery writing, the ink faded and slightly smudged, I could just make out the words: *Gift from Rev. G. Robinson, Rabaul 1908.* 'Yes, that's right,' she said as I read it out to her. 'New Britain – Rabaul is in New Britain.' She sounded ill-at-ease as though conscious that her resentment of my intrusion was uncalled for. 'They belonged to my grandfather. I'm afraid they're – well, a little crude if you see what I mean. But exciting.' She gave a quick nervous laugh. 'I wouldn't like to have to sell them. They're all I've got left. ` . . .' Her voice trailed away on a note of sadness, or was it something else? The atmosphere of the house was strangely oppressive.

The carving was in some black heavy wood not unlike ebony, but rougher, perhaps ironwood, and it was certainly crude, the frightening features elongated to what was almost a beak and an exaggerated phallus equally long. 'This isn't the only one you have then?'

'No.'

I hesitated, looking down at it and wondering at the primitive mind that had carved this travesty of the human figure. It both repelled and fascinated, so that I guessed it was good of its kind, and now that I knew where it had come from I could remember seeing similar carvings in the junk shops of Singapore.

She must have sensed my reaction for she said hesitantly, 'You think it's valuable, do you?'

I looked at her then, seeing her eyes staring at me, dark-ringed and very large in the gloom of the hallway, her face framed in a frizzy cap of golden-red hair that was almost orange and matched the freckles on her clear skin. She wore no make-up, her mouth a tight defensive line and her nose oddly flattened as though it had been broken at some time. 'Look, Miss Holland,' I said, feeling the need to reassure her, 'it's entirely up to you what you sell and what you keep. You say it's not to go on the list and it won't.' And then, out of curiosity, I asked her how many of them she had.

She shook her head a little awkwardly. 'I – can't remember. I stored some of them away in a trunk in the loft. If you want to see them . . . it's very dusty, I'm afraid. I haven't had time to go up there for so long. But I suppose, if they're valuable . . .' Her voice trailed away.

'No,' I said. 'I don't think they're valuable, just interesting. If it was a case of insurance, or you did decide to include them in the sale, then I think I would advise an expert opinion. Primitive art of this sort is a specialized field and I haven't the faintest idea what they're worth.' I put the carved figure back in its place. 'I'll exclude them, shall I?' I was certain that was what she wanted, though she was very hesitant, thinking it over a few moments before she finally gave a quick decisive nod. 'Yes. I wouldn't want them to go for next to nothing at a local sale. It will be a local sale, won't it?'

'Yes, Ipswich probably. Or we may feel we could get a better price by putting the furniture into our Chelmsford auction room.' I had already glanced through into the sitting room, my eyes, accustomed now to the gloom, taking in the worn chintz covers, the threadbare carpet, the rather sparse furniture and the absence of antiques. It was all down-market stuff and I hoped she wasn't relying on the sale to support her brother in the nursing home for long.

'And those carvings, they would go to London?'

'I would think so.'

'Good, then I can always change my mind, if I have to.'

'So long as you can find somebody to house them in the meantime.' I said it jokingly, but her eyes remained large and serious and she didn't smile. I opened my briefcase and got out my clipboard. 'Now, if you care to leave me to work steadily through the house from room to room I'll make the inventory.'

'And you're valuing everything, aren't you?' When I told her it was only a rough valuation, she said, 'So long as I have some idea what we can expect to get out of the sale.' She stood there for a moment longer, staring past me into the sitting room, a withdrawn look on her face, so that I didn't know whether she was regretting the need to part with treasured possessions, which is something one gets used to in this business, people feeling the accumulation of inanimate objects as somehow personal to themselves, or whether she was thinking of her brother and mentally trying to equate the sale proceeds to the nursing home charges. 'Well, I'll leave you to get on with it,' she added, suddenly making an effort at brightness.

'It won't take me very long,' I said. 'Two hours maybe.'

She left me then, a slim figure in jeans, her movements quick and decisive. She was younger than I had expected and somehow disturbing, an impression that stayed with me as I got down to the job of listing the contents. Normally I dealt with the agricultural side and it was some time since I had handled this sort of a sale. I had never liked it. Almost always there is some female member of the family hanging possessively around as you prepare the catalogue and either they are emotionally upset at the loss of familiar things that have become dear to them over the years or else they are there as predators, trying to figure out just how much it is going to cost them to get their hands on old Aunt So-and-So's cherished table, desk, commode, whatever it is. Here it was somewhat different in that, except for the carvings and some of the pictures, the contents were mostly functional and not items anyone would become greatly attached to. But all the time I was working on the inventory I was conscious of the presence of that young woman in the house, and it was a strangely disconcerting presence.

She made hardly a sound, and yet all the time I was working steadily round the downstair rooms, I was aware of her being there in the house with me. And the house itself, it had an unpleasantly sombre atmosphere, so that I found myself thinking about the man who was the cause of the sale, the man who had been ill here and was now in a home. It was as though something of his personality still lingered, or else the pain of his suffering. This brooding presence, this sense of something hanging over the house – it was in such startling contrast to the happy brilliance of the day outside. And in every room there were those bizarre carvings.

I was in the dining room when I heard the clatter of the loft ladder. I had the cutlery out on the table, all of it EPNS and badly worn, and I stood there wondering what it was she had hidden up there. But there was no sound of movement, everything very still, and I got back to the inventory, anxious only to get out of the house, back into the sunshine.

By the time I started upstairs she was in the kitchen and the loft ladder was back in place. The larger of the two bedrooms had obviously been her brother's. There was a swing table and the bed had an invalid rest against the headboard. The hospital aroma of sickness and medicine still lingered. There were no wood carvings in that room, but the pictures on the wall attracted my attention. They were bright primitive paintings of palms and flat calm seas, also faded photographs of ships that looked like small trading schooners taken against towering, jungle-covered mountains. The room seemed different then, my mood changing as I realized that the sick man belonged to a world I only knew in my imagination. The pictures, those carvings – the South West Pacific, she had said. Of course, the carvings were like the designs on some of the Papua New Guinea stamps. I no longer felt depressed, only curious that the family should have abandoned such a colourful world for England and this wretched little house, which now had an exotic feel to it, wild relics of a dead past cocooned in an almost suburban wrapping.

I had moved to the smaller bedroom, and was staring at a large wooden mask hanging on the wall above the bed, when her voice startled me: 'I thought you might like some refreshment, Mr Slingsby.' I turned to find her standing in the doorway, a tray of tea in her hands, some books under her arm, and for the first time I saw her clearly, illumined by the sunlight pouring through the window. The hair and the freckles really did match, and her eyes, which were large and brown and slightly prominent, were fixed on me in a most disturbing way. She was no longer dressed in jeans. She had changed into a cotton frock, green and quite plain, her small breasts thrusting at it in a very demanding way.

'Thank you,' I said quickly. 'Some tea would be great.' I was staring at her, conscious of her figure, everything about her. Conscious, too, of the effect she was having on me. It wasn't just her youth, or even the protruding breasts, that extraordinary cap of brilliantly coloured hair now catching the sun. It was something much more powerful, a deep current passing between us, so that I just stood there watching her as she crossed to the dressing table, put down the tray and laid the books carefully beside it. 'Milk?' she asked and I nodded, feeling overwhelmed and at the same time a little ridiculous at being dumbfounded by something I'd never experienced before. In an effort to pull myself together, I said, 'This is your bedroom, is it?'

'Yes.' She had turned and was smiling at me, the full lips turned up at the corners, a glint of laughter in her eyes. 'You're wondering how I can go to bed with that dreadful face hanging over me.' The smile broadened, a flash of long, very white teeth. 'You must think my taste very odd, but I've lived with them all my life. They remind me of the world I used to know.' She turned her head, staring out of the window towards the sea. 'It made life more bearable.' Her voice, intense and tinged with nostalgia, was husky, barely above a whisper. Then she seemed to collect herself, bending quickly to pour the tea. 'Do sit down. It's very hot and you haven't stopped — ' She stood for a moment, the cup in her hand, staring out of the window. 'You can see the sea up here. It's the only room in the house that looks out to the sea. Sugar?'

I shook my head, looking round for somewhere to sit other than the bed. There was nowhere except the dressing table stool. She handed me my cup, and having poured her own, perched herself on the broad window ledge. Seeing her there, against the light, she seemed like something caged-in and on the verge of flight, her hair in the sunlight red-bronze, like a burnished helmet. There was a long silence as she sat there drinking her tea and staring out of the window.

'I had a bathe before I came here,' I said. 'It must be nice living so close to the sea.'

She nodded abstractedly. 'I used to swim, once. But my father was a sick man, and then Tim came back. I never had

19

time after that.' And she added almost harshly, 'My brother was paralysed, you see.' There was another silence. Then she said very quickly, 'It's been a long time, and now he's dying.'

I thought perhaps she wanted to talk about it and almost without thinking I asked her what he was dying of.

'Sorcery'. She said it so quietly, so matter-of-factly that I thought for a moment I must have misheard her. But then she added, still in the same tone of voice as though she were talking about something as common as cancer, 'As a kiap – a patrol officer – he had a lot of experience of that sort of thing. Of course, the doctor says it's the effect of the accident, some sort of stroke following the spinal injury. But I told him it wasn't that.' She gave a nervous little giggle. 'It was really very funny, his face. Sorcery! Dammit, the silly little man thought I was out of my mind. He started prescribing sleeping pills, pain killers, all that rubbish. Not that it mattered, no doctor's going to cure him of sorcery or enter that on a death certificate, is he? Not here in England. But that's what it'll be. Tim's had a death wish put on him, and he knows it.'

I stared down at my inventory, feeling confused and wondering to what extent she was suffering from shock. 'He was a patrol officer, you say,' I heard myself murmur. 'Was he in the Army then?'

'No, not the Army. Civil Administration. In the Goroka District. He was very badly injured and invalided home.' She hesitated, but before I could ask her where Goroka was, she said, 'It's been a long time, and now . . .' She shrugged. 'With him gone I feel a little lost.' Again that effort to collect herself. 'You're just about through now, aren't you? This is the last room.'

'Unless there is anything of value in the loft that you want included in the sale.'

She hesitated, then shook her head. 'No, nothing.'

'Any jewellery you want disposed of?'

She laughed. 'All that went long ago.' She was silent then as though recollecting, then she gave a little sigh. 'Mother left me her things. They were beautiful, mostly native work. But they didn't fetch much.' Her eyes fell involuntarily to her hands, which were strongly formed and capable, the wrists slim and bare, no rings on the short, broad fingers. 'I hated parting with them. But I kept the carvings.' She said it almost defiantly. 'My grandfather gave them to me and I've nothing else to remember him by.'

She sat there for a moment as though thinking about him. Then she said, 'Do you have a safe in your office?'

'Yes.' I concentrated on my tea, wondering what was coming, still thinking about her brother and his mysterious illness.

'I was hoping perhaps you'd have room for these two albums.' She nodded to the books on the dressing table. They were old leather-bound volumes with metal clasps.

'Yours?' I asked, not quite certain on whose authority the sale was being made, was on her brother's.

There was a momentary hesitation, then she said, 'Yes. Yes, I suppose they are now.' She was staring towards the sea again. And then as though conscious that she had been speaking as though her brother were already dead, she went on quickly, 'They were among his things when he was sent home. He couldn't speak at all then, but I knew they were important. We were very close, you see. And then Jona wrote – that's my elder brother – he said if Tim ever recovered he thought he'd want to make some enquiries about them. So I kept them here, hidden in the loft.'

'What are they, diaries?' I asked.

'No. Stamps. It's a collection of stamps.'

I didn't say anything for a moment, the collector's instinct suddenly taking hold, a feeling of excitement. Only once before in the years since I had switched from marine engine salesman to estate agent had the job given me the opportunity to acquire a collection direct from the owner. My eyes were fastened on the albums, wondering what was inside those battered leather covers. They looked Victorian, in which case there could be some early GBs. But this was a young woman I was dealing with, not a business man. 'You could put them in the bank,' I said, 'or it might be better to let the solicitors hold them.'

She shook her head, those large prominent eyes of hers staring at me intensely. 'I'd rather you kept them,' she said.

It was an odd request. 'Why? If they're valuable. . . .'

'It isn't that – though I wondered, of course, when things became really difficult. Anyway, I didn't know how to go about selling them, and there was never any time. . . .' She hesitated, still staring at me, but her gaze had turned inward. 'No. I just want to know they're safe, that's all. I don't want them in the house any more.' That husky voice of hers was low-pitched now, almost a whisper, her thoughts a little disconnected. 'Something Jona wrote in a letter. I keep on remembering. He's never been much of a letter writer, too wrapped up in his ship. He did write to me about Tim's future. I'd cabled him about the nursing home charges, but even then his letter was all about the need for an engine overhaul which meant Australia and no cargo earnings. It's very expensive running a ship, I know, but – '

There was a long pause, and then she suddenly looked at me again and said. 'But about those stamps, he did write that Tim had been very excited when he discovered them. I don't know why. That was just after the accident and I couldn't get any sense out of Tim, of course.' Her eyes went to the windows again. Another, longer pause, then she said, 'You've got to remember he wasn't very coherent. There was brain damage as well. That's why I put them in the loft. I thought he might suddenly want them. He had moments when he could communicate, after a fashion. But he was very strange, very unpredictable. About a fortnight ago, just before I finally persuaded the nursing home to take him – they're some sort of charitable hangover from colonial days and very choosy, it seems, about who they take – he suddenly seemed to want to see them again, and when I brought them down to him he lay staring at them most of the day. Then he suddenly lost interest. He was like that.' Her voice was very low, falling almost to a whisper. 'If ever I catch up with the man who did that to him, I'll kill him.'

It was said so quietly, without emotion, in the same matter-of-fact way she had mentioned sorcery. If she had said it wildly I could have put it down to her being overwrought. But she wasn't overwrought or in any way hysterical. She just sat there, making a flat statement, and that made it all the more frightening. I didn't know what to say. 'Can I have a look at the albums?'

'Yes, of course.' Her eyes were staring past me at the mask above the bed, her tone offhand.

I put down my cup and picked the albums up. They were identical, measuring about eight inches by five, the leather dark green, almost black, and very thick, the clasps gilt, two to each album, and the hinges damaged. The pages were loose-leaved, a heavy cartridge paper, the stamps carefully presented, sometimes only one to a page, sometimes complete sets. Many of them were unused and in the case of the sets most of them were overprinted SPECIMEN. No early GBs, no Queen's heads, virtually the whole collection devoted to views, ships, a sprinkling of animals, and all about the turn of the century. Nothing very early and every stamp stuck down, which was a pity.

The first volume I looked through contained nothing but Canadian provincials and Australian states. There was a Specimen set of Tasmanian scenes which was particularly attractive and the last two pages were taken up with what looked like proofs. But it was the second volume that interested me, an exclusively island collection; Malta, Papua, North Borneo, Samoa, Tonga, Bermuda, Cook Island, Jamaica – ships, canoes, galleys, coats of arms, island scenes, and in the case of Samoa a page of the EXPRESS stamps. There was a nice Specimen set of Turks and Caicos to the full 3s. value, all with ships, and a very battered imperforate stamp, blue with a white sailing ship and the script letters *LMcL* underneath, stuck to the centre of the page so that it caught my eye. It was pen-cancelled and rang some faint bell in my memory.

'Well?' she asked as I sat looking at it, trying to remember an island that had issued a stamp with no designation on it, only a monogram. 'I read somewhere that old stamps had kept pace with inflation.'

I nodded. 'Better than most things. But I couldn't give you even a rough idea what these are worth, not till I've checked them through with the catalogue. Even then I won't be certain because of their condition.'

'I think my brother realized we were short of money. That day when he lay there staring at them, I was helping him over his lunch – ' She stopped there, a muscle in her cheek twitching at the memory. 'I don't know whether I understood him right, but I thought he tried to tell me they would be worth a lot to somebody.'

I thought she meant a collector, or a dealer, and I said, 'I think I should warn you they won't fetch anything like the catalogue value. It's an interesting little collection, well arranged, but I don't think there's anything very rare and none of them are in mint condition. They're stuck down, you see. Mint condition requires that the original gum on the back is intact.'

'I see.' She frowned. 'You're not a stamp dealer, are you?'

'No, but I collect them.' And I told her how as a kid I had used any money that came my way to buy pictorials. 'They were quite cheap then and it was a sort of displacement activity, I suppose, a world in which I could forget that my parents were at each other's throats and only staying together on account of me. Lately I've been taking advantage of the rise in market values to switch into line-engraved issues, concentrating on Great Britain and the Caribbean, islands like Antigua, St Kitts, St Vincent, Turks and Caicos.'

'So you know some of the dealers?'

'Two or three, yes. When I get the chance I buy at auctions. It's usually cheaper at auctions.' I hesitated, not sure what she wanted. 'Would you like me to get a valuation for you?' And as I said it I knew it had been prompted by a desire to see her again.

'Could you?' She was silent a moment, thinking about it. 'Thank you, yes, I'd be very glad if you would.'

It was as easy as that and feeling slightly pleased with myself I finished my tea and picked up the clipboard. Knowing something of her circumstances now I said, 'Is there anything else – anything I've missed – that you want either included in the sale or else for me to value for you while I'm here?'

'No, I don't think there's anything else. Just about everything that's left belongs to Tim, I suppose. I don't own very much now except my clothes.' And she added, 'There was a time when we were quite well off, but when my father finally died – ' She hesitated. 'I knew he'd been financing Jona, but not the extent of it. There wasn't much left for Tim except the house, and these last two years I've sold off what I could. There's nothing of any real value here now. Can I give you some more tea?'

I thanked her, studying the inventory as she refilled my cup. The contents I had listed wouldn't fetch enough to keep him very long, even if the nursing home was charity-run, and to get her mind off the subject of finance, I asked her about the carvings. 'Was it your grandfather who collected them?'

'My great-uncle.'

'He was a missionary, was he?' I was thinking of the label on the base of that wooden figure downstairs.

She seemed amused. 'No, he was the black sheep of the family. An inveterate liar, that's how my grandfather described him. But he wouldn't talk about him, except once long ago I remember he said his brother had got into some sort of trouble. He shipped out on a wool ship to Australia and wasn't heard of again for several years. Then he suddenly turned up in England boasting he owned an island and some schooners and had become king of a lot of cannibals in a world where they believed their ancestors were butterflies.' She gave a little shrug. 'My grandfather was always reminiscing about people with strange backgrounds, so I didn't take much notice. I was a child at the time, but I liked the bit about the butterflies.'

'It was his brother then who gave him the carvings?'

'Yes, his younger brother Carlos.'

'And he gave him the carvings to convince him of his improbable story, I suppose.'

She laughed. 'No, I think he just left them with Grandpa so they'd be safe. I've often wondered about that, whether he had some sort of premonition. He was drowned, you see, on his way back to the Pacific. He had come to England to raise money for the purchase of a steamship and was drowned when it sank.' And when I asked her where it had sunk, she said, 'In the Pacific, somewhere east of Papua. But God knows where. There weren't any survivors. He had named her the *Holland Trader*.' And she added, 'It happened a long time ago, in 1911. Sad, isn't it?'

She turned her head from the window and smiled at me. 'That's all I ever got out of my grandfather. He wouldn't talk about him. The subject was taboo. So maybe you're right. Maybe Carlos Holland did bring those carvings home to prove he was telling the truth for once.' And she added in that husky whisper, 'I think of him sometimes. An odd name, Carlos – for an Englishman. And the man himself a complete mystery. If only he had kept a diary.'

'Is that why you've hung on to the carvings?'

She nodded. 'It's teasing to know so little – no letters, nothing; just those carvings, and the stamps. You'll find his name inside the albums.' I thought her interest in the man was the natural reaction of somebody whose life had been very restricted, but then she said, 'Strange I should still have relics of his world and nothing left of my grandfather's. He had marvellous things – native head-dresses and spears. But they were all left behind when my father sold Kuamegu. I can only dimly remember them now, and the brilliance of the poinsettias, the women with their bare pointed breasts and the men wearing nothing but a few broad grass fronds – arse grass we called it – hanging from a waist cord.' She gave that little shrug and got to her feet. 'It was all very primitive, wonderfully colourful.' She began gathering up the tea things. 'You have finished, haven't you?'

'Yes.' I was thinking how wrong I had been, her background so very different from my own. 'You were born out there?'

'At Kuamegu, yes. It was a coffee plantation in the Highlands about five thousand feet up in the Chimbu country.' She stood there for a moment, very still. 'Buka wasn't the same, hot and

humid, always raining. And living at Madehas. . . .' She turned
away. 'After Mother was killed we came here. That was
something different again, and when you've no money. . . .' She
stopped abruptly, gave a little self-derisory laugh and picked up
the albums. 'I don't know why I'm talking to you like this.
Stupid of me. I'll get these wrapped up.'

She left me then and I sat there for a moment, the clipboard
on my knee, wondering where Buka was, what part of the
Pacific she had been talking about. Doing my National Service
in Singapore as a junior officer on landing craft, I had had just a
glimpse of the Pacific, the only exciting bit of travel I had ever
managed to achieve, and here was this strange young woman
talking about it as though the Pacific islands were more home to
her than England. What would she do now? *If I ever catch up
with the man. . . .* those shocking words came suddenly back to
me. But with her brother to support, the sale of the contents
wouldn't get her out to the Pacific, and from what she had said I
guessed the house itself was mortgaged. I wasn't certain what
age she was – late twenties, early thirties, it was difficult to tell.
And the way she had looked, sitting there, staring out at the sea.
If she intended going back, then the stamps were her only hope,
and as I got to my feet I was wondering whether I could find the
money to buy them from her. Stuck down like that they couldn't
be worth more than two or three hundred pounds.

I put the clipboard in my briefcase and stood staring out of
the window at the sea. It was milky calm, the horizon lost in
haze. I thought of all the times she must have stood here in her
bedroom looking out at it, and at night in moonlight, longing to
be away. If it had been anybody else, if she hadn't talked like
that, then I could have made her an offer for those stamps and
she would probably have taken it. I don't know why I wanted
them so badly. It wasn't the stamps themselves. I had some of
them already and the others I could have bought from Josh
Keegan or one of the other dealers in the Strand. No, it was
something in the careful way they had been stuck into those
albums, the planned choice of subjects, almost as though there
had been some purpose in collecting just those items and

presenting them in that particular way.

I knew it was foolish of me. Even that second album didn't contain a single stamp of the islands on which I was now concentrating. But collecting is like that. You see something and suddenly, for no apparent reason, you want it. Would she take £400 for them? I could probably raise that much on a quick sale of some Penny Blacks. But as I started down the stairs I knew I couldn't do it. Without a valuation it would be taking advantage of her, and I had promised to get them valued.

She was waiting for me at the bottom of the stairs, and as she saw me to the door, handing me the albums neatly wrapped, all I said was, 'I'll do what I can for you, Miss Holland. There's a member of my sailing club, a retired naval commander, who deals in stamps. I'll ask him to have a look at them. But please don't bank on their being worth very much.'

She shook her head and the light coming from the door showed a deep scar running back from behind her left ear into the orange-red cap of hair. 'Of course not. I no longer expect anything to be made easy for me.' And then with a quick lift of her chin – 'I'll find a way.' It was said to herself, not to me. She held out her hand. 'Thank you. I'm glad you came, you've been very kind.'

I was thinking about her, and about the way she had said *I'll find a way* for most of the drive back to Chelmsford. I just couldn't get her out of my mind. I couldn't think of any girl who had made such an instant and deep impression on me, and God knows I've never been short of girl-friends. But it had always been physical before. This wasn't physical. I didn't know what the hell it was. I'd read about people falling in love, but that was in books. The real life relationship was sex, the physical meeting of two bodies. It was what men and women were all about. But not this one. The impact had been entirely different, an emotional intensity, an emanation almost of something totally alien to me as though she had the power to project herself into my mind. It wasn't her face, or her figure, or even those extraordinarily prominent breasts that I was remembering now. It was the impression she had made, her strange background, those dreadful words of hers and her face so set, and that reference to the death certificate, talking of her brother as though he were already dead. 'You think your brother will die then?' I had asked her, and she had replied, 'Unless I can do something about it, get that death wish lifted.'

It seemed such nonsense, in the hot sun driving down the A12. But in that house, in her presence, talking to her, it had all seemed real enough. And there were those two battered green albums lying on the seat beside me. It was almost as though she were there herself, so powerful had been the impact of her personality.

That evening, instead of going down to the boat, I drove straight home, taking the albums with me. Great Park Hall, at the end of almost a mile of dirt farm track, was a very lonely place, which was the reason the rent was within my means. To call it a hall made it sound grander than it was; almost any old farmhouse in East Anglia can be called a hall. It was, in fact, little more than a cottage full of centuries old beams with the remains of a moat taking up most of the overgrown garden. I was fending for myself now and with a tankard of beer and some chicken sandwiches I settled down to check the stamps against the catalogue.

My British Commonwealth catalogue was two years old, but at least it would give me a rough idea of what the collection was worth. And as I worked through the albums page by page my excitement grew. I was the only collector who had ever seen them, and whether she wanted to or not, I was certain she would sell them in the end. She knew she'd have to. Why else had she wanted them valued? The question was, what was the fair price?

It took me just over two hours to list them. There were 247 stamps ranging in value from almost nothing to £65 for the Turks and Caicos Specimen set of nine sailing ship stamps. The total added up to £1,163, excluding the proofs and the ship stamp with the script lettering *LMcL*.

By then the sun had set and the light was fading. I sat there for a long time idly going through the thick pages of the albums again, wondering what sort of a figure a dealer would put on them. I thought perhaps half, or even a third, of the catalogue value, for the more valuable unused and Specimen stamps were not only stuck down, but many of them showed signs of discolouration caused probably by damp.

I suppose it was the island scenes that started me dreaming of the Pacific. Ever since my Singapore days I had wanted to see more of the Pacific. I didn't switch on the light, but sat there in the half dark, thinking about my own future and what I should do if Rowlinson did offer me the job of looking after his Australian interests, something I had been angling for even before I knew the partners weren't going to let me in. He had rung me up two days ago saying his manager had finally promised him the figures for the Queensland station within a week. If that LCT I had served on hadn't poked its nose into the Pacific north of Indonesia, maybe I wouldn't have been so pleased at the prospect of Australia. But my appetite had been whetted and since then I hadn't been out of England except to sail my Folkboat across to Holland and spend a few days in the Dutch canals.

And that girl – she had spent most of her life out there . . . *very primitive, wonderfully colourful.* I was remembering the way she had said that, the nostalgic whisper of her voice. And now she was free.

If I offered her five hundred, would that be enough to take her where she wanted to go?

I switched on the light then and spent an hour running through the catalogue, searching for that stamp I hadn't been able to identify. I had an uneasy feeling that it might be valuable, even though it was spoilt by an ink cancellation; also it was slightly creased and appeared to have been cut into at the top righthand corner. I even tried an old Stanley Gibbons World Catalogue, concentrating all the time on the islands of the Pacific, but in the end I had to give it up. I just couldn't find it. Nor could I identify the proofs, which were printed in black on thick paper and showed what looked like a seal in a rectangular frame and also the frame separately.

It was not until Sunday evening that I was finally able to contact Tubby Sawyer. He had been north along the coast as far as the Deben estuary for a few days and I called across, inviting him over for a drink, as he drifted up on the tide to his moorings. He was a short stout man with blue seaman's eyes in a round babyish face, and coming alongside in his tiny plastic dinghy he looked like a frog balanced precariously in the cup of a waterlily. 'And to what do I owe the doubtful pleasure of being offered a gin on your old Folkboat?' he asked, squeezing himself in through the hatch and lowering his heavy bottom into the space at the head of the only berth. He wore a tattered blue sweater, oily jeans, and his bare toes were poking out of his salt-stiff deck shoes. 'First time this season.' He grinned at me, leaning frayed woollen elbows on the makeshift table. 'There must be a catch in it.'

'There is,' I said. 'I want you to value some stamps for me.'

'Free of charge, I suppose.'

'Of course.' And I explained about Miss Holland's circumstances as I poured him his pink gin.

'Any particular period?'

'Victorian, most of them.' I gave him his drink and put the albums down in front of him. 'See what you think. There's one I haven't been able to identify, and where there's just one stamp to the page like that it makes them look important even if they aren't.'

He sat there for a moment gazing at the worn leather covers with their gilt fastenings. 'These are the sort of albums Victorian ladies used for drawing miniatures, writing poems, pressing flower collections, that sort of thing.'

I poured myself a drink and watched him as he opened first one, then the other, leafing quickly through the loose pages. 'You're right about the period, anyway. The end of Queen Victoria's reign, most of them stamps in issue in the late 1800s, and all of them stuck down tight.' He shook his head sadly. 'Still, it's probably better than if they were hinged with gummed strips from the sheet margin, a very common practice in those days.' He turned to the island album and began going through it slowly, page by page, until he came to the blue stamp with *LMcL* below the ship. He paused there and sipped his drink. 'This the one you couldn't identify?' And when I nodded, he said, 'Try Trinidad. The "Lady McLeod". Its value may surprise you.'

I sat down on the berth opposite him, watching his face which was lit by the evening sun slanting in through the open hatch. He was turning the pages again and I couldn't be sure from his expression whether the stamp would put the collection beyond my reach. He came to the end and lit a cigarette, leaning back, his eyes half closed. 'Well?' I asked.

'Don't be so impatient. I haven't finished yet.' He smiled. 'But it's interesting – very. I'll tell you why in a minute.' And he leaned forward again and began working his way through the second volume. It was so quiet on board I could hear the ticking of the ship's clock and the gurgle of the tide making against the bows. And then, when he came to the proofs, he held the two loose leaves up to catch the light, peering at them closely. 'Do you use a magnifying glass when you're charting?'

'Yes, do you want it?'

'Please.'

I found it for him and he went over those last two pages again, examining the proofs through the glass. 'Know anything about the person who put this little collection together?' He seemed quite excited.

'A little,' I said. 'But I'd rather hear what you think first.'

He hesitated, the corners of those bright blue eyes crinkling. 'Want me to stick my neck out, do you? All right, but tell me something first. This client of yours who's had such a poor time of it, does she want to sell, or don't you know yet?'

'I think that would depend on the price,' I said cautiously.

He laughed. 'I never doubted you were a good agent, Roy, but don't get too excited. We're not dealing with the earlies here, no Mauritius or other rarities, except for the "Lady McLeod". Put it this way, is she after a quick cash sale, or is she going to send them to auction? You can tell me that surely.' And he added, 'At auction, as you very well know, it could take four months, even longer, before she got her money.'

'Are you interested in them personally then?' I hadn't expected that.

He hesitated, then said, 'Yes. Yes, I think I might be. Not because of the value of the stamps, but because of the collection as a collection. It has a distinct curiosity value.'

'How do you mean?'

'You've looked through it. Didn't anything strike you?'

I nodded. 'New Zealand and those Australian states, you'd expect a man living somewhere in the South Pacific to collect them. But there are Canadian provincials as well, a lot of Newfoundland. And most of them unused, so it looks as though he visited the eastern seaboard of Canada, maybe traded there.'

'It's possible.' But he sounded doubtful. 'My guess is he simply wrote for them so that he could see what they were like.' He picked up the last two pages and turned them round so that I could see them. 'Know what these are?'

'Proofs,' I said. 'But it did occur to me they might be fakes.'

'Look again.' And he pushed one of the pages towards me.

I bent forward, examining once again the two little rectangles of thick yellowish paper, one showing the frame of the stamp, the other simply the unadorned shape of what looked like an Arctic or North Atlantic seal. On the other page there was just the one rectangle of paper showing the seal inside the frame. 'Doesn't anything strike you now?'

I shook my head. There was no value given, no indication of country, the frame surround all black.

He turned the pages round, lost in thought as he stared down at them. 'I'm not quite sure if they're die or plate proofs. That's why I wanted the magnifying glass. The whole process, as you know, starts with the die and it is from this original picture, engraved on the flat, that the roller impression is taken by rocking it back and forth over the die under pressure. This transfer, or roller die, is then used to transfer the impression, again by rocking back and forth, on to the actual plate from which the final stamp will be printed. Now, I *think* these are die proofs. That's to say, they're taken from the original flat engraving; in the case of the one showing the seal inside the frame, both dies have been used on the same sheet of paper, the proofs being struck off singly. They have that extra sharpness. If they were plate proofs they would have been taken from the plate itself after it had been hardened for printing the full sheet of stamps.' He leafed back through the album, pausing several times. Finally he turned again to the pages with the proofs. 'Very interesting,' he mused. 'The collection itself, I mean. As you say, no Queen's heads. The stamps are all of ships and views, with a sprinkling of animals. Recess or line-engraved printing, mostly Perkins Bacon, the first printers of postal labels and specialists in line-engraving for banknotes.'

He leaned back and I guessed I was in for one of his lectures. He loved giving tongue on the printing of stamps, and though he could be very interesting on the subject, he always talked as though the other person knew nothing at all about it. 'Perkins Bacon now. They produced the Penny Blacks of 1840, all our early stamps, the Penny Reds and Twopenny Blues. Then De La Rue took over, printing by the letterpress process – surface printing. Not nearly as attractive, and the colours harder. So anybody collecting stamps in the ordinary way at the turn of the century would almost certainly have included some of the early line-engraved GBs.' He picked up his glass, which was empty, and held it out to me. 'While you're pouring another drink you might fill me in on the background, or didn't you ask her?'

'About the man who made the collection?'

He nodded. 'Carlos Holland. Was that his name? It's on the fly leaf of each album.'

'Why do you want to know about him?' I asked. 'It can't make any difference to the value of the stamps surely.'

'I'm curious, that's all. This isn't an ordinary collection. I think he put it together because he was exploring design possibilities before ordering stamps he required for his own official use. He was probably a colonial governor, somebody like that.'

'And the die proofs at the end represent the design of his choice, is that what you're saying?'

34

'Yes, that's about it.'

'Well, I can tell you this, he wasn't a colonial governor.' I reached for the gin bottle and the angostura. 'But you're right about the name.' And I passed on to him what little I had been told about Carlos Holland.

'So the ship was a total loss. It went down with all hands.'

'That's what I understand.'

'Then he couldn't have had this collection with him at the time. If he had, it would be at the bottom of the sea. So how did it come into Miss Holland's possession?'

'As I understand it the albums were among her brother's things when he was invalided home.'

'How did he come by them?'

'I've no idea.'

'Didn't you ask her?'

'No.'

'Very odd,' he murmured, shaking his head. 'This man Carlos Holland leaves a collection of carvings with his brother, but not the stamps. And then, somewhere on his way out to the Pacific, at some port of call, he suddenly decides to leave these albums ashore. And there's something else,' he said, gazing abstractedly at the albums. 'What about the sheets?'

'Sheets?'

'Yes, the sheets,' he said almost irritably. 'The printed sheets of the final stamp.' He looked up at me over his tumbler. 'You say he owned some schooners and came back to England to add a steamship to his fleet. That suggests he required stamps for the franking of mail carried in his vessels. So where are the sheets?'

'Presumably at the bottom of the sea.'

He nodded, but I could see he was not wholly convinced. 'Very odd,' he said again. 'And the design . . . I can only recall having seen two ship stamps, and like the "Lady McLeod" stamp, they both carried the picture of the ship. This stamp doesn't, the picture enclosed in the frame is of a seal. Doesn't that strike you as odd?'

'The collection includes quite a few stamps with ships on them.'

'Exactly. And he chooses a seal as his emblem. Seals don't swim around coral reefs in the warm waters of the South Pacific. Not the grey or Atlantic seal, which I think this is.' He gave a little sigh. 'Pity the girl isn't here to answer a few questions.'

'I don't think she'd be able to help you. She didn't seem to know very much about the stamps. All she said was that they were among Timothy Holland's things when he arrived back in England and that another brother, Jona Holland, wrote that he'd been very excited by the find.'

He nodded. 'Well he might be if he knew anything about stamps.' He was silent for a while, sitting there staring at the black impression of the proof. 'But no sheets,' he muttered. 'I wonder. . . .' He sat back, toying with his glass. 'If I'm right, then there must have been sheets of those stamps. I wonder where they are. Somebody must have them.' He shrugged, closing the album slowly and with a certain reluctance. 'I think I'd better take this collection along to somebody who knows more about ship stamps than I do. Josh Keegan is the best bet. And if he doesn't know he'll tell me who to go to. I've a feeling . . . I'm not sure, mind you, but I think a stamp rather like that die proof came up for sale at a Robson Lowe auction some years back. Josh may have been at the sale.' He downed the rest of his drink and got to his feet. 'I've got to go now. Mind if I take the albums with me?'

I hesitated, unwilling to let them go now that I knew he was interested. 'Yes, of course,' I said. Obviously he couldn't give me a valuation on the spot.

'Good.' He had noticed my hesitation and smiled. 'Don't worry. I'll take good care of them.' He picked up the albums, holding them out to me. 'Pop them in a polythene bag, will you. Don't want to get them wet rowing ashore.'

He had a supper date with friends near Maldon and when he had seated himself carefully in his dinghy he looked up at me, his bright eyes twinkling. 'I could have valued the collection off the cuff, made you an offer and, given the girl's circumstances, she'd probably have accepted. Instead, I'm seeking expert opinion for you. Greater love hath no man.' He picked up the oars, and as I tossed the painter into the bows, he began to drift away on the tide. 'I'll tell Josh to ring you direct if he's anything of interest to report. Otherwise, I'll come back to you myself and make an offer for the lot.'

'You really want it then?'

He nodded, smiling at me like an amiable frog. 'Yes, I do. First time I've ever had a collection in my hands that was made for the purpose of choosing a design. Three or four days and I'll hope to be back to you with that offer.'

'Well, see that it's a fair one,' I said.

He laughed, back-paddling against the tide, the plastic dinghy so low in the water it looked on the verge of sinking. 'Suspicious bastard you are. Whatever the business ethics in your world, Roy, stamps are still a gentlemanly occupation.' And with that he swung the little boat round and headed for the nearest landing pier.

As soon as I was home I got out the catalogue and looked up Trinidad. There it was, the first Crown Colony stamp listed, a 5c. blue. A note underneath read: *The 'Lady McLeod' stamps were issued in April, 1847, by David Bryce, owner of the s.s.* Lady McLeod, *and sold at five cents each for the prepayment of the carriage of letters by his vessel between Port of Spain and San Fernando. Used examples are pen-cancelled or have a corner skimmed off.* The value of it unused was given as £6,000, used £2,000.

I sat there staring at it for a long time. Even though the Holland stamp was used, or rather pen-cancelled, and the condition of it not that good, it put the collection in a different class, quite outside my range. To buy it I'd have to sell most of my carefully acquired GB stamps. Either that or the boat.

I put it out of my mind after that, which wasn't difficult since I was loaded with all Packer's work. And on top of that Rowlinson sent me the figures for Munnobungle asking me for my comments as soon as possible.

It was not until the following Friday that I heard from Tubby, a formal letter that read:

37

Dear Mr Slingsby,

I have now gone through the whole collection with a view to valuation. Excluding the 'Lady McLeod' and the die proofs on the last two pages, the theoretical value is £1,273 based on the latest Stanley Gibbons catalogue. Bearing in mind their condition, my estimate of the actual value is around £500 – at auction they might well reach a little more, equally they might fetch less.

The value of the die proofs is impossible to estimate. A copy of the actual stamp does exist, in deep blue, but it did not go through the post in the normal way. It was apparently on a cover (i.e. envelope) which bore an Australian postage-due stamp. In other words, the Australian postal authorities refused to accept it, regarding it as no more than a private label. This cover was sold at a Robson Lowe auction about two years ago for £220, a high price considering it's an unknown and so had curiosity value only. Josh was at the sale and recalls that it was bought by a dealer handling European accounts. In the circumstances, I think it fair to value the die proofs at the same figure.

As regards the 'Lady McLeod' Trinidad ship stamp, this is more difficult to set a value on. In prime condition the current value of a pen-cancelled example is put at £2,500. What this particular example would fetch at auction is anybody's guess, but Josh was quite prepared to give £550 for it, so I think £600 would be a fair valuation.

Thus, my valuation for the two albums is £1,320 and, as agreed, there is no charge for this.

I think it would be a great pity to break this collection up and sell the stamps piecemeal. I remain personally interested in it as a curiosity and am prepared to offer £1,500 for the collection as it stands. Perhaps you would convey this offer to Miss Holland. I do not honestly think she will do better than this and I will keep the albums here in my safe until I hear from you.

No sailing this week-end. I promised to go down for my son's half-term.

Sincerely, J. L. Sawyer.

I did something then on the spur of the moment that was pretty daft. I wrote to Miss Holland telling her that I was enclosing Cdr Sawyer's letter valuing the stamps and offering for them. And then I added that I was personally interested as a collector and asked if I could drive over and see her as I might be able to offer her slightly more. To this day I don't know how much I was motivated by my interest in the collection, how much by my desire to see her again, and it was only after the letter had gone that I began to worry about raising the cash. But if Rowlinson did decide to offer me the job in Australia I would be selling the boat anyway, and that would more than cover it.

Almost a week passed and no word from Miss Holland, nothing from Rowlinson, though I had sent him an outline of my ideas for halting the losses on his Queensland property. And then, after a deadly dull morning arguing with bureaucrats and tenants over rent increases for a row of tenement houses, I returned to the office to find that Rowlinson's secretary had phoned to say he would call at my home at 7 p.m. Also Eric Chandler had been trying to get me. The only business we had with Rose, Walker & Chandler at that moment was The Passage valuation and sale of contents, and when I rang him back to point out that I had sent my rough estimate of the current value of the house the previous week, he said, 'Yes, of course, and that's all being dealt with.' He had a high-pitched East Anglian voice. 'But now we need her signature and she's disappeared. I wondered whether you could help me. You met her, I take it, when you did the valuation?'

'Yes.'

'When was that?'

'About a fortnight ago.'

'Was she alone?'

'As far as I know.'

'I see.' There was a pause and I asked him what exactly he had meant, saying she had disappeared.

'Gone away,' he said, 'leaving no address. Most extraordinary. There's a mortgage on the house and we're negotiating with the mortgagors on the basis of your valuation. Obviously she can't sell the property unless they agree to termination and are satisfied there will be sufficient funds to cover everything as a result of the sale. And now she's gone. I had written to her twice – there's no phone there, you see – and when she didn't reply I told one of my staff who had to call on a client in Woodbridge yesterday to go on up to Aldeburgh and see her. She didn't answer the door and when he enquired of the neighbours he was told she had left. At least, they had seen her leaving in a taxi with two large suitcases. That was on Saturday, and no forwarding address. He enquired of the neighbours, the local shops, and checked with Aldeburgh Post Office. Milk and paper delivery had been stopped and the bills paid. I thought you might be able to help.'

'In what way?'

'Well, I haven't seen her since her father died. That was three or four years ago. You've met her recently and I was wondering whether she'd given you any indication she might be going away – to stay with a relative or friends. She can't have had an easy time of it these last few years looking after that brother of hers. He was very badly injured, you know. Now, can you help me at all?'

'I'm afraid not,' I told him. 'I was expecting a letter from her myself, and she certainly didn't say anything about going away.'

'You talked to her then?'

'For a short time, just before I left when she brought me some tea.' I started to tell him then about the wood-carvings and Carlos Holland, but he interrupted me:

'Yes, but what was her frame of mind? I'm just trying to decide whether I ought to do something about it. I can't ever remember a client going off suddenly like this without a word when we're trying to get a mortgage position cleared up. And it was at her request, I may say. But the point is this . . . well, life hasn't exactly been a bed of roses for her, first her father, then her brother – I wondered whether you'd been able to form any opinion of her mental state. She'd no relatives in the country, nobody she can turn to, I do know that.'

'If you're worried she may be suicidal,' I said, 'you can forget it. That was not her mood at all.' And I added, 'She's got another brother I believe. Why not contact him? Presumably you have his address.'

'I don't think that would help. He's out in the Pacific somewhere.'

'Had she any money of her own at all, money she could use to fly out there?'

'I can't answer that.' There was a pause, and then the high crisp voice said, 'Well, thank you. Thank you very much for your help.' And he put the phone down.

There were a lot of papers piled on my desk, but it was difficult to concentrate, wondering if I had been justified in declaring so categorically she was not in a suicidal state. Nothing in our conversation had indicated that she had any friends in England, and though she apparently had the money to pay her bills and hire a taxi, that didn't mean she had enough to do whatever it was she had in mind. And here I was with a bid of £1,500, which I had offered to increase, and no means of contacting her.

And then, just as I was packing up to leave, stuffing Rowlinson's papers into my briefcase so that I could refresh my memory before he came to see me that evening, the girl in the outer office rang through to say a Mr Berners was on the phone wanting to speak to me personally. I told her to find out what it was about, but she had already done that; all he would say was that a Miss Holland had told him to contact me.

I thought perhaps it was to give me her address, but when he was switched through it was the stamps he was interested in. He was a dealer and he had heard from somebody in the trade there was a collection available that included proofs of a stamp he thought might interest a client of his. 'When I go to see Miss Holland I find she don't have the collection any longer. You have it, so now I am asking you what time tomorrow is convenient for me to see it.'

'When was it you saw Miss Holland?' I asked.

'On Thursday. Last Thursday afternoon.'

He had an accent I couldn't place and it irritated me. 'How

did you get her address?'

'From a Mr Keegan who is making some enquiries of me. He made a note of it when he is asked to consider the authenticity of the die proofs. So now, when can I see the proofs please?'

I remembered there had been a label with her name and address on the brown paper she had wrapped the albums in and I had used the same wrapping before putting them in a plastic bag and giving them to Tubby. 'I am afraid the collection is not available for viewing here.'

'But you are handling the sale, Mr Slingsby. If it is not with you, where is it please?'

'It's being valued. My instructions at the moment do not go beyond obtaining a valuation.'

'I do not understand. Miss Holland tell me you are handling the sale for her and I must go to you to see the proofs.'

'I think you misunderstood her.'

'No, I do not misunderstand her. She said to go and see Mr Slingsby and she gave me your address in Chelmsford. So, if you are handling the sale you cannot just tell somebody who is interested to go away. It is your duty to co-operate and make the collection available for anybody to view who wishes.'

'I don't need to be told my duty,' I said sharply. A door slammed down the corridor and I looked at my watch; rush hour already. 'If you give me your address, Mr Berners, I'll be in touch with you as soon as I've contacted Miss Holland.'

'Do you have the valuation yet?' he asked.

'Yes,' I said. 'And I also have a firm offer which I have passed on. . . .'

'How much?'

'I'm afraid I can't tell you that.'

'Okay then, the valuation. How much does your dealer friend value it at?'

There was something about the way he said 'your dealer friend' that I didn't like. 'I think you will have to ask Miss Holland that.'

'How can I? She is gone abroad and I am asking you because you are handling the sale.'

'I am not handling the sale,' I repeated angrily, irritated beyond measure at his insistence. 'All I have agreed to do is obtain a valuation.' By that time his words had registered and I asked him how he knew she had gone abroad.

'She tell me, of course. She tell me when she said you would be selling the collection for her. Now, this dealer friend of yours – he has valued the stamps and I take it also made the offer for them. In the circumstances, I think you have to tell me one figure or the other. It would be most unethical for an agent to conceal a professional valuation in order to protect his friend's bid for a property. Eh, Mr Slingsby? So, now you give me the figure please.'

I was greatly tempted just to slam the phone down, but he was so obviously a trouble-maker it didn't seem worth it. 'All right,' I said, 'the collection has been valued at £1,320.'

'And the proofs? I am only interested, I think, in the die proofs. I take it he has valued them separately.'

'Yes, at £220.'

'Ah yes, of course, £220. How many die proofs are there?'

'Three, two on one page, one on the other.'

'Can you describe them for me?'

I did so and he said, 'Good. That confirms what I have been told, that these are die proofs of the Solomons Seal. Kindly do not dispose of them until I have had the opportunity to view and put in a bid. I will call at your office in Chelmsford tomorrow afternoon, say three o'clock. Please have the stamps available then.' And before I could say anything further he put the phone down.

I sat there for a moment, thinking back over the conversation, still annoyed by his manner and the inferences he had drawn. But for all I knew the valuation might be too low, particularly for the Trinidad ship stamp. I reached for the phone again and dialled Tubby's number. Fortunately he was at home and his voice sounded cheerful as he said, 'She's accepted, has she? I'm probably paying over the odds, but – '

'No, she hasn't accepted,' I told him. 'She's gone off somewhere, leaving no address, and now there's somebody else showing an interest.'

'Who?'

'A man called Berners. A dealer.'

'I see.' His cheerfulness had suddenly evaporated. 'So you want the collection back?'

'He's coming in to see it tomorrow.' And I told him briefly what the man had said, adding, 'It appears your profession is not so gentlemanly after all.'

'Berners is not exactly typical,' he growled. There was a pause. 'You want to pick up the stamps right away, do you?'

'I think it would be best. I'm not a stamp dealer and I didn't like his attitude.'

'All right.' I was just about to ring off when he added, 'I was going to phone you this evening anyway. Something very odd has come to light. Tell you about it when I see you.'

2

That evening the traffic was particularly heavy and by the time I reached Woodham Ferrers I was running short of time. Tubby's cottage overlooked the Crouch and when I finally got there I found he had some half dozen pages from the collection laid out on his desk and there was a pile of books with markers in them stacked to one side. 'You in a hurry?' he asked as he poured me a whisky. 'I could knock up an omelette later, or we could go down the pub for a bite if you doubt my cooking.'

'Is this going to take long?' I asked. 'I've got a client coming to see me at seven. I mustn't keep him waiting.'

He sighed. 'No, it won't take long, Roy. Come over to the desk here and see what I've dug up about this collection.' He switched on an anglepoise lamp. 'Newfoundland and Western Australia. That's what was puzzling you, wasn't it? I spotted it

44

at once, of course, but I didn't say anything. I wasn't sure. I'm not sure yet, not really. How the hell did he manage to get hold of the dies? Or did he choose the designs and employ an engraver to copy them?' He reached for the page that showed proofs of the frame and centre of the stamp separately. 'The seal first. Now that, unless I can't tell a copy from the original, is the seal from the American Bank Note Company's printing of the Newfoundland 1865 five cent brown.' He picked up the Gibbons catalogue from the top of the pile on his desk, opening it at a marker. 'There's the picture of it, under the Codfish two cent stamp. *Seal-on-Icefloe*. Now compare that with the die proof. Same shape, same background, same blank area of white representing the icefloe. Agreed?'

'Looks the same.' But I hadn't called on him for a lecture on stamp design. 'Who is this man Berners?' I asked.

'I'll come to him in a moment,' he said impatiently. 'Just concentrate on this now.' He selected another page from the collection. 'Here is an example of the stamp itself – a five cent blue, the edges rouletted, not perforated. It was issued in 1876 and like the two previous issues it was printed in New York by the American Bank Note Company. Nice condition, too, except that it's stuck down tight and the original gum lost. Worth, I suppose, a tenner or so, but if it had been the five cent brown of 1865 it would have been worth a lot more.' He looked up at me, smiling. 'Like angling, isn't it, the big fish always just out of reach.'

He turned to the end of the catalogue. 'Now take a look at the frame. This is less obvious, but I'm pretty certain it's the Perkins Bacon design for the first Western Australia stamp, the black one penny of 1854.' He held the catalogue under the light so that I could see. 'Almost square, but slightly rectangular, with a sort of four-leaf clover shaped cross in each corner. The words Western Australia on the two sides, Postage at the top and One Penny at the bottom.' He placed the page with the die proof alongside the illustration so that I could compare it. 'The die proof omits the words, of course. Presumably they were to be included, together with the value, in the roller die from which they would prepare the final plate before going to press.'

'Any idea what the words would have been?' I asked.

'No, I haven't been able to find that out. Not yet.' He put the page back on the desk and closed the catalogue. 'You might ask Arnold Berners that. He was the dealer who purchased the cover I mentioned in my letter, so he will know.'

'Why didn't you contact him then?'

He gave a little shrug, smiling at me. 'I'm a collector as well as a dealer. No point in alerting the opposition when you've made up your mind you want a thing.'

'That's not very ethical when you've been asked for a valuation.' I didn't tell him I was behaving just as badly, trying to raise his offer without telling him.

'Perhaps not, but my offer was fair, even generous. I doubt he'll offer more. Anyway, he operates from Switzerland. Presumably he came over for last week's Harmer's auction and stayed on to see some of his clients.' And he added on a note of envy, 'The little bastard has managed to get his hands on some of the Arab oil money.'

'You don't like him?'

'No, none of us do. Operating out of Switzerland with clients like that, he can outbid us any time he wants. But mostly he buys privately. Two months ago he acquired a unique collection of Japanese Malayan Occupation stamps for a figure that is believed to have been in the region of £18,000. That's a hell of a price, but then he's like a professional burglar – he never grabs anything unless he knows he has a market.' He was gazing down at the pages of the collection left out on his desk, 'I can't match him if he's got a wealthy client interested in this. Did he say he had a client interested?'

'Yes.'

He nodded and there was a trace of wistfulness in his voice as he said, 'Probably the same one he sold the cover to. I wonder what he charged the poor devil for that? A lot more than the £220 he paid for it at auction, I'll bet.' And he added, 'It carried the only example of this very odd stamp in existence. What do you suppose happened to the others? Went down with the ship, eh?' He shook his head. 'And I don't even know what the finished label looks like. There was no illustration of it in the auction catalogue. Josh dug it out for me. It just said: *Cover with unrecorded ship label in deep blue with Port Moresby cancellation dated 17 July, 1911, also Australia 1909-11 Postage Due 2d. cancelled at Cooktown. Some stains, otherwise fine, unusual.* The estimated value was £50 plus.'

'Berners referrred to it as the Solomons Seal,' I said.

'Did he now?' He leaned forward and picked up the page containing the proof of the entire stamp. 'So that's one more piece of the jigsaw fallen into place. Presumably Holland's ships operated out of the Solomon Islands. Anything else he told you?'

I shook my head.

'Oh well, no point in going on, not now that I know Berners is after the collection.' He began to gather the pages, putting them back in their albums. 'Whoever has that cover is probably prepared to pay over the odds for the die proofs, and there'll be others after them when they realize . . . ' He gave a little shrug, his words hanging on the air. 'Another Scotch?'

'No.' I glanced at my watch. 'I've got Rowlinson coming in to see me and I'm running it fine as it is.'

'The frozen food man?' And when I nodded, he said, 'Wish more of my clients were as successful as that. Tell him to put his money into stamps. One of the few things that have never gone down in value.' He put the albums back in their original wrapping and handed the parcel to me. 'For the sake of the girl, inform Berners you've got an offer of £2,500. See what he says to that.'

I stared at him. 'Are you serious?'

'Yes, I think so.'

'A figure like that, it could frighten him off.'

He nodded, a speculative look in those bright blue eyes. 'If it does, then I've got the collection, haven't I?' And he added, 'But I doubt whether it will, not if his client is rich.'

'I think,' I said, 'I had better have that offer of yours in writing.'

47

'Don't trust me, eh?'

'I wouldn't trust anybody making a bid like that.' My voice was sharpened by disappointment, the sense of opportunity lost. But at least it disposed of my own offer. I couldn't outbid him at that figure.

He sat down at his desk and pulled a sheet of notepaper from a drawer. 'You're sharp, Roy,' he said heavily. 'What I had in mind was for you to quote him my offer so that he'd be forced to pay Miss Holland a thumping price.' He was gazing questioningly at me. 'Then if it did scare him off you'd let me have the collection for the figure I'd originally offered.'

'That would be dishonest,' I said.

He stared up at me a moment longer, not saying a word, then he wrote down his revised bid and signed it with a flourish. 'You know, I must be mad,' he said, slipping it into an envelope and handing it to me. 'But it's not often I've wanted anything as badly as I want that collection.'

'It's your money,' I told him.

He laughed. 'You remember somebody suggesting a long time ago that ocean racing was like tearing up fivers under a cold shower? Well, stamps are a bit like that. You get a hunch, a feel about something, and then you become so obsessed you've got to have it whatever the cost.'

He saw me to my car and as I was getting into it I remembered what he had said to me on the phone, that something very odd about those die proofs had come to light. I asked him what it was, but he laughed and shook his head. 'When you've got more time and are prepared to show a little more interest – '

'I'm a lot more interested now you've upped your bid by such a large amount.'

'If I get the collection, then I'll tell you. Okay?'

I was annoyed with myself then, wishing I wasn't already late for my appointment. All I could think of as I drove fast through the quiet Essex countryside was his extraordinary behaviour. I had no idea what his financial position was, but he lived quite modestly, certainly within his pension, and though he presumably made a profit out of buying and selling stamps, I was quite sure an offer like that would be stretching his resources. I had seen quite a bit of him since his wife had died a couple of years back. I liked him and, not doubting for a moment that his original valuation had been arrived at in good faith, I was afraid he had been carried away and was offering too high a price.

I was almost a quarter of an hour late when I turned into the concrete driveway and from two fields away, just after I had hit the dirt track, I could see Rowlinson's Aston Martin standing outside the Hall. I found him sitting under the walnut tree by the moat watching a pair of mallards, his dark, almost Welsh features brooding and sullen.

'Sorry I'm late,' I said. 'Can I offer you a drink?'

'No thanks.' He tossed the broken half of an old walnut shell into the water. 'I'm afraid I've some bad news for you. I'm selling.' He didn't look up, just sat there staring into the water. 'Not your fault. Your ideas were fine and I think they'd have worked. But I can't fight Bessie and the board. We've decided to expand further and we need the money.' He picked up another walnut shell, breaking it between his fingers. 'Doesn't look as though I'll have time for any more long trips, so no point in hanging on to the property. Pity. But there it is.'

I stood there, not saying anything. There was nothing to say with my hopes dashed like that. I had known Chips Rowlinson for about six years, ever since I had sold him a new engine for his boat and arranged its installation. Then, after I had taken the job with Browne, Baker & Browne, I learned he was looking for a larger residence. I was lucky, I managed to find him a lovely old manor house near Tolleshunt D'Arcy, and I got him the land to go with it much cheaper than he expected. As a result, he had come to regard me as his land and agricultural adviser, which was why he had turned to me when the rundown sheep station with the ridiculous name of Munnobungle had become a problem. I had looked at the rainfall figures in that part of Queensland and I was certain deeper boreholes and a switch to cattle and sorghum would help to make it profitable. It just needed somebody there to get the place back on its feet.

'I'm sorry you've decided to sell,' I murmured.

'So am I.' He got slowly to his feet. 'Don't think I want to. I've had a lot of fun out of it. Marvellous country.' And he began talking in that quick, energetic way of his about the climate and the people, the sense of space and trips he had made out to the Barrier Reef in fishing boats and in a Cessna he had hired from an outfit called Bush Pilots Airways. He was pacing up and down the edge of the moat, his head up as though sniffing the air. 'You know, I've half a mind to pack it in here, let the tax boys have their last bite at me and go out there for good. There's a sense of freedom, like a breath of fresh air. The sea, the fish, all that coral, and over the horizon to the north-east islands hardly anybody has ever seen. The Solomons, the Bismarcks; I never got as far as that. Only Papua New Guinea. But that was enough. One of the last lost primitive frontiers.'

'Primitive enough to believe in magic?' I asked. 'Death wishes. That sort of thing?'

'Oh yes. It's witchcraft really, but they call it sorcery.' He had stopped and was staring out at the moat. 'I was at Mendi and there was a young Australian lawyer staying at the hotel with me, running a course for local village magistrates, and he had just come face to face with this problem. What the devil does a magistrate, or a High Court judge for that matter, do when a case is brought against a man for putting a death wish on another? Is it murder? Difficult under our laws. No physical attack, no weapons. But they know it's murder, and if the law doesn't act, then the relatives will. They'll take the law into their own hands. They call it pay-back. It's feuding, of course. Can go on for generations.'

'And the Administration, the District Officers – a Patrol Officer, for instance, would he believe in it?'

'Yes, I imagine so. I did see it once myself. Not in Papua New Guinea, in West Africa, when I was a Sapper there. I had a company out in the bush throwing a Bailey bridge over a swollen river and my best sergeant went sick on me. Nothing obviously wrong, only that he'd had a go at another man's wife in a nearby village and the local witch doctor had been paid to put a spell on him. Medicines didn't do any good,' so I had to go and search the old wizard out, buy him off and the injured man as well.'

'And your sergeant recovered?'

'Oh yes, once he knew the death wish was lifted. Funny thing is that this sort of magic doesn't seem to be an oral, or even a visual art. The sorcerer seems able to do it by remote control, by telepathy.' He was silent a moment, still staring into the moat which was now becoming shadowed from the rays of the sinking sun. 'Quite honestly,' he said quietly, 'it's something I can do without. It's quite beyond my comprehension and I don't want to know about it.'

His acceptance of it, the way he had reacted to it – a hard-headed business man . . . I was appalled. Here in England, in this most mechanical, most material of all ages. . . . 'When you were out there,' I said, 'did you ever hear the name Holland mentioned?' And when he looked at me with a surprised lift of his eyebrows, I added, 'There was a Carlos Holland ran ships in the islands around the turn of the century.'

He shook his head. 'Queenslanders aren't much interested in the past. Life's too hard and they live for the present. What they talk about mostly is the price of sheep or cattle or sugar, and how that randy old sport out at Dead Horse Springs has shacked up with some raw kid up from Brisbane. And if they do mention the past at all it's to curse the Chinks for mining out all the gold on the Palmer River.'

He had spent a week up in the Highlands of Papua New Guinea and he talked about that for a moment, how the people there had developed their pig and cassowary economy to a degree of complexity that was quite as difficult for the uninitiated to comprehend as the City's dealings in stocks and shares. 'But the rich man, the banker as you might say, doesn't lend, he borrows, so that individuals, sometimes whole clans, become tied to him. Spendid fellows,' he added. 'A real fighting people who are not averse to a little cannibalism if it will increase their virility.' I think he saw my mind had strayed, for he suddenly switched back to my question: 'No, the only Holland I ever heard of was a fellow called Black Holland. He was killed by an abo half-breed in a bar brawl up near Ingham. Lewis, that was the abo's name. He was tried for murder. Queer fellow, you buy him a drink and he'll tell you a tall tale about some forgotten gold mine.'

'How would an aborigine have come by a name like Holland?' I asked.

'His father, of course.' His tone was terse, as though suddenly bored. 'If the father is white they'll cling to the name, like all those hyphenated Smiths. Human nature is much the same everywhere. But Black Holland wasn't an abo. He was from the islands. Bougainville, I think.' He dropped the subject then. 'Now, about Australia. I know you were very set on the idea of going out there to look after my interests. That's why I wanted to tell you the situation myself. The final decision to expand was only taken yesterday.' He was staring up into my face very intently. After a moment he said, 'But I do need somebody I can trust to go out there and organize the sale of the property. Will you do that for me? All expenses paid, of course.'

I didn't say anything for a moment as I tried to readjust to this totally different offer. It wasn't at all what I had been hoping for, but at least it would give me a chance to see whether there was more of a future for me out there than there seemed to be here in England. I think he misunderstood my silence, for he said, 'I'm not leaving it to some smart-alec land agent out there. Like as not he'd take me for a ride. Can't blame him, a Pommie with a lot of land and nobody looking after his interests. I'd be a sitting duck. Well?'

'I'll think about it,' I said.

He stared at me a moment longer. 'Tell you what I'll do. You've been through all the figures. You know what I paid for the place. I'll give you a percentage of the net difference between my purchase price and whatever you manage to get for it. Say ten per cent. Would that help?' And without waiting for a reply, he turned abruptly and walked to his car.

He had bought Munnobungle early in the seventies when

Australian land prices were almost at bottom. There had been massive inflation since then, and with a good local agent the price should be very much higher now even if the exchange rate was against him. As soon as he was in the driving seat he lowered the electric window. 'You get a good deal for me and you'll have a nice little packet of Australian dollars. Not a bad start if you're thinking of settling there.' He was looking up at me, smiling. 'We're having another board meeting day after tomorrow, a lunch afterwards. Why not join us? One o'clock at the factory. That gives you time to think it over.' And he drove off, taking my acceptance for granted.

At the office next morning there was a handwritten envelope marked Personal among the correspondence lying opened on my desk. It was a brief note from Miss Holland to say she had been offered a job as stewardess on a cruise ship and would I be kind enough to sell the stamps for her and forward whatever I got for the collection, less commission and any expenses, to the credit of her account at the Southampton branch of the National Westminster Bank.

The writing was small and neat, slightly angular, so that it was not noticeably feminine, and she signed herself Perenna Holland. I had never come across the name Perenna before. There was no address and the note had been scribbled on what appeared to be a half sheet of typing paper. The cheap buff envelope in which it had been enclosed was postmarked Southampton. I dialled her solicitor's number and as soon as I was put through to him he said in that high, precise voice of his, 'I was just about to phone you.'

'You've heard from Miss Holland, have you?'

'Yes. She's sent me a Power of Attorney and asked me to arrange for the sale of the house as well as the contents as soon as possible. Fortunately I now have the agreement of the mortgagors so we can go ahead. I'd like you to handle that for us, if you will – since you were kind enough to give us a rough guide to the market value.'

'Who drew up the Power of Attorney?' I asked. 'Was it a firm in Southampton?'

'Ah, you've heard from her, too, have you? Yes, it was a Commissioner for Oaths at Southampton. And you were right when you said she seemed anxious to get away. She's got a job on a cruise ship.'

I asked him for her address, but it was the same she had given me, the bank. She hadn't said what ship she was sailing on or where it was going. It was all 'very odd' he thought. I told him we would deal with the sale of the house, and after I had put the phone down I rang Lloyd's Intelligence Services at Colchester. It took them only a moment to check the Southampton sailings with the computers. A Greek cruise ship, the *Lemnos*, had left at 20.30 hours the previous evening for the Caribbean calling at Madeira en route. No other cruise ship was due to sail from Southampton for the next eight days.

'When will the *Lemnos* return?' I asked. But they weren't sure she would dock at Southampton again. It was a fortnight's cruise finishing up in Bermuda. The ship would then embark mainly American passengers for a further cruise through the Panama Canal to the Galapagos, then down to Callao and Valparaiso, finishing up at San Francisco on 2 August. That was as far as their information went.

It wasn't much, but at least I knew that she had sailed, and on a vessel headed for the Pacific. I sat there for a moment remembering the things she had said, the atmosphere of that house, wondering how much Eric Chandler knew about the family.

I was still thinking about that when the phone rang. It was the chairman of the Rotary Club. Would I take the chair for him at today's lunch as his wife had suddenly been taken ill? There was a lot of work to get through and it was only as I was leaving that I remembered Berners was coming at three. I gave the two albums to Miss Paget and told her to remain with him the whole time he was looking through them.

By the time I got back from lunch Berners was in my office with Miss Paget, the albums open on the desk in front of him. He was a small, thrusting little man, expensively dressed in a dark grey suit, rather square at the shoulders, and a gaily patterned bow tie. He got quickly to his feet, bowing slightly and giving me a limp handshake. As soon as we were alone he said, 'Your description of the last few pages of the collection was exact, Mr Slingsby. They're undoubtedly die proofs and the stamp is the one that interests my client.' He folded his neat pale hands across his stomach, a signet ring glinting in the sunlight that streamed in through the open window. 'Now, if I make you an offer are you in a position to deal?'

'Yes.' I sat down at my desk, waving him to the chair opposite.

'So, you have heard from Miss Holland.'

'This morning.'

'Then perhaps you will inform me what figure I have to beat.'

'A high one,' I said, wondering once again whether Tubby really wanted the collection at that price or if I should try and get him off the hook. But looking at Berners I didn't think I could. He was so obviously a hard bargainer.

He stared at me for a moment, his eyes coldly grey and very shrewd behind thick-lensed glasses. 'How much?'

'Suppose you name a figure?'

'This is not an auction.' His thin lips were compressed into a sour little smile and he shook his head. 'First let me say that the value of this collection for anyone not specifically interested in the Solomons Seal label – and it is no more than that, you understand, it is not in any sense a postage stamp. . . .' He hesitated. 'The value is perhaps £1,000. That is to a dealer.'

Allowing for the fact that he was pitching it as low as possible it was close enough to Tubby's valuation to make nonsense of his subsequent offer. I said, 'But you are interested. So what is your offer?'

He shook his head, still with that sour little smile. 'I don't make any offer until I know how much I have to beat. I think in fairness to your client, to Miss Holland, you have to tell me that. You say it is high.'

'Very high,' I told him.

'Higher than £1,000?'

'Much higher.'

He frowned, his hand moving up to his blue jowls and the high dome of his forehead catching the light. The hand came away, the head thrust forward. 'You have this offer in writing?'

'Yes.'

'Show me. I don't believe it.'

I started to tell him that I wasn't accustomed to having my word doubted, but I checked myself. The figure was so preposterous that in his shoes I would have been equally incredulous. 'All right,' I said, and I took Tubby's letter from the drawer in my desk and handed it to him.

He picked it up, holding it close to his face. 'C'est incroyable!' he breathed. 'Who is this?' He peered closely at the signature. 'J. L. Sawyer. A dealer?' he asked. 'Yes. I remember now. I have met him. An amateur.' He said it half in contempt, half in wonder. And then he looked at me over the top of the letter. 'Have you had any other offers?'

I shook my head.

'Then why does he go directly to this very high figure of £2,500? It cannot be for the 'Lady McLeod' Trinidad stamp, that is in too poor condition.'

'I've no idea,' I said. 'He just seems fascinated by the collection as a whole, and by the proofs, of course.'

'Why? What is his interest?'

'He seems to think it has great curiosity value.'

'He wants it for himself then, not for a client?'

'Yes, for himself.'

He shook his head as though in wonderment at the stupidity of it. 'Well, I'm not sure now. For myself I would not go beyond £1,500, maybe a little more. But above this figure, no – not on my own responsibility, you understand.' He had been speaking slowly, more to himself than to me. Then abruptly he put the bid letter down on the desk. 'You must give me a little time. I have to consult my client about this.'

'Miss Holland needs the money,' I said. 'If you would like to use my phone.'

But he shook his head. 'My client is not in England any more. He is somewhere in Europe, I think. You must wait a little, until I can contact him.'

'How long?'

'A fortnight, three weeks – I'm not sure. Shall we say a month? I expect him to be in England again sometime next month.'

I hesitated. A month would take us to July 23. That would be running it fine if she were leaving the ship at Callao or Valparaiso. 'I'll give you three weeks.'

He seemed about to argue, but then abruptly he nodded. 'Three weeks then. Meantime, I have your word that you do not sell to this man Sawyer before I contact you again.'

'You have until 16 July,' I told him. 'If I haven't heard from you by then –'

'You will hear from me. That I promise you.' And he got to his feet, 'It's very strange,' he said, shaking his head and frowning again. 'I don't understand why Sawyer is making this bid. It can only be that he hopes to twist my client's elbow.' He suddenly spun round on me. 'You think he knows who my client is?'

'I've no idea.'

He seemed puzzled and uneasy as I showed him to the door. I, too, was beginning to wonder about that client of his. I was wondering about a lot of things, particularly the sheets Tubby had talked about. If the proofs were worth this sort of money, what would a whole sheet be worth, a solid block of 120 or 240 of the printed stamps?

Though Packer was back by then I decided to deal with the preliminaries of the Aldeburgh sale myself. I could then have a look at that loft. A lot of papers and records are usually left behind by the occupants when a house and its contents are up for sale. There was sure to be something there, and a closer look at those old photographs might help. But first I needed more information about the family's background. I rang Chandler and asked him to have a drink with me before lunch at the County Hotel next day.

I thought he might be a little less reticent over a drink than if I saw him at his office. Unfortunately I was delayed and he had already bought his own drink by the time I got there. It started us off on the wrong foot. 'I can only give you a quarter of an hour,' he said primly.

'And I've got to be at Rowlinson Fast Freeze by one.' I wasn't in the best of tempers. I'd just had a long session with Sam Baker, who had told me bluntly that if I went off to Australia to do a job for Rowlinson on my own account it would be the end of our association. With business the way it was I knew he was taking advantage of the situation to edge me out. In the end we had had a blazing row and I had walked out, telling him he'd better start advertising for another office boy right away. I got myself a drink and steered Chandler to an empty table.

'So you're lunching with Chips Rowlinson.' He was looking at me the way a thrush eyes a worm, his eyes bright behind his glasses. 'There's talk that they're expanding again. If I can assist in any way. . . .' He left it at that. 'Well now, you want some information on the Hollands. May I ask why?'

I explained briefly about the stamps, but when I asked him about Carlos Holland, he said, 'I wouldn't know about that. Before my time. In any case, I'm not at all sure I'm at liberty to discuss their affairs with you.'

'Then why did you agree to meet me?'

He smiled suddenly, his glasses catching the light. 'Like you, perhaps I'm a little curious. Also I don't like loose ends. I ought to have been informed. She should have told me she was going abroad, not written to me so that I only received the letter after she had sailed.'

I asked him how long his firm had been acting for them and he said, 'Since January 1922. I had one of my juniors check through the files. Fortunately they were in store here when our Moorgate office was gutted in the blitz. The first conveyance we handled was for the sale of a London office property, then shortly afterwards a house in Surrey. Of course the partner who dealt with that is dead now.'

'Presumably he was acting for Miss Holland's grandfather.'

'Yes. Lieutenant Colonel L. D. Holland. He sold up and

went abroad shortly after the First World War.'

'Do you know where he went?'

'Singapore. His address was care of a bank in Singapore. We had to have his bank address as he had arranged for us to manage his affairs. At that time all his funds were invested in this country. Later, he instructed us to sell most of his investments and remit the proceeds to a bank in Sydney, Australia. In 1923 he changed his address again to a Post Office Box number at Port Moresby in Papua. After that there's nothing on the file until his son, Captain Philip Holland, arrived in England with his family and we handled the conveyancing, first for a farm near Snape, and then when he sold that for the purchase of the house at Aldeburgh.'

'I take it her grandfather was dead by then?'

He nodded. 'Apparently Colonel Holland disappeared the same year they came to England.'

'When was that?'

'About six years ago.'

'You say he disappeared.'

'Yes. Made an end of it, that was what she said. He took a native boat and just sailed off into the blue.'

'Did she say why?'

'No. She wasn't there at the time. Anyway, she had come to see me on business and that was a private matter. I didn't ask her.' He was silent for a moment. 'I don't know whether I should tell you this, but she was badly injured, and her mother was killed, in some sort of an outbreak of native hysteria. I think perhaps this preyed on the old man's mind. He must have been over eighty, and at that age, nearing the end of his life . . .' He sighed, a solicitor's acceptance of the vagaries of elderly people. 'That's what decided Captain Holland to sell up and come to England. Wanted to get away from it all.'

'You met him, did you?'

He nodded. 'When he bought the farm, and again when he sold it and purchased the little place in Aldeburgh.'

'What was he like?'

'An odd-looking man, mixed blood you see. Not very sure of

himself. Quite out of his depth running a farm here in England.'
He leaned back, his eyes half-closed. 'Can't recall him very
clearly, only that there was something about his manner that was
a little strange, and his features – the nose rather broad and
without character, large eyes and a low forehead under a mop of
brown hair. Thickset, but rather shrivelled. He wasn't at all well
the last time I saw him, some disease of the tropics, hepatitis
probably. He had a darkish skin that had a tinge of yellow in it.
He died shortly afterwards. That's when Miss Holland came to
see me.'

'What nationality was her mother?' I asked. 'English?'

'No, Australian, I think. Captain Holland had been educated
in Australia and had served in the Australian forces at the end of
the last war. He probably met her then. At any rate, they were
married shortly after.'

'You say he had mixed blood?'

He nodded. 'According to the information we dug out of the
files Colonel Holland's first wife died just after the Kaiser's war.
The 'flu epidemic, I imagine. She would have been quite a
young woman. Probably why he sold his shipbroking business
and went out to Papua New Guinea.'

'To see if he could discover what had happened to the ship
that went down with his brother?'

'Something like that, I imagine. It would have given him a
purpose.' He hesitated, then said, 'You're wondering about that
young woman, I suppose. Well, no reason why you shouldn't
know. Miss Holland's grandmother was from the islands, I can't
remember which. She was the daughter of a French trader.' He
said it as though that explained everything. 'I suppose Holland
was finding it pretty lonely up there in Papua New Guinea. He'd
bought some land, a place called Kuamegu according to the
photocopy of the deeds we have. That was in 1923 if I
remember rightly and he married this island girl the following
year.'

'Was Captain Holland the only child?' I asked.

'No, there was a sister. She's married and lives in Perth.'

'So why did he come to England?'

'God knows. Probably because of his son, the younger one who had just left school.'

I asked him about Timothy Holland then, but he couldn't tell me much, only that he had failed at Sandhurst and had then gone out to Australia. 'As you know, Australia became administrators for Papua New Guinea after the war, from I think 1952 until Independence a few years ago. He was an officer in that administration.'

'She said he was a patrol officer. Was he on duty when he was injured?'

He shrugged. 'I presume so.'

'How did it happen? Was he attacked?'

'No, it was an accident apparently. He was examining a ship while it was unloading and was hit by the cargo sling swinging on its boom. It knocked him into the hold. Just one of those things,' he murmured, finishing his drink and glancing at his watch.

'Can you tell me anything about the elder brother?' I asked. 'Have you met him?'

'No, I've never met him. Why?'

'My guess is she intends joining him. He's something to do with ships, I believe.'

'Yes. Runs his own vessel, a landing craft if I remember rightly. The Hollands have always been interested in island trading.'

'He was being financed by his father, I believe.'

He looked at me sharply. 'Did Miss Holland tell you that?'

'Yes. She said that's where all their money had gone.'

He nodded. 'I advised against it, but yes, that's true I'm afraid. And now he's gone in with a rival shipowner, a relative of some sort.' I asked whether he had any information about the man, but he said, 'No. Captain Holland was very reticent on the matter. But I do know this, he wouldn't have approved of his son's involvement. Some sort of family feud.' He checked himself there. 'I can't go into that, you understand, or into the financial details. But as far as Miss Holland's money is concerned, I tied it up as best I could so that she now has quite a large stake in this ship of her brother's. Something I'll have to look into, but I fear it'll take time and no way I can see of converting it into cash.' He got to his feet, muttering in a very petulant tone, 'She should have told me what she was doing so that I could advise her.'

I was standing beside him, downing the rest of my drink, when he continued, speaking slowly, almost reflectively, 'If you're right about Miss Holland going out to join her brother, then I am afraid it will be a difficult journey for her, a very unhappy one. I can't help wondering . . .' He shook his head, and when I asked him what he meant, he pursed his lips and murmured something about it being no place for a young woman. 'It means she's going back to the very island where her mother was murdered, where she herself was injured.'

'What island is that?' I asked.

'Madehas, near Buka. And it was in the Buka Passage that Timothy Holland had his accident.' He shook his head again. 'Her grandfather, too. It's not been a lucky place for the Hollands.'

'And that's where her brother is now?'

'I suppose so. His base anyway. The last I heard he was living on board his ship. He had just the one and he was running it himself, trading in the islands and around Bougainville.' He seemed to think he had said enough, for he turned to leave. But then he paused. 'Those stamps you mentioned. Are they worth anything?' I told him she should clear at least £2,000 and he seemed pleased. 'That's good. I'd like to think she had some money coming to her.' And then with his usual caution he added, 'I take it you have a buyer.'

'Two,' I said, 'so it may pay to auction them. I'll be going up to London on Friday and if I have time I'll look in on a dealer I know and get his advice.'

He nodded. 'Well, I'm sure you'll do the best you can for her.' He was turning to go and I reminded him about the house and that I'd need the key. 'Ah yes, I should have told you. She left it with a Mrs Clegg next door, a house called Wherry Haven.' And he added, 'Have a good lunch and if you're being

asked to deal with anything local you might remind Rowlinson
we did the conveyance on his present residence.'

It was well past one when I got to the factory on the Maldon
road. They were standing around in the boardroom and a girl
was serving drinks. All the directors were there, including
Chips's wife, Bessie, a nice homely woman, but with a very
good head for business. Shortly after they were maried the two
of them had begun smoking salmon in a shed attached to their
cottage on the Blackwater using the traditional oak chips, which
was how he got his nickname. That was the start of it all, and
now, even the new factory was too small for them. The board
meeting had been considering details of the latest expansion
programme and they asked me about the availability of the
adjoining land and its probable cost.

It was after lunch, when we were having coffee, that Bessie
Rowlinson drew me aside and said, 'You realize what this means.
That sheep station will have to go. Chips is needed here. He can't
go out and see to the sale himself.'

And later, when I was leaving, Chips took me by the arm and
saw me to my car. 'Bessie had a word with you, did she? When
do you think you can leave?'

'As soon as I've got my visa.'

'Your firm agrees?'

'Not exactly.' And I told him the result of my interview with
the senior partner.

'I see.' He looked at me, a sly little smile. 'But you're not
worried.'

'No, not really. It's time I moved on.'

He nodded. 'Good. I'll dictate a letter of agreement for you
this afternoon.'

Three hours later I had cleared my desk and was on the A12
driving north to Aldeburgh. It was a bright, still evening and
the house when I reached it looked less neglected with its
brickwork glowing in the slanting rays of the sun. Wherry
Haven was only a few yards down the road. I had phoned Mrs
Clegg that afternoon and as she handed me the keys she said,
'I'll be glad when it's sold. My husband didn't think I should be

saddled with the responsibility, not at my age, but I couldn't very well refuse. First her father, then that poor brother of hers. She needed to get away.'

She was grey-haired, her hands showing signs of rheumatism, but her eyes were bright and intelligent, her movements still energetic. 'How long have you known the Hollands?' I asked.

'Let me see now. We came here when my husband retired. He was very keen on sailing. That was just over four years ago and they came soon after.'

'You knew her father then?'

She nodded. 'He used to walk down to the yacht club and chat with us while we were working on the boat. We had a small twenty-footer then. He had lived a lot of his life abroad. In Papua New Guinea.'

'He came to England when his wife died, I believe.'

'Yes. But he never talked about that. She was killed, you see. By the natives. It was a very primitive place and they had some sort of cult. Something to do with ships and cargo.' She hesitated as though trying to remember something, then went on: 'The Hollands were a shipping family, that's why he was interested in boats. He'd have a drink with us sometimes and then he'd talk about the incredible blackness of the people, the incessant rain and the war when his father had lived close under an active volcano and had fought the Japanese, things like that. It was all very interesting and colourful. But he never told us what happened. He was a strange man, very withdrawn, very nervy. And that poor boy. You'd never think they were father and son, would you?'

'I never met either of them,' I said, wondering what she meant.

'Oh well, if you'd seen them together. The father was quite a dull little man, very English in his manner. But that son of his with his red hair, those strangely flattened features, and the eyes . . . you've met Miss Holland, haven't you?' And when I nodded, she said, 'Yes, I thought I saw you here about a fortnight ago, before she left. She has something of the same features. Very striking, don't you think – unusual?' She was suddenly silent, as though she had been trying to convey something to me and was at a loss for words. 'Oh well, I mustn't keep you. You'll bring back the keys.' And she added, 'I hope it's sold soon. I never liked the house – inside I mean. All those terrible carvings.'

The first thing I noticed when I went into the house was that the carvings had gone, and most of the pictures, too. I went through it quickly, noting down the rough measurements of the rooms and drafting out the sale notice. The reddening sun cast a lurid light and the empty, abandoned feel of the place made even a professional visit seem like an unwarranted intrusion. It didn't take me long to check the contents against the inventory I had made on the previous visit. All the furniture was still there, but she had cleared out every drawer. No papers, no photographs, nothing to show the sort of people who had occupied the place. She had made a clean sweep of everything. Even the loft was empty. The trunk she had mentioned was gone, presumably into store. The place was dusty, still hanging in cobwebs, and in a corner close under the rafters my torch picked out a small pile of books. They were most of them old Army manuals, a copy of Queen's Regulations, some pictures of Sandhurst, one of a group of cadets, several dinner menus. And then, tucked into the pages of a book called *Black Writing from New Guinea* I found the photograph of a man in khaki shirt and shorts, a black and white picture taken against a background of round thatched huts exuding smoke in the shadow of sombre mountains.

I took it down with me to the window of the room that had been her bedroom. The picture had been taken in the fading evening light when the cooking fires were burning in the thatched village, the whole scene very dark, no humans, only that single figure and a pig with its tail up scurrying away from him. But some trick of the light, a shaft of sunlight perhaps shining through a gap in the mountains, illumined the man's face. He was a young man, clean-shaven, hair standing up like a brush on his bare head, and the face rather square, a jutting jaw and wide-set eyes above a flattened pugilistic nose. It was a face that was both pugnacious and gentle, the nose and jaw contrasting oddly with the appearance of almost childlike innocence, the overall impression one of clean living boyishness.

I looked up from the picture and saw her as I had last seen her, sitting on the window ledge staring out to sea, the same brooding, dreamy look, the same nose and jaw, only the hair different. They must have been very alike, the way twins are; I knew why she had gone then, understood her purpose, and it scared me, so that without thinking I stuffed the picture into my pocket and hurried downstairs, out into the fresh air, closing the front door behind me.

The sun was setting now, the sky cloud-galleoned and flaring red. The stillness and the brilliance, the peace of an East Anglian summer evening – my mood changed. The sense of something appalling and beyond my comprehension that had clung to those empty walls was gone. Like a bad dream I could not even recall what it was that had so disturbed me, just the memory of her face and how she had stared out towards the sea.

I still had to calculate roughly the acreage of the garden and I went round the back of the house to pace it out. At the far end, where it backed on to the garden of the house in the next street, there was a toolshed. I checked the contents, adding them to my list, then continued my pacing. A garden fork was stuck into the ground by the remains of a bonfire. I pulled it out and was about to put it in the shed where it belonged when I realised that the heap of ashes in front of me was not an ordinary bonfire. There were charred scraps of paper scattered around it. This was where she had burned the contents of the drawers, all the papers and rubbish that had accumulated in the loft.

I began turning over the half-burned scraps with the fork. There were cheque counterfoils, remains of bank statements, old Christmas cards and scraps of newspapers. Not our newspapers. The words were English, but the names were foreign. A headline caught my eye – *Meteor Falls near Goroka village*. The paper was yellowed with age. And there was the remains of a letter. I bent down to read the charred fragment of notepaper and found myself staring at something that lay beside it, a tattered travesty of the human figure, a sort of doll about ten inches high, burned black but with the head still recognizable, a birdlike mask of wood and bones and feathers.

I picked it up. The wood was driftwood, smooth and hardened by the sea, the feathers seagulls' feathers, and there were shells as well as the thin little bones of seabirds. I had a sudden mental picture of her striding along the beach, the brassy helmet of her hair blowing in the wind, gathering up the sea's hightide offerings and taking them back to her brother, and that young man propped up in his room, half-paralysed and alone, struggling to fashiom this feathered monstrosity from the bits and pieces of her beachcombing.

I dropped it back on the ashes, standing there staring down at it, feeling sickened that he should have believed in sorcery to the extent of trying to defeat death with that – thing. In a sudden feeling of revulsion I raked the remains of the fire over it and in doing so uncovered something else, a thin sliver of carved wood like a long barbed needle. It was white with ash and badly charred at one end, but when I had wiped it clean on the long lawn grass I saw that the pointed end was coated with red paint.

The actual point was about six inches long and below that· were several barblike nicks. It looked like the head of a very thin-bladed wooden spear, or perhaps an arrow. But what caught my eye, because it was so strange, was that, below the nicks, were three long slits cut into the shaft. They had been fashioned with great care and there was no doubt at all about their purpose. Driven into the body of a man and wrenched back, those slits would cause the hard narrow splines of wood to spring outwards, tearing into the flesh and holding fast.

It was a weapon fashioned by somebody with experience and understanding of a deadly primitive craft, and the red paint on the tip, traces of it still clinging to the slits, right back to where the fire had burned it off, could be nothing else but a simulation 'of the blood of the intended victim. The masked doll and the weapon, the two together . . . and the blood-red sky fading above me. I felt suddenly cold and appalled, the concentrated hatred, the deadly fear that had made him do this lying there in his bed, working away at this murderous copy of a weapon that symbolized a death wish – somebody else's death – and his face so innocently boyish, his body crippled! What primitive knowledge had driven him to it? A patrol officer in a civil administration, and yet somehow he had been infected, possessed almost, by the primitive beliefs of the people he had administered. His grandmother's people. Was he a throwback to the island woman Colonel Holland had married? And who was the enemy for whom it had been intended, who was the intended victim whose death would save him? Or was it all just the figment of a dying man's superstitious imagination?

I slipped it into my clipboard with the intention of getting an expert opinion. Sorcery, she had said. I could hear her voice, the way she had said, *You can't enter that as the cause of death, not in England*.

My God, I thought, and she's gone back there, alone. She's gone to do what her brother could not do. I was still thinking about that as I took the fork to the toolshed and completed my pacing out of the garden. Then I went down the road to return the key to Mrs Clegg.

She must have been watching for me, for the door opened before I had even rung the bell. 'You've finished then?'

I nodded, my mind still groping for a rational explanation.

'Is it true the house is up for sale, too?'

'Yes.'

'When will it be, do you know?'

'We'll be advertising the date in the local paper. I think some time next month.' And I handed her the key.

'You want me to keep this?'

'The lawyers will be in touch with you.' And I added, 'Some of the things have been put in store. Do you know where?'

But all she could tell me was that a small van had been there about ten days ago. 'It was just a trunk and several suitcases. There was no furniture moved. You'll be selling the furniture, too, I suppose?'

'The contents will go into one of our weekly sales at Chelmsford.'

'I wonder who will come to live here. It makes so much

difference in a road like this. We all know each other.'

'Yes, of course.' I hesitated. 'Did they have many visitors?'

'No, they kept very much to themselves. I went in occasionally, but Miss Holland didn't make friends easily, and then there were all those extraordinary carvings. It wasn't that people here didn't care, but the house had a strange, rather unpleasant atmosphere. I always felt uneasy when I visited.'

'What about strangers? Has anybody been to see them just recently?'

'No. Not just recently.' She stared at me, a little hesitant. 'Perhaps I shouldn't say this, but earlier, talking about Miss Holland's appearance – it was the red hair, you see. It reminded me.'

'Reminded you of what?' I asked, for she had stopped there as though she had changed her mind about telling me.

'This man. It was about two months ago. Dick – that's my husband – he was out so I answered the bell. He seemed to have mistaken the house. He was asking for the Hollands and really he looked so like Miss Holland's brother, the same coloured hair, you see, and his face tanned by the sun, almost leathery. A rather aggressive manner. Australian I think. He had that sort of accent.'

'Did he say who he was?'

'No. He asked if this was the Hollands' house and when I said No and pointed it out to him, he just nodded and went straight there.'

'A relative?'

'Oh yes, I would think he must have been, with hair like that and coming to Aldeburgh specially to see them. Do you think that's why she left? He was there a long time, several hours. I asked her about him when I next saw her. Two days later it would have been and she just stared me down, making it obvious she didn't want to discuss it. He was quite handsome in a way, but there was a hardness; the eyes I think.'

She couldn't tell me anything else and I left her, wondering whether there was any connection between this stranger and the things I had found in the ashes of that fire.

I stopped for sandwiches and beer at The Spaniard near Marks Tey, sitting at a table by myself and staring at that arrowhead. Now that I had a chance to examine it closely I knew it wasn't an old weapon, certainly not one of her grandfather's collection of spears and arrows. The red coating came away quite easily to the scratch of my thumbnail and the wood underneath was pale. The coating itself wasn't hard like paint, it was softer, more like dried blood.

Who had taught him, I wondered, to fashion such a weapon, and for such a deadly purpose? I had never met him, yet holding that wicked little sliver of wood in my hand I seemed to feel his presence. I could see him, propped up in that bed with the pictures on the wall in front of him, pictures that represented his real world, and labouring to trim the point and cut the slits, and death in his heart as he struggled to control and direct the movements of his hands. And she had thrown it on the fire, hating it. The doll, too. And now, to save him from himself, she was working her passage back to the world he had come from, where she had been born.

Pay-back, Chips Rowlinson had called it. *If I catch up with the man* . . . I felt a chill run through me though the darkened bar was heavy with the day's heat trapped in the crush of people eating and drinking. An English pub, everything so ordinary, and the sliver of wood in my hand, the memory of her words. And those stamps. They were part of it, too. I was certain of it, so that sitting there, drinking the rest of my beer, I wondered how Timothy Holland had come by them. He couldn't have inherited them, not from his father at any rate, otherwise the albums would have been at Aldeburgh all the time, not as his sister had said among personal belongings sent home with him from Papua New Guinea. No, he had either discovered them or been given them out there. But where? And had he known they were valuable, or was his interest in them in some way connected with the disappearance of the *Holland Trader*?

Unfortunately, I had other things to think about next day in London, and when I discovered the stamps were probably worth even more than Tubby had offered for them I ceased to worry

about their real significance. If you're hungry you don't enquire
where the manna comes from.

*

Canberra House, where I had to go for my visa, is near the Law
Courts so that it was only a short walk to the Strand Stamp
Arcade and on my way to the Qantas office to pick up my airline
tickets. This philatelic hypermarket almost next door to the
Savoy has the atmosphere of a bazaar, a sort of Aladdin's cave of
stamps. I preferred it to Stanley Gibbons on the other side of
the Strand because you were not confined to any one dealer and
could wander from counter to counter looking at stamps,
chatting to dealers, meeting other collectors, and no pressure on
you to buy anything. However, since I had got to know Josh
Keegan personally most of my purchases had been through him.
He was expensive, handling nothing but the best, but if you
could catch him between Continental buying trips he was
fascinating to talk to, full of stories of deals he had pulled off,
fakes he had exposed, and of course his latest acquisitions,
which were always superb and mostly beyond my modest
means.

His stand was at the far end of the arcade: J. S. H. Keegan,
Specialist in GB & Commonwealth. It was just before lunch
when I arrived and his manager, Jim Grace, was invoicing some
early St Helena he had just sold to a thickset man flourishing a
German credit card. The only other customer at the counter was
picking over some Specimen GBs neatly packaged in plastic
envelopes.

'Is Josh Keegan in?' I asked.

Grace nodded. 'Just back from Birmingham. Our first auction
is next week.' To look at this small stand in a crowded arcade it
was difficult to realize that he had a partner in Zurich, another
in Munich and had just gone into partnership with a firm of
auctioneers in the Midlands. 'If it's about that little collection
Commander Sawyer brought in, I know he'd like to see you.'
He reached for the credit card, jotting down the number on the

invoice. 'He's upstairs in the office if you'd like to go up.'

I had only once before been to his office on the third floor, that was when Tubby had introduced me to him. It had originally been one large room, now it was partitioned off into small cubicles where his staff sorted, packaged and priced the material he acquired, most of it from private collectors. His own office was little bigger than the others, a desk, two chairs, a window looking down on to the Strand and the walls lined with small filing tray cabinets. He was standing at the window when I went in, a neatly dressed man with a shock of grey hair. He might have been a musician, except that he had a block of orange stamps gripped in a pair of tweezers and was holding it up to the light, his glasses pushed on to the top of his head and a jeweller's magnifying glass screwed into his right eye.

He turned and smiled at me. I think he was Irish, the smile and the charm all part of his stock-in-trade. 'Ever seen a block of four £5 orange? Lightly cancelled, too. I thought they might be fakes, but no, they're all right and it's the blued paper.' He held the block out for me to see. 'Superb, isn't it?' His eyes were shining with enthusiasm.

'What's it worth?' I asked.

He shrugged. 'What anybody will pay for it — £4,000, £5,000, I don't know. But it's something to bring the dealers down to Birmingham when we hold our big auction there in the autumn.' He slipped the brilliant orange block back into its plastic case, his eyes already fastened on the parcel I was carrying. 'Is that the Holland collection you've got there?' He sat down at his desk, clearing a space with a sweep of his hand. 'Are you going to let us auction it for the lady or is she prepared to sell direct? I'll make you an offer for it if you like.'

'Tubby has already made an offer,' I said. 'And I've given a man named Berners until 16 July to better it.'

'Two dealers after it already, eh?' He smiled and rubbed his hands together. 'Tubby won't get it, of course, poor fellow. I've already been on to my Zurich partner and I've just heard that one of our clients over there is willing to go to £3,500, probably more, provided the background is substantiated. In that case I might even go to £4,000 myself.'

I stared at him. 'But you were only willing to give £550 for the Trinidad ship stamp.'

'It's not the 'Lady McLeod'. Didn't Tubby tell you what he had discovered?'

'He said something very odd had come to light, but I was in a hurry and wasn't prepared for one of his lectures. I thought it was some finer point of printing – '

'Some finer point of printing?' He laughed. 'You could certainly call it that.' He leaned back. 'So you don't know. And if I'd offered you £4,000 you'd have taken it?'

'There's Berners,' I said. 'Also I'd have had to get advice about exchange regulations.' And I told him about Perenna Holland's movements. 'As a UK resident, I think it might require Bank of England permission to send money out to her.' That was before exchange controls were lifted.

'No problem, if you're willing to let us auction the collection.'

I hesitated. But it was what I had been hoping for. 'Provided you can let her have some sort of payment in advance.' And I explained her position and also that I was booked out for Sydney on Sunday evening.

'Sydney, Australia?' He looked at me with sudden interest. 'That could be very helpful. But before I promise anything let's have another look at those die proofs. It's the die proofs that make that collection unique.'

'Because they're ship stamps?'

'No, because they could explain something that has always puzzled students of the Perkins Bacon printing house. Come on, open it up and let me have another look at them.' And he added as I undid the wrapping, 'The catalogue description would have to be very circumspect, but we could certainly say enough to bring every major GB and Commonwealth dealer running to have a look at it.' He opened the albums, searching out the two pages with the proofs, placing them side by side on the desk in front of him. 'Forgeries, fakes, re-entries, inverted watermarks, doubled surcharges, there are examples of every vagary of stamp printing. But stolen dies that were later used to prepare the transfer roller for a plate of ship labels – that's something quite new. Hard to believe in connection with a firm like Perkins Bacon.' He put the glass to his eye, peering closely at the seal in its frame. 'Solomons Seal. That's right, isn't it? That's how Berners described it to you.'

'Yes.'

He nodded, still examining the proof. 'Tubby rang me about it, said he thought the label on the cover auctioned a couple of years ago must have had the word Solomons on it – Solomons Shipping Company, something like that.' And he added, 'I checked with a friend of mine at Robson Lowe. He couldn't remember what was on the label so I asked him who had put the cover up for auction. He rang me later to say that it had been sent to them by a dealer in Sydney.' He reached to a box file on the window ledge behind him, searched out a card and copied an address on to a slip of paper. 'Cyrus Pegley, that's the dealer's name.' He handed me the slip. 'Since you're going there, do me a favour, will you? Go and see him when you're in Sydney, find out all you can about that cover, where he got it from, what was printed on the label – anything at all that will help establish the provenance of these die proofs.'

The address he had given me was Victoria Street, King's Cross, presumably a suburb of Sydney. 'I won't have much time,' I murmured.

'Then make time. It's important if you want these die proofs to fetch the sort of figure I think they could.' He was leaning forward again, peering intently at the pages, the jeweller's glass back in his eye. 'Solomons Shipping Company,' he murmured and shook his head. 'I don't believe that would fit. Berners didn't tell you who his client was, I suppose? No, of course not.' He sighed. 'A pity. We need to know a lot more. It's so incredible, so incongruous.'

'What is?'

'The seal. Particularly the seal on its icefloe. Do you have the *Perkins Bacon Records*?' he asked without looking up. 'The first volume dealing with the Colonial issues. You'll find it in that, towards the end. A very odd admission for a firm of security

printers that was known chiefly for the printing of banknotes.'
And when I told him I hadn't got the books, he said, 'You
should have. Those two volumes are the meticulous record of
every letter, every transaction connected with the design,
printing and delivery by Perkins Bacon of stamps for the
colonies, and for several foreign countries, too. It took Percy de
Worms years to compile it and he died before he had completed
the work. Every collector of early line-engraved issues should
have them.'

'Well, I haven't,' I said. 'So perhaps you'll tell me what it's all
about.'

He hesitated, then shook his head. 'Better ask Tubby. He
spotted it first, not me.' He took the glass out of his eye, closed
the albums and leaned back in his chair. 'He'll enjoy telling you,
so I won't spoil it for him. And now, having had another look at
the proofs, I have a suggestion to make, bearing in mind your
client's needs and the fact that you'll be out of the country for a
time.'

What he proposed was to have the collection entered on the
books of his partner in Zurich who would then advance Miss
Holland the equivalent of £2,000 in Swiss francs. This would be
paid into an external account at her Southampton bank, thus
enabling her to draw on it for payments in any currency. The
only stipulation he made was that I sign an undertaking on her
behalf that the collection would be put up for sale at his
Birmingham auction house. 'We'll put it up in the autumn when
I hope to have a really big sale and I won't charge her any
interest on the monies advanced. Okay?'

It was as good an arrangement as I could have hoped for, and
with my departure for Australia so imminent I was relieved to
have the whole thing settled. It was only when I was out in the
Strand again that I remembered what Tubby had said about the
Seal-on-Icefloe stamp having been printed by an American bank
note company. It couldn't have been anything to do with
Perkins Bacon. But that was Keegan's problem now. As far as I
was concerned the collection was out of my hands. Perenna
Holland had £2,000 spending money in the form of a guaranteed

minimum, and the prospect of at least double that if he were right about the interest the collection would arouse.

As soon as I got home I wrote to her care of the bank. Then I rang Tubby. There was no reply. I rang him again later that night when I had broken the back of the things that had to be done before I left. There was still no reply. My curiosity unsatisfied, I got out my own collection. It always gave me a feeling of satisfaction to look through the colourful print mosaics of my careful lay-outs and to realize that most of the stamps had been acquired long before inflation had got into its stride. But not this time, for I was very conscious that there was nothing in my collection that was in any way out of the ordinary, nothing that would get Josh Keegan talking the way he had about the Solomons Seal.

In the end I locked the albums away and went to bed. It was after one. An owl was hooting from the big cedar across the moat, and though it was already Saturday, and tomorrow I would be on my way to Australia, the forlorn sound of it seemed to reflect my mood.

A new country, the possibility of a fresh start – I should have been feeling eager, full of anticipation. Instead, the feeling I had was one of despondency, almost foreboding. And that night I had a very strange dream. I was back in that empty house and everywhere there were masks and strange obscene figures staring at me, and a voice was calling. I don't know whose voice it was or what it was trying to say; it just boomed meaninglessly around the empty rooms and I woke with the feeling that somebody, something had been trying to get through to me.

I don't often dream and when I do my dreams are usually fairly innocuous. But this wasn't and I automatically reached out to the next bed for comfort. But it was empty, as it had been for far too long now, and I lay there in the dark, trying to remember some detail that would provide a rational explanation.

In the end I switched on the light, got myself a Scotch and took it back to bed, thinking about that girl, and about Australia. What would she do when she got my letter? The memory of her was very vivid in my mind, and I lay there sipping my drink, telling myself it was nothing to do with me and no chance our paths would cross again. It was finished, but the knowledge that she was gone out of my life for good didn't stop me indulging in fantasy. And all the time I was remembering that booming, unintelligible voice.

Dawn was breaking before I dozed off, and when I finally woke it was past nine. I rang Tubby, but again I got no answer. I didn't bother about breakfast, but drove straight down to the Crouch. His boat was gone. I went on board my own then, got the anchor up and beat down the river against the tide, tacking through the first yacht race of the day until I was out in the fairway and thumping around in a growing nor'easter off Foulness. It did me a world of good, the voice of my dream and that dreadful little house blown away by the stiff onshore breeze funnelling up the estuary.

Back at my moorings I cooked myself a meal, and afterwards I sat in the cockpit with a drink in my hand wondering whether I would ever see my boat again. The wind had died with the setting sun, the Burnham waterfront gleaming white in the fading light, everything very still except for the ripple of the tide against the bows and the waterborne sound of voices from the last yachts drifting up on the tide. No sign of Tubby, so clearly he was away for the weekend. The pale glow of the town, the estuary, the tide . . . I had lived in East Anglia ever since finishing my National Service and the thought of leaving it for good filled me with nostalgia. Would I always have to be shifting from job to job? Was that the pattern of my life, some flaw in my character, a lack of stability? Two months past forty and here I was planning to start all over again.

I finished the bottle, slept the night on board, and in the morning drove home, closed up the house and took an afternoon train to London. The following morning I was breakfasting at over 30,000 feet and looking down on the bare arid hills of Muscat and Oman.

PART TWO

CARGO

===

1

It was 2 July that I arrived in Sydney, a southerly buster blowing and low cloud obscuring the harbour as we came in to land. It was Australia's winter so no problem in finding the people I needed to contact in their offices. I saw little or nothing of Sydney the first two days, moving from office block to office block in the central part around George Street, so that my first impression was of a rather drab, modern, dollar-hungry city full of scurrying raincoats and umbrellas. It took me those two days to decide on Kostas Polites & Co. as the estate agents I wanted to handle Rowlinson's Munnobungle station. They were an old-established firm of Greek origin commonly referred to as Castor & Pollux, and they had a branch office in Brisbane, which would enable the sale to be pushed locally with the farming community in Queensland as well as with the institutions in Sydney.

It was lunchtime on Thursday before I had settled all the details. I had a word on the phone with Cooper, the manager of their Brisbane office, told him I would be flying up to see him the following day, and having booked out on the Ansett flight, I took a taxi to the Ferry Terminal. It was only a short walk along Circular Quay to the sail-like complex of the Opera House and I had lunch there looking out to the Harbour Bridge and the bustle of ferries coming and going. The wind was still kicking up little whitecaps in the broad expanse of Port Jackson, but it had stopped raining and the clouds were broken. I should have been in a buoyant mood, everything fixed and fleeting glimpses of sun through the plate glass windows. But now that I was on my own with time to think about my own future, I found myself depressed by all the stories I had heard of large properties that had broken the backs of their owners. No doubt the estate agents had exaggerated to emphasize the difficulty of disposing of a place like Munnobungle, but the cases they had quoted were undoubtedly true and I was beginning to realize how huge and hostile the outback of Australia was.

I had intended having a look round the docks on the offchance I might pick up information about the Holland ships, but then I remembered the stamp dealer Josh Keegan had asked me to visit. The slip of paper on which he had written Cyrus Pegley's address was still in my briefcase where I had put it the night I had packed my things. I paid my bill and walked through the Botanic Gardens and The Domain to the crowded streets of Woolloomooloo.

In just over half an hour I was in Victoria Street, in a narrow-fronted shop packed with stamps and coins, talking to a little wisp of a man with an untidy mop of black hair and bright bird-like eyes that peered at me from behind steel-rimmed spectacles of extreme magnification. When he heard why I had come he handed the counter over to a plain young woman with pebble-thick glasses who might have been his daughter and took me through into an office at the back where two more girls were busy sorting stamps.

Yes, he remembered the cover. He also remembered the lettering on the Seal ship label. 'It was a blue label, deep blue to be exact. The vertical lettering HOLLAND SHIPPING. SOLOMONS at the top and at the bottom a space for the amount to be inked in and the word PAID. I'll show you.' He picked up a pencil and began sketching it for me. 'A smudged postmark, I remember, the clerk in a hurry presumably and cancelling it when he should have hand-stamped it with a capital T and the amount due of ten centimes. Instead, it was left to the Post Office clerk in Cooktown to slap a Postage Due twopenny red and green on.'

And he added, 'I was reminded of that cover only the other day, something I read in the *Herald*. A Holland ship in for engine repairs. It hadn't occurred to me the company was still in existence.'

'How long ago was this?' I asked.

'Last week, I think. It was only a short paragraph and it caught my eye because it was headed WAR HERO'S GRANDSON SAILS IN. I read anything about the war. I caught the last two years of it, finishing up at Darwin.'

'What sort of ship was it?'

'An old warship. Landing craft I think it said.'

'Is it still here?'

'Couldn't tell you. It was only mentioned I think because of the name and the association with old Colonel Holland. He was one of the coast watchers on Bougainville. Stuck it there until the Americans arrived.' He turned the piece of paper round so that I could see the sketch he had made. 'There you are. That's what it looked like.

Unusual, isn't it? And the way it came to me was unusual.' He turned to a filing cabinet and began rummaging through a thick wad of letters.

'You don't happen to have any more of those ship labels, do you?' I asked hopefully.

He laughed and shook his head. 'Wish I had. I did well out of that sale. But if I'd had any more I'd have probably sold them anyway. A man came here two or three months ago . . . Ah, here we are.' And he handed me a letter written on cheap paper with a Mission address stamped on it in purple.

I am writing on behalf of Mr Minya Lewis, it began, and a little further down I found the information Keegan wanted . . . *his mother died in Cooktown on 16 February of last year. Being her only son and his father not having been heard from since 1911, I am satisfied that he has right of possession to anything that was hers, and particularly to this letter which was in his father's writing. She was apparently a very old woman and he found the letter in a box under her bed. As I believe there is some value in old stamps . . . .*

Lewis! Was this the same Lewis that Chips had talked about, the half-breed aborigine who had killed a man named Black Holland? 'Can I have this photocopied?' I asked.

He hesitated, then gave a little shrug. 'You can keep it if you wish. I can't see that it's any use to me now.' He asked me about the collection I had mentioned, and when I had satisfied his curiosity he insisted on showing me some of his recent purchases. In the end I came out with a real bargain, a superb mint pair of the first issue Turks & Caicos Islands 2s. purple showing salt-raking against the background of a ship under sail; also a used set of the Papua New Guinea first issue of 1952, which attracted me because they were line-engraved and all of them different, the full set of fifteen stamps conveying a vivid picture of the strange primitive world that lay less than a thousand miles north-east of where I would be in two days' time.

I must have been in that shop over an hour, for the evening rush hour had started when I reached the Ferry Terminal, intent on checking the docks to see if Holland's ship was still there. But though the ferry I boarded gave me a good view of the docks I saw nothing that resembled a landing craft, the ships all too big to be trading in the islands. It was dark by the time we docked at the quay again, a cold blustery evening. I took a taxi across Pyrmont Bridge to Union Street, found a way into the docks and began searching the wharfs on foot. My mood was quite different now, despite the wind and the bitter cold. Chance had presented me with a priceless opportunity, a ship I understood and bound for the Pacific islands. What more could

I ask? I felt she must be there, and in the end I was proved right. I found her at last, up in the northern end of the docks, lying with her square stern close against some dilapidated sheds in a part of the docks that hadn't been modernized, one of the Mark VIIIs or older even, and she had HOLLAND LINE slapped across her rusty side in red.

There was no glimmer of light showing and when I tried to go on board I was shouted at by an old man with a beard who was walking a mongrel bitch as old and shaggy as himself among the empty beer cans littering the dirty quay. He knew nothing about the owners, wasn't interested. The agents had given him the job and as long as he was the watchman nobody went on board without written permission from them. The only information I got from him was that the engineers were still working on her.

I walked slowly the length of the vessel, recalling the cramped quarters, running my eye over her battered plates. She looked old and tired, which was hardly surprising considering she had been built over thirty years ago. But at least the bridge housing looked well cared for. Her name, painted in black on the stern, was just visible below the flukes of the stern anchor: *Perenna – Buka*. The fact that Holland, after purchasing the vessel presumably from the Ministry of Defence, had re-named her for his sister started me thinking about her, wondering whether she had got my letter yet, if she was even now on her way to join him here.

Before returning to my hotel I asked the watchman the name of the agents, and all the way back, walking briskly through the lit city with ragged clouds glowing red and the moon showing intermittently between their torn edges, I was remembering other nights of velvet humidity when I had stood on the compass platform of just such a ship conning her through the Molucca Straits. The things you do as a youngster remain incredibly vivid and the more I thought about it the more I was attracted to the idea of trying for a passage on the *Perenna* when the engine overhaul was finished. There was always the possibility that job prospects in the Solomons might be better than they seemed to be in Australia. But I knew bloody well the

real reason was curiosity and the thought that if I could stay
close to her brother I might see her again, perhaps even be able
to help her.

I rang the agents from the airport next morning, but was told
the man dealing with the *Perenna* was out. Whoever it was
speaking could give me no information about her sailing date,
and when I asked whether it was Holland himself who had
brought the ship to Sydney, he wanted to know my business and
why I was making enquiries about her. In the end he suggested
I rang again later and put the phone down.

By then my plane was being called and once we were airborne
I put all thought of the ship out of my mind, concentrating on
Munnobungle and the notes in my briefcase. The sun was
shining when we landed in Brisbane and I spent most of the
afternoon in the Kostas Polites office going over the details with
Ted Cooper. We finally agreed that the auction should be in
Brisbane on 22 August, six weeks being, in his view, the
minimum required to obtain full coverage for the sale in such a
large area as Queensland. That evening he and his wife gave me
an excellent dinner of mud crabs in a restaurant overlooking the
Brisbane River, and the following day I went on to Townsville.

Townsville was the nearest airport to Munnobungle and
McIver, the station manager, was there to meet me. I found him
in the airport lounge, a craggy, sun-dried Australian in khaki
shorts and open-necked shirt. He was in conversation with a
black man neatly dressed in a tropical suit that was almost sky
blue, a marked contrast to McIver's sweat-stained bush gear.
'You want a beer before we start?' he asked in a grating voice
without any friendliness in it.

'Just as you like.' He had every reason to resent my arrival
and I was wondering how best to handle him.

'Well, I bloody do. Had a flat on my way in so I only just got
here in time.' He went over to the bar and came back with two
cans and glasses. The black had drifted off and we drank in
silence. Finally McIver said, 'How's Rowlinson?'

'All right,' I said. And, because I wanted to get things
straight at the start, I added, 'Look, the fact that he's selling has

got nothing to do with the results for last year. He doesn't want to sell, but he's under pressure — from his wife, and from his business associates.'

'That's what he wrote, but it's hard to believe. I liked the bastard, and I thought he understood. You'll see when you get to Munnobungle. It's a tough station.'

There were quite a few people waiting in the terminal, many of them blacks, some very black indeed with frizzy hair. 'Most of the people here are from Papua New Guinea,' McIver said, making an effort at conversation. 'The Port Moresby plane is in and they're waiting to board.'

'Are there many of them in Australia?' I asked him, thinking of the man Chips had called Black Holland.

'Not many in Australia, but here in Queensland, oh my word, yes. They come over to work in the sugar plantations. Not that fella I was talking to, he's a PNG government official. Been down in Sydney buying road building equipment.'

The loudspeaker suddenly burst into voice, announcing the departure of the Air Niugini flight for Port Moresby. The blacks began gathering up their belongings and I watched them move to the exit. McIver said something, but I didn't hear it, lost in the knowledge that here I was at the gateway to that primitive world so beautifully depicted on the stamps I had bought, the world that Chips had talked about with such nostalgia. 'Another year,' McIver was saying, 'an' I reck'n we'd have turned the corner.'

'That's got nothing to do with it,' I told him irritably.

'No? Then why doesn't he come out himself, tell me what the problem is to my face?'

'Rowlinson's got a business to run in England. He hasn't the time.'

'So Munnobungle was just a bloody toy. Is that what you're saying?'

'If you like to put it that way.'

'Jesus! An' I've worked my guts out. . . .'

We finished our beer in silence and went out to the parking lot. The Fokker Friendship was taxi-ing now. It took off just as we were driving out of the airport and, seeing its wings glinting silver in the sun as it banked eastward over the sea, I was wishing I was in it, not seated in a dirty utility with a disgruntled man who was worried about the future.

We were headed west and it was a long dusty ride, gravel rattling against the mudguards, the last twenty miles all dirt. Having seen the deeds and maps, his report, all the figures, I thought I knew what Munnobungle would be like. But I was wrong. Nothing, not even Chips's description of it and the fact that three sheep to the hectare was the best they could do, had prepared me for the aridity of the place. They had had almost a month without rain, which was unusual in winter, and the place was little better than a dust-bowl, the scrubland running out to a distant view of purpling hills, and everything hazed in the sun's glare with the leaves of the eucalypts shimmering to a slight breeze.

I spent three days there, driving more than a hundred miles in the Land Rover and covering most of the 60,000 odd hectares. And the more I saw of it the more I wondered how Chips had ever imagined he could make a profit and who the hell would be fool enough to buy it off him. The percentage rake-off he had promised me faded like a desert mirage. 'Looks different when we've had some rain,' McIver said hopefully that first evening. And his wife, a quiet, solid woman, added, 'It's real beaut then, the grass coming green, and the flowers.' They had two young kids, a boy and a girl. They were a nice family and I was sorry for them, hoping that whoever bought the station would let them stay on. They seemed to love the place, something it was hard for me to appreciate, seeing it in a dry spell with nothing growing and the sheep looking gaunt and half-starved.

But by the third day Munnobungle was beginning to get under my skin, the wide skies, the sense of space, and the birds flocking round Deadman's Hole, a pool in a dry tributary of the Burdekin. It was only five miles from the homestead and about the only water I saw on the place. I was riding a horse that day and beginning to understand why Chips had so enjoyed the time he'd spent on the station.

It was my last day there and that evening I persuaded McIver to drive me over to the hotel at Mushroom Rock on the Burdekin, which was the nearest place I could buy him a beer. I still needed clarification on some of the sale details I had prepared and I thought it would be easier to discuss them away from the homestead. By then he had become resigned to the inevitable and we were on reasonably friendly terms, so that when I had got the information I required I began to tell him about my own problems. I think that was when I first saw him smile. 'So we're both of us in the same boat, eh, wondering where the hell we go from here?'

He was no help to me, merely repeating what the estate agents had said, but more colourfully and in greater detail. 'It's a tough life, a tough country. No place for a Pommie unless he's got a helluva lot of capital and doesn't mind how much he loses.' When I asked him about the islands, he shrugged. 'There's the copper – mining and plantations, that's about it. Some smart boys, Canadians some of them, are doing well selling to the indigenous population. That's in PNG, government contracts mainly. It's what I hear anyway. I never bin there. But I might,' he added thoughtfully. 'I might pack it in here and try my luck, 'cept that I got a family to provide for.'

I told him about the Holland Line then and asked him whether he knew anything about it, or the family. But he shook his head. 'There was a Holland on Bougainville became something of a war hero. One of the coast watchers. I remember my father talking about him. Stayed on when all the others had left and fought his own private war.'

'Was that Colonel Lawrence Holland?'

'Could be.' He nodded. 'He was a colonel, that I do remember.'

'Did Rowlinson mentioned a man named Black Holland?' I asked.

'Yes, that's right. He did.' He frowned. 'I remember now. He came back full of some story about an aborigine he'd met. Tried to sell him a share in a mine. The Dog Weary gold mine. That was it.'

'What was his name?'

'Oh, I don't recall that. Only the name Black Holland. It seems the abo killed him in a brawl over the ownership of the mine. I remember Rowlinson was full of it at the time, thought it a damned funny story.' And when I asked him whether the killing had happened locally, he said, 'Oh dear, no. Cooktown I think. Rowlinson had just been to Cooktown to see where Captain Cook had repaired the *Endeavour* after she'd hit the reef.'

He couldn't tell me anything more, but when we got to the homestead, and I showed him the letter the stamp dealer in Sydney had given me, he agreed the aborigine's name might have been Minya Lewis. 'Reck'n that's it. Welsh and Cornish miners, they were in on all the gold strikes, and the Palmer River was full of the stuff until the Chinks mined it all out.'

He could tell me nothing more except that there was an amazing graveyard out beyond Cooktown that included a Chinese burial place, also an old Edwardian hotel with frosted glass windows and a large wall painting that included some of the old-timers that still hung around the bar. He had been there only once. 'Took the wife and kids up there, but it's a helluva journey unless you fly up with Bush Pilots Airways.'

Had I gone to Cooktown then I might have had some warning before I got myself involved in the tangled background of the Hollands. As it was I flew back to Sydney next day knowing nothing about the trail of greed and death that had its origin in the Dog Weary mine, or the relevance of that stamp collection, only that there was probably some connection. I had a window seat and coming in low over Sydney Harbour Bridge in the late afternoon, the sky clear and the sun just setting, I thought I could see the repair yard where the LCT had been lying. But now there was only a coaster alongside. The plane tilted slightly, giving me a view of the bridge and the whole broad expanse of Port Jackson right out to the Heads. That was when I saw her, a squat little toy of a vessel out beyond Fort Dennison. I thought for a moment I had missed my chance and she had sailed. But as we steadied on our course for the airport on Botany Bay, craning my head I caught another glimpse of her below the tailplane. I could see the wake then. She wasn't outward bound. She was heading back into port.

As soon as we landed I rang the agent. This time I had no trouble, probably because the man who answered was in a hurry to get home. The *Perenna* had just completed her engine trials. There were still some minor adjustments to be made. These would be carried out tomorrow. She would be taking on cargo Friday morning and sailing for Bougainville the same day. It didn't give me much time, for I still had the legal side of the Munnobungle sale to deal with, as well as currency and land sale regulations to check. I went straight to my hotel, left my bags and took a taxi to Observatory Park where I knew I would have a good view of the dock area.

It was a cold, very clear evening, and from the steps above Kent St. I looked across Darling Harbour to wharves thick with shipping and more vessels anchored off in the dark expanse of water. It was some time before I picked her out. She was half hidden by a big container ship, just her bows showing, and then she was completely lost to sight for the container ship was under way with two tugs in attendance.

When the container ship was clear I could see her plainly, small and slab-sided among the freighters over towards Peacock Point. There were no taxis and it was a long walk across Pyrmont Bridge to the dock area and the gate leading on to the wharves. I was almost an hour wandering about under the stars among ships and cranes and the blank walls of the storage sheds before I was lucky enough to find a launch lying alongside some steps out by Donkey Island. It was taking on the crew of a Japanese freighter anchored off and the coxs'n, who spoke a few words of English, agreed to drop me off at the LCT. It was just on eight when we left, a stiff breeze blowing up the harbour and all of us huddled under the canopy. He made for his own ship first and when we were alongside there was a great sorting out of packages and souvenirs before the crew members finally went chattering like a group of starlings up the gangway. 'Your ship ex-war?' the coxs'n asked me, his teeth showing in a grin.

'Not my ship,' I told him.

'You visit?'

I nodded and he turned the launch towards the LCT, now only 3 or 4 cables away. 'How you get shore?' he shouted above the sound of the engine and the crash of the bows.

'They'll have a boat.'

'No boat.'

I didn't say anything, watching as we approached the familiar shape of her. She looked even older than when I had seen her last, the paint flaking from her flat side, the letters HOLLAND LINE showing red and streaked with rust in the glimmer of the shore lights and her plates all buckled by years of work. And then that name again as we rounded the stern to come alongside under her lee.

No gangway, and no sign of anybody on board, only a light high up in the bridge housing aft. It came from what used to be the wardroom. I hailed her, but there was no reply. A rope ladder lay flat against her side and I seized hold of it as the launch bumped. 'You send a signal *Yamagata*', the little coxs'n said, 'I come take you shore.'

I thanked him and then the launch was swinging away and I was climbing the rusty side. And when I reached the catwalk, and stood looking down at the empty tank deck with the storm and ramp doors at the far end, it was all so familiar that it was like that first time I had gone aboard an LCT at Helensburgh, a young National Serviceman nervous at the thought of going to sea in such a strange craft.

'You, what you like?'

I turned to find a man in thin blue trousers and a heavy sweater standing below the bridge housing. He was very black with a great mop of frizzy black hair. 'Is the captain on board?' I asked him.

He stared at me, the whites of his eyes showing, and there was a long silence. 'You like to see him?'

'Where is he? In the wardroom?'

'What you want him for?'

I hesitated. 'Is his name Holland?'

'He not seeing anybody.'

'Tell him I have news of his sister.' I had moved along the catwalk and was now quite close to the man. He was shivering slightly and the glossy smoothness of his black skin had a blue tinge as though he had been dipped in indigo. 'You'll get cold out here,' I said, moving past him towards the bridge ladder.

'Okay. I take you.'

'Don't bother. I know the way.' I went up the ladder to the bridge wing and slid back the door to the wheelhouse. It was dark inside, only the glow of the shore lights to show me the dim outline of the wheel and the engine-room telegraph. It was very quiet, no sound of movement or voices, not even a radio, and the hum of the ship's generator muted to a gentle persistent murmur deep down below me. I went through into the passage leading aft, past the captain's cabin and the signals office with its radio equipment. Light showed in the heat cracks of the wardroom door and I pushed it open.

The lay-out hadn't changed, a black grease-stained leather settle around two sides of the mess table, some chairs and the inevitable ship photographs and Service plaques on the walls. The mess table had a chart spread half across it and there were books open, one of them an Admiralty Pilot, and beside it a sheet of paper with some notes. There was also a half empty bottle of whisky and a china jug with the lip broken. All this I took in at a glance, my mind slipping back twenty years and my eyes fastening on the man slumped at the far end of the settle under the porthole, his legs up and his head leaning back against the corner. He had dark hair, almost black, a square freckled face, very sallow with deep lines creasing the forehead and his mouth hung slightly open.

He looked ill and tired and I thought for a moment he had fallen into a drunken coma. But then his eyes opened, staring at me wide with shock. Suddenly he sat up, a quick startled movement. 'Who are you?'

'You're the captain, are you?' I asked him.

He nodded slowly, his eyes still wide and that startled, almost frightened look. I told him my name, but he didn't seem to take it in. 'Who sen' you?' His voice was soft, a little slurred. 'Wha' you want?'

He wasn't ill. He was just scared. I could literally smell his fear, the nerve twitching a muscle in his cheek, his self control almost gone.

'It's all right,' I said, trying to reassure him. 'I just came to see if you had room for a passenger. They told me you'd be sailing on Friday as soon as you had taken on cargo.' I was talking fast, trying to give him time to accustom himself to my presence. 'I'm from England, on business, but I've got over a month to kill and I thought –'

'Who told you I'd be sailing on Friday?'

'The agents.'

'An' you wan' come with me, on this ship?' The creases on his forehead deepened as he forced his brain to concentrate. 'Why? Who put you up to this?'

'Nobody,' I said. 'I've just told you, I've time to kill and I've never been to Bougainville or the Solomons. I'd like to sail with you, that's all.' And then, because he bore no resemblance to Perenna Holland and I wanted to make doubly sure of his identity, I asked him if he were the owner as well as the captain.

'Yes, I own this ship.' He was staring at me, breathing hard. 'Didn't you know that? Didn't they tell you?'

'You're Jona Holland then.'

'Who told you that? My name's Jonathan Holland. Nobody calls me Jona, 'cept – 'cept my sister.' He sounded confused, fear giving way to resentment. 'I don't know who you are, what you're doing here. I've got things to consider – decisions – must think clearly, work it out.' He pushed his hand up through his hair, staring with glazed eyes at the bottle. 'Tomorrow night and the nex' night and the nex'. No sleep. Five nights and then –' He looked up at me suddenly. 'You know Perenna?'

'I've met her.'

'In Suffolk?'

'Yes, at the house in Aldeburgh.' And I started to explain the circumstances, but he wasn't listening. Even when I told him she wasn't there any more, he didn't seem to take it in, muttering to himself, 'She doesn't understand. About money, I mean. The difficulties – ' He checked himself, staring at me with a surprised look as though suddenly conscious of my presence. 'Sit down. Have a drink.' He waved vaguely to a chair. 'Strange girl, Perenna. Tough. She won't stay there, will she? Not now she's put him in a home. Did she tell you she'd killed a man? She was with Mother in the kitchen when they burst in an' she fought them off with a meat cleaver. Killed one and wounded another before they – ' His eyes were wide open, re-living the scene. 'She was only seventeen. Blood everywhere. Always remember it. Terrible sham'les.' I thought for a moment he was going to burst into tears, but then he pulled himself together, a conscious effort. 'Glasses in cupboard. Wha' d'you say your name was?'

'Slingsby,' I said. 'Roy Slingsby.' I got a glass and poured myself a drink, appalled at the scene, at his vivid recollection of it. 'What caused the natives to behave so violently?' I asked.

'Cargo,' he muttered darkly. 'Bloo'y cargo. They go crazy.' He shook himself as though to get rid of the memory. 'Why d'you want to go Bougainville anyway?' He pronounced it Boganville.

'I've always wanted to visit a Pacific island.'

'Coral beaches, white sands, blue sea, blue sky, eh?' He laughed, but on a high tense note. 'Bougainville's not like that. Just rain and mountains and rain forests, and copper, bloo'y copper. Copper and gold. Gone to their silly heads.' He reached for the bottle, looking round vaguely for his glass which was lying on the floor. I got it for him and he mumbled his thanks. Then, suddenly suspicious again, 'Who you going to see on Bougainville?'

'Nobody. I don't know anybody there.'

'Bloo'y liar.' The bottle rattled against the glass as he poured the whisky. 'Nobody goes to Bougainville without a reason.' He looked up at me, his eyes focusing, his forehead creased with the effort. 'You going to make trouble, start organizing things?'

I hesitated, but his behaviour was so odd . . . 'Are you expecting trouble?' I asked. 'Is that why you're scared?'

'Scared?'

'Yes, scared. You're scared of something.'

He shook his head vaguely. 'Drunk too much,' he muttered, pushing the glass away. 'Copper an' gold. They think it's Cargo. You know about Cargo?'

It seemed a pointless question, but when I said, Yes, of course I did, he got very excited. 'You've been briefed. They've briefed you and now you want me – '

'Look,' I said, 'I'm just an estate agent acting for a friend of mine in England. I know nothing about Bougainville, only that you operate out of the Buka Passage.' I told him about Munnobungle then and having to wait until 22 August for the sale. 'I've time to kill and this seemed a good way of doing it.'

'You mean just a tourist trip. To Bougainville!' He said it incredulously, glaring at me, his bloodshot eyes still doubtful. 'Why don't you fly then?'

'I like the sea.'

'An old bucket like this? If we got another southerly buster you'd be sick as a dog and so bloo'y frightened – '

'I know what these ships are like in a blow.'

He didn't seem to hear me. 'She rolls and rattles and flops around like a limp sheet of tin. One day she'll break her bloo'y back.'

'You don't have to tell me. I've sailed on LCTs before.' And I added, 'Maybe on this one. I served in three of them.'

That got through to him at least. 'Three? You've been on three?' He put his glass down carefully, leaning forward, the frown deepening as he tried to concentrate. 'This one came from Singapore. There was a number on her. Can't remember now. I've got it somewhere. The British were pulling out and they were going to scrap her. She was so old they wouldn't risk sailing her back. Were you in Singapore on LCTs?'

I nodded. 'I had almost a year there. Before that I was on the St Kilda run. The Outer Hebrides and the North Atlantic. I wouldn't think you could throw anything worse at me down here than we had on that run.'

He smiled then. 'You were Army, were you? These ships

weren't Navy ships. They were run by a Maritime Detachment of the Army.' His uneasiness returned. 'What was your outfit?'

'RASC Water Transport. I was doing my National Service.'

He hesitated, then nodded. 'Yes, of course. They changed the name. Were you an officer?' And when I told him I had been newly commissioned as a 2nd Lieutenant he said almost eagerly as though now, suddenly, he wanted to believe me, 'A deck officer?'

'Yes. A very junior one.'

'How much do you remember about running these ships?' His voice was no longer slurred, his manner almost urgent. 'You say you like the sea. Have you done any navigating since?' And when I told him I owned a sailing boat and occasionally raced her in the East Anglian offshore races, he leaned back, laughing quietly to himself. 'And you just walk on board, like manna from bloo'y heaven. You know these buckets, you sail your own boat – Jesus Christ, there must be a catch in it somewhere.' He paused, staring at me hard. 'If I gave you a berth would you be prepared to work your passage, take a watch? Not officially, of course. Officially my first officer is Pat McAvoy. But unofficially?'

'What's wrong with McAvoy?' I asked.

'He's an alcoholic. He's ashore now. He's been ashore all during the engine overhaul. I know where he is, an' his condition. But he's on the list and I'll get him on board before we sail so they can't stop me.'

'What about the second officer?'

'Luke? Luke is from New Britain. Inshore he's fine, but not on this run. A fisherman's son, passed his exams, but can't be left to navigate an ocean passage. He knows the theory, but panics when he's out of sight of land.'

'So you're on your own.'

'For the run to Bougainville, yes. Coming over I was five nights on the bridge. Five bloo'y nights with no sleep.' He straightened up, leaning forward, his voice urgent again as he said, 'Well, is it a deal? You sign on as a deckie, as one of the crew, then once we're at sea I make you an acting ship's officer,

94

okay? There's no union where I come from, so no problem, and that way, if anything goes wrong I'm covered.'

'Nothing I'd like better.'

He laughed then, suddenly relaxed as he reached for the bottle and poured me a stiff drink, slopping some of it on to the table in his excitement. He tipped the rest of the bottle into his own glass, then raised it. 'Welcome aboard, Mr Slingsby. If you're what you seem, then for once I'll have had a slice of luck.' He gulped down most of his whisky. 'Bit of a change that. Luck and I don't seem to have been on speaking terms for a long while.'

We finished the whisky and as I was about to leave I asked him whether he had ever come across an aborigine half-cast named Lewis. But the name meant nothing to him and he had never heard of Black Holland. 'Red Holland, yes – but no' Black Holland. No blacks, only mixeds in my fam'ly.' And he gave a drunken titter. He tried to get up to see me off, but by then he was almost out on his feet. Slumped back on the settle again, he pulled himself together sufficiently to say, 'See you Friday morning.' And then with a great effort, 'You meant it, didn't you? 'Bout standing watch.'

'Yes,' I said. 'Send a boat for me at nine. Darling Island. I'll be there.'

He nodded. 'Dar'ing – 'arling Island. Nine. Boat. I'll be there. Tell Luke.' His head lolled back, his eyes rolling, the whites yellow.

'You all right?'

'Sure. Sure I'm awright.' His eyes closed, his mouth falling slightly open.

I hesitated, wondering what it was had started him off on a lonely drinking bout. Something he was scared of, but it wasn't the sea or the condition of his ship. And it wasn't the prospect of five sleepless nights. Well, doubtless I'd get it out of him in due course. I went back through the wheelhouse and down the bridge ladder. I didn't have to signal the *Yamagata*; there was a big inflatable with outboard at the bottom of the rope ladder and the man who had greeted me ran me the short distance to the wharf steps.

Before stepping ashore I asked him his name and he said, 'Luke Pelau.' I told him who I was and that I'd be sailing with him. 'Remind Captain Holland to meet me here at 09.00 Friday morning. Meanwhile, get him to bed.' I was on the point of making some comment, but he didn't look as though he was in the mood to respond to a touch of humour, his black face blank, almost sullen. 'Gutbai,' he said and gunned the engine, swinging the inflatable out into the dark waters of the harbour, heading back to the slab-sided hull of the LCT, a black silhouette now against the headlights streaming across the Harbour Bridge.

It was a long walk back to the hotel and I had plenty of time to consider Holland's strange behaviour. I suppose it was that, and the realization that in two days' time I would be at sea with him, that started me thinking again about Carlos Holland and the disappearance of the *Holland Trader*. I had sandwiches brought up to my room and scribbled a note to Josh Keegan, passing on to him the stamp dealer's description of the Solomons Seal ship label and enclosing a copy I made of the missionary's letter confirming Lewis's ownership. As soon as I had posted it I went to bed, but I couldn't sleep. I was too excited. It was the thought of being on the bridge of an LCT again, this time heading out into the Coral Sea towards an unknown Pacific island – I was as excited as I had been that first time, years ago joining ship in the Clyde, and as nervous. But it was a different sort of nervousness now, more a feeling of uneasiness, almost trepidation.

First thing the following morning I went to the Maritime Services building in George Street. To my surprise they not only had records going back to the year 1911 but were able in a very short time to produce the details I wanted. The *Holland Trader* had arrived from England via the Cape on 4 July 1911. She had discharged one member of the crew, a seaman, and had signed on two others. She had taken on coal and sailed for Port Moresby on 10 July. They were even able to give me the names of the crew members who had been shipped at

Sydney. One of them was named Lewis – Merlyn Dai Lewis. He had been signed on as a stoker.

I would have tried the newspaper offices then, to see what had been said about the ship's disappearance, but I hadn't time. The restrictions covering currency remittances overseas was still very tight so that I had the bank as well as the lawyers to contend with. In the end I only just managed to purchase the additional items of clothing I thought I would need before the shops closed.

Friday morning everybody seemed to be checking out of the hotel at the same time and on top of that I had to wait for a taxi. It was past nine before I reached the Darling Island docks, sun glinting on the water and the wharves seething with activity.

He was there waiting for me, pacing up and down, a stocky figure in dark blue trousers and jersey, cap pushed back from his forehead. His face lit up as he saw me. ''Fraid you'd had second thoughts about it.' There were dark circles under his eyes, but otherwise he seemed himself. He was even smiling as he took my bags. 'Well, let's get the formalities over.' He passed my gear to the two blacks manning the inflatable, told them to wait for him, and then we took my taxi on to the Maritime Services building where I signed on.

Just over an hour later we were back on board, the engines thrumming under my feet and the anchor coming in. We loaded at a roll-on, roll-off ramp, the cargo reconditioned Haulpaks for the Bougainville copper mine, and shortly after noon we had cleared and were steaming out under Sydney Harbour Bridge.

I was in the wheelhouse then, checking the instruments and following our course through Port Jackson towards the Heads. Besides the helmsman and the pilot there was just Holland and Luke Pelau on the bridge, no sign of McAvoy, and when I asked Luke where the first officer was he said, 'Mr McAvoy little tired this morning.' Holland heard him and laughed without humour. 'You won't see Mac on the bridge unless he's in one of his moods. Then he'll come and tell us how to run the ship. That's right, isn't it, Luke?' And the black officer nodded.

'How long has he been like this?' I asked.

'Since my grandfather's death. They'd been together a long time and he never forgave himself for being away after a woman when the Colonel started out on his last voyage.' He was staring out towards the Heads, which were separating now to show the empty heaving expanse of the Pacific in the gap. 'Go down and check those Haulpaks are properly secured, will you. She'll be rolling a bit when we get outside.'

Down on the tank deck the Haulpaks were huge, their fat rubber tyred wheels standing taller than myself. The crew, all black, were tightening up on the securing chains. The bos'n, an elderly man with a great mop of frizzy black hair streaked with grey and a broken-toothed smile, was standing over them. The ore trucks were larger than anything they had carried before, but he knew his stuff and though I went round every vehicle I had no fault to find.

Already there was movement on the ship, the faint beginnings of the swell coming through the Heads. I went for'ard to the storm door and, having checked that, climbed the vertical ladder to the port catwalk. For'ard, under the ladder to the foredeck, was the bos'n's locker and workbench. The watertight door leading to the controls for the electric motor powering the bow door thrusters was open. One of my jobs had always been to check the bow doors and the ramp before sailing. I ducked through to the narrow platform that looked down into the well behind the bow doors and there I got a shock. The steel cross-members that should have been bolted into their transverse position to hold the bow doors securely shut were still in their vertical housing.

I hurried back and yelled for the bos'n, telling him to get some men on to the job right away. But he didn't understand what I wanted. Even when I took him with me and showed him, he only shrugged and pointed to the hydraulic thrusters, indicating in a complicated mixture of Pidgin and English that that was what kept the doors shut. 'No use ol ain girders,' he added, referring to the cross-members.

'Well, you use them this trip.' And I told him to get on with it. Good God! With the sort of seas we might encounter on the run across to Bougainville the bow doors could be burst wide open. What really appalled me was the knowledge that they must have come all the way to Sydney with the bow doors held on the thrusters only. This was apparent as soon as the cross-members had been dropped into position. They couldn't find the securing bolts. 'Better get hold of the Chief Engineer,' I told the bos'n, who seemed to understand what I said even if he couldn't speak proper English. 'If he hasn't got any the right size, then he'd better make some quickly.'

He was just leaving, looking puzzled and unhappy, when one of the crew, squatting on his hunkers below the work bench, held up one of the missing bolts. All eight of them were there where they had fallen, covered with dirt and a pile of steel and wood shavings. The place looked as though it had not been cleaned out since the ship had been handed over by the Army.

I stayed until the cross-members were securely bolted together, then I took the bos'n with me up to the bridge. Holland had to be told. A first officer who was drunk, never took a watch, never checked the cargo, was one thing. But not checking the bow doors, leaving those cross-members unsecured – that was something different; gross negligence that endangered the ship and everyone in her. But we were dropping the pilot and Holland wasn't on the bridge, only Luke. I turned to the bos'n. 'Where's Mr McAvoy's cabin?' I was so angry I decided to have it out with the man myself. 'Where is he?' I repeated as the bos'n stood there gazing dumbly at his feet.

'Okay, kum,' he said reluctantly. 'Mi suim.'

I was thinking McAvoy must have some hold over his captain, otherwise Holland would never put up with it. But that was no reason why I should. And then to find him tucked up in his berth in the obvious place, in the first officer's quarters right across the alleyway from the spare cabin I had been allocated aft of the wardroom. He was lying flat on his back, his pale blue eyes wide open, a vacant stare, the skin of his face haggard and drawn, and so drained of blood he looked positively yellow as though he were suffering from jaundice. 'McAvoy. Can you hear me?'

He must have been getting on for sixty, a hard little monkey of a man with battered features and a scar running white under the hairs of his half bare chest. 'Why aren't you up on the bridge? Why haven't you secured the bow doors?' I didn't expect any reply, but I thought I saw a flicker of comprehension in those dull lifeless eyes. They were like two pebbles that had dried out and lost their lustre. 'Where do you keep the stuff?'

That at any rate got through to him, his eyes suddenly wide and alarmed, 'Fu'off. None of your fu'ing bus'ness.'

I started searching his cabin then, emptying drawers, lockers, the lot, and flinging everything on to the floor. 'Ge'out,' he screamed. 'Ge'out, d'ye hear me.' He had hauled himself up to a sitting position, his head gripped in his hands as he groaned. 'Wha'ye looking for?'

'You know bloody well what I'm looking for.' I reached over the bunk and shook him. 'The bow doors. Don't you know enough to have them braced? Now come on. Where is the stuff?' He started to fight me off, his nails clawing at me, his teeth bared. 'All right,' I said, flinging him back on the bed. 'I'll find it in the end. And when I do I'll break every goddam bottle. Understand?'

'You do that,' he breathed. 'I'll kill ye. Aye, I will.' He was staring at me, his eyes alive now with malevolence. 'Wha' are ye doing on this ship anyway?'

'Standing in for you, you useless bastard.'

The malevolence deepened to blazing anger. 'You call me that again – '

'I'll keep on calling you that until you're on your feet and sober enough to do your job. You're supposed to be the first officer. You're a bloody menace. A danger to the ship, do you hear me?' I left him then, knowing I had got under his skin and wondering just how dangerous he'd be when the drink was out of him. If I hadn't been so angry I might have been a little gentler with him.

The bos'n was waiting outside the door and I made him show me all the likely places. In the end we found it tucked away in a locker behind the life-jackets, half a dozen bottles of whisky and two of vodka. We carried them through the wheelhouse and out to the bridge wing, where I jettisoned the lot. We were out through the Heads now and the ship was rolling.

Holland came into the wheelhouse just as I was getting rid of the last bottle. 'What's that you're throwing overboard?' he asked me. And when I told him, he said, 'You shouldn't have done that.' He didn't wait for me to explain, but added as though to justify his forebearance, 'He suffers from melancholy. He's a manic-depressive. I think that's the medical term. Without a drink inside of him he's no good at all.'

'Well, he's no good with it, so it makes no difference.' And I told him about the bow doors. 'If you'd had that southerly buster when you were coming down the coast. . . .'

'Well, we didn't,' he said sharply. 'Anyway, they'd have held. We never use those cross-members. Takes too much time. And Mac,' he added, 'he needs his liquor. Without it he goes crazy. He's afraid.'

'Of what?' I asked.

He shrugged. 'Death. Devils. All the dark imaginings that inhabit men's minds. He's quarter French and quarter Mortlocks.' He didn't tell me what the other half was. He didn't have to. It was Glasgow Irish, the accent unmistakable. 'He was with my grandfather through the war, and afterwards. Fought with him, ran the schooners, taught me most of what I know about the sea. Never mind,' he added. 'I'll see he gets enough.'

I was about to argue with him, but then I thought better of it, knowing that men who have been together a long time develop ties that are sometimes closer than blood relations. Shelvankar would fill me in on the details. It was Shelvankar who had shown me to my cabin, a talkative little Indian from the island of Fiji who acted as radio operator when he wasn't dealing with stores, fuel, cargo inventories and bills of lading. He came in shortly afterwards with the latest weather forecast. It was good; easterly force 3 decreasing, sea calm with a slight swell, some rain showers, visibility moderate. The general situation indicated that conditions would further improve as we headed north to the Queensland coast.

Holland spiked it and turned to me. 'Care to take over, Mr Slingsby?' I nodded, the formality not lost on me. 'Course 010°. Keep her about five miles off shore.' He stayed there for a while, watching as I entered up the log, checked the chart and the Pilot. Apparently satisfied, he said, 'Luke will relieve you at four. I'll take the last Dog.' And he left me to it.

There was only one ship in sight, a coaster heading north up the coast and about two miles ahead of us. A shower of rain was drifting across the sea to the north-east. I stood for a while by the windows watching it as it swept across the coaster, enjoying the movement of the ship under me, the lift and roll as the blunt bows breasted the swell, the steady throb of the engines under my feet. The tank deck below me, made strange by the ungainly bulk of the Haulpaks, rose and fell, the heavy vehicles straining at the chains as she rolled. Once, trying to make the lee of Barra, we had been caught out in Force 10. If we'd had this sort of a load, I thought, we'd have gone to the bottom.

I was alone except for the helmsman, everything so familiar, yet because of him it was different, the skin of his face a glossy black below the woolly halo of his hair and no means of communicating with him except in Pidgin. He was from Shortland Island. I checked it out on the Solomon Islands Chart 214; it was a small island just south of Bougainville. 'Are all the crew from the Solomons?' I asked him.

He shook his head. 'Sampela long Bougainville en Buka. Buka bilong Solomons wantaim. Nau Papua New Guinea.'

I went back to the charts, found the one that gave the planned details of the Buka Passage, and with this and the Admiralty Pilot I began to familiarize myself with the approach. It was something I always did. I have an orderly mind and I like to know what lies ahead of me before I make any sort of a passage. When I had finished with that I turned back to the chart we were currently using, the Pacific Ocean 780, South West Sheet. It was old and faded, much used, with many pencil marks only half rubbed out in the area of the Solomons. Looking at it, I wasn't surprised that Holland was worried about navigation. Sometime in the second night out we would be off Sandy Cape.

We would have to leave the Australian coast there, just short of the Great Barrier Reef, and head north through the hazards that littered the chart between Queensland and New Caledonia. Variation between true and magnetic at that point was given as 10°E.

'You know where Captain Holland is please?'

I turned to find Shelvankar behind me, a message pad in his hand. 'Isn't he in his cabin?'

'No, not in his cabin or the saloon. Maybe in the engine-room.' He smiled. 'It's about the two extra vehicles we take on tomorrow night. It can wait.' He put his thick lensed glasses firmly into place, peering at the charts. 'I have entered you as acting first officer now. On Captain Holland's instructions. You are a good navigator?'

'Why do you ask?'

'He is damn nearly asleep on his feet when we come south to Sydney.' His English was very precise, spoken with a high-pitched lilt that reminded me of a Welsh friend of mine who lived on an old Thames sailing barge up the Blackwater. 'The sea is not my natural home and when the captain is tired and his mind is on other things – ' He gave a little shrug expressive of an unwilling fatalism. 'I am relieved to see you checking the charts so conscientiously.' He said it on a note of uncertainty and I realized that he knew nothing about navigation and was afraid I might be trying to pretend I knew more than I did.

'Don't worry,' I said. 'I can navigate all right. It's just that I don't know these waters.'

'So you find out from the chart and the Pilot.' He nodded, smiling his relief. 'That's fine. That's very fine, very sensible.'

'What's this about loading two extra vehicles?' I asked, glancing down at the tank deck where the four Haulpacks had been loaded aft in a tight huddle that left a clear space between the lead vehicle and the storm door.

He didn't reply and when I asked him what the message was he said, 'It's nothing important. Just a change in the time the vehicles will be at the beach.'

'At the beach? Are we loading direct off an open beach?'

He nodded, a shade reluctantly.

'What about Customs?'

'No Customs.'

I stared at him, conscious of his reluctance to talk, remembering Holland's strange behaviour two nights back when I had walked unexpectedly into his wardroom. 'Where is this beach?' I pushed the chart towards him. 'Show me.'

But he shook his head. 'You ask Captain Holland. I not know where it is.' And he scurried out like a small spider that has weaved a bit of a web and then been frightened off it. He could have kept his mouth shut. But I realized that wasn't in his nature. As a source of information he would always be unreliable, but at least he was a source, somebody I could talk to, and I guessed he had been with Holland quite a time, knew the family's history.

Luke arrived in the wheelhouse a little before four, which was a good sign. He seemed to know nothing about the beach. And when I raised it with Holland in the saloon over tea he refused to discuss it, his face blank. 'Two trucks, that's all. Nothing to do with you.' And he began discussing navigation, confirming that we'd leave the Queensland coast at Sandy Cape steering 05° Magnetic to pass between Saumarez Reef and Frederick Reef, both lit. I had already pencilled this probable course on the chart. 'Where's the beach?' I asked him.

He hesitated, then said, 'In the vicinity of Tin Can Bay, just south of Fraser Island.' It was at the northern end of Fraser Island that Sandy Cape marked our point of departure for the Coral Sea.

He wouldn't tell me anything more, sitting there sucking on an empty pipe, the creases in his forehead deepening and his mind far away. He was so tense, so uncommunicative that I was certain this was what had started him drinking that night. I went to my cabin and lay on the bunk, but I couldn't sleep. There were some dog-eared paperbacks on the shelf above my head, including Conrad's *The Nigger of the Narcissus*, but I couldn't concentrate, which was probably just as well since it wasn't the ideal book to read in the circumstances.

I was on watch again at eight and as Holland was handing over to me Shelvankar came in. It was dark now and I was concentrating on locating the stern light of the coaster ahead of us. I heard a muttered curse and turned to find Holland staring down at a message in his hands, his face gone pale and looking as though he couldn't believe it. He was staring at it so long he could have read it through half a dozen times, and the little Indian standing close beside him as though enthralled by its dramatic potential.

Suddenly Holland turned to me. 'Didn't you tell me you'd met my sister?'

I nodded.

'When was that? How long ago?'

'About a month.' And guessing what the message must be, I said, 'She's on her way to Sydney, is she?'

He didn't answer that, staring at me, very tense. 'How did you come to meet her? Was it about the house?'

'Yes.' And when I started to explain he said, 'I know all about the sale. But that was to provide for Tim, and she'd taken a job as a stewardess. I didn't expect her out here for at least another month. Somebody must have given her money.'

He sounded so suspicious that instead of asking him about his brother, I found myself having to explain the value of the stamps. And all the time I was speaking he was staring at me, very pale, and still with that tenseness. 'So you arranged for £2,000 to be put to her credit in a bank at Southampton. And you didn't tell me.' His voice was harsh, a little out of control. 'Why are you here? Did she ask you to contact me?' And without waiting for a reply, suddenly aware of the little Indian standing close beside him avidly taking it all in, he said, 'We can't talk here. Hand the bridge over to Luke, then come to my cabin.' And he left abruptly, the flimsy still clutched in his hand.

His cabin was next to the wheelhouse and as soon as the second officer had taken over I joined him. He was sitting on his bunk, staring fixedly at nothing. 'Why didn't you tell me?' he muttered again, almost petulantly. 'If I'd known she was going to fly out . . .' He looked up at me. 'That night when you came on board, if I'd known then . . . you should have told me.'

'I didn't think it was the moment,' I said.

He stared at me, finally nodding his head. 'No, perhaps not. And you seem to have done the best you could for her. I'm grateful.' He said it as a matter of form, nothing more. And then he was silent for a long time, lost in his own thoughts. The odd. thing was he didn't seem at all happy at her imminent arrival, his reaction one of alarm rather than pleasure.

'When did you last see her?' I asked.

'What? Oh, let me see, it must be about five years ago now. I went over to England, to discuss things with my father.' Remembering Mrs Clegg's description of the father, I thought he probably took after him, and wondered what the mother had been like, the two of them, brother and sister, so completely different. 'She shouldn't have come,' he muttered to himself.

'What did you expect her to do?'

He shook his head vaguely. 'It's no place for her,' he mumbled, but I knew it wasn't that. For some reason he was afraid of her. 'I never thought she'd come, not suddenly like this. She talked about it, of course. She was always writing to me. Once a week, regularly.'

'She'll have told you then – about your brother. She says it's sorcery.'

But he didn't seem to take that seriously. 'Ever since Mother was killed. . . .' He shook his head, his mind on something else. 'It's Hans,' he murmured. 'It must be Hans.' He looked up at me. 'Hans Holland,' he said. 'We have a partnership arrangement. Perenna doesn't approve.'

'He's a relative, is he?'

He nodded. 'A bit removed you might say.'

'Was he in England two or three months ago?'

'Yes. I think he's still somewhere in Europe. He's got big ideas, you see, and he's looking for an ore carrier now.'

'And he's got red hair, has he?'

'Yes, why?'

'I think he visited them in Aldeburgh.' It seemed to worry

him and I said, 'Are you afraid your sister will ask awkward questions, about the partnership I mean? You're still a separate company, aren't you?'

'Yes.' I had his attention now, his eyes on me, his fingers drumming nervously. 'And the ship's still mine'. He sounded defensive. 'I've had to borrow, of course, but we're still solvent. It's been a company since 1947 when my grandfather started it going after the war. He was running all sorts of craft then. Even when I took over we still had some schooners. But it wasn't until Hans began to undercut us that things became difficult. He started from scratch with two of those ugly little ramp-propelled lighters. RPLs. I had to make a deal with him then, and for that we needed something better than beat-up old coasters and the schooners.'

'So you bought this vessel and named her after your sister?'

'Yes.'

'So why don't you want her out here?'

I thought for a moment he wasn't going to answer, but then he said, 'Perenna and I. . . .' He gave a little shrug. 'The point is, whether it's a house or a ship or a business, she wants to run it herself. The last I heard from her she was at Southampton. That was before I left Buka. Now there'll be letters waiting for me at Chinaman's Quay.' He smiled warily. 'If I'd been at Madehas instead of in Sydney I'd have known all about you and those damned stamps.' He sighed. 'What the hell do I say to her? This – ' he tapped the message – 'is an inflight from a Qantas aircraft en route from Singapore to Perth. She knows I've been in Sydney for engine overhaul and she expects me to meet her at the airport. You think she'll have enough cash with her to fly on to Bougainville?'

'Why not tell her to meet you at that beach you're putting into?'

'No.' He said it quite violently. 'No, she can't come on the ship.'

'Why ever not?'

He stared at me, a puzzled frown and his eyes worried. 'There's no place for her, no proper accommodation. I can't have a woman on board. Not Perenna. She'd – she'd be difficult.' He had got to his feet. 'I'll tell her to contact the agents. That's the best thing. They can arrange hotel accommodation and fix it for her to fly on to Kieta. Better still, she could stop off at Perth and stay with her aunt for a while. Yes, that would be best.' And he nodded, smiling nervously as he pushed past me, pleased at having worked out a solution.

I went back to the bridge and took over from Luke again. The coaster was still there ahead of us and nothing to do but follow her. The chart showed Kieta as the main port of Bougainville. I tried some star fixes then. The night was very clear, ideal for sextant practice, but after I had twice made a nonsense of my calculations I gave it up. I just couldn't concentrate, my mind on Perenna Holland instead of star charts and correction tables. I slid the starboard bridge wing door open and stood thinking about it in the cool night air. Well, I had done my best. I had tried to explain and if he didn't share his sister's belief about sorcery it was none of my business. But it still didn't make sense expecting her to fly on to Kieta when she could so easily join ship at this beach we were putting in to. And she certainly wouldn't stop with an aunt in Perth, not when she had come so far, working her passage until I'd got her the money to fly the last part.

I found myself gazing for'ard over the backs of the empty Haulpaks to the gap left for the two trucks we were going to load from a deserted beach in the small hours of tomorrow night. No Customs, the Indian had said. I wondered what those trucks would be filled with – drink, cigarettes, or was it something more serious? Drugs? Was that what he was afraid of, that she'd find out he was smuggling drugs?

There was a light on in the signals office and suddenly my mind was made up. I went back to the chart table, wrote out my message and then took it to Shelvankar. He was alone, sitting at a portable typewriter, a cigarette burning in an old tobacco tin, the air thick with smoke. The place was littered with cardboard boxes and as he glanced up at me, dark eyes magnified by the thick lenses of his glasses, he looked more like a storekeeper than a radio officer. I handed him the message I had written. 'I want that sent right away.' He read it, taking his time. Finally he put it down.

'You know Miss Holland?' he asked.

'Yes.'

He shook his head uncertainly. 'I will have to ask the Captain.' He was getting to his feet, but I pushed him back into his chair. 'Just send it,' I told him.

'But Mr Slingsby. I cannot do that. It is very difficult, you see. Captain Holland has already sent quite different instructions to his sister. She is to fly to Kieta.'

'At his expense?'

'No, he don't say anything about who pays for the ticket. He just tells her he can't meet her and if she doesn't stay with her aunt at Perth she must fly on to Kieta.'

'So, after coming all across the Pacific to see him, she's fobbed off with an aunt or else she has to fly up to Townsville, get the Air Niugini flight to Port Moresby, then switch to another flight to Bougainville.'

'Is none of my business, Mr Slingsby. If you do not agree, then you talk with Captain please.'

'I've already talked to him. He's worried about that beach cargo.' I hesitated, sure that this little man knew what it was, but not certain I could wring it out of him. 'You keep the ship's accounts, don't you?' I saw a flicker of uncertainty in his eyes. 'Well, don't you?'

'Yes. But I don't see – '

'Then tell me this. Just how much are you in the red? You've been losing money – '

'The Hollands, they run very good shipping line. Is very important for the islands.'

'I'm not talking about the Hollands. I'm talking about this ship. It's been losing money, hasn't it?'

He was silent for a moment. Then he said, 'There is a recession, you know. All over the world. In the Solomons and Papua New Guinea, too. Everyone is affected by it. But we were all right until we have to go to Sydney for engine repairs. This is very old ship now.'

'And Holland's in debt – to his partner?'

He didn't have an answer to that, and because I had already come to the conclusion that Jona Holland was no business man and relied entirely on this man for cargo arrangements and all the accounts, I said, 'You know everything that goes on in this ship, Mr Shelvankar, so I'm sure you have discovered what my normal business is. I deal in land and big estates, which means I know all about figures and can read your books the way an accountant can. Do you want me to get Captain Holland to let me check through them?'

There was a shocked look in his eyes as he said quickly, 'I assure you, Mr Slingsby, there is no need for that. Everything is accounted for very meticulously. I am a most meticulous person.'

I knew I had him then. In total control of the business side it wasn't in his nature not to fiddle something. 'You send that message. Quote the flight number and ask for it to be delivered to Miss Holland on board the aircraft.'

For a moment he sat there staring up at me. Then he nodded. 'Okay, I send it. But on your responsibility, you understand. I am not responsible.'

'Just send it.'

2

The last night watch is always a lonely one, but at 04.00 that morning I felt lonelier than usual. Tiredness may have had something to do with it. I had been on the bridge until past midnight and had had very little sleep. But that wasn't the real reason. It was the strangeness of the ship, the crew all islanders who didn't speak my language, and a coast I had never seen before. Standing there on the bridge, the night dark and overcast, a black helmsman at the wheel and only the lights of that coaster ahead for company, the sense of isolation was very strong.

My eyelids gradually became heavy, almost gummed together with sleep, and to keep myself awake I began thinking about Bougainville, what future the island might hold for me. Then my mind switched involuntarily to the trucks we were going to load off that beach and to Perenna Holland – wondering whether she had got my message in time, what she would do. Would she stay with her aunt in Perth or fly on to Sydney, hire a car and drive up to Tin Can Bay? I knew so little about her I didn't even know whether she had a licence and could drive. And if she did manage to locate us in the dark, what prospect was there for the development of any close relationship here on board with her brother and his problems always present? Even my memory of her was now overshadowed by that vivid drunken picture he had given me of her wielding a cleaver in the blood-bespattered kitchen where their mother had been murdered. An outbreak of native hysteria, the lawyer had called it. But hysteria is a symptom; there had to be a cause for such an outbreak of violence.

Luke relieved me as dawn broke reluctantly under the overcast, the ship tramping steadily on over a leaden sea and the coast of New South Wales just visible, a dark line on the horizon to port. He had a reasonable command of English and I stayed with him for a while. He was from a village at the eastern end of New Britain. He showed me the position of it on the Pacific Ocean chart. It was on the coast facing towards Hixon Bay and a high mountain called The Father. He was an important figure in his village, he said, but to retain that position he had to return at reasonable intervals to hold a feast and give presents. 'I have two worlds, you see.' He was smiling a little sadly. 'They do not understand this world. They know I am a navigator and have a ship. That they can understand for we have always lived partly by the sea. But they can only see that I am a navigator if I go there and prove to them I am rich. It is a very poor village.' And he added quickly, 'But the life there is good.'

I asked him why he wouldn't stand a night watch or navigate out of sight of land. He hesitated a long time before replying. Finally he said, 'Mr Sling'by, believe me, I can do it.' His deep voice was suddenly urgent. 'But I do not have confidence when the Captain is all time watching me. In the islands he knows I am a good navigator, but at night, or on a long voyage like from Louisiade Archipelago to Sandy Cape, he has no trust, so I am afraid I don't do it right and make some very abominable mistake.' He looked at me then, his black, broad-nosed face reflecting a deep-felt sense of wrong. 'It is a long time since you serve in a ship like this, but he does not watch over you.' He said it almost accusingly.

Looking into his face, I realized that beneath that black, markedly different shell, was a very proud man. 'Would it help,' I said cautiously, 'if you shared a night watch with me? Later in the trip.' And I added, 'It would certainly help me if you did. I don't know these waters and I'd appreciate having you check my navigation.'

He hesitated, his large brown eyes fixed on me intently. Finally he nodded. 'Yes, I do that.' And suddenly he was smiling at me, a great broad smile that had extraordinary warmth in it. 'I think you understand.'

I left him then to find the wardroom empty, breakfast already over and the table littered with the remains of the meal. I was tired and didn't feel like food anyway. I slipped down the companionway to the main deck, got a mug of tea from the galley and took it to my cabin, turning in straight away. Holland was having a long lie-in in preparation for the night ahead and I was due on the bridge again at noon.

Luke called me a little before twelve so that I had time to eat before going on watch. There was nobody else in the wardroom and Samson, the big burly steward, served me in lonely splendour. When I finally joined Luke in the wheelhouse I found the weather had deteriorated. There was no sign of the coast now, visibility down to about two miles. 'This evening I think it rain,' he said.

'You've got a new forecast, have you?'

He shook his head, laughing. 'Don't need forecast to tell me what this weather will be. I know.'

I was to discover that in this, as in many other things, his instinct was infallible. But he knew nothing about sorcery, or pretended not to, though he admitted it existed and that it was still practised in the islands. Talking to him, I found him a complicated mixture of pride and diffidence. He was also one of the most likeable men I had ever met.

He relieved me again at four and by then there were rain clouds building up to the east of us. 'Compass course is due north,' I said. 'And the radar shows the coast six and a—half miles off. Have you had some tea?'

'No, I have coffee.'

I got some tea from the galley and took it up to the wardroom. There was nobody there and when I had finished it I started on a tour of the ship. It was the first opportunity I had had to look around. I started with the engine-room. They were still clearing up after the overhaul, but already the copper and brasswork gleamed and the whole hot mass of machinery had a cared-for look. The chief engineer was from Rabaul, an old grey-haired man who introduced himself as Ahab Holst. Of mixed German blood, and German trained, he was a cheerful, friendly man, and his regard for his engines was in the nature of a love affair. The others in the engine-room were different. They were from Buka and I was unpleasantly conscious of the sullenness of their manner.

Outside of the engine-room the ship was in a poor state, dirt and rust everywhere and no sign of anything having been painted for a long time. Even essential gear looked neglected and nothing seemed to have been done to clean up on deck after the period in dock. The galley on the main deck of the bridge housing was far from clean and in the crew's mess for'ard I sensed that same sullenness. They were most of them from Buka and the coxs'n was there with them, a squat bearded man, the skin of his face so glossy black it looked like polished ebony. He said his name was Teopas and when I asked him why he didn't stick to his own mess aft, he affected not to understand, though

113

I learned later he had been to school at a Marist Mission and spoke quite good English. I told him to come with me and check some of the things that urgently needed attention, but he just stood there staring at me with surly insolence, not saying a word, and the devil of it was there was no way I could enforce the order.

I went aft then to what had been the segeants' mess, which was where he should have been. The only occupant was the bos'n, and when I asked him about the attitude of the Buka men, he said, 'Buka bilong Solomons. No laikim Papua New Guinea gavman. Buka pipal laik ind'pendence. Bougainville tu.' He was from Kieta and he said something about his father having been killed by the Australians during the war. At least, I think it was that. He said, 'Papa bilong mi and ol Australia maikim dai.'

Finally I went up to my cabin feeling distinctly uneasy. A ship with a political bombshell ticking away in its guts, that wasn't what I had been looking for when I had come out to her in Darling Harbour. Lying on my bunk, thinking about it, it was hard to realize it was only thirty-six hours since I had come on board.

I was back on the bridge at 20.00 after a greasy overdone steak, apple pie and coffee. Holland was there, pacing restlessly back and forth. Nobody else except the helmsman. 'We're closing the coast now,' he said. 'I altered course about an hour and a-half back, shortly after we came on to the continental shelf. I'm not sure, but I think I've got the loom of Double Island light fine on the port bow. We're in sixty-five fathoms at the moment. When you get below thirty fathoms put the engines at Slow Ahead and give me a call.'

'What's your ETA at the beach?' I asked him.

'Between midnight and 04.00 was what I told them. I guess we should be there about 01.00, probably a little before.' He went over to the chart. 'That's our position.' He had pencilled in a cross with 20.00 against it. 'When you raise the light keep it fine on the port bow and whatever the depth call me at 23.30. We should be less than an hour's run from the beach then.' He turned to me with a quick nervous smile. 'I hope you're enjoying yourself. It's a great help to have you on board and I'm grateful.'

I nodded. 'Glad I'm of use.' I turned to him then and the smile faded as I said, 'There's just one thing. Those two trucks you're lifting off the beach, what's in them?'

'I don't think that need concern you.' His tone was abrupt, slightly defensive.

'That depends,' I said. 'You're loading off a deserted beach at night, no Customs Officer present, and if it's contraband. . . .'

'The cases will be Customs-sealed, papers, everything dealt with.'

'Yes, but what's in them?'

'I'm afraid I can't tell you that.'

'Does that mean you don't know? You're accepting cargo off a deserted beach and you don't know what it is?'

He stared at me uneasily, then turned away. 'It's simply to save them trucking it all the way down to Sydney.'

'You could have picked it up at Brisbane.'

'I don't know why they chose this method,' he said irritably. 'I didn't fix it. But I need that extra cargo to cover my fuel bills.'

'If you didn't fix it, who did?'

'My partner.'

'Through your agents in Sydney?'

'It'll be on the manifest. I don't know what agent he used.'

'And you don't know what the cargo is.'

He turned on me then. 'Look, Mr Slingsby, either you're a passenger on my ship or you're acting first officer. Whichever it is, you're under my orders. The cargo is nothing to do with you. But if you feel there's something wrong, then there's nothing to stop you going ashore as soon as we're on the beach and the ramp down.' He was facing me, his head down, his voice trembling on a high note. 'It's up to you,' he added and went quickly out as though afraid I'd persist with my questions.

I stood there for a moment, staring at the chart and thinking over what he had said. I was certain that there was something

illegal about those trucks. All the time I had been questioning
him I had sensed his doubt. But, as he had said, no reason why
I should be a party to it. I was free to walk off the ship as soon
as we reached the beach, except that I had radio-ed that message
to his sister. 'Kepten!' The helmsman was pointing. 'Lukluk
kepten. Double Island lait.'

I picked up the glasses and went out to the bridge wing. The
night was very dark. Away to the north a flash of lightning lit
the low cloud base. It was some time before I saw it, picking up
the flash as the old tub crested a swell. It was too low on the
horizon for positive identification, but it couldn't be anything
else. During the next half hour the echo-sounder recorded a
gradual decrease in depth, finally steadying at between 39 and
34 fathoms. By then the light was very clear. But during the
next hour it became increasingly difficult to see as rain came in
from the north, very heavy at times so that it even blurred the
trace of the coast I was getting on the radar screen. At 23.30 I
called Holland. We were then in 32 fathoms, the indistinct radar
trace showing us six miles off.

I got him some coffee, then stayed with him in the wheelhouse, but we didn't talk. He was completely absorbed in his
navigation. However, when we were barely two miles off, at a
point when I would have expected the ship to have his full
attention, he came across to me and said, 'I think I should tell
you something. When we bought this ship it was a question of
survival. It still is. I've never been much of a business man. It
was Hans who saw the advantages of landing craft that could
bring copra and coffee cargoes direct from the plantations. He
bought a war surplus RPL, and traded with it so successfully
that within a year he had bought another. He's over in England
now arranging finance for this new ship. That's the sort of man
he is, and when he puts something my way I know it will be to
my advantage and all the details thoroughly worked out.' He
looked at me sideways. 'I've been thinking over what you said
and I felt I ought to tell you the position.'

I thanked him, not sure whether this explanation wasn't in
part to convince himself. 'Of course, mostly the cargoes are

arranged by Mr Shelvankar. He does it by radio. All the isolated plantations have radio now, some of the bigger ones even have their own airfield.' He reached for his oilskins. 'Think I'll con us in from the upper bridge. It's not going to be too easy to see the track down to the beach in this muck.' Dressed, he tightened the strings of his hood. 'Hope I've set your mind at rest. I wouldn't want to lose you just as we're starting the long haul across to the Solomons.' His smile was friendly but tense as he pushed back the door and went out into a drenching downpour of rain.

The rain was so heavy now it had completely blotted out the scanned outline of the coast. The upper bridge telegraph rang for Slow Ahead and the revs died to a sluggish beat. We were half a mile from the shore and nothing visible, the circling illumination of the Double Island lighthouse no more than an intermittent glimmer in the darkness. Ahead of us was nothing, only blackness. A few minutes later he signalled Slow Astern and called the crew to stations on the ship's loudspeakers. We backed and filled with constant alterations of course. Luke came through the wheelhouse on his way to the upper bridge, barely recognizable in his oilies, and for'ard I could see oilskin-clad figures flashing torches as they got ready to open the bow doors and lower the ramp. I heard the stern anchor let go and almost immediately afterwards the gleam of headlights showed through the rain. The telegraph rang for Stop Engines and a moment later there was a slight lurch as the ship grounded.

There was an oilskin coat and sou'wester hanging on a peg at the back of the wheelhouse. They were too small for me, but at least they gave some protection as I climbed down to the tank deck. By the time I reached the bows the doors were open and the ramp was being lowered. Fortunately the sea was calm, flattened by the rain, for we were grounded at least a dozen yards from the shoreline, and the ramp, when it touched bottom, was half under water. Holland waded out to the end of it with the water up to his knees as he tested the bottom with his feet. Apparently it was firm for he signalled them to drive on with his torch.

There was no difficulty with the first vehicle. The driver took it slowly in low gear and four-wheel drive, coming up the ramp without a check and parking himself neatly against the steel side of the hold, nose right against the wheels of the first Haulpak. He didn't get out of his cab and when I went over to him and asked whether he had seen anything of a young woman, he said, 'Sure. That beach is crowded with them, all in bikinis.' He had a broad-brimmed hat on his head and a hard-bitten face. 'You think I carry a harem around with me, an' in this weather?' He grinned down at me. 'You expect a lot with this sort of a consignment.' The second vehicle was already coming down the beach and I had to move out of the way. It came too fast, had to check at the ramp and the engine died. After that it was a winching job.

It took the better part of half an hour, winching and manhandling, to get it positioned. Finally it was done and the two drivers waded ashore to the back-up car that was waiting for them at the top of the beach. No sign of Perenna Holland. Either she hadn't been able to make it or she hadn't got my message. Maybe Shelvankar had never sent it. I went up to the signals office and asked him again, but he assured me he had sent it at once, looking offended that I should doubt his word. He was busy checking the papers the drivers had brought on board. 'What's the cargo?' I asked him.

'Japanese outboard engines.' He showed me the manifest. 'You see. They are all cleared by Customs.' I had already checked that myself. The trucks had been stacked with heavy wooden crates, each crate wired round and sealed with a little leaden seal. Back in the wheelhouse I found the bow doors closed, the ramp up and the ship already moving astern as Holland hauled her off the beach on engines and stern anchor winch. Ten minutes later we had recovered the anchor and were headed out to sea. He came down then from the upper bridge. 'Went quite well really.' He looked tense, the muscle on the side of his jaw twitching slightly, his oilskins dripping water. 'Rain's taking off now.' I could almost feel him trying to unwind. 'Didn't like it running in. Lot of tide around here. Not too sure of the chart. Conditions didn't help either.' He was pulling off his oilskins. 'What about some coffee?'

'I'll go and see about it,' I said.

'Thanks, and put something in it. You'll find a bottle of Scotch in my cabin.' He was already at the chart table, leaning over it and at the same time keeping an eye on the echo-sounder. Luke was standing by the helmsman. 'Coffee?' I asked him and he nodded.

When I got back with four mugs, some sandwiches, and the bottle of whisky the rain had almost stopped and the light on Double Island Point showed as a distant flash low down on our starboard quarter. Our course for the gap between the Saumarez and Frederick reefs took us close inshore the whole 100-mile length of Fraser Island. Only when Sandy Cape was abeam would we be in deep water. Holland drained his coffee, put the mug on the chart table and turned to me. 'I'll relieve you at four. That all right with you?'

I glanced at the clock at the back of the wheelhouse. 'That gives you barely two hours' sleep.'

He nodded. 'Can't be helped. It's the same for both of us. Just keep your eye on the depth and the radar. Call me if you're in any doubt. The Double Island light gives you a perfect back bearing and if the rain holds off you should have it in sight until just before I relieve you.'

It gave me a certain sense of satisfaction that a man who spent his whole life navigating the island-infested waters of the South West Pacific should have sufficient confidence in my navigation to leave me in charge of his ship running close along the shore of an island I had never seen before. 'Just don't go to sleep, that's all,' he added as he went out.

I sent Luke to check that the bow doors had been properly secured. He was gone a long time, finally reporting that he had had to rout out the crew again and oversee the job himself. 'They don't think it important.'

'And you?' I asked.

He shrugged. 'We never do it before.'

'That's because you could always run for shelter under the lee of an island. This voyage you can't.'

He stayed with me for the first hour of my watch. It was a help, for once the effect of the coffee had worn off the whisky in it took over and I began to have difficulty keeping my eyes open. The rain, the constant strain of peering into the darkness, the nervous tension of the beaching and the fact that I had been on watch now for almost seven hours, all in a climate that was quite different from England, had made me very sleepy. I was sorry when he finally left me. We hadn't talked much, but his company had been comforting.

Alone, I paced back and forth, thinking about Holland's problems, wondering where his sister was, vague fantasies flitting through my mind. Oddly enough, it was those damned stamps and the fate of the *Holland Trader* that was the recurring theme of my thoughts. There had to be some connection, some connection that was relevant, not just to what had happened in 1911, but to *now*, to this ship, to Jona Holland, Perenna, that wretched arrowhead, all those masks and pictures in the Aldeburgh house.

My brain went round and round, chewing at it like a mincing machine, like the echo-sounder interminably making its trace. Periodically I stood watching it, half mesmerized – 22 fathoms, 21, 24, 18, 20 . . . and then I would go out on to the bridge wing, take a bearing with the hand compass on the Double Island light, now barely showing above the horizon. And all the time my mind half occupied with strange thoughts that gradually resolved themselves into the conviction that what had happened to the *Holland Trader* would happen to the *Perenna*, that we'd mysteriously disappear to become a ghost ship, a latter-day *Flying Dutchman* damned for ever to steam the South West Pacific, always heading for Bougainville and the Buka Passage, but never making it. Lost in the Coral Sea – 19 fathoms, 20, 18, 17 . . . I was back at the echo-sounder but couldn't remember how I got there. A coral reef? But that would have left her a wreck with at least her mast and her upper works showing. A volcanic disturbance? That would account for it. And there was a volcano on Bougainville, something about

Rabaul also; hadn't it been half destroyed about the turn of the century? Or the sea cocks, perhaps they had been opened, in error, or purposely. There could have been an explosion in the engine-room, boilers bursting, something that had blown a hole in her bottom. But the stamps. And that cover. There would have been a letter inside it. What the hell had it said? To get that stamp the man must have been on board the ship and I wondered whether that half-breed aborigine up in Cooktown still had the letter or could remember what it said. Even if he couldn't read, his mother might have told him. I wished Perenna Holland were here. So many questions, and the need of somebody to talk to, somebody to share the half-formed fears that had begun to take root in my imagination.

'Lait, Kepten.'

I turned, peering vaguely towards the helmsman, my eyes barely open, my thoughts still confused. 'Where? On the port bow?' But the Sandy Cape light was still fifty miles away.

'Lukluk!' He was pointing to starboard.

I saw it then, two tiny pinpoints widely separated. A ship southbound down the coast. I noted it in the log, and the time, which was 03.47. Only another thirteen minutes before I called Holland. Watching the slowly changing bearing of that ship gave me something to occupy my mind, and ten minutes later I went to Holland's cabin and gave him a shake. He started up abruptly, his eyes looking wild. 'What is it? What's happened?'

'Your watch,' I said.

He shook his head, smiling thinly, his hair hanging over his eyes limp with sweat. 'Dreaming.' He pushed his hand up over his face. 'I dreamed we were aground and then. . .' He shook his head again. 'What's the time?'

'Just coming up to 04.00'

He nodded. 'I'll be glad of some air.' He swung his legs off the bunk and sat there staring at me. 'You all right?'

'Tired, that's all. Everything's okay. We're in seventeen fathoms with the coast about eight miles off.' I left him then and a few minutes later he came into the wheelhouse, his hair slicked back and looking fresher. The helmsman had already been relieved and I didn't linger.

Back in my cabin I didn't bother to switch on the light, undressing quickly, dumping my clothes on the foot of the bunk. And then, as I went to get into it, my bare feet stumbled against something on the floor. I just managed to save myself, cursing, my hand on the bunk and something moving under it. Then the bunk reading light went on and I was standing there in my vest and pants staring at her stupidly. She was sitting up, the orange-red hair falling across her face, her eyes blinking in the light. 'Sorry if I startled you.' She wasn't wearing much, some sort of a slip, and she was smiling a little uncertainly. 'I borrowed your bunk. I was a bit tired. I hope you don't mind.'

I shook my head, still feeling dazed. It was her bag I had stumbled against. 'How did you get here? You weren't at the beach.'

'Yes I was. I was on that first truck. You talked to the driver, remember? I kept low because I was afraid Jona would send me ashore if he knew.'

'You were taking a chance with a man like that,' I muttered, remembering the hard-bitten face, that crack about a harem. She laughed and shook her head, her hand reaching up to a leather thong round her neck. 'How did you persuade him to smuggle you on board?'

I don't know what she replied, I was too astonished at the sight of her sitting up in my bunk, the freckled face still flushed with sleep, her hair a tousled mop, and dangling from its thong like a barbaric pendant between those thrusting breasts a native knife in a worn leather sheath. 'I was quite safe, you see.' She was smiling at me. 'You look almost as shocked as that Aussie driver.' She slipped it back and said in that husky voice, 'Buka isn't quite the same as Aldeburgh, you know.' She pulled the coverings back, shifting herself close against the partition. 'Come on. You'd better get some sleep. You're almost dead on your feet.'

'I'll take one of the blankets and kip down in the wardroom,' I told her.

'No. That would look odd.' She didn't want her brother to

know she was on board until we were clear of the coast. I was looking around, wondering where else I could put myself in that tiny cabin when she said, 'Don't be silly. Are you afraid I'll seduce you? You look too tired for that. I know I am. I worked till I dropped on that cruise ship, every day an endless delay, thinking of Tim all the time, wondering . . . And the men on board,' she added, seeing me still hesitating; 'I've had all the men I need for the moment.'

The brazenness of her admission shocked me more than the knife. 'You mean you've been sleeping. . . .' I checked myself. It was none of my business who she slept with. 'I'm sorry.'

She laughed, an angry snort. 'What did you expect on a cruise?' Her tone was one of contempt. 'And after being cooped up in that house I'd have had every justification – except that I had other things on my mind.' She patted the bunk. 'Now come on. You look silly standing there in your underclothes.'

There was just room on the bunk and she had no intention of vacating it. I was too tired to argue. I got in beside her and was instantly aroused by the warmth of her body close against my back. 'I haven't thanked you,' she said. I could feel her hair against the back of my neck, the soft whisper of her breath, and I thought she said something about her brother, but I lost it, my brain gone blank, my body tumbling into sleep.

When I woke sunlight was streaming in through the porthole, and somebody was calling, 'Breakfast.' I sat up and there she was, fully clothed, opening the door. McAvoy came in with a tray, his hands trembling and the cups rattling. He put it down on the shelf table, then looked at me, his bloodshot eyes creased up in his wizened face. 'I wouldn't be doing this for anyone but Perenna, you understand.' He turned to her. 'He's asleep now so you can move around the ship without his knowing. By the time he wakes for his midday meal we'll be a good twenty miles clear of the coast. You can tell him then.'

'Is that far enough?' she asked.

'Aye. He'll not go twenty miles back on his tracks. It'd cost him too much in fuel.' He hesitated. 'Do you want anything in your coffee, to perk you up?'

She shook her head, smiling at him. 'Thank you, Mac.' And she added, 'It takes me back, seeing you. It really does – reminds me of the good things. Thank you for the breakfast. And I'm so glad to find you're still with him.'

He didn't say anything, nodding dumbly and staring at her with those watery blue eyes. Then he seemed to pull himself together, starting for the door, but pausing with it half open. 'Last time you were at Madehas wasn't so good. Let's hope it's better this time.' The way he said it he seemed to be sounding some sort of a warning.

'That man,' she said when the door had closed behind him, 'he used to be skipper on one of my grandfather's schooners. I've known him all my life.' She handed me a plate of bacon and eggs and then, as she was pouring the coffee, she said, 'When we were children we'd go down to Port Moresby and he'd be there waiting for us. Every year we'd sail to Madehas, the whole family, all except my father, of course. He was running Kuamegu. I used to look forward to those voyages. We'd be anything up to a week at sea, sometimes more, putting in at all sorts of places. And when I was bigger I was allowed to join my brothers on trading runs through the Solomons, to Choiseul, Santa Isabel and New Georgia, once as far as Guadalcanal and San Cristobal. And always with Pat McAvoy. My grandfather wouldn't allow me to sail with anybody but Mac. He was the best skipper he had. I didn't mind the stink of the copra. I was most of the time on deck anyway. I even slept on deck. It was marvellous lying there watching the sails against the stars on a hot tropical night.'

I couldn't make up my mind whether she was talking to cover her embarrassment that we'd spent the night together in the same bunk, or because she was nervous at the prospect of meeting her brother. 'What about school?' I asked. 'Presumably you went to school in Australia.'

She shook her head, the cap of orange hair brilliant in the sunlight slanting in through the cabin porthole. 'Jona was educated at a boarding school in Sydney. Tim followed three years later. But I never had any proper schooling. Mother was my teacher. That's probably why we were so close. And there was a Mission not far away. That helped. Then, of course, I read a lot. My grandfather had a very good library.' She paused, sitting in the chair there, her head bent over her coffee, lost in thought. 'It was a marvellous life, so free. And the Chimbu village was quite near so that I grew up with their children, looking after the pigs and cassowaries, attending their sing-sings, learning how to shoot with bow and arrow, how to throw knives, spears, axes, and at the Mission how to nurse the sick, how to keep accounts and barter for trade.' She gave a little laugh. 'You know, I sometimes think I had a far better education than my brothers. What's the use of learning to read if you aren't given the right books, or doing algebra when you've no experience of trading? And ball games, football for instance, that's no substitute for the real thing – two fight leaders in armed combat with their supporters behind them, all roaring encouragement.' She looked at me, smiling. 'Remember, when you came to Aldeburgh, I said I was born to colour and excitement. I don't think you believed me, but I really did have a very full, very exciting childhood.' And she added, 'It didn't exactly prepare me for all the time I had to spend in that dull little seaside town.'

'And now?' I asked.

'Now . . .?' She hesitated, her mouth hardening, the crease-lines deepening. 'How long will it be, before we get there? Four days?'

I nodded. 'About four.'

'Ships;' she murmured, draining her coffee and getting to her feet. 'I love them. And this is mine, partly mine. But they're so slow. In that aircraft, I felt I was moving then, getting there fast. But now – four days! Do you think he'll let me send a cable? By radio. All this time . . . I don't even know whether Tim's still alive.' And then she added, her hands clenched, 'Yes I do. I'd know if Tim were dead. I'd know it instantly.'

She had turned and was staring out of the porthole. 'Strange! Tim, that house – now, with the sea out there sparkling in the sun, and the warmth, the sense of movement, it seems like another world, another life . . . so far away, almost unreal. But it is real, isn't it?' Her hands were clasped together, the fingers locked tight. 'All those years – Father dying, then Tim . . .' Her voice faded and she stood silent for a moment, her eyes staring out at the sea with great fixity, as though by concentration she could leap the distance of half a world and talk with her brother. Suddenly she turned to me, a quick gesture of hands, and smiling now: 'I'm sorry. I haven't thanked you. First you got me the money, then you told me how to find the ship. I can't tell you what it meant to me. Those weeks on the *Lemnos*, struggling towards Buka . . . . It's there, you see, on Buka Island, whatever it is that's killing Tim. And I hadn't the money, no hope of getting there before – ' She gave an awkward little shrug. 'I tried to thank you last night, but you were asleep.' Her lips spread in a smile, a conscious effort. 'You went out, just like that.' She clicked her fingers almost gaily. 'More coffee?' She reached for the pot. 'Four days! I'm going to try and relax now. Nothing I can do will get us there any sooner.' She was refilling my cup. 'I had no idea those stamps could be worth so much.'

I told her briefly how their value had escalated, about my visit to Josh Keegan, but I don't think she took it in. 'Where did your brother get them?' I asked. But she didn't know. She was back at the porthole then, staring out at the water, and it was only when I produced the letter the stamp dealer in Sydney had given me that she showed any real interest. 'Lewis?' She had turned, frowning in concentration. 'Didn't you say Carlos Holland had those ship's stamps specially printed? That means the father of that abo was on board the *Holland Trader* with him.' She stared down at the letter. 'Cooktown. And you were in Queensland. I wish you'd gone up there.'

'I hadn't time.'

'No, of course not. But to have killed a man called Holland. Black Holland. It's such a coincidence. Do you think he still has his father's letter?'

'I doubt it.'

'But you said the dealer only received the envelope.'

'The aborigine's mother was dead. I don't imagine he kept

the letter.'

'But if he had . . . It's so strange. I'll ask Mac whether my grandfather ever said anything about that mine. The Dog Weary gold mine. You can just imagine a man at the end of a long trek into the Australian outback calling it Dog Weary. Or perhaps there were two of them.' She was silent then, thinking it over. 'I've often wondered where Carlos got the money to buy a steamship. A gold mine would explain it.' She laughed, handing me back the letter and turning to the porthole again. 'I can still see the coast.' And then she asked about her brother. 'How is he?' And when I didn't answer, she said, 'You've been standing in on the night watches. You must have formed some impression.'

'He's tired,' I said. 'We're both tired.'

'Yes, I know.' Her voice was sharper. 'But that doesn't explain why he radio-ed advising me to stay with my aunt in Perth. He didn't want me on board, and he didn't want me in Buka – why?'

I hesitated. But it wasn't for me to tell her he was scared of something. 'You're part owner of this ship, aren't you?'

She nodded.

'Maybe that's the trouble.'

'The ship's still losing money, is it?'

'I think so.' And then I asked her about the partner her brother had gone in with. 'D'you know anything about him?'

'Yes.' Her face had suddenly altered, the jaw clenched, the lips a tight line and her eyes coldly staring. 'What's Hans got to do with it?'

'He seems to handle the business end and I thought perhaps—' I left it at that, shocked at the violence of her reaction, standing there staring straight at me, gripping hold of the back of the chair so tight that her knuckles showed white.

'He should never have gone in with Hans Holland,' she said in that husky voice, her mouth clenched tight. 'I knew it wasn't right. Tim was against it and that day when – ' She shook her head, her eyes very wide. 'But Jona came over to England specially. He talked Father into it. Said the sins of the fathers shouldn't be visited on the children, that Hans and he were another generation and if they wanted to join forces and build a new Holland Line together the past of the two families shouldn't be thrown in their faces. I haven't seen Jona since.'

'And what were the sins?' I asked.

She let go of the chairback and turned to stare out at the sea again. 'I'm not sure. It was something that happened during the war, but Grandpa wouldn't talk about that – ever. Nor would Mac. All Grandpa ever told me was that Hans's father handed the Holland schooners over to the Japanese.'

'A collaborator?'

She nodded. 'He went over to the Japs. That's why he was killed. I think maybe my grandfather had a hand in that. And Hans – the same red hair, but he's Buka really.' She paused there, frowning, and when I asked her if it was Hans who had visited them in Aldeburgh some months back, she nodded vaguely, muttering to herself, 'Buka through and through.' And then she seemed to jerk herself out of her reverie, lifting her head and looking straight at me again as she abruptly changed the subject. 'So Jona's in financial difficulties, is he?'

'He needed this cargo. That's all he told me.' I got off the bunk and reached for my clothes. It was up to her to find out about that. 'Talk to Shelvankar,' I said. 'He's radio officer and cargo agent all in one and I would imagine the best source of information on board. And if you know any of the crew . . . Do you understand the Buka language?'

She shook her head. 'Not Buka. But Pidgin is the same all through the islands. I'm sure that will come back to me quite easily.'

'Then have a look round the ship, talk to some of the crew while I get dressed.'

'And what about Jona? You haven't told me what impression you've formed of him.'

'No, and I'm not going to.' I had my back to her, rootling around for my shaving kit. 'I'm a visitor on board this ship and if he has problems it's none of my business.' I was still tired and her persistence irritated me. The old belief that a woman on board meant trouble may have had something to do with it.

Silence for a moment, then she said, 'Very well, I'll leave you to dress now.' I heard the door close. She was gone and I breathed a sigh of relief. I went to the heads then and had a shower. By the time I was shaved and dressed it was past 10.30. I lay on my bunk and tried to read, but my mind wouldn't concentrate, wondering how well she knew her brother, how much he had told her in letters. It was five years since she had last seen him. A long gap, and some time in the next two hours she would confront him with the fact of her presence here on board his ship. And those two trucks. Like me, she must be wondering what the hell was in them, why the secrecy?

She had flown from Sydney to Brisbane and then hitched lifts up to within a few miles of the beach. That much I got out of her when I went into the wardroom for a quick bite of food before going on watch. But that was all. Holtz was there, and Shelvankar, both of them treating her very formally, and beneath the formality I sensed a mood of caution as though she were something to be handled with extreme care. Shelvankar, in particular. He was unusually silent, his eyes every now and then glancing at her furtively. And she herself was not at all communicative, sitting there quite still as though bracing herself for the moment when her brother would come in.

The steward brought me my coffee and then went along the alleyway to give Holland a shake. It was just past noon and time for me to relieve Luke. I excused myself and took my coffee along to the bridge. The course was due north, visibility good and the sea calm, a long shallow swell coming in from the south. We were already clear of the continental shelf, no reading now on the echo-sounder and no sign of any land. I took a sun sight and was pleased when my calculations coincided almost exactly with our DR position. There was little for me to do then and the watch passed slowly.

Any moment I expected Holland to come in and ask me why the hell I had gone behind his back and sent that message to his sister. Maybe she dissuaded him, but nobody came on the bridge during the whole of the afternoon watch and when he relieved me at 16.00 he never mentioned it. He didn't even refer to her presence on board. He was tight-lipped and very tense, the lines on his forehead deep creases, and he had been drinking. I could smell the whisky on his breath. 'Have some tea, then get your head down,' he said tersely. 'You're on again at 20.00 hours.'

'What about McAvoy?' I asked.

'No.' And when I suggested he had looked sober enough to stand a watch, he almost shouted at me. 'I tell you, no.'

The door to McAvoy's cabin was open as I went down the alleyway to the wardroom. He was standing there, a glass in his hand, staring at his bunk which had an open suitcase on it and a pile of clothes. An empty drawer lay upside down at his feet. He turned slowly, sensing my presence in the doorway. 'You're out of luck.' He smiled at me slyly. 'She's having my cabin tonight.' He waved the glass at me. 'Thought you'd cleaned me out, didn't you?' The smile broadened to a grin, but behind the grin he looked old and tired. 'Care to join me in a drink? It's here somewhere.' He looked vaguely round for the bottle. 'Well, say something, can't you?' His voice was suddenly petulant. 'Bloody amateur doing my job.'

'It's your own fault,' I murmured.

'My own fault, you say.' He nodded slowly. 'Aye. Maybe it is.' He looked down at the glass still clutched in his bony hand and smiled. But it was only a drawing back of the lips from yellowed teeth. There was no humour in the smile. 'I haven't the guts, you see, to make an end of it. Not alone. I've tried, but I canna do it. So. . . .' He lifted the glass to his lips, swallowing quickly. 'You're lucky. No dark Celtic streak in you.'

He stood there, staring at me, and I didn't know what to say. But there were things I wanted to ask him and in his fuddled state I thought perhaps it was as good a moment as any. 'You knew Colonel Holland very well, I believe.' His bloodshot eyes were suddenly wary and hostile. 'Miss Holland said you were his best skipper.'

'Aye. He wouldn't let Perenna sail with anyone but me.' His voice was firmer, a touch of pride.

'Would you tell me something then? As I understand it, Colonel Holland took a canoe and sailed off into the Pacific. Why?'

I thought at first he wasn't going to answer. He was glaring at me angrily. Then, as though it were being dragged out of him, his voice quivering, he said, 'It was the custom. When you're too old . . . to lead the fight . . . it's the way the old Polynesian navigators used to go when they'd come to the end of their lives. God damn it! It's better than dying in bed, to sail away, to the horizon, going on and on until in the end you meet your Maker, still proud, still alive, sailing the way you've always sailed.' And he added, 'He loved the sea. He had courage. He was the finest man . . .' He jerked back the words, turning away, tears in his eyes. 'Blast you!'

'I'm sorry,' I murmured. 'But what I need to know is why he suddenly decided his time had come. Was he ill?'

'No.' He was staring down at the empty glass in his hand.

'Then what decided him?'

There was a long silence. Then he raised his hand and smashed the glass on the floor. 'I told you,' he shouted, turning on me. 'When a man's too old to fight any more . . . he was eighty-three.' He was glaring at me. 'You – you're in the prime of life. You're hard, callous – you think the world's at your feet. If you want anything, it's there and you grab it. But you wait. You just wait. Wait till you're old and tired and can't face youngsters. Can't fight the world any more. Then you'll understand. An old bull . . . he was like an old bull . . . too proud to go under . . . too old to fight.'

'To fight what?' I asked.

But he had turned away, surveying the cabin. 'I have to clear up here,' he murmured. 'Perenna won't like it if it isn't tidy.'

I hesitated, but he was already kneeling on the floor picking up the pieces of broken glass with trembling fingers. I left him then and went to my cabin, lying on my bunk and trying to visualize the world towards which the monotonous throb of the ship's engines was steadily driving me, the world that Colonel Holland had been too old to fight. Across the alleyway I could hear sounds of movement and Perenna's voice.

The cabin door opposite me was closed when I went along to the wardroom for the evening meal. She didn't appear, nor did her brother. Luke had taken the last Dog watch and I relieved him at 20.00. The sky had clouded over and beyond the lights of the ship all was darkness. The watch passed slowly. I wasn't accustomed to a helmsman who had no English and I couldn't even take star sights to pass the time.

I had just entered up the log for 22.00 and was working out the DR position on the chart when I became conscious of somebody else in the wheelhouse. Perenna was standing on the starboard side staring straight ahead at the reflection of herself in the glass of the porthole. She was dressed in jeans and an open necked shirt, the same clothes I think she had been wearing when she had first opened the door to me on that sunny summer morning back in England. She turned her head as I crossed towards her. 'Mind if I share your watch for a bit?'

'Of course not.' She was no more than a shadow in the darkened wheelhouse and though I couldn't see her features clearly I was conscious of a withdrawn mood. 'How did it go?'

'Oh, all right. At least he didn't throw me off the ship.' She had turned back to the porthole. 'It's very dark tonight. Do you think there are sharks out there? In the islands the crew used to catch sharks. For sport, not to eat. They'd tie their tails together and push them back into the sea. Sprit-sailing, they called it.' She went on talking like that for a time, about nothing that touched either of us, treading cautiously as though unwilling to destroy the quiet peace of the night with the questions that were in her mind. 'Where are we now?'

I took her over to the chart table and showed her, conscious of the effort she was making to behave normally, not to show her impatience at the slow progress towards Buka. 'Another six hours and we should pick up the light on the north-east edge of Saumarez Reef.'

'Is that named after the Admiral who served with Nelson? His descendants live in Suffolk.'

'How do you know about Admiral Saumarez?' I asked.

She shrugged. 'At Aldeburgh I had a lot of time for reading, especially at night. I got books out of the library, sea books mainly. I think I take after my grandfather. He started in the City of London, the family shipbroking business, but his real interest was the sea. Jona's the same. It's in the blood.' She paused then and there was a long silence. 'I'm sorry you don't know Tim,' she said suddenly. 'He's different, very different.' Silence again. 'Has he told you anything about this voyage? The cargo, I mean, and where he's delivering it.'

'No.'

She nodded. 'I can't get anything out of him either.' All this time she'd been staring down at the chart. Now, suddenly, she turned to me. 'Those trucks. While we were waiting on the track leading down to the beach I had a look in the back. They were full of crates. Do you know what's in them?'

'Outboard engines.'

'Are you certain?'

'It's on the manifest.'

She nodded. 'That's what Jona said.'

'And you don't believe him?'

She was silent for a moment. 'I don't know. I don't know what to believe.' And then in a whisper, speaking half to herself: 'Japanese outboards. It makes sense. It's the sort of equipment that would sell well in the islands. . . .'

'Well then?'

'It's the secrecy I don't understand. And those drivers. I don't know what sort of men go in for trucking in Australia, but they didn't seem like ordinary truck drivers to me. And the back-up vehicle to take them home wasn't a ute or anything ordinary like a Holden. It was an English Jaguar.'

'Did you find out anything about them?'

'No. They weren't the sort of men you ask about their backgrounds. I did ask Nobby, the one who drove me on board, where his home was, and all he said was, 'You want my telephone number, too?' And then after a long pause. 'There's only one way to find out what's in those crates.' And when I reminded her they were Customs sealed, she smiled. 'It wouldn't be the first piece of cargo that got dropped and fell open by accident.'

I didn't say anything and after a moment she asked about the watches. 'It's just you and Jona then?'

'During the hours of darkness, yes.'

'So we either do it now or just before dawn.'

I told her it was out of the question, that the cargo he carried was his own affair and anyway I was his guest on board. She stared at me. 'I've a right to know. And so have you.' I thought she was about to press me further, but then with a quick goodnight she was gone.

There was less than an hour of the watch to go and I spent it pacing up and down, my mind going over and over what he had said that first evening when I had come on board in Darling Harbour, remembering how scared he had been, his conviction that I had been sent by somebody. Who? And why had he been scared, so scared that he had set out to drink himself into a stupor?

Midnight came and went. I entered up the log, then went to his cabin to wake him. But he wasn't asleep. He was sitting there, a glazed look in his eyes, a glass of whisky beside him. His face looked pale, almost haggard, beads of sweat on his forehead. He lifted his arm, a slow deliberate movement, and peered at his watch. 'Thirteen minutes after midnight.' I could see him struggling to pull himself together. 'You should have called me before.'

'No hurry,' I told him and went back to the wheelhouse.

It was about five minutes before he came in. He had had a wash and seemed more or less himself. I gave him the course and was turning to go when he said, 'Has Perenna been talking to you?'

'She was here for a while.'

'What did she say?'

'Nothing very much; she talked about the sea, about the schooners she used to sail in.'

He was staring at me, his eyes unblinking, holding himself very carefully. 'Anything else?'

I hesitated. I was on watch again in less than four hours and I wanted to get my head down. But then I thought, to hell with it, the moment was probably as good as any to get the truth out of him; now, when he was still mentally exhausted by his sister's suspicions. 'She was asking me about those two trucks,' I said.

He turned away from me then, to the high chair that was still in the wheelhouse, relic of the ship's Service life. 'God in Heaven!' He slammed his hand down on the wooden back of it. 'Why did she have to come now? If she'd done what I told her, stayed in Perth . . .' I thought he was about to reproach me for sending that cable, but instead he asked me in a very quiet voice, 'What did you tell her?'

'That the crates contained outboard engines.'

He nodded. 'Did she believe you?'

'No.'

'And you?' He turned suddenly and faced me. 'You think I'm smuggling something, don't you?'

I shrugged. 'It's none of my business. You made that perfectly clear.'

'Well, understand this. I don't know what's in those crates any more than you do. They may be outboards. They could equally be full of cigarettes, or whisky. It's nothing to do with me. I'm being paid to put them ashore on Buka Island. If she wants to know what's in them she'll have to ask Hans. He fixed it. It's his responsibility.'

'What if it's drugs?'

He shook his head firmly. 'Hans wouldn't ship drugs.'

'Stolen silver then, something like that?' In Sydney the papers had been full of a wave of silver thefts by armed raiders. 'It's your ship that's delivering them to Buka and if the police find out, start an investigation . . .'

'They won't. Buka is a long way from the centre of the civil administration at Arawa.'

'And there's no Customs?'

'No. Not where I'm going to put those trucks ashore.'

Again I was remembering that first meeting with him, and now that same driven look. 'Why did you ask if I was going to

135

Bougainville to stir up trouble?' I said it quietly, not wishing to push him too far.

'Did I?' He was staring at me, shaking his head. 'I don't remember.'

'When I came on board that first time.'

'I wasn't myself. I was very tired.'

'You were worried about something.'

'Yes, I remember now. You said I was scared.' His voice had suddenly risen, his face flushed, his eyes angry. 'You'd no right to say that. I was worried about the ship, about my ability to stay awake for five nights. It's not so bad this way, but coming south it's a long haul to the two reefs we'll be threading our way through in a few hours' time. Even so, there's the Louisiade Archipelago. There aren't any lights on the Louisiades. Yes, I was scared if you like. I didn't want to lose my ship the way Carlos Holland did.'

He hadn't answered my question, but I didn't feel this was the moment to ask him about the sullenness of the Buka element on board. 'We'll talk about it tomorrow,' I said. 'But if I were in command of this ship I'd certainly want to know what was in those crates. If it's drugs –'

'It's not drugs,' he said quickly. 'Hans would never handle drugs.'

'On moral grounds?'

He didn't answer for a moment, standing there, thinking it out. Finally he said, 'I don't think he'd necessarily see it that way. He's a business man. It's just that there'd be no profit in it. There's no demand for drugs in the islands.'

'But he could be shipping the crates on – South East Asia, Singapore, and no questions, even if the contents have been stolen.'

He shook his head, frowning, and that muscle moving on his cheek.

'Well, if I were you I'd check.'

I turned to go then, but he stopped me. 'I've told the coxs'n nobody is to go on the tank deck without my permission. You understand? That includes you, and Perenna.'

It was so utterly illogical that I was on the point of telling him it didn't make sense, one minute convincing himself that the crates were no more than innocent contraband, the next giving orders to ensure that he couldn't be faced with the hard evidence of their contents. But seeing him standing there, gripping the back of the high chair, so tense that his hands were shaking, I thought better of it. 'See you at 04.00,' I said.

He didn't seem to hear me, his head turned to the porthole facing for'ard, his eyes wide, and I realized he was staring at those trucks, their tops just visible above the cab roofs of the Haulpaks. I didn't bother about a warming drink. I went straight to my bunk and was asleep as soon as my head touched the pillow.

Dawn was beginning to break when I woke. He hadn't called me at 04.00 and when I went into the wheelhouse he was at the chart table. He nodded to me. 'Just managed to get a bearing on the Saumarez light while it was still dark enough.' His face looked pale and drawn, but he seemed pleased and he was quite relaxed now. He was a man who thrived on navigation, his mind totally absorbed in the necessity of picking up that light. 'Had to rely on dead reckoning. No star sights. Thick cloud all night.' The course hadn't changed. 'I'll send Luke up to keep you company as soon as he's fed.'

I have never liked the dawn watch. There is a timelessness about it, daylight spreading but the day not yet come, the world in limbo, everything a little unreal. I went out on to the bridge wing and climbed the ladder to the upper bridge, letting the wind blow the sleep out of me. It had freshened. Away to starboard the clouds were greying. A glimmer of whitecaps showed in the dark blur of the sea and a light drizzle touched my face, clinging to my sweater like dew on a cobweb. Once I thought I caught a glimpse of the light away to port, but the drab dawn was strengthening all the time and I couldn't be sure. For'ard I could just see the trucks, dim, canvas-covered shapes.

I thought of all the times I had been at sea, sometimes wet and cold, sometimes frightened, but never before with any doubts about the purpose of the voyage or my own involvement in it. And now, standing in the boxed-in area of the open bridge watching the coming of that reluctant dawn, I knew she was right. Somehow Holland had to be persuaded to check that cargo, and if he wouldn't do it himself, then we'd have to do it. Cigarettes or liquor was one thing, but I wasn't going to be party to the delivery of stolen goods, drugs, any of the things the police might investigate.

Back in the wheelhouse I found Luke poring over the chart. He looked up and smiled, a flash of white teeth in a broad black face. 'Not very good morning, Mr Sling'by. I think it blow soon.' He nodded to the barograph. 'Pressure already falling.' And this was the Coral Sea. When Shelvankar came in with the latest forecast it was for strong to gale force winds, sou'sou'east veering sou'westerly, rain heavy at times with moderate to poor visibility.

The sea was already getting up by the time I went off watch, the movement uncomfortable and the fiddles fixed to the wardroom table. The others had finished breakfast, Holland sitting beside his sister smoking a cigarette. 'Any sign of the Frederick Reef on the radar?'

I shook my head. 'The trace is getting blurred by the break of the waves and the rain is quite heavy now.'

He pushed the bell for the steward and got to his feet. 'When you've finished take a look round the ship and see that everything's secure, will you? Particularly the Haulpak fastenings. They may need tightening. I'll tell Teopas to go with you.' He poured himself another cup of coffee and took it with him to the wheelhouse.

The steward came in with my bacon and eggs. This time there was no fat. 'I hope you like it,' Perenna said. 'I've had him grill the bacon instead of frying it.' She smiled. 'Getting him to cook vegetables properly may be more difficult.' She seemed unaffected by the movement, face fresh and the freckles very noticeable with no make-up.

'We'll be hove-to before the day is out,' Holtz said gloomily. 'It's not so good down below when she's hove-to.'

I didn't think it would be much better up top. I could

remember how I'd felt last time I'd been hove-to in one of these ships. We had been off South Uist then and I'd been sick as hell. I hoped I wasn't going to be sick this time. An LCT is very different from a sailing boat. It never conforms to the wave pattern.

We were already slamming heavily by the time I started my tour of inspection. Down on the tank deck I found the coxs'n already tightening up on the securing chains of the first Haulpak. We were about a quarter of an hour checking the other three, then we came to the trucks and I glanced up at the bridge. I could just see the top of the helmsman's head, nobody else. 'I'll look after these,' I told Teopas. 'You check the bow doors and ramp.' It meant he would have to go up to the catwalk and through past the work bench to the platform above the cross-members. As soon as he had vanished from sight I unfastened the back of the starb'd truck. The movement up here in the bows was very violent and as I clambered in with the bag of tools the slam of the bows plunging into a breaking wave pitched me against the first of the crates. It took me a moment to recover myself, and then, as I was searching the bag for a cold chisel and hammer, my ankle was gripped. I turned to find Teopas staring up at me angrily. 'Ol bilong mi pipal.' He was shouting to make himself heard above the noise of the sea. 'What you doing there?'

For a moment I considered trying to persuade him to help me, but the dangerously hostile look in his eye made me think better of it. 'Just checking to see that the crates haven't shifted.' But he had seen the hammer in my hand and he didn't believe me. 'You come down. Nobody go inside truck. Kepten's orders.'

I jumped down, landing heavily on the deck beside him. 'They seem okay,' I said. 'I told you to check the bow doors.'

He reached into the truck for the tools and then fastened the canvas back of it. 'First we check the trucks. Then we check the doors, ugh? Together.' The deep guttural voice was solid and unyielding, and I turned away, uncomfortably aware that this was a man of considerable authority in his own world. 'Well, let's get on with it.' I felt I had lost face and my voice sounded peevish. Perhaps it was the movement, the constant slamming. By the time we had finished I was suffering from nausea and a feeling of lassitude.

I got used to it, of course, but the constant plunging and twisting, the bracing of muscles against the staggering shock of breaking waves was very exhausting. There was no let-up in the tension, even when I was flat on my back in my bunk, and though we were never actually hove-to, I was conscious all the time that we were steaming close to the limit for an old vessel of this type.

The gale lasted a full two days, something I had never experienced during my National Service, and when the wind finally died it left us wallowing in an uncomfortable swell, no slamming, but the movement equally trying. One thing I remembered afterwards – the appearance of McAvoy on the bridge. It was in the early hours of the second day. I was on watch and he was suddenly there beside me. He didn't say anything, he just stood there, his face very pale, his eyes staring wildly. He stood there for a long time, quite silent, staring into the black darkness out of which the brilliant phosphorescence of broken wave tops rushed at us. God knows what he saw out there, but something, some haunting product of his drunken imagination.

'What is it?' I asked, unable to stand it any longer. 'What are you staring at?'

He turned then, facing me reluctantly, his features crumpled by the intensity of the emotions that gripped him. He mumbled something, gripping hold of my arm, but the sound of his voice was lost in the crash of a wave. The shock of it flung us against the front of the wheelhouse. Involuntarily I ducked as spray spattered the portholes like flung pebbles and when I had recovered myself he was gone, leaving me with the odd feeling that his presence there had been nothing more than a ghostly apparition. I was thinking about him all the rest of that watch and it was during those black lonely hours that I began to understand the depth of the man's attachment, the terrible burden he carried in his heart, living all the time in the past. I was certain that what he had seen out there was the corpse of an old man alone in a canoe.

I was on duty every four hours during the gale, sharing the watches with Holland. He wouldn't trust Luke to know when to heave to. In the end I was too tired to keep anything down, living on coffee and falling into my bunk dead to the world the instant my watch ended. Sometimes Luke was in the wheelhouse with me, but he didn't talk much and I was only vaguely conscious of his presence. And Perenna. She'd stand there for hours on end during the day, staring dumbly ahead as though searching the grey line of the dipping horizon for the imagined outline of Bougainville. But everything was so chaotic, a vague blur of sleeplessness and tumbling waves, that I don't remember whether we said anything to each other or not.

And when it was finally over it took time for body and mind to adjust, muscles still tensing for the slams that no longer came, eyes bleared and heavy with sleeplessness. We were all of us exhausted. That afternoon the sun came out and I was able to get a fix. Within an hour the clouds were lying in a cottonwool pile to the north of us and we were steaming in a bright blue world, blue sea, blue sky, the surface of the water oily calm, and it was suddenly hot.

Perenna was in the wheelhouse then, looking fresh and bronzed in shorts and a sleeveless shirt. She came over to the chart table, leaning her bare arms on it and watching as I entered up our position. It put us at least twenty miles to the west of our dead reckoning and thirty miles ahead of it. We were getting very close to the Louisiade Archipelago now. She reached for the dividers and measured off the distance to Bougainville. 'About 300 miles to go,' I said.

She nodded. 'So this is our last night at sea.'

'Not quite. There'll be another night as we work our way up the coast to Buka.' I had forgotten all about those damned cases. 'Better leave it till then.' I pushed my hand up over my eyes and through my hair. I was too tired to care.

'No. We must do it tonight.' Even whispering her voice was

implacably determined. 'Tonight, while everybody's still exhausted.' And she added urgently, 'I must know.'

'Tonight,' I said, 'all that matters is getting safely round the end of the Louisiades.'

'He's been worrying about that all morning.' She ran the point of the dividers along the 200-mile outline of the archipelago. 'Do you think that's where my great-uncle Carlos went down?' She was tapping gently with the dividers, leaning forward and staring at the chart, and for no apparent reason I was suddenly reminded of McAvoy. Perhaps it was the *Holland Trader* he had seen out there in the luminous break of the waves, and not Colonel Holland at all. 'Tonight,' she said. 'It must be tonight.'

'Oh, for God's sake!' I said. 'Leave it till we're off the coast of Bougainville. Tonight we've more immediate problems.'

She put her hand on my arm, gripping it urgently. 'Please. This is our best chance. Jona comes off watch at midnight. You'll be alone then.'

'He won't leave the bridge, not until we're past the Louisiades.'

'And that will be when?'

I pointed to the eastern tip of the archipelago. 'Rossel Island is nearly 3,000 feet high. We should pick that up on radar within the next four hours.' I glanced at the bulkhead clock. 'That means we'll clear Cape Deliverance around 02.00.'

'And once we're past the Cape it's open sea again.' She looked up from the chart. 'Then he'll go to his bunk till he relieves you again at four.'

'Probably.'

'That means you'll have two hours alone here.' She straightened up. 'All right then. I'll check with you at 02.00 and if there's nobody about. . . .' She turned to go, but then she said, her voice a little cold and distant, 'No need for you to be involved. I should be able to manage it on my own.'

Cape Deliverance was broad on the beam when I came into the wheelhouse at midnight, the radar trace showing our distance off nine miles. Holland had already altered course to 350°. The tension had eased out of him and he stayed chatting to me

142

until we were clear of the Cape and into the open waters of the Solomon Sea. Then he went below, leaving me with nothing to do except admire the brightness of the stars. The port wing bridge door was open, a warm breeze ruffling the pages of the Admiralty Pilot.

I had just entered up the log for 02.00 when Perenna appeared dressed in jeans and dark top. 'I've had a look round. Everybody's asleep.' Her voice was low, a little strained.

'Have you got a torch'

'Yes, and tools. They're in my cabin.'

I hesitated, but only for a moment. The wire fastenings might be difficult for her and now that I was rested the urge to know what was in those crates had returned. 'Tell the helmsman I'm going to check the vehicles. I'll be gone about ten minutes, quarter of an hour.' He was a Buka Islander and she relayed the message in Pidgin, then I followed her to her cabin, picked up the tools, and we climbed down into the tank deck. It was very quiet down there, the sound of the sea rushing past the ship's sides muted. Somewhere a chain was rattling and the black bulks of the Haulpaks, outlined against the stars, seemed to sway with the movement of the ship. There was nobody anywhere for'ard of the bridge housing to challenge us. I chose the starb'd truck, knowing the canvas back was easy to unfasten. Once inside I shone the torch on the first of the crates and set to work with hammer and chisel.

It took longer than I had expected. The top of the crate was very securely fastened, long four inch nails, and the steel walls of the tank deck echoed to the sound of my hammering, the reverberations magnified in the still night. I felt nervous, remembering the way Teopas had hauled me out of the back of the truck two days before, so that I found myself glancing up every now and then, half expecting that deep voice to challenge me out of the darkness. Before I could prise open the wooden top the two securing wires had to be severed. There were no wire cutters in the toolbag she had borrowed from the engine-room. I had to use a hacksaw and it took time. 'Hurry,' she whispered as the first wire parted with a twang. 'The helmsman comes from the same village as Teopas.'

Her face was very close to mine, sweat shining on her freckles in the torchlight as she levered at the top of the case, using the long cold chisel. 'Is that important?' I asked.

She pushed her hair away from her eyes. 'They're in a funny mood. You must have noticed it.' And she added in a fierce undertone; 'I don't trust the Buka people when they're like that.'

With her hair pushed back I could see the scar in the beam of the torch. 'Is Teopas responsible for their mood?'

'He's their leader, yes.' She straightened up for a moment, easing her back. 'There's something brewing. I don't know what. Something . . .'

The second wire parted. I took the hammer and chisel from her and in a moment the nails were pulling out, the whole top of the case lifting. I put all my weight on the chisel and my end came loose, enabling me to get my hands under it and force it back, the nails at the other end tearing out of the wood. Whatever it was in the case it wasn't bottles, and it wasn't anything in cartons. The thick brown covering paper yielded to the touch. She tore at it with her hands, ripping it clear. 'Oh, my God!' She stood frozen, shocked into immobility, staring at the contents. 'Guns!'

They were neatly chocked into wooden supports, half a dozen machine pistols in the top layer, the plastic grips gleaming, the dull steel coated with grease.

She looked up at me. 'Do you think he knew? He must have known.'

'He probably guessed.'

'All these cases. And another truckful of them.' She was peering into the back. 'And there'll be ammunition, too.' She turned to me. 'Who's getting them? Where are they being sent?'

'No idea.' I started folding the lid back. 'If you're in the armaments business, I don't imagine you ask yourself questions like that.'

'He'll have to ditch them.' Her voice was trembling. 'I won't be a party to it. Automatic weapons like that. They'll land up in the hands of terrorists – innocent people getting killed. God! What a fool! No wonder he didn't want me here. What a bloody stupid mindless fool to get mixed up in a thing like this!' And before I could stop her she had jumped to the deck and disappeared among the black shapes of the Haulpaks.

3

The small hours of a night watch are not the moment I would choose to face up to a decision involving moral principles. There was nothing to occupy my mind, the course set, no navigation required . . . time passing as I paced back and forth, wondering what the hell to do and conscious all the time that there were guns on board and a sullen crew – an explosive mixture.

Every now and then I glanced at the clock, the minutes dragging, wondering whether she would persuade her brother to get rid of them, expecting him to burst in on me at any moment. Suddenly the deck lights came on and there were men down there at the for'ard end of the tank deck, dark figures in the shadows gathered around the back of that starb'd truck. The cox'n's head appeared, coming up the ladder from below and storming into the wheelhouse. 'Yu. yu opim kes?' He was naked to the waist, the muscles rippling under the velvet skin of his bare arms as he stood glaring at me. 'Why yu do it? Cargo bilong Buka pipal. I tell yu before, bilong Buka Co'prative. Where I find Kepten Holland, in his cabin?'

I nodded, too surprised at the man's anger, his proprietorial sense of outrage, to say anything.

'Okay, I tokim. An' yu – ' He was still glaring at me – 'Yu stay out of cargo deck. Nobody go on cargo deck – nobody, yu savvy, only Buka men.' And he went through into the alleyway. I heard the door of Holland's cabin thrown open, the sound of voices, then silence, only the murmur of the engines, the rattle of the cups on the ledge below the porthole.

A few minutes later Holland came in. 'I'd like a word with you. Not here, in my cabin.' He was wearing sandals and cotton trousers, nothing else, his face pale and that muscle twitching along the line of his jaw. I followed him into his cabin, the ceiling light blinding. There was a bottle and glasses on the desk and Perenna was there, sitting withdrawn and very still, the tension in her filling the cabin. 'I thought I'd better tell you. There's nothing I can do about it.' He had seated himself on his bunk, his body slumped. 'By morning it'll be all over the ship. Everybody will know we're carrying guns.' He reached for his glass as though to a lifeline. 'Perenna wants me to ditch them. But I can't. I can't do that.' And he added, 'She thought I should tell you.'

I looked at her, expecting her to say something, but she remained silent, drawing on a cigarette in quick short puffs. I hadn't seen her smoking before. 'What's their destination?' I asked.

'Queen Carola Harbour in the north-west of Buka. The Co-operative takes them on from there.'

'Yes, but who gets them in the end?'

'How the hell do I know?'

I glanced at Perenna again, but still she didn't say anything, her eyes avoiding mine, drawing nervously on her cigarette, inhaling deeply. 'So you don't care where they're going.' I had turned back to her brother. 'Or even what they'll be used for?'

He shook his head as though to push that thought aside. 'There were fuel bills,' he muttered. 'I told you. And the yard – the engine overhaul cost more than I thought.' And then, still trying to justify himself, 'Hans has always co-operated with the indigenes.' He was looking across at his sister again. 'He's very close to them, so close that sometimes – ' He shrugged. 'Well, you know his background. He's almost one of them.'

'He came to see Tim.' Her voice sounded strained, a little wild. 'I wrote you about it. At the end of May.'

'Of course he came to see you. He was in England and the accident happened on a coaster he'd chartered, so naturally – '

'Don't you ever read my letters? Tim was getting better, slowly. He was winning. And then suddenly there was no will left. He just seemed to give up. Hans was with him for the better part of an hour and it was after that – '

'For God's sake, Perenna! You're letting your imagination run away with you.'

'Am I? Don't you see what Hans is? A child of four hidden in thick forest under Mt Bei until the war was over, then brought up in Lemankoa by that man Sapuru. Red hair and a white skin, but underneath he's Buka through and through. Grandpa saw that, why the hell can't you?'

'The Old Man was prejudiced. He thought Hans hated him. God knows he'd every reason – '

'Why?' She was leaning forward, her eyes fixed on him. 'Why should Hans hate him?'

'His father was killed during the war.'

'Lots of people got killed in the war.'

'He was killed in a raid on Carola Harbour. His schooners were based there and it was the Old Man who led the raiding party.'

She stared at him a moment, then nodded. 'I see.' She said it huskily, her voice barely audible. 'So that's why he wouldn't talk about it.' And she added in a whisper, 'Now I begin to understand.'

'I hope you do. Red Holland was a collaborator, but from his son's point of view – well, if it were my father who'd been killed ...' He left it at that, leaning forward and continuing quickly, 'So don't go on about Hans. And stop imagining things. He's been very helpful.'

'What about the guns?' I asked.

He glanced at me, suddenly reminded of my presence. 'I told you. That cargo belongs to the Buka Trading Co-operative.' And then he had turned back to his sister, taking up where he had left off: 'Hans helped found the Co-operative. He's provided most of the finance and given it proper commercial direction. I admire him for that. Some return for their having saved his life during the war and looked after him until he was old enough to go to school in Australia.'

'And you admire him?'

'Yes. Yes, in some ways I do.' And then, soothingly, 'It's just a trading organization, Perenna. Nothing else. And it makes sense for us to have a close association with it. No white company can survive in the islands without being involved locally. Not any longer. It's a matter of politics.' He turned to me. 'It's happening all over the world. So why not in the Solomons? Don't you agree?'

'Trade is one thing,' I said, 'but guns – '

'Governments deal in guns, don't they? Your government, every government – they're up to their necks in the arms trade. Just because I have to get them secretly, off an open beach, what's the difference?'

'Cargo,' Perenna said. 'That's the difference. It's Cargoism.'

He turned on her angrily. 'Now don't start on that again. What happened when you were last at Madehas was quite different. I know how you feel, but this is strictly a business proposition. It's got nothing to do with the Cargo Cult.'

'The Hahalis Welfare Society called it *bisnis*,' she said wearily. And then, leaning towards him, 'I've never been able to ask you this to your face, but when Tim was sent to Buka, was it to deal with a new outbreak of Cargoism?' He didn't say anything, the silence seeming to last a long time. 'Well, was it? I asked you in letters, but you never replied. . . .' She was staring at him and he sat there, eyes fixed dumbly on his glass. 'I see. First Mother and me, then Tim. But now it's *bisnis*, nothing else – and two trucks full of guns.' She stubbed out her cigarette, getting slowly to her feet.

I thought she had finally made up her mind and was going to tell him that if he didn't dump them overboard she'd notify the authorities. He seemed to think the same, for he started to tell her again that trading in arms wasn't very different to trading in any other commodity, but his voice trailed away as he saw the look of contempt on her face. Then suddenly, without a word, she turned and left the cabin.

He didn't say anything for a while, sitting motionless, his

head in his hands. At length he finished his drink and looked up at me, an effort at a wry smile as he said, 'That's why I didn't want her out here. She's very emotional and last time she was at Madehas . . . you know about that, do you?' I nodded and he went on, 'She's right. It was Cargoism then. And when Tim was injured, that was Cargoism too. But this is different. The Buka Trading Co-operative is just like any other co-operative anywhere in the world, entirely commercial. Those guns are being shipped to make a profit and they'll be passed on to some dealer, a friend probably of one of the traders at Chinaman's Quay in the Buka Passage. They'll finish up somewhere in South East Asia, I imagine. It's just a business deal.'

'And Teopas?' I asked. 'Where does he come into it?'

'He's only looking after the Co-operative's interest. It's run by a man called Sapuru. Teopas comes from the same village.' He glanced at his watch and got to his feet. 'You shouldn't have let Perenna persuade you to check the contents of those cases. The crew are mostly Buka men and monkeying around with Co-operative cargo makes them suspicious. Just stick to navigation in future.' And he left me to go on watch.

Neither of them had offered me a drink, so I helped myself, drinking it standing there and wondering about the Hollands, what the hell was going to happen. I had two small whiskies, then I went to my cabin, half expecting to find her there. But it was empty, and in a way I was glad. I was too damned tired. The questions could wait for the morning.

They were talking about it when I went in to breakfast shortly after eight, Shelvankar saying, 'How was I to know it is not what it says on the manifest?' And Holtz shaking his head and muttering, 'It had to be something bad, but I never thought he would be such a bloody fool. . . .' He checked at the sight of me, self-consciously burying his face in his cup.

I sat down to an awkward silence. 'Is Captain Holland still on watch?' I asked and Holtz nodded. 'Where's Luke then?'

He didn't say anything, both of them sitting very still, watching me. My breakfast arrived and I ate in silence. 'The forecast is good,' Shelvankar said. Silence again, an uneasy sense of waiting. Then Luke appeared. 'They don't let me go near the trucks.'

'How many of them?' Holtz asked.

'Four, five, I not sure. They say nothing to do with me. Is their cargo.' He hesitated, his eyes flitting nervously. Nobody said anything. Finally he turned to the door. 'I tell Kepten. Buka men very funny about Cargo.'

'What's that mean?' I asked Holtz.

'Trouble.' He stared at me, his eyes hostile. 'Did you know what we were shipping off that beach?'

'Not until early this morning.'

'So, it is you who break open those crates.' He seemed relieved. 'I thought perhaps you were on board as an agent – ' He gave me a little apologetic smile. 'My engine-room is full of rumours this morning.'

'You mentioned trouble. What sort of trouble?'

He shook his head, wiping his moustache and getting to his feet. 'Maybe it is nothing.' And he muttered a formal apology, escaping back to his engines. Shelvankar, too, got to his feet, excusing himself. 'I must go to the radio.'

As soon as I had finished breakfast I went along to the wheelhouse. Holland wasn't there, only Luke and the helmsman. At the far end of the tank deck I could see several of the crew standing by the trucks. 'There are four now,' Luke said. 'All Buka men.'

'Has Captain Holland been down there?' I asked him.

'Yes. He talk to them. But they don't let him go near.' And he added, 'Is it true, Mr Sling'by, that you and Miss Holland find guns in those trucks?' I nodded and I heard his breath sucked in between his big white teeth. 'Tha's bad.'

'Why?'

He shrugged. 'I don' know. The war, I think. There was a bad war in the islands, very bad on Bougainville and Buka. The Japanese, the Americans, the Australians, they bring so much cargo.' He didn't say anything more, staring morosely through the porthole, and when I asked him to explain the significance of that word Cargo, he gave a high, nervous laugh. 'All Buka people laik Cargo. My people also. But Buka people, they laik very much because their ancestors send it to them from across the sea.' He gave a shrug, laughing nervously again. 'Is what they believe.'

I went over to the chart table, staring at the pencilled cross that marked our 08.00 position. We were already more than halfway across the Solomon Sea. Soon the high mountains of Bougainville would show up on the radar. I turned to Luke again. He was still gazing nervously for'ard at the tank deck. 'Have we any weapons up here or in the officers' cabins?'

He shook his head. 'I not seen any.'

And two truckfuls down there. I left him then and went to my cabin. The sun streamed in through the porthole, the small space hot and stuffy. I hesitated, but I knew rest would be impossible, so I went down the alleyway, past the empty wardroom, to what had once been the quarters for tank officers and other Service passengers. I pushed open the door. The same 2-tier bunks and McAvoy lying there unshaven, his clothes piled in a heap on the upper berth, and a stale, old man's smell pervading the cabin. His eyes were open, pale moonstones in rheumy sockets, the whites still bloodshot. 'Come in and shut the door. That galley stinks.'

I sat myself down on the bunk opposite. I don't think he had been drinking, but his eyes looked vacant, staring into space, and when I asked him about the Cargo Cult he didn't seem to hear me. 'You read much?' he asked.

'A little.'

He nodded. 'Thought mebbe you did. Myself, I never had the time. But there's a writer man buried out here. On Samoa. I've climbed to the top of the hill overlooking the sea and seen his gravestone. *Home is the sailor, home from sea.* That's what he wrote for them to put on it.'

'Stevenson,' I said.

'Aye, that's the man.' He pulled himself up by his elbows till he was sitting propped up against the soiled pillow. 'Care for a drink?'

I shook my head. 'I've only just had breakfast.'

'That's when you need it.' He looked vaguely round the room, his eyes fastening on the locker below the porthole. 'You'll find a bottle and some glasses yonder. Pour me a dram, will you, and help yourself or not as you please.' I got the bottle out and as I poured him a drink he went on, speaking slowly, 'I've been thinking about that poet in his island grave. If they buried me at sea now . . . Just give it to me neat, will you. Burial at sea, I've never really liked the thought of that.'

I helped myself to a drink while he rambled on about death and not giving it a thought until he was damned near sixty. 'When you're young, somehow it don't seem very important. Just a fact of life. But dying. . . .' He was staring dully at the porthole where the sun blazed in a blue sky. 'I was on a dhow once, in the Red Sea. We had gold on board and we were pirated. Threw the *nakauda* and his crew overboard to the sharks, all except me. I was just a kid bumming my way from place to place. White, not Arab, so they figured I'd do as a hostage if they got caught. Missed India by a full point, hit the Maldives instead. That was my first experience of coral, wrecked on the outer reef of Suvadiva. But it never worried me.'

'What happened?' I asked.

'Got picked up by a *vedi* on its way back from Java to Addu Atoll.' He shook his head slowly. 'Death never worried me, then or later. I didn't give it a thought until the Old Man went. . . .'

Silence then, his neck showing white crease-lines, his Adam's apple moving as he swallowed. 'Never gave it a thought,' he muttered again. 'You leave it that late an' it suddenly hits you. Wondering what it's all about – life, death, the whole pointless bag of tricks. I lie here thinking . . . Then, by Christ, I need another drink.' He held his glass out and as I filled it, he said, 'Wondering what to do about those Buka boys and their cargo, are you?'

'You've heard then?'

He nodded. 'Perenna. She woke me in the middle of the night to tell me.' He leaned forward suddenly, spilling his drink. 'Leave them be, Slingsby. That's what I told Perenna. Now I'm telling you. It's Cargo. You try getting it away from them and they'll turn nasty.' I asked what was meant by the words Cargo Cult and he began telling me about the missionaries and how the ships that had supplied them from Europe and America were responsible for it all. 'It was Cargo, from out of the sea. How would the islanders know where it came from? They got the new God mixed up with their old religion of ancestor worship an' came to believe that if it worked for the missionaries, then why shouldn't it work for them? That's how it started.' He leaned forward, hunched over his knees, holding his glass carefully. 'Missionaries! They're half the damned trouble.' He didn't like missionaries. He was an atheist himself. 'They only got themselves to blame. . . .' He went into a long tirade, his words confused and difficult to follow. Then suddenly he said, 'Pako. That was the fellow's name. He started the Cargo Cult on Buka and it spread to Bougainville. And Muling. Muling was the original Cult wizard.'

'When was that?' I asked.

'Oh, a long time ago. Before the Kaiser's war. The Germans held Bougainville then. But the second war, that's what really did it. First the Nips, then the Americans, finally the Australians. Can you blame them? All those ships stuffed with everything they'd ever dreamed of.' He gave a low, cackling laugh. 'Jesus! It's a funny world. War material sent by God. And if you believe your ancestors make just as good gods, then why the hell shouldn't they deliver the goods to their own descendants?'

That was when I asked him about the Welfare Society Perenna had mentioned. 'It was a co-operative, wasn't it?' He didn't say anything for a long time, sitting there, nursing his drink, staring at nothing. Then at length, he mumbled the name. 'Hahalis Welfare Society. I saw the start of that.' He was speaking very slowly, his voice barely audible. 'There was a woman, in a village just north of Hahalis. I was there when those two young devils, Hagi and Teosin, abandoned their Mission schooling and came back with their heads stuffed full of the business methods they'd picked up. Communism, and baby gardens to increase the working population!' A long pause, then he said, 'But Cargoism was a fact of life in the islands long before the war. When I first joined the Holland Line. . . .' He was nodding to himself. 'And he was in it up to his neck, of course.'

I thought he meant Colonel Holland, but when I asked him why Colonel Holland had got himself mixed up in the Cargo Cult, he turned on me as though I had said something blasphemous. 'No, it was the other one. Him and the Old Man, they were like as two peas. 'Cept one of them was rotten. Aye, and something else, too – ' He frowned, groping for a word, then struck his fist against his knee. 'Pagan. That's what he was. Pagan bad.' He was staring at nothing, silent, lost in the past.

'Who?' I asked him. 'Who are you talking about?'

'Red Holland, of course.' He almost snarled the name. 'We burned the bastard. Alive.' His head turned, eyes staring wildly. 'Why do you ask? He's dead now and none of your business.'

Shocked at the violence in him, I waited, expecting him to calm down. Instead, he suddenly screamed at me, 'Get out!' And then muttering to himself, 'They're dead, all of them dead, the schooner captains, too. Lot of silly sheep, doing what he told them. Welcomed the Nips with open arms.' He smiled, baring his teeth as though relishing the recollection. 'We killed all four of them, took their ships back and sailed them for the Allies. Got a medal for that, but didn't get *my* ship back. Finest little schooner I ever had and I sank her in the Buka Passage.' He was silent then, nursing his drink, his eyes with a glazed look. Finally he whispered, 'Get out, d'you hear. Leave me be.'

I left him then and went along the alleyway to the wheelhouse. Jona Holland was there talking to Shelvankar, his sister standing silent beside the helmsman. 'Makes sense.' He was staring down at the message in his hand. 'He'll take them up to Queen Carola and we go straight to Anewa.' He turned at the sight of me. 'There's a slight change of course. I've just heard from Hans. One of his RPLs is going to meet us off Shortland Island.'

'Will Hans be on board?' Perenna asked, her voice sounding sharp and brittle.

He nodded. 'Looks like it. I didn't know he was back, but he says he sailed from Carola at first light, and he's got Sapuru on board. He's the head of the Co-operative.' He glanced at his watch. 'Should make the rendezvous about five this afternoon, which means we'll be shot of those guns by nightfall and can head round the south of Bougainville to deliver the Haulpaks to the copper port.'

'You haven't changed your mind then?'

He jerked his head round, staring at her angrily. 'No. And if you want to know the destination of that cargo, you can ask Hans.' He was already moving towards the door. 'Work out that course, will you,' he said to me and escaped into the alleyway.

Perenna watched him go, then gave a little shrug. I thought it was a gesture of defeat, but then she turned to me. 'What would you do? Come on, tell me. If you were captain . . .' She was staring straight at me. 'Would you hand those cases over, just like that? Well, would you?'

'I can't answer that,' I said, turning away to the chart table.

'But I want to know. I want to know if another man would behave the way Jona is behaving.'

'We're all different,' I murmured, picking up the chart ruler. 'We behave differently. Right now I don't see that he's any alternative.'

'Meaning you would never have got yourself into this sort of situation.'

I didn't answer, bending over the chart and concentrating on the Shortland Island course, conscious all the time of her eyes still fixed on me. After a while she said, 'Anyway, I'm glad you're here.' By the time I looked round she was gone.

Shelvankar gave me the rendezvous, which was off Gomai Point to the west of Shortland, and after taking some sun sights and establishing our position, I altered course to 27°. But for that damned cargo I would have been enjoying myself, standing there on the bridge of an LCT steaming through a milky haze in the Solomon Sea to a landfall on my first Pacific island. When I relieved Luke after the midday meal Shelvankar had the ship's radio tuned to the Brisbane station. I don't know what its normal range was meant to be, but that morning we were receiving it loud and clear, music mostly, interspersed with local items of news and the odd interview. It must have been about three in the afternoon. I remember the faint trace of Bougainville's Mt Taroka had been showing on the radar for ten minutes or so and I had just fixed our position. Then the disc jockey interrupted a Heron Island waitress playing a guitar and trying to sing like Joan Baez to announce a news flash: Queensland police had traced the driver of a stolen Jaguar found abandoned in the Glass House Mountains. He had been picked up at Toowoomba with A$500 in cash on him and an air ticket to Sydney. The Jaguar had belonged to a car dealer in Sydney. The police had not released the name of the man who had stolen it, only his statement that he had driven it up to Tin Can Bay to pick up the drivers of two trucks that had been shipped out from the beach at about 2 a.m. on Sunday night. *The description of the ship indicates some sort of a landing craft. Police enquiries have already established that an old wartime tank landing craft of the Holland Line cleared Sydney on Saturday morning bound for Bougainville. They have alerted the PNG authorities and Bougainville has been requested to search the vessel on arrival. The trucks are suspected of carrying contraband, possibly stolen silver. A search is now being made for the two missing drivers.*

The newscast ended and I went at once to Holland's cabin. He wasn't there, but then I heard his voice coming from behind the closed door of the signals office opposite. I pushed it open to find him sitting with Shelvankar at the desk, his face pale and bloodless, his hand trembling as he held the microphone to his mouth. 'I tell you, I'll have to think about it. Over. . . .' He listened for a moment, then he said, 'I know there's a lot of money in it, but it's me they're after. They don't know anything about you. They don't know you're involved. You should have told me. It's a hell of a shock. I don't know what's best to do. I'll just have to think. Over. . . .' And after a long pause, he nodded. 'Well, if you're sure they'll stick to that if they are picked up. But I'll keep tuned to Brisbane. If there's nothing new comes through before we meet up we can discuss it then, decide what we do. Over and out.'

Slowly he put down the microphone and switched off the VHF. 'You heard the news, did you?' He jerked his head at Shelvankar and the little Indian sidled out. The muscle on his jaw was moving, his eyes as scared as when I had first seen him. 'Well, come in and shut the door. I don't know what the hell to do. Bloody stupid business. I never handled contraband, anything like that before. But guns. . . .' He half buried his head in his hands. 'Christ! Everybody on the ship must have heard it.' He dropped his hands, raising his head to stare at me again. 'What are you going to say if they question you?' He was like a man under sentence appealing for some way out.

'That's what I came to tell you.' His eyes went blank, knowing what I was going to say. Then the door opened and Perenna came in.

She closed it behind her, standing there, her face set as she stared down at him. 'That settles it,' she said. 'You'll have to get rid of them.'

He seemed to brace himself, shaking his head. 'He's already at the rendezvous, waiting. I was talking to him on the radio when that news flash came through.' And then, speaking much faster, 'All they know is that two trucks were loaded off the beach. They don't know there was anything in them and Hans says there's no way they can find out. The drivers will say they were empty. He'll take just the crates. I put the trucks ashore at Kieta. Empty trucks. The District Commissioner can't make much of that. It's not a crime. We're always putting empty trucks ashore in the islands.'

'You're going to tell them that?' She stared at him in disbelief. 'What about Roy here? What about me? Do you expect us to swear those trucks were empty?'

'Hans says once those cases are on board his RPL there's no way anybody can prove . . .'

'And you trust him? Well, I don't.' She was leaning forward, half bending over him, her voice urgent: 'For God's sake, have some sense. You're the one who's implicated, not Hans. You'll never have a moment's peace. . . .'

'What the hell do you suggest then?'

'Get rid of them. I've said that all along.'

'But I can't. He's out there, waiting for them. Waiting to take them off me.'

They went on arguing about it, taking no notice of me as I stood watching through the porthole, the sun gradually overtaken by rain clouds, the sea losing its sparkle as though reflecting their mood. Behind me the murmur of their voices, and the sun disappearing, the sea all grey to the horizon; I thought I could see the vague silhouette of a small vessel lying broadside on to us against the drab backcloth.

Holland suddenly gave in. 'All right,' he said. 'If that's what you want. . . .' He got up abruptly and went through into the wheelhouse. I followed him. I saw Luke give him a startled look as he pushed past him, reaching for the handle of the engine-room telegraph and slamming it to Stop. The engine pulse died and he disappeared out on to the bridge wing, hurrying down the ladder to the catwalk, calling to Teopas to get the bow doors open and the ramp lowered to sea level. It began to rain, big drops hitting the deck and drying instantly.

Gradually we lost way until we were lying stationary. The bow doors were open, the ramp coming down; soon I could see the length of the tank deck to the sea beyond. The men were hauling the crates out of the trucks, piling them at the top of the ramp, and Holland climbing the ladder to the catwalk. I had lost sight of the other ship, rain moving towards us across the sea in a solid mass, and when it reached us the scene up for'ard was almost obliterated as the downpour hammered our steel plates with a noise like a waterfall.

Work stopped, black bodies glistening with water huddled for shelter under the Haulpaks, and Holland standing just inside the doorway leading to the bow door control gear. McAvoy suddenly appeared in the wheelhouse and stood staring at the scene, swaying slightly and blinking his eyes. 'Thought we were on a reef, in the surf.' He was leaning close to me to make himself heard, his breath smelling of whisky.

The full weight of the cloudburst lasted only a few minutes, then the rain eased and the crew got back to the job of hauling the crates out on to the ramp. Whether Teopas realized his skipper was going to jettison them or whether he felt the bow door thrusters were his responsibility, I don't know, but whatever it was he was suddenly scrambling up the ladder to the catwalk. All the crates were out now, the canvas flaps of the two trucks being fastened down again, and Holland and his coxs'n facing each other, both of them talking urgently. Finally, with an angry gesture, Holland made to push past him through the watertight door that lead to the control panel. Teopas flung him back so that he fell against the steps leading to the upper foredeck. I heard Perenna give a startled cry and turned to find her looking wildly round. Then she wrenched a fire axe from the wall and was out in a flash, tumbling down the ladder to the catwalk.

I followed, calling to her. I can't remember what I said, but I was suddenly scared that the sight of her with that axe in her hand would start a riot. By the time I reached the catwalk she was already facing Teopas, the axe poised in her hand as though she were going to throw it at him, and he stood there, staring at her, his big mouth hanging open, his eyes rolling. 'Get back,' she screamed at him. 'Get back down!' She indicated the ladder down into the tank deck, the axe swinging, the blade with its red paint bright in the falling rain, and the way she held it, balanced and purposeful, I thought, 'She knows how to use it, and my God she might'.

Teopas must have thought so, too. The muscles of his body had tensed momentarily for a quick rush at her, but then he thought better of it. 'Cargo not bilonging you, Misis. Bilonging Buka pipal's co-operative. You understand?'

'No, I do not understand.' Then she was talking to him in Pidgin, something about guns, all the time moving slowly nearer him, step by step. Holland had picked himself up, but he didn't do anything, just stood there. Suddenly Teopas moved, pushing past him up on to the foredeck, moving fast and shouting orders to the crew below as he crossed to the starboard catwalk and flung himself back down the vertical ladder on that side to rejoin his men on the tank deck.

All this time Holland had stood quite still as though unable to move, staring at his sister. She yelled at him to get the ramp down to the full stretch of the chains, but he seemed incapable of movement, while down on the tank deck Teopas and the crew were hauling the crates back, stacking them on the solid deck, clear of the ramp.

And then a shot rang out. The rain had stopped and the sound of the shot was very loud in the stillness.

On the tank deck the crew froze into immobility, all eyes turned to the port bridge wing where McAvoy stood above me, gazing down at them, smoke curling from the muzzle of a heavy revolver gripped in his hand. I don't know what he said. He spoke to them in their own tongue. But there was no doubt about the way he said it. He might be a drunk, but he had years of command behind him and the ring of authority that demanded instant obedience was there in his voice. I saw Teopas's shoulders sag, a shut look on his face and resignation in every line of his body. The crew, too. It wasn't the gun. They could have handled that in weaker hands. It was the man, the powerful biting anger in his voice, the knowledge that he'd seen war, been one of the old-time Holland Line skippers, that drunk or sober he was still a Master.

It was a very strange moment, everything in limbo, all of them staring at him. Holland and his sister, too. He held them like that for a long minute, gazing down at them, his eyes moving from face to face, resting on each man individually till they were all of them avoiding his gaze. 'Coxs'n. There will be no more trouble. You will obey orders. Understand?' And when Teopas had been forced to nod his head in silent acknowledgment, he turned to Perenna. 'Bring that axe back here please, Miss Perenna.' And when she had brought it, he handed it to Luke. 'Put it back where it belongs.' Slowly he pushed the revolver into the waistband of his trousers. He was gripping the rail, his shoulders beginning to droop. 'Captain Holland. Your ship.' And he was gone, back into the wheelhouse, staggering a little, but his face still set, one eyebrow raised as he glanced fleetingly at me as though to say why the hell hadn't I done something, his bloodshot eyes shining balefully.

It was only then, when he had gone, that I became aware of the sound of engines and turned my gaze to the open end of the tank deck. The bows of the RPL were just coming into view. She was less than two cables off and already turning, a slab-sided, ugly, flat-iron of a vessel streaked with rust. No chance now of getting rid of those crates, everybody watching as she manoeuvred to come in bows-on to us, looming larger and uglier every minute until she was hanging motionless off the end of the tank deck, her bow ramp coming down to drop with a hollow clang on our own ramp.

They had two light trucks and some motorcycles on board, and over their loudhailer a voice boomed in English, 'I see you're all ready for us. Get the crates across fast. We may not be able to hold our position long. Move, Teopas! Move!'

Holland shouted something, but the crew were already galvanized into action, grabbing at the crates and manhandling them across the grinding steel ramps. He scrambled down the ladder, pushing past the men and walking quickly on to the open deck of the lighter, heading for the squat wheelhouse aft. Perenna followed him, but more slowly. I watched her as she climbed down the ladder and walked slowly, almost reluctantly, out through the open bows on to the deck of the other ship. There she stopped suddenly, standing very still as though rooted to the spot. And then I saw him, red hair like hers, standing at the starb'd rail by the wheelhouse door of the RPL talking to Jona Holland; a short, energetic man in white shirt and shorts, his body leaning forward, his sunglasses catching the light as he turned and stared at her down the length of the ship.

The way they faced each other, both of them quite still, both of them staring – even from that distance I was conscious of something – lust, hate, I don't know what – sensing it only as a current running between them. They were like that for what seemed a long, breathless minute, and then he had turned abruptly to question her brother and she was moving resolutely between the trucks, climbing in slow motion up the ladder to the bridge deck. They didn't shake hands, the three of them standing there, talking heatedly, and a man watching them from the wheelhouse, a black wrinkled face framed in one of the windows. Hans Holland jerked his head, a peremptory gesture of command, and they went inside.

I had only once seen an RPL, and that from a distance. I had never been on one. I walked along the catwalk to the for'ard ladder and climbed down into the tank deck. Two crates had already been shifted on to the lighter as I crossed the ramps. It was much smaller than an LCT, less than a third of the length, the bows square, everything very basic – a utilitarian motorized barge. The original grey showed through patches of different coloured paint, the flat steel sides of the cargo deck flaked and pitted by long years of work in the salt and heat of equatorial islands. The motor cycles roped to the sides were Japanese Hondas, four of them and all brand new. But the two small trucks were old American Dodges. It was very hot enclosed in those steel walls, the ramps grinding and the velvet black backs of the men labouring over the crates glistening with sweat.

Perenna appeared on the bridge ladder, climbing down and walking past me without a word, a blank, set look on her face. She was like a person in a trance, I don't think she even saw me. After watching her cross the ramps, still walking slowly, still locked in her thoughts, I turned back to the trucks, squeezing between them with the intention of seeing what they carried.

'You there. Who are you?' The voice, an Australian accent, came from above me. 'What are you doing there?'

I came out from behind the truck, looking up to see him standing at the top of the ladder, his red hair bright against the flaking white paint of the wheelhouse. 'Hans Holland?' I asked.

He came down the ladder at a run, squeezing past the first truck to stand facing me, the sunglasses hiding his eyes, but his mouth a hard line in a hard, tough face. 'Who are you?' he asked again. I gave him my name and he said, 'The name doesn't matter. What's your job? What are you doing on that ship?'

'Passenger, acting as first officer.'

'Passenger? I wasn't told of any passenger.' He was worried

and he didn't believe me. 'What the hell would a passenger know about running an LCT?' I started to explain, but he cut me short. 'Get off this ship. You've no business — ' He checked himself. 'No, you wait there.' And he dived back up the ladder shouting for Jona.

I stayed there, wondering what he would do now that he knew I was witness to the contents of those crates. Somebody was shouting from across the ramps. The RPL was slewing, Teopas calling for more power, the plates vibrating against the soles of my feet as the engine revs increased. Then he was back, smiling now and more relaxed. 'So you're a trained LCT officer and looking for a job out here. That right?' I nodded. 'Stick around then. I'll see you later, on Bougainville.' He tapped me on the shoulder. 'Maybe I could use a trained landing craft man. Not easy to find now.'

I was conscious of him watching for my reaction behind his sunglasses. 'What sort of a job?' I asked.

'We'll talk about it later. But I promise you this, it will be a ship of your own. You think about it, eh?' He stared at me for a moment, then switched his gaze for'ard. 'Better get back now. Looks like that's the last crate coming across. Just keep your mouth shut when you get ashore. Understand?'

He left me then, hurrying back up the ladder to the wheelhouse.

The two vessels were slewed almost at right angles, the ramps barely touching as I crossed to the LCT. The last crate was shifted across. I waited in the bow door opening for Jona Holland. He only just made it, jumping a gap that was opening up between the ramps. 'Well?' I asked him. 'Did he tell you the destination of those guns?'

He didn't answer me, only shook his head as he turned aft, moving quickly as though to avoid further questions. The RPL was backing off, the flat steel square of the bow door rising. Somebody shouted to stand clear and then our own ramp was lifting, the bows closing. By the time I reached the bridge the deck was throbbing under my feet again and we were heading east to turn the end of Shortland Island. The rain had passed seaward, visibility good, and away to port the massive forest-clad bulk of Bougainville showed bright green in the slanting sunlight.

PART THREE

ISLAND OF
INSURRECTION

=

1

With the guns gone it was as though the ship had been relieved
of an incubus, the mood almost carefree as we gathered for
drinks in the wardroom before the evening meal. Luke was on
watch, McAvoy in his cabin, otherwise we were all there,
including Perenna, and nobody referred to what had happened
before the RPL had taken the cases from us, talking about other
things as though it were best forgotten. 'We'll be off Kieta at
first light, get rid of those trucks, then go round to the copper
port.' Jona Holland turned to me. 'If you'll stand in till
midnight that'll be it as far as you're concerned and you can
have a good night's sleep before going ashore. Luke and I will
manage the night watches. I'm very grateful to you for all your
help.' His tone was friendly, his manner almost lighthearted.

Darkness had fallen in a steady downpour of rain, but when I
relieved Luke the island was a black silhouette against the stars
and the group flash of the Shortland Harbour light just visible to
port. Out on the bridge wing I could smell the land, a damp
smell of sodden vegetation mingled with some indefinable
aromatic scent. Most of that watch I was thinking about Hans
Holland and his offer of a ship. He was buying my silence, of
course, but much of my life had been connected with boats and
I didn't have to like the man, just so long as the driving

ambition I had sensed in him gave me the opportunity I was looking for.

Jona relieved me at midnight. There was something on his mind and he was ill at ease, keeping me there, talking about nothing in particular. And then, when I said I was tired and going to bed, he suddenly came out with it: 'That job Hans offered you, are you going to take it?'

'I might,' I said.

I don't know whether that was the answer he expected, but he didn't say anything, just stood there frowning as though working out some complicated pattern in his mind.

'Why? Does it matter to you?'

'No.' He shook his head. 'No, not at all.' He managed a small smile. 'Good to have somebody I know skippering one of the ships.' And he turned quickly away to the chart table.

Back in my cabin I stripped, had a quick shower, then fell into my bunk, naked except for a sheet, with the luxury of a whole night's sleep ahead of me. I dropped off immediately, the steady murmur of the engines like the refrain of a song beating out a vision of Pacific islands. At that moment I was strangely content, a new world opening up before me and a feeling that here was something that I could make my own.

I don't know what woke me – the door maybe – but my eyes were suddenly open, searching the cabin. A shadow moved in the pale light filtering through the porthole and I sat up. 'I'm sorry if I startled you.' It was Perenna's voice, a husky whisper barely audible. 'I couldn't sleep.'

'Why? What's wrong?'

'Nothing. I just couldn't sleep. That's all.'

I could see her now, standing like a ghost just inside the door, a thin dressing gown held tightly round her.

'It's the heat,' she said in a small voice. 'Do you mind?' And then, as though conscious of a need to explain her presence, she added, 'I don't know why, but I'm scared.'

'Scared?' She was so different from her brother that it hadn't occurred to me that she could ever be scared of anything. 'What of?' I was still only half awake.

'I don't know. Everything. The future, what's going to happen. . . .' Her voice trailed away.

'Do you want to talk about it?'

She came towards my bunk then, moving so slowly, so silently she might have been walking in her sleep. 'I had an awful telephone conversation with the doctor at the nursing home. Tim was worse and there was nothing he could do. Just a matter of time, he said. That's why I left Aldeburgh in such a hurry. I felt if only I could get to Buka I might be able to do something . . . Stop whatever it was from reaching Tim – destroy whoever it was that was killing him, switch it off.' She hesitated, then went on, her voice faltering, 'Now – now that I'm on the last leg of this long journey . . . I don't know what I'm going to do – ' Her voice fell to a whisper. 'I'm so afraid of Buka. And Sapuru. He was there with Hans.'

'I'll switch on the light,' I said. 'We can talk – '

'No. No, I don't want to talk.' And I knew then she had come to me for comfort, like a little girl afraid of the dark. 'Can I come in with you – just for a little while?' She was standing close to me now and I could smell her; no scent, just her own natural female smell. She slid in beside me, drawing the sheet over her shoulders, her body close against mine. The bunk was so narrow the only place I could put my arms was round her. 'Just hold me,' she whispered. 'Don't do anything. I just want to be held.'

Snuggled close against me I could feel her body naked under the dressing gown. She was trembling slightly. 'I keep thinking of Mother. That's why I couldn't sleep – wondering whether it would be the same this time. Blood and violence, the worship of ancestors . . . when I was growing up in the Chimbu area – there were still cases of cannibalism. And the fight leaders. There was always fighting somewhere.' Her breath was hot on my shoulder, her body close against me. She must have felt the beat of my blood for she withdrew slightly. 'I'm sorry, it's not fair.' Then with a sudden giggle, 'I only brought pyjamas and it's too hot to wear them.'

I tried to kiss her then, but she turned her head away, lying

167

quite passive. 'You don't want to talk, you don't want to make love, what the hell do you want?'

'Nothing,' she murmured, 'Just don't do anything. I'm tired.'

'You said you were scared. What is it? What are you afraid of?' I was being gentle with her then, the sexual urge in me dying. 'Is it really what happened when you were last here? Or is it those guns, the fact that your brother is involved?'

'No, it's not Jona.'

'Hans Holland then?'

She lay there, withdrawn, not answering. But I had felt her stiffen at the name. *Pagan bad*. The words came back to me. It was such an odd description. And Red Holland's son brought up after his death in a Buka village. Did that mean a pagan background? 'Did you know I'd killed a man?' she said quite unexpectedly. I only just caught the words, her face close against my chest.

'You don't want to think about that,' I whispered gently. 'History doesn't repeat itself and anyway it wasn't deliberate.'

'I was fighting mad,' she breathed. 'I was covered in blood and I didn't care.'

'It was a long time ago. Stop thinking about it.'

I felt her shake her head. 'I can't. There's Tim . . . and Jona – he's such an innocent.' And then, to distract herself, she began talking about the elder brother, how the sea had been his life ever since he had left school, how their grandfather had encouraged him. 'He thought he could mould Jona into a likeness of himself so that, when he was gone, there would be somebody left to build up the Holland Line again. He didn't see that Jona wasn't made that way, that it wasn't trade and ships that interested him, but the sea itself.' Her breath touched me in a little sigh. 'Since I've been on this ship I think I've become more worried for Jona than for myself. He just doesn't understand the sort of man Hans is.'

'And what sort of a man is he?'

'How would I know?' She spoke sharply, suddenly on the defensive. 'I've no experience, not of men like that – ambitious, driving. . . .' She was silent a long time, but I sensed that she was still thinking the question over. Suddenly, with what seemed total irrelevance, she said, 'Grandpa had a Christian upbringing. He was a morally upright man.' And she went on quickly, 'I suppose I'm talking about good and evil. Grandpa was a good man. He may have done things during the war, terrible things – destroying, killing. But that was war. It doesn't alter my impression of him.'

'And Hans Holland isn't a Christian.'

She didn't answer, lying very still.

'What happened when he visited you in Aldeburgh?' I felt her stiffen again. 'Did you leave him alone with your brother?'

'Yes. Tim wanted it.'

'And where were you?'

'Somewhere – I don't remember.'

'In the house?'

'Of course.'

'So you could have heard what was said between them – if you'd wanted to.'

'Yes.' The words seemed forced out of her. And then in a fierce whisper she said, 'I won't answer any more questions. I don't want to think about it.'

'You're twins, aren't you?'

'Yes.'

'And his illness – the reason he's dying . . . it's sorcery. That's what you told me. Don't you remember?'

'No.' She pulled back the sheet and started to get out of the bunk, but my arms were still round her and I held her. 'Is that what you're scared of, that you've come out here with one object in mind – to kill the man who put a death wish on your brother?'

I heard her draw in her breath. 'Do you think I'd kill him?'

'It's what you said you'd do, that day I came to do the sale inventory.'

There was a long silence, and then in a whisper she said, 'Yes, I remember now.' She drew in her breath, speaking with sudden urgency – 'But that was just after Tim had gone. It was part of the nightmare. Please believe that, Roy. I was living a nightmare. It's different now.'

But I knew it wasn't. It hadn't been a nightmare. It had been real, so far as she was concerned. It was paganism she was scared of. I started to tell her that I understood, that I knew about the arrowhead and the horrible little doll and that there were ways of dealing with sorcery and evil things like that. I knew nothing about it really, thinking of exorcism, crucifixes, the Christian faith . . . 'Please.' Her hand touched my face. 'Let's not talk about it any more. I don't want to think about it now. I don't want to think about anything.' She lay staring at me in the darkness and the touch of her fingers on my cheek stirred me. I tightened my arm about her and gradually the tension in her body relaxed. She murmured something, and when I tried to kiss her again she didn't turn her head away, only whispered, 'Let's get some sleep now.'

Silence enclosed us, only the beat of the engines, and the cabin dark in shadow as she lay there beside me, relaxed now and seemingly unaware of what she was doing to me. Yet I knew she could feel the hardness of me against her. Gently I took her face in my hands and kissed her eyes, her mouth. She didn't turn away, only whispered, 'No.' But her breathing was quicker now, her lips responding and suddenly she pushed me away. 'Oh, hell – why not?' She sat up, slipped out of her dressing gown, and then she was back beside me and my hands were holding those extraordinary thrusting breasts as she reached down to touch and caress me.

I had never experienced a woman like her, so total in the expression of a passionate nature, so absolutely uninhibited. And yet, through it all, was a tenderness, the sense of our being one. And when it was over and we lay there, drained and exhausted, I caught the whisper of a sigh as she murmured, 'Thank you. Now I can sleep.'

When I woke in the morning she was gone, the sun streaming in through the porthole, steep slopes of tropical green sliding past. I washed and shaved, slipped on a pair of shorts, and went through into the wheelhouse. The ship was just emerging from the narrow passage between Bakawari Island and Bougainville.

Ahead was a great bay with a curving shoreline and old wooden houses half-hidden in the shade of palm trees. 'Kieta,' Jona said when I joined him on the upper bridge.

A big yacht lay at anchor off the jetty, some local craft closer inshore, and almost abeam of us was a dusty-looking wharf with a small cargo vessel moored alongside. But it wasn't the port and the great sweep of its natural harbour that held my astonished gaze. It was the slopes beyond. They were emerald green in the sun, a towering vista of endless rain forests reaching up to pinnacles of grey rock etched sharp against the hard blue of the sky.

There was still a trace of dawn freshness in the air, the sea, the land, everything sparkling in the sun, and Jona standing there with a pipe in his mouth, wearing nothing but a pair of shorts and his peaked cap. That's how I shall always remember Bougainville, the picture in my mind as vivid now as when I first saw it in the lingering freshness of that blazing morning. There was an overpowering sense of magnificence in those endless towering vistas of jungle green. 'The copper mine is over there, beyond those hills.' Jona pointed the stem of his pipe towards the forest-clad slopes above Kieta. 'You'll get a glimpse of the road they blasted up to it when we move on along the coast to Anewa Bay.'

He ran the ship straight in to the beach, close under the main part of the town, where a little knot of islanders stood waiting. There always seems to be a sense of anticlimax when finally arriving in port, the contact with the shore and its officials being in marked contrast to the excitement of the landfall, the sense of achievement at the end of a voyage. On this occasion the change of mood was very noticeable. As soon as the bow doors were open and the ramp down an official from Provincial Government Headquarters came on board accompanied by a police sergeant. Jona did not go down to meet them. He left that to Teopas, waiting with his sister in the wheelhouse. The two drivers sent to take over the trucks remained on the shore.

We watched as Teopas unfastened the back of each truck. The inspection was very thorough, the police sergeant even crawling

171

underneath the vehicles to check the chassis. The Haulpaks, too, were examined. 'He'll want to see the manifests now,' Perenna said.

'Hans has the manifest.'

'Then how are you going to explain the trucks?'

To my surprise he seemed almost relaxed. 'Teopas will tell him we shipped them to help the Co-operative. And Hans has kept his promise; Nasogo is from Buka.'

The official was coming up the ladder now, thick-set and very black with a little wisp of a beard and dark glasses. He was dressed in grey-blue trousers and a white short-sleeved shirt that was freshly laundered. Teopas stood waiting close behind him as he shook hands with each of us murmuring 'Joseph Nasogo' in a soft, gentle voice. Then Jona took them to his cabin and we waited, the heat and the humidity growing all the time.

At length Perenna asked, 'What happens if he doesn't accept Teopas's explanation?'

I looked at her and gave a little shrug. 'I'm a stranger in these parts.' I said it lightly, but there was no answering smile as she stood by the open door to the bridge wing staring down at the trucks. The drivers were getting into them now and the police sergeant was standing on the ramp talking to a little group that had collected to gaze at what I imagine they regarded as a pretty odd craft.

Perenna never moved from her position by the open door to the bridge wing. She seemed totally withdrawn inside herself, the tension in her affecting me, so that I wondered whether she was still scared of something or merely locked up in her memories of the place. And then McAvoy appeared briefly, swaying slightly as he stood staring for a moment at the green hills behind the port, his eyes screwed up against the glare. '*Kapa*,' he muttered. 'Bloody *kapa*.' He turned to Perenna. 'I suppose you'd gone before this copper thing started?'

She nodded. 'There was a lot of talk, of course, and they'd started drilling. But I never saw anything of it, nothing had been built.'

'Well, you'll see a lot of changes now. Not so much in the rest of Bougainville, and nothing in Buka. But here. Aye, there's been a great change, an' all too dam' quick if you ask me.' His gaze switched to the little group framed in the open bows. 'The Black Dogs,' he growled. 'Wouldn't think it to see them now, standing there so peaceable, but this was where they came from. The Rorovana. That was one of the *wantoks* involved. Nasty fighters, all of them.'

'This was during the war, was it?' I asked.

'Aye. They were the young men of several family groups, all based on Kieta. Claimed they were for the Japs, but what they were after was independence, from the British, from everybody. Caused us a lot of bother, those bastards did, and now they drive great trucks up at the mine or work in the crushing plant. No independence at all, just slaves to machines. And all in less than a decade.' He shook his head slowly. 'I don't understand,' he murmured. 'The world changed, and then again nothing changed, man being what he is and his nature just the same.' He stood for a moment, silent, his body sagging as though bowed down by the weight of his thoughts. And then he was gone. Back to his cabin and his drink without another word.

It must have been a good half hour before Jona came back into the wheelhouse, his manner almost jaunty as he saw Nasogo to the top of the bridge wing ladder. Back in the wheelhouse he informed the two of us that we should tell the Immigration Official at Anewa that our visas would be issued at the offices of the North Solomons Provincial Government Headquarters in Arawa that afternoon.

A few minutes later Nasogo drove off with the police sergeant in a small Japanese car. The engines of the trucks had already been started up. We watched them bump their way down the ramp into the water and up the beach to the road. 'Well, that's that,' Jona said, and there was a sigh of relief in his voice. 'We'll be round at the copper port by lunchtime and tonight we can all have a good lie-in.' The ramp clanged shut, the bow doors closing. He rang for Slow Astern and the big winch drum aft began winding in the anchor. The crew were so used to this manoeuvre that orders were unnecessary.

173

As we headed north between the high green slopes of Bakawari Island and the Kieta Peninsula I wandered round the ship, mingling with the crew. No solemnness now, the Buka men all smiling. But they weren't singing at their work and they didn't talk. I couldn't figure out what the mood was, except that I was conscious of an undercurrent of excitement, all of them locked up inside themselves and the bared teeth not so much a smile as a grin of expectancy. I thought I must be imagining it, but when I spoke to Luke he evaded my questions. All he would say was, 'Buka pipal bilong old days. For them this mine and all the great development here and up in the mountains is a kind of Cargo.'

We cut north-west through the narrow passage inside the small island of Arovo and then we were heading just south of west direct for Anewa Bay. Already it was too hot to con the ship from the upper bridge. We were all of us in the shade of the wheelhouse and as we came clear of the Kieta Peninsula the broad curve of Arawa Bay began to open with the modern township spread out on the flats behind it, a pattern of buildings and palms all hazed in heat. 'Used to be a big expatriate plantation,' Jona said. 'Now it's got the largest shopping centre and superstore in the South West Pacific.' And behind the town, merged now into the jungle green of the mountains, were the faint scars of blasting where the highway to the mine hairpinned its way up to a gap on the skyline. 'The mine is just over the other side. In a car it takes about quarter of an hour, maybe twenty minutes from Anewa. It's low grade copper mixed with gold and some silver.' And he added, 'The taxes paid by that mine is what keeps the new state of Papua New Guinea going. Without it they'd be broke.'

'How do the Bougainville people feel about that?' Perenna asked.

He glanced quickly over his shoulder, then said, 'I'm not sure how they feel about it down here, but in Buka they don't like it.'

'Rather similar to the attitude of the Scots on North Sea oil,' I said.

'No, not at all similar.' His voice was suddenly sharp. And

then to his sister he said, 'It's not a question I would make a habit of asking if I were you, some of them are very sensitive on the matter.' He lapsed into silence then, staring straight ahead, no longer relaxed, the tenseness back in him as though reminded of something he had temporarily forgotten. Abruptly he said, 'The headquarters of the Bougainville District is over there.' And he indicated the eastern end of the small bay. After that he seemed to withdraw into himself and I became conscious again of the oppressive heat building up in the wheelhouse. Even the air blowing in from the open bridge wing doors was heavy and humid. Wisps of cloud were beginning to drift over the green heights as the forest growth gave up moisture to the air.

Anewa Bay was opening up ahead of us and soon it was possible to make out the details of the shore buildings. The storage sheds and loading wharf for the copper concentrate were on the northern arm of the bay, the power station in the centre and the fuel storage tanks showed as silvery roundels to the south. The only vessel in this very modern looking port was a small tug moored alongside the wharf. Jona straightened up from the chart table, glanced at his watch and picked up the microphone for the ship's loudspeakers. 'Attention deck crew. Stand by for berthing 12.30 hours. I repeat 12.30 standby.'.

Anewa was very different from Kieta. This was the Company port for one of the biggest copper mines in the world, everything mechanically sophisticated, from the pipeline that carried the liquid concentrate across the Crown Prince Range from the mine sixteen miles away at Paguna, to the filtering plant and drying kilns. The power for everything, including the mine, even the electricity for the new township of Arawa, came from that one power station with its Japanese turbines humming away close under the green slopes at the head of the bay.

By the time the formalities of our arrival had been dealt with, it was the hottest part of the day, and with no ship loading at the wharf the port fell into a deep sleep, nobody stirring and only the steady roar from the power station turbines and from the drying plant to indicate that the giant up in the hills beyond the Crown Prince Range continued in full production. Just before

15.00 the crew began straggling in twos and threes up the slipway on which our ramp rested to assemble on the quay, waiting for transport into Arawa. Their jet black skins and fuzzy mops of hair identified them as Buka men. Perhaps that was why Jona refused to let his sister go with them. 'I'll have a word with the power station engineer. There'll be somebody going into Arawa who can give you both a lift to Government Headquarters.' That's the old District H.Q.'

Above the shimmering green of the rain forest the clouds had thickened, lying heavy over the heights. Teopas joined the little cluster of men on the quay. It began to rain, big heavy drops that seemed to be squeezed out of the humidity that hung over us. Seaward the sky was still a blinding white haze. The truck appeared, one of the two we had put ashore at Kieta. Teopas got in beside the driver, the rest of the crew scrambling into the back for shelter as the rain increased. The truck splashed off down the road past the power station and ten minutes later Jona came hurrying back along the empty quay under the shelter of a borrowed umbrella. One of the engineers would be going into the hospital at Arawa to visit a patient in about an hour's time and would give us a lift.

He arrived in a heavy downpour of rain, driving a company car and wielding a large umbrella. 'Standard equipment at this time of day,' he said as he escorted Perenna from the bridge to the car which he had parked halfway down the slip. His name was Fred Perry. 'Same as the old-time tennis star,' he said without a flicker of a smile. He was Australian, thirtyish and thickset with sandy hair and sharp features that reminded me of a fox terrier I had once known. He had been with the Company since the first steel girders of the power station had been erected and, with no prompting at all, began telling us the story of its building as he backed up the slipway and headed out on the road to Arawa. 'You must like it here,' I said.

He half turned his head. 'No worse than Tom Price or Parraburdoo. I had a two year sabbatical up in the iron cauldron country of Western Australia. But I'd rather be in Sydney any day.'

'You come from Sydney?' Perenna asked.

'No, Wagga Wagga.' And he went on to tell us about the building of the port, all the cargoes of massive machinery that had been shipped in. Once we were clear of Anewa Bay, the forest closed in on us from either side, the rain bouncing on the tarmac, steaming between the primordial green walls, and frogs everywhere – they turned out later to be toads – squat and motionless, soaking up the moisture.

We came to an intersection and turned left. 'If you're going up to the mine that's the road to take,' he said. 'As good a piece of highway engineering as you'll see anywhere in the world.' He talked about that for the rest of the way into Arawa, how it had had to take a 50-wheel transporter to get the 80-ton crusher up to the ore treatment plant. 'Remember that when you're driving up. This whole operation is on such a massive scale it's difficult to imagine what it was like when we started. It was all very primitive then, the people too. Now we've got training and recreational centres, a technical college, everything they could possibly want. The whole concept, right from the very beginning, was that the indigenous people would eventually take over. The concentrator, for instance. It's the largest in the world and almost entirely operated by local men. The power station, too. They've been very quick to learn, though we do lose a lot of them after training. They're ambitious and they seem to like doing their own thing. Transport, shops, engineering, construction work, even import-export, any service operation where there's a demand and they can make money seems to appeal to them. Funny isn't it, when you consider that they had very little experience of money before we began this monster operation. Like I say, they've caught on bloody quick.'

The forest fell away, the road opening out to a rain-drenched view of buildings widely spaced on the flat of a valley floor. 'Arawa'. He pointed out the shopping centre and superstore as we turned right off the Kieta road, left by the swimming pool, then skirted the edge of the residential area till we came to the hospital. The rain was still bucketing down, and when he had parked, he turned to me. 'It could go on like this for a couple of hours or more. You've got a licence, have you? Then you'd better take the car.' He gave me directions to the Provincial Government Headquarters. 'Pick me up when you're through.' He was seeing a fellow engineer who had been operated on for appendicitis and didn't seem to mind how long he stayed. 'Eddie is pretty well recovered now. Eddie Flint. They'll know at the desk where to find me. And I'll leave you the umbrella. You'll need it.'

He ran for the entrance and I moved into the driving seat beside Perenna. He had told us where we could get instant pictures taken in the shopping centre, and when we had them, I drove to the Government offices. By then it was near their closing time, but even so the waiting room was still crowded and we were the only whites.

I noticed him as soon as we entered the room. He was the centre of a little group in the corner by the windows, all of them short, barrel-chested men with bare splayed feet like shovels and heavy broad-nosed features. He was dressed in immaculate white shirt and shorts, white stockings and black shoes, but he was of the same ethnic type, broad-shouldered and stocky with a large, heavily-boned head. He stood out from the others, not just on account of his dress, but because of the brightness of his eyes, the vitality in his face, his dominant personality. One of his group nodded in our direction and he turned, his mouth open on a word, staring. And Perenna, beside me, said on a note of surprise, 'I know that man. I'm sure I do. It's Tagup. He's one of the Chimbu tribal chiefs from the Kuamegu area.' And she started towards him.

The man detached himself from his group and came over to her, smiling now, his hand outstretched in greeting. On the pocket of his white shirt a silver shield gleamed. I watched the two of them for a moment as they greeted each other, the white girl with the orange-red cap of hair and the black man from the Highlands of Papua New Guinea in his white European clothes. They made a strange, contrasting pair. Then, as they continued talking, I went over to the desk clerk and explained our business. He said he would see the Immigration Officer as soon as he was free and I lit a cigarette and took up a position against the wall where I could survey the room. I didn't go over and join Perenna. It didn't seem important, not then, and anyway they were talking in a mixture of Pidgin and some local language. After a few minutes the man from Papua New Guinea was called away to lead his group into one of the offices and Perenna rejoined me, excited at this unexpected renewal of contact with the people she had grown up amongst. 'It *was* Tagup. A marvellous man! I was telling him about Tim – I knew he'd understand and I thought he might help me – ' She broke off abruptly, hesitated, then went on quickly in an artificially light voice – 'He's one of their fight leaders. I didn't expect to find men of the Chimbu people here, and he is from a village quite close to Kuamegu. As a kid I used to cheer them on.' She laughed. 'It's rather like a football match really, a sort of fight display, a show. Unless they've really got something to fight about, then it's serious. But he's a Councillor now. That's the silver shield he was wearing.'

'What's he doing here then?' I asked. 'He's not looking for a labouring job surely.'

'No, he says he's come to find out what the magic is the whites have discovered here that is making so much money for the PNG government, and also for the Chimbu people who come to work in Bougainville. He says it's disrupting village and clan life, that men who are no better than rubbish men – he called them that – come back with money to buy pigs and cassowaries and are able to display more property at the sing-sings than the chiefs and elders.' The clerk caught my eye and indicated the door marked Immigration. 'He was very concerned about it,' she said.

'Disturbs the village pecking order?'

She nodded and I pushed open the door for her. 'It's a very complex, very paternalistic social structure, and if it is undermined there'll be chaos. They're fighters. They're a fighting people. . . .'

It was almost 17.30 when our passports were finally stamped and we went out to the car. The rain had eased, but humidity remained heavy, the daylight fading so that we could see lights in Arawa glimmering through the trees. In the bay behind us there was nothing visible at all. 'Is it always like this?' I asked Perenna.

She nodded. 'Most days the humidity builds up to rain by late afternoon. It's different in Buka. Buka is comparatively low, but this is a very mountainous island.' I knew that from the chart. The Crown Prince Range was over 5,000 feet and there were other mountains along the spine of the island that were a thousand or more feet higher. 'As soon as the sun sets and it starts getting cooler, the rain gradually exhausts itself. You'll see. A couple of hours from now the stars will be out and it will be a lovely evening.'

We got into the car and I started the engine. 'What do you plan to do?' I asked her – 'now that you're here and you've got your visa. Will you just stay on the ship with your brother or are you going to get a job?'

She didn't answer for a moment, sitting very still and gazing ahead through the clicking windscreen wipers. 'I don't know,' she murmured huskily. 'I had it all planned – when I was on that cruise ship. If Tim was ever well enough to look after himself, I was going to come out here and look after the business side so that Jona wouldn't have anything to do but run the ship. And when you got me that money . . .' She was smiling. 'Well, it seemed like an omen, everything suddenly simple and straightforward, and those stamps a symbol of good luck for a change. But now . . .' The smile had faded. 'Now it all seems different, so many things I don't understand. Jona, for instance. He's not a bit as I remember him. He used to be so carefree. And Mac . . .' She hesitated, shaking her head. And then, her voice livelier, 'Better drive back to the hospital. I think Fred will have had enough of his friend's operation by now.' She turned to me, smiling again, her mood suddenly relaxed, almost intimate. 'I've got quite a lot of Australian dollars left and the Immigration Officer said they were just as good currency as the local *kina*. If we can find a decent restaurant I'd like you to have dinner with me.'

'This isn't our car,' I reminded her.

'No. But I'm not spending the evening listening to how they built one of the greatest mines in the world. There'll be taxis.' Her hand touched mine. 'If not, we can thumb a ride or else walk. Or don't you want to walk me home to my ship?'

Her eyes were laughing, a direct invitation. I put my arm round her and kissed her. The softness of her mouth, the leap of my blood at the feel of her through the thin cotton shirt, I suddenly had other ideas. 'If he's tired of his friend, he can always chat up one of the nurses.' I was trying to recall a suitable place to park. Two blacks passed, a man and a woman, both of them huddled under an umbrella. I put the car into gear and drove out of the parking lot on to the narrow ribbon of tarmac. The glare of headlights showed ahead, tree boles became moving shadows, the lights swung, undipped and blinding. It was a truck and as I pulled in to the side to let it pass, just before dipping my headlights I caught a glimpse of the driver.

I heard the catch of Perenna's breath and suddenly she reached across and flicked the dipper back to high beam. The truck was barely twenty yards away and I saw him clearly, his teeth showing in a big grin, his broad face frowning in concentration under his woolly head of hair. It was the bos'n's mate, a man called Malulu, and Teopas was sitting in the cab beside him. The truck roared past us with a sudden burst of acceleration, the same truck that had come down to the port to pick up the crew, and turning my head I saw the back of it was full of men.

She caught hold of my arm, her head twisted round, her voice urgent: 'Were they all from the ship? What are they doing here? This road only leads to the Government offices and on down to the shore. Do you think there's a café there or a liquor store?' She was staring at me, suddenly very tense, so that I wondered whether she, too, had seen the glint of metal among the packed bodies. It had only been a glimpse in the red glow of our rear lights and I couldn't be sure . . . 'I think we should go back,' she said.

'No.' I parked the car and switched off the engine. Darkness closed in on us, the trees dripping. 'You wait here.'

But she was out in a flash. 'If they're up to something I want to know.'

I turned on her, facing her across the roof of the car. 'Just do what you're told. Please. Get in the driving seat and wait for me.' I didn't stop to see what she did. I just started back down the almost dark road, moving quietly and stopping now and then to listen. I could hear the sound of voices and then shadows emerged out of the gloom ahead. They were moving in a bunch down the road towards me. I slipped in among the trees and watched as the people from the waiting room hurried past. They were talking amongst themselves, but I couldn't understand what they said, only that they seemed excited about something, constantly glancing back over their shoulders.

When they were beyond the bend I stepped back on to the road. My watch showed that it was now after 17.40. They could have been ordered to leave because the offices were closing and their excitement no more than anger at having to return next day. But somehow it hadn't sounded like that. And when I turned the next bend, and was in sight of the headquarters, there was nobody in the parking lot, the official cars still standing dark and empty and all the lights on in the offices. The truck was parked outside the main entrance. Its lights were off and I could only just see it. Had I been mistaken? Was this merely some sort of a deputation to the District Commissioner? Beyond the truck a man moved in the shadow of the trees. I wouldn't have seen him except that the entrance door had been opened and for a moment he was illumined in a shaft of light.

I knew then that I had not been wrong. The light glinted on the short barrel of the machine pistol cradled on his arm. A voice spoke and he moved towards the door. It was the driver, Malulu. I retreated softly into the shadows, wondering whether to wait for some confirmation of what I was beginning to fear or drive straight to the police. But all I had seen was a man with a gun. Hardly sufficient to convince them of a hold-up or perhaps the kidnapping of a senior PNG official.

And then a light suddenly blazed out from a darkened room on my side of the building. There was a shout, the sound of feet on a wooden floor and the window was flung open, a man starting to climb out. He saw me and hesitated. A door banged. He turned his head, his mouth opening in a scream, but the scream was cut short as the outline of his head and shoulders was jerked away from the window. I heard the soft thud of a blow, a gurgling gasp followed by a dragging sound, then silence.

The light went out and I stood there, shocked into immobility. Malulu came round the corner of the building and stood looking over the parked cars. Then he went back to the main entrance. I began to move cautiously through the trees bordering the road. As soon as I reached the bend I stepped out of concealment and began to run.

I met Perenna coming towards me. 'I thought I heard a shout. That Chimbu chief – Tagup . . .'

'Get back to the car,' I told her. 'Quick!'

'What is it? What's happened?' She was running beside me. 'Tagup said they had been ordered out of the office they were in, all of them, by a gang of armed men.'

We had reached the second bend. The car was still there and no sign of anybody near it. 'Get in.' I flung myself into the driving seat and had the engine on and the car moving before she had shut her door. 'What else did your Chimbu friend tell you?' I switched the headlights to high beam. 'Did he know what they were up to?'

'No. He didn't seem to understand what was going on. He was worried about the safety of his people. He's a redskin, you see. . . .'

'What's that supposed to mean?'

'Anybody from Papua New Guinea. They're lighter skinned and it seems there's been trouble between them and the Bougainvilleans.' We reached the main road and I turned right, towards the town. 'Was it really a hold-up? What happened?'

I told her briefly and by the time I had finished we were at the first house. I parked right against the entrance, jumped out and beat on the door. A woman answered it. 'May I use your

.phone please?'

She looked at me, startled, a small, pale face under a fringe of dark hair. 'Why? Has there been an accident?'

'Excuse me.' I pushed past her. 'Where is it?'

'The phone?' She seemed slightly dazed. A record player was blaring in the background. 'It's over there, by the kitchen. But you can't use it. Not now.'

'Why not?'

'Something's gone wrong with it. Sandra – that's my daughter – she was trying to ring a friend. Then I tried, but it's out of order, I guess. I'm sorry. Can I help at all? If it's an accident. . . .'

'I'll try the next house,' I said, and left her standing there with her mouth agape.

It was a man who answered the door this time. He worked in Community Relations and knew the number of the police. But when he tried to get it for me he found the phone was dead. 'Looks like there's a fault in the line for this part of the town. If it's urgent you'd find it quicker to drive there.' He started to give me directions, but now that I was faced with people in their houses, living their normal lives, I was beginning to realize how difficult it was going to be to convince anyone of what I had seen. 'I'll go direct to the hospital,' I said.

'It's an accident, is it?'

'Something like that.'

'Anything I can do? If you've hit somebody, run down one of the indigenes –'

'No. It's something else.'

He stood in the doorway, watching me as I drove off, a puzzled, uncertain look on his face. 'We'll go to the hospital,' I told Perenna. 'We can get Perry to ring the police from there.'

'You didn't get them then?'

'No. His phone was out, too.'

She was silent for a moment, then she said quietly, 'Do you think we'll find all the phones are out?'

The same thought was in my mind, but it was something I didn't want to think about. 'We'll know when we get to the hospital.' I was wishing now I had told the man what had happened. In Community Relations he might have known if there was any trouble brewing. I glanced at Perenna, sitting tight-lipped beside me. 'Did your brother give you any hint about what those guns might be used for?'

'No.' And she added quickly, 'He's not involved. It's Teopas.'

I didn't say anything, knowing that Teopas was a man who obeyed orders. He would never have planned a raid on the Government offices. I should have brought that Community Relations man with me. Phil Brewster. That was the name he had given me. The hospital showed up ahead and I turned into the entrance.

At the reception desk I asked for Perry. 'He's with a patient of yours, Eddie Flint.' The woman picked up the house phone, spoke to somebody and then said Mr Perry would be right down. I asked her to get me the police then, but she said, 'I'm sorry. The outside lines are out of order.'

'Since when?'

'About quarter of an hour.' She glanced up at the wall clock. 'We haven't been able to contact anybody since before six.'

We waited in silence until Perry appeared. 'You've been a hell of a time.' He was smiling, relieved that we had finally turned up. 'What happened? Did you lose your way?'

'Let's get out to the car,' I said. 'I'll tell you what happened as we drive to the police station.' And I hustled him out, Perenna talking quickly all the time, telling him about the two houses we had stopped at to telephone. 'All the phones are out, even the hospital.'

'That's a matter for the telephone engineers, not the police.'

'Don't talk, just listen.' I pushed him into the passenger seat. I don't know why. It was instinctive, not reasoned. I just didn't want him to drive, his reactions were too slow. He protested, of course, but by then I was behind the wheel and had the engine going. 'Just tell me where to go.' And as I followed his instructions I gave him a brief account of what I had seen at the Government offices. He didn't believe me, of course. 'An armed band?'

And then Perenna in the back seat was telling him what the Chimbu man had said.

'You don't want to believe anything they tell you,' he said. 'They're plain stupid. Rock apes, that's what we call them.'

I heard the angry intake of her breath. 'I'd have you know, Mr Perry, that I was brought up with the Chimbu people – '

'There's police headquarters now,' he interrupted her, pointing to a white building away to our left. 'Do you really expect them to believe that there's some sort of a plot – '

'They'll soon find out when they get over to the Government offices.' Perenna's voice was controlled now, but very tense. I was swinging left into the parking area and then I slammed on the brakes. Standing by the front entrance was a closed truck. 'A Dodge, isn't it?' I was remembering the trucks I had seen on Hans Holland's RPL.

'What is it?' Perry asked. 'Why have you stopped?' His voice was pitched a shade higher, suddenly nervous.

'I think that truck belongs to the Buka Trading Co-operative.'

'Then they must be delivering something. There's no reason to believe – ' His voice cut off abruptly in a gasp. A group of policemen were coming out of the building, their hands above their heads. Two men armed with machine pistols followed. I switched off our lights, leaving the engine running, and we watched as the policemen were herded into the back of the truck at gunpoint. Then everything suddenly went dark.

I glanced back over my shoulder. Not a light showed anywhere in Arawa. The township was in total darkness. I heard Perry mutter, 'Christ! They've got the power station.'

With the engine just ticking over, and in low gear without lights, I turned the car and felt my way back on to the road. Government Headquarters, the telephone exchange, the police and now the power station. The thing that had been in the back of my mind, that I had feared all the time, had happened. It was a coup, a carefully planned coup. 'Now we know what those guns were for.' I turned to glance back at Perenna. 'Did your brother know?'

'Of course he didn't.' But there was no conviction in her voice.

I didn't say anything, remembering that first night when I had found him drinking alone in the wardroom. He may not have known, but he'd had a pretty good idea. No wonder he had been scared.

'What do we do now?' She was leaning forward so that I felt the urgency of her breath on my ear.

'Get a message out.' I switched the lights on full and started driving. It was a loosely sprung car, the road holding poor, but it had a big engine and out on the main road I got her moving. I glanced at Perry sitting hunched in his seat, his face pale and frightened. 'Where's the transmitter – up at the mine?' He nodded. 'And they have emergency generators?'

'Yes.' Suddenly he grabbed hold of my arm. 'Do you think – those men – do you think they're up at the mine already?'

'That's something we won't know till we get there,' I said as we crossed the bridge over the Bovo River. The town was behind us now, the trees closing in. The road still steamed, but the rain had stopped and there were fewer toads. 'Shouldn't there be some traffic on this road?' We hadn't met a single vehicle.

He nodded. 'It's usually quite busy at this time of the day. Men going home – ' He hesitated. 'Perhaps we should go down to Anewa and check at the power station. There may have been a breakdown.'

'Does that happen often?' I asked.

'No.'

'Well then – ' The speedometer was reading eighty. At any moment we would reach the intersection where the mine road came in from the left. I eased my foot on the accelerator. Suppose they had a road block there? Or had they sealed the mine road higher up?

'How many work up at the mine?' Perenna asked.

'I don't know,' he said. 'It varies. Two or three thousand.'

'What about whites? At any rate, men with cars. How many would normally be coming down at this time of day?'

She never got the answer to that, for suddenly, clear in the headlights, there was a figure in a white shirt with a furled umbrella standing in the middle of the road. He stood facing us, signalling us to stop and pull into the side. A rope was stretched across the roadway between two oildrums and in the middle was a large notice board. 'Have you got a torch in the car?' I asked. The man appeared to be unarmed.

Perry reached into the glove locker and handed me a powerful plastic torch. I stopped with my bonnet close against the rope barrier. The board had the words BRIDGE BLOCKED – PLEASE PROCEED ANEWA FOR INSTRUCTIONS painted on it with an aerosol spray. The man came up to my side, leaning down to peer in at the window. 'You go to Anewa plis.' His face was broad and very black, his hair standing up like a golliwog's.

'That's where I'm going,' I said.

White teeth showed in a big smile. 'Gutpela. Anewa okay.' And he went to the oil drum on the left, undid the rope and pulled it clear. The glow of a vehicle showed through the trees coming from the direction of Anewa. I switched off my lights and called him back to my window. 'That notice,' I said. 'The bridge isn't blocked. We've just come over it.' Uncertainty showed on his face. 'I'll remember you,' I said, shining the torch full in his eyes. And then, while he was still blinded, I slammed the gear lever home, pushed my foot hard down, and with the engine roaring shot away from him, the tyres slithering on the wet surface as I took the sharp turn on to the mine road. I did it without lights, only switching them on when I was out of range of any pistol he might have been carrying. 'How far to the mine?'

'Ten miles I'd say,' Perry said.

'And the surface?'

'You don't have to worry about that. Tarmac all the way.'

The road stretched ahead of me, straight and smooth, the gradient only slight, so that I was again doing eighty in top gear. 'When do we start climbing?'

'Some miles yet. Then it gets rapidly steeper as the road claws its way up the side of the mountain. You need to be careful then. There are a number of hairpin bends and a nasty drop on the left.'

Perenna leaned close to me. 'That man. Did you recognize him?'

'No. I find these black faces confusing. He was from Buka, wasn't he? That very black, glossy skin, and the hair. Why? Is he one of your brother's crew?'

'Not Jona's. But I think I saw him helping to shift those cases on the RPL.' And then she tapped me on the shoulder. 'There are headlights now, down the road behind us.'

I glanced in the mirror. They were just coming into sight round a shallow bend, presumably the vehicle coming from the direction of Anewa that had allowed me to make it on to the mine road without lights. 'Is it gaining on us?'

She was twisted round in the back seat, watching it. 'I don't think so,' she said at length. 'In fact, it looks more like a truck. The headlights are too high off the ground for it to be a car.'

Either they had made certain of the Administration and the port before moving on to the mine or else we were going to find ourselves trapped. The jungle of green growth bordering the road did not look at all inviting as a way of escape, and higher up there would be scrub and rock and precipitous slopes. The gradient was already getting steeper, a breeze blowing off the tops and the road drying. Stars were beginning to show, so that ahead, beyond the gleam of the headlights, I was getting glimpses of the crest of the range etched as a jagged line against the night sky. We crossed a bridge over a rock gulley. Nothing visible to the left, just the blackness of a sheer drop.

'Can you still see that vehicle?' I asked Perenna.

'Just a glimpse now and then. And I think there are two of them, but they're a long way away now.'

The first real bend was coming up, the tarmac running into gravel on the broad verge as the road swung round to the right. 'Must be a good view from here.'

'Wait till you get to the big hairpin just short of the pass,' Perry said. 'You can see the whole coastline from there, all the lights.' He waited till we were round the bend. 'I was forgetting the power had been cut off.'

Steep, blast-hewn slopes of red earth and rock rose above us, lightly clothed by regeneration. 'When we get to the top, how far to the mine?'

'Not far. A mile, perhaps a little more.'

'And the offices, where are they?'

'They're the first thing you come to, on a sort of plateau overlooking Paguna.'

'Will the mine manager be there, do you think?'

He shook his head. 'I couldn't say.' We were into a double bend now, and when we were round it and snaking out over a black drop, he added, 'Normally he'd have left by now. Like the rest of us he lives in Arawa. But with the power off, he's probably still there. A power failure means the crushers, the concentrator, all the vital machinery comes to a standstill. That's a major crisis as far as he's concerned, so he'll be around somewhere.'

As I went into a long curving right hand bend I was thinking that, if I were managing one of the biggest mines in the world, and the power and telephone systems failed, I certainly wouldn't be sitting in my office. I would be out making sure something was being done about it. The slopes to the right of us were so sheer they had been terraced. We were running out to the long buttress of an outcrop, another black void opening up below us, the outline of the tops very close, and as we approached the next backward loop, I slowed the car, stealing a quick glance to the left. Far below in the dark void I could see the road up which we had climbed, a tiny thread of tarmac lit by headlights. Two vehicles, a long way behind now.

'They're moving very slowly,' Perenna said. 'And they've closed up. They're almost head-to-tail.'

I drove on round the loop. Old trucks, full of armed men – it would take them at least ten, perhaps fifteen minutes to grind their way up to where we were now. I slipped into bottom gear, my foot hard down as the road rose steeply to skirt an outcrop that faced to the right. We were almost at the top. Round the outcrop, we were into a defile, and suddenly we were on the level, our speed increasing as I went up through the gears, and Perenna's voice behind me saying, 'Strange, we haven't met a single car.'

'Not strange at all,' Perry answered her. 'A power failure causes a lot of problems. They'll all be staying up here trying to cope.' And then to me, 'It's downhill for about a mile and then there's a cut-off to the left. The offices are there.'

Lights glimmered in a great bowl in the mountains. Driving fast now, I couldn't see any details, but I got the impression of a scarred and terraced crater, a sort of moonscape. The road dropped quickly, a glimpse of trees and suddenly the cut-off was there, the shallow slope of roofs beyond. 'Left now,' Perry shouted and I slammed on the brakes, tyres slithering as I made the turn, and then we were up on a plateau and I had stopped at steps leading to the verandah of a long, low single-storey building. 'This it?' Perry nodded, his door already open.

We rushed in, the three of us, to be faced by a young woman looking cool and neat. But when Perry asked for the mine manager she informed him that he had flown to Melbourne two days ago. 'Then we'd like to see Mr Tooley.'

'I'm afraid he's busy right now.'

'Is he in his office or not?' I asked her.

'No, I'm afraid – '

'Just tell us where he is then. It's urgent.'

'I'm not sure. I know he was going down to the concentrator first. There's a power failure, you see, and the telephone – '

'Who's in charge here?'

'Well, nobody really. I think I'm the only one here now. They're all down at the mine. We're on auxiliary power – '

The mine area, when we got down into it, was huge. It was an open-cast mine, a stupendous gravel pit of an area with huge drag cranes shovelling ore into the Euclids and Haulpaks that lumbered like mammoths over the dirt road. We spent an exasperating ten minutes wandering round the massive complex of the concentrator with its electrolytic tanks, driving from one dusty building to another, before we finally ran him to earth at the auxiliary generating shed.

He was a tall, rangy Canadian, and he didn't take it in at first, his mind on other things. 'Are you trying to tell me there's been some kind of an uprising?' That was after I had described what we had seen at police headquarters. Then he turned to Perry. 'You're one of the power station engineers. Why the hell didn't you go down to Anewa and see what the situation was for yourself?'

Even with the power off and the telephone out, I don't think he would have accepted our version of what had happened if I hadn't told him about the arms we had trans–shipped off Shortland Island. That finally convinced him. 'Christ!' he muttered as he got into the car with us. 'Bloody politics! We try to keep out of politics, but it's there all the time waiting to trip us up.' By the primary crushing plant I had to pull in to let one of the Haulpaks past. 'After all we've done for them, the work we've put into this place. Turn left here.' We were on to the exit road then, climbing in zig–zags up towards the administration block. 'Do you think they'll be there now?'

I glanced at my watch. Twenty minutes since we had stopped at the offices. 'Bound to be.'

'What do you plan to do?' Perenna asked him.

'Talk to them, I suppose. Find out what they want. What the hell else can I do?' And he added, 'If it had been trouble with those Chimbu labourers of ours I could understand. The Administration has had trouble with them before.'

'Have you any weapons up here at the mine?' I asked.

'Of course not. We run the mine, that's all. This is PNG territory. They're shareholders in it and they look after the civil administration. It would happen when Bill is away in Melbourne. I'm just a mining engineer. I'm not interested in politics.'

At the cut-off to the offices I stopped the car, suggesting that he and Perry went in on foot. 'We'll wait for you here in case you want to get out in a hurry.'

'Okay. If we find they've occupied the offices I'll send Fred back. See if you can get him down to the power station. I'll be staying here.' The two of them went off up the road, their

figures blending into the shadows. Perenna and I sat there in the
darkness waiting. Ahead the tree-covered outline of the pass was
a black shadow against the sky. The murmur of the mine was
just audible from the dust bowl behind us. There was no other
sound. 'Do you know where the transmitter is?' I asked. But of
course she didn't. I was thinking about that, certain it must be
somewhere up here where the radio mast would be clear of the
mountains, when I saw a shadow moving down the road from
the offices. I switched on the ignition, the lights showing Perry
running towards us.

They had found the offices just as we had left them, the girl still
there on her own. No vehicles had driven in from the coast. They
had tested the telex and it was still working.

'Has he sent a message out?'

'No.'

'He doesn't believe us, is that it?' I started to get out of the
car, but he stopped me.

'He wants me to go down to Anewa and check on the situation
there. He refuses to do anything until he knows for sure, but if I
don't report back by ten tonight, then he'll send that telex.' He
got in beside me. 'What do you think has happened to those
trucks that were following us?'

'We'll soon know.' I started the engine, then hesitated,
wondering whether to go up to the office myself and get Tooley
to send to Port Moresby while it was still possible. But what
would he tell them? In his shoes I would be reluctant to stick
my neck out on the hearsay of a young engineer and two
strangers. Nobody likes making a fool of themselves, and
anyway, perhaps it wasn't part of the plan to cut off all
communication with the outside world. 'Let's see where they've
got to,' I said and drove off up the road to the pass.

We reached the head of the pass, came out of the defile and
started down round the buttress to the loop that ran out on to a
shoulder of the mountain. When I reached the hairpin, I
switched off the lights, pulled on to the verge and stopped the
car. Far down the shadowy scar that marked the twisting line of
the road tiny figures moved in the glow-worm lights of two

S.S. – G

vehicles drawn up side by side. I turned to Perry. 'Isn't that where the road goes over a gulley?'

He nodded, sitting tense, his head thrust forward as he peered through the windscreen.

The stars were very bright now, the mountain slopes dark in shadow. If they intended to cut the mine off from the coast, that was the obvious place to do it. 'Are there explosives down at Anewa?'

'Probably.' He nodded. 'We use a lot of explosives for blasting the ore. Yes, I think there's bound to be some in store at the port.'

'And this road is the only way out?'

'There's the old tote road, also a rough track that follows the line of the Jaba River to the other side of the island. And of course we've got helicopters. But as far as vehicles are concerned, yes. If they blow the road and set up a guard post, then the mine is virtually sealed off from the port.'

The simplicity of it! No supplies, no spares, nothing – until terms had been agreed. And what was it they wanted? The mine couldn't grant them independence. Perhaps it was money? 'How much does the mine pay the Papua New Guinea government by way of taxes?' I asked him.

'I wouldn't know. I suppose it's in the yearly report. There's royalties as well as tax. I've heard it said that in all it amounts to a third of the PNG annual revenue.'

'So the islanders would be pretty rich if they could get their hands on it.'

'Yes. But how could they possibly do that? They don't control the armed forces in Papua New Guinea, or the police. Bougainville comes under the PNG government, and that's in Port Moresby.' He sat there for a moment longer staring intently at the lights on the road below. Suddenly he opened his door and got out. 'I'll drive now.' He came round to my side. 'I suggest you and Miss Holland wait here. No point in risking your necks. If I don't get through, then you can walk back to the mine.' He had pulled open my door. 'Come on. It's my car, my problem.'

'What do you propose to do?'

'Talk to them, find out what it's all about.' His voice was tense and by the look on his face I knew he had made up his mind. 'If they won't let me through, then I'll come back and pick you up.'

I got out of the car. 'Okay,' I said. 'But don't do anything stupid. They'll be armed.'

He nodded, settling himself in the driving seat. Perenna got out. 'Why are you doing this? You don't have to. Leave it to the manager.'

He gave her a nervous little smile. 'I happen to believe in what we're trying to do here. We've achieved so much.' And when she started to argue, he said, 'Believe me, I know. I lecture in my spare time at the Technical College.'

He started the engine then and she seized hold of my arm. 'Stop him,' she said urgently, her face white in the glow of the lights. 'He doesn't understand. They're from Buka and this is Cargo. The mine is the biggest Cargo they've ever had.'

He smiled at her again, trying to appear confident. 'I've been here six years altogether. I guess I know as much about these people as anyone. I'll be all right.'

'Just one thing.' I said. 'You mentioned an old tote road. Where is it?'

'About halfway between here and those trucks. It crosses the highway at the second loop of the double hairpin. But it hasn't been used in years. If you're thinking of walking out . . . Here, take the torch.' He passed it to me and then, with a quick wave of the hand, he started down the hill.

'You should have stopped him.' Her hand was still on my arm and I could feel her trembling. 'He doesn't realize what they're like. Cargo is magic. It's like a religion. They're not open to reason when they're in the grip of it. If he tries to stop them they'll cut him to pieces.'

'Better sit down,' I said. 'Nothing you can do about it now and we may have a long, rough walk ahead of us.'

We sat there on the gravel verge watching the blaze of his lights dwindle as the car swung down under the scarred terraces of the mountainside. They disappeared for a time behind the buttress that hid the double hairpin, then came into view again, a tiny glow now as he came on to the final straight before the gulley. He was driving fast and the figures moving in the lights of the truck froze. I thought I saw the glint of a gun barrel, then he was slowing down. Finally he stopped, the car's lights shining on the little group in front of the trucks. They waved him back, but he was out of the car now and walking towards them.

Time passed – a minute, perhaps two, the huddle of men moving closer to him. One of them held a gun. I saw it distinctly as he ran past him and Perry, turning, was suddenly engulfed. I couldn't see him after that. 'The fool!' Perenna breathed. 'The stupid, quixotic fool!'

'He'll be all right,' I said. But I wasn't at all sure. It depended how tensed up they were. But at least we had heard no sound of a shot.

His car was driven on past the trucks and parked down the road. After that there was a burst of almost frenzied activity. It went on for about ten minutes and then the trucks were started up and manoeuvred back and forth until they were turned and could be driven down to park behind the car. We waited, certain of what was going to happen as tiny figures straggled down the road to crouch in the shelter of the vehicles. Suddenly the road surface burst upwards in a flash of flame and smoke. The sound of the explosion followed, a protracted, rattling boom that reverberated against the mountain slopes and slowly died away in the distance.

'Well, that's that,' I said, getting to my feet. 'You going back to the mine or coming on with me to find that tote road?'

She didn't seem to hear, still sitting there, her eyes wide and shocked, a frozen look on her face. 'They'd never have thought of that on their own.' She looked up at me. 'It's all been so carefully planned – the arms, the way they've taken over the vital centres, everything. But what does he hope to get out of it?'

'Who?' I was still gazing intently at what was happening on the road below.

'Hans, of course. It has to be Hans. The arms, the trucks, the timing . . .' Her voice was low and husky, barely audible. 'But why? What does he want?'

I wasn't at all certain about that myself. There was no smelting operation on Bougainville. The gold and silver wasn't separated from the copper, it was shipped out as a mineral concentrate. I had checked that with Tooley. 'Bulk cargo contracts, I imagine. According to your brother, when he was in England he was looking for an ore carrier.'

She didn't seem to take that in, sitting hunched on the gravel, grasping her knees. 'Power,' she whispered. 'He's a man who wants to dominate everything – everybody.' A shudder ran through her. And then, not looking at me, still in a whisper, speaking her thoughts aloud: 'He fascinates me and appals me . . . he's . . .' She seemed to choke on the words, falling silent, her mood tense, overwrought. I sat down again and she gripped hold of my hand, very tight. There was a long silence, and. I waited, knowing she wanted to tell me something, needed to explain. Finally, in a small voice, she said. 'Roy. I'm scared – scared of him, of myself – everything. How's it going to end?' And under her breath she murmured, 'God, what a mess!'

I was still waiting, expecting her to tell me what it was that so appalled her. But she just sat there, wrapped in silent misery. In the end I asked her about the day he had visited them at Aldeburgh. I knew it had to be that. 'Tell me what happened?' I asked gently.

She shook her head slowly. 'No.' She was like a child lost in darkness, some terrible darkness of her own making. I shifted my position, put my arm round her shoulders. She was shivering, but not with cold. 'One day perhaps . . .' And she turned to me, burying her head in my shoulder. 'Don't ask me, not now. Not till I'm ready.' She was crying now, crying because something had happened, something in that house that could never be wiped from her memory. 'Hold me. Just hold me.'

I held her and gradually the shivering ceased. After a while she lifted her head and pulled away. 'Silly of me.' She had her handkerchief out and got quickly to her feet. 'I'm sorry. I get these moods sometimes.' Her voice was firmer. 'Maybe it's the mixed blood. We're a bit of a mixture, you know.' She said it with forced gaiety, 'Come on.' She reached down and took hold of my hand, pulling me to my feet. 'Let's see what that old tote road is like.'

'It will be badly overgrown,' I warned her. 'Probably take us all night to reach the ship. Are you sure you want – '

'The ship! Of course. I'd almost forgotten.' Her face, her whole mood was suddenly brighter. 'If we can find Jona, he can take us out of here.'

I didn't think Jona would be much help, but I didn't tell her so as we started down the road. The trucks were driving off now, leaving the car still parked there, just visible in the starlight. And when the glow of the trucks' lights had finally been swallowed up in the night, there was no glimmer of light anywhere, the world a darkened silence, broken only by the distant murmur of water and the periodic croaking of frogs or toads.

2

We had reached the first loop of the double hairpin and were standing on the verge, trying to make out the line of the tote road, when a glimmer of light showed from down the slope towards Anewa. We stood, watching in silence, as it climbed steadily towards us. There was sudden movement where the road had been blown, three figures standing by the parked car. The sound of an engine came to us faintly as the twin lights of the approaching vehicle emerged from the trees. It was being driven fast, and soon the headlights were shining full on the three armed men, all blacks, their fuzzy mops of hair distinctly visible. The car stopped just short of them, the headlights dipped now.

Two men got out and I heard Perenna give a little gasp as they moved forward into the beam of the headlights to talk to the guards. One of them wore a white shirt and his hair was red in the lights. I couldn't be certain who the other was, only that he was an islander. They stood there for a moment, talking, and then the whole group walked up the road to stand on the edge of the dark line where the charges had blasted the surface. The beam of a torch showed, a pinpoint of light sweeping the gap in the tarmac.

Hans Holland and his companion were there about ten minutes. Then they went back to their car. We watched as the headlights blazed on the figures of the men standing there, the weapons in their hands clearly visible, then swept the red rock of the gulley edge as the car turned. 'So you're right,' I said.

Perenna nodded. 'I said it was Hans. It had to be. Nobody from the Buka villages could have planned this.' Her words, whispering in the night, had an undertone of excitement. It was almost as if, against her will, she admired the man for what he was doing. Pictures of Nazis, seen in old films, flickered through my mind. The figure had been tiny, but even at that distance I couldn't help noticing a swagger in his walk. 'For tonight,' I said, 'he's a sort of Führer, a little Napoleon.'

She didn't say anything, standing very still, gazing intently as the car's lights dwindled, so intently that I suddenly had the feeling her mind was reaching out to him, that she was imagining herself in that car, a part of the plan he had conceived. Then she seemed to collect herself, and in a cool voice she said, 'Better get started if it's going to take us all night.'

I nodded and we moved back on to the tarmac, walking quickly down to the second bend, where the old road was just visible in the starlight. To scramble down to it would be rough, the darkness of the valley full of croakings. 'I shouldn't have come.' She was standing on the road, staring down into the forest growth below.

'You couldn't help it,' I said, thinking she meant the drive up to the mine. But she shook her head. 'Tim, I mean. I shouldn't have left him. I didn't realize –' She hesitated. 'It's all so different, and now this plan . . . I can't do anything for Tim here.'

But I was still thinking of Hans Holland inspecting the blown road like the commander of a military operation.

'You think he'll pull it off?'

'Probably. I don't know.' She shook her head. 'But Tim needs me. I know that – I feel it. And there's nothing I can do, no way I can help him. Only pray . . .' She looked up at me suddenly, her eyes luminously large in the dark. 'Have you ever prayed? I mean, really prayed.' She sensed my hesitation and added, 'I tried prayer in Aldeburgh. But it didn't work. I think – deep down . . . I found myself believing, but not in God, in something else . . . the powers of darkness, evil, I don't know what, but it was there in my heart. It scared me. Even there, in England, it scared me. And now, out here – ' My hand was on her arm and I felt a shiver run through her. 'It's stronger out here.'

'Come on,' I said. 'If we're going to get back to the ship we'd better get started.'

'Yes, the ship.' She squared her shoulders, bracing herself. 'Jona's different, isn't he? Much more practical, a seaman, no imagination . . .' She forced a little laugh and then she had stepped off the verge and started down the bulldozed debris of the steep slope leading to the shadow line of the old road. It was a hard scramble requiring all our concentration so that we didn't talk, either then or when we reached the tote road, for the line of it ran close below the highway and with every step down the remains of the steep track we were approaching the gulley. I dared not use the torch, so that our progress was slow. In places the track was completely obliterated by the rubble of the roadworks above and there were muddy stretches where the rainwater lay trapped.

It took us over half an hour to reach the gulley. There were trees to our right and it was very dark, only the sound of water to indicate that we were right below the guards. The track here dropped steeply down the face of the mountain range and we were a long time scrambling through the tangle of new forest growth that had almost obliterated it. Finally, well hidden from the highway, I began using the torch.

I think if we hadn't returned to the highway we should never have made it, for the lower we went, the worse the going became, the jungle growth almost impenetrable and patches of swamp water. It was past midnight and we were both of us very tired when I finally made the decision to force our way up the slope to the road. We reached it just over an hour later, hot and dirty, our clothes torn and soaked with sweat. After that it was easy, just a long downhill walk. Twice we had to seek shelter among the trees, once for a car going up full of men and again when it came down. Presumably the guard at the gulley was being relieved.

It was during that long walk down the highway that my mind began to grapple with the implications of what was happening. Now that I was sure Hans Holland was behind it I tried to put myself in his shoes, but the more I thought about it the less I understood it. It was quite inconceivable that he could hold such a large and important company to ransom, a company that had international connections and a worldwide market. And if it wasn't money, but power he was after, how could he possibly achieve that with three or four old landing craft and a group of cargo-crazy islanders? Tooley was probably correct in saying that the mine administration tried to keep clear of politics, but even if the white expatriates stood by and did nothing, there was a large work force drawn from Bougainville and other islands in and around the Solomons. How would they react? And the fact that Papua New Guinea had only become independent a few years back would not prevent them from reacting very vigorously to the threat of secession, particularly as Bougainville provided such a large slice of their revenue. And any action they took would presumably have the moral support of the UN, the co-operation of those countries where the copper was marketed and the active support of the Australian government.

It just didn't make sense. That he could achieve a temporary success was obvious. He appeared to have done that already. But how could he possibly hope to build on it to the point where Bougainville could successfully achieve a unilateral declaration of independence? There had to be some advantage to him, something that he was certain he could negotiate before the initial success of the plan collapsed under the longer term strain of forces that must in the end prove too powerful for him. But what? Perhaps he didn't see it that way. Perhaps he believed that the people of Bougainville and Buka would combine to make the whole thing politically possible.

It was a fascinating possibility, and toying with it in my mind I began to wonder how I could turn it to my own advantage. Providence had brought me to this island at a moment of intense political activity where events would produce either change or chaos. Whichever it was there would be opportunities. A selfish point of view, perhaps, but when you're out of a job and looking for openings in a new world, it's not unnatural to relate events to your own personal problems. By the time we reached the intersection with the Kieta road I had more or less made up my mind.

There was no road block now, and no guard. With the mine road blown there was no need. The time was 02.17. Four hours since Tooley would have sent his telex. I wondered what he would have said, what they would think of it at Port Moresby. Or would he notify his own head office in Melbourne and leave them to inform the PNG Government? The latter probably, in which case nobody would do anything about it till morning. It would probably be midday before Port Moresby appreciated the situation and then, even if they were able to establish communications with the mine, they would still have to convince themselves that it had really happened, and only then would they start considering what should be done about it. It could be thirty-six hours at least before any positive action was taken.

I was thinking about that as we approached Anewa. A lot could happen in thirty-six hours.

The dark rain forest walls that had hemmed us in since we had struggled up on to the road fell back. We were into a clearing, the tarmac shining wet under the stars, and round a bend storage sheds black in shadow. It was cooler now, a faint smell of the sea and the sweat on my body ice-cold. A bridge over a stream, another bend and the road straightening out with the power station's fuel oil tanks looming above us, everything dark except for the double flash of the light tower on Takanupe Island marking the passage seaward. Perenna paused, her head on one side, listening. 'I thought I heard the sound of a generator.'

We had just passed the second fuel tank and through the gap between that and the next I could see the huge bulk of the power station itself. It stood in total darkness. 'Maybe it's the ship.' I was close beside her, staring at the road ahead. Beyond the last tank was the sea. It was lighter there, the road bending round to the left to pass in front of the power station. I was wondering where they would have set up their guard post.

She seemed to read my thoughts, for she said, 'If we keep to the road we'll walk straight into a trap.'

But there was nowhere else we could go, the sea and the stream to our right, and the fuel tanks to our left surrounded by a wire fence.

'They'll probably have control of the ship anyway.' Now that we had reached the port I wasn't at all sure what to do for the best.

'I don't care whether they've got the ship or not.' She was tired and her voice sounded petulant. 'I just want to get back on board. To my bunk, a shower, familiar surroundings, Jona.'

We went on, moving cautiously under the shadow of the last fuel tank. We could hear the sea, a soft lapping of tiny wavelets. And then, round the bend, suddenly there was the glimmer of lights and the familiar, homely shape of the LCT. It was no longer at the slipway, but tied up alongside the loading wharf. 'It's still there.' She said it in a tone of weary relief and quickened her pace.

The road all the way to the ship was clear under the stars and it was empty, no vehicles, no sign of movement, nothing, and the power station a huge black block above it with no sign of life. I thought we'd make it then as we hurried on past some small buildings and into the shadow of the power station. Several company cars were parked in front of it, and with the whole building silent and dead, they had an abandoned air like cars in a film sequence depicting some nuclear disaster. I was wondering what had happened to their drivers, to all the men who would have been on the night shift, when the trap was sprung. A powerful spotlight blazed blindingly out from the ship, and turning away from the glare of it I saw a torch signalling from one of the small buildings back down the road and figures with guns in their hands running towards us.

I put my hands up, told Perenna to do the same, and waited. There were five of them, and when they were close to us they slowed to a walk, talking excitedly among themselves. One of them seemed to know who we were. He spoke briefly to Perenna in Pidgin, all the time watching me as though I were some sort of prize exhibit. 'We're to go to the ship,' she said. The blacks hemmed us in and we started walking. 'It seems there's been a search party out looking for you.'

'For me? Why me?'

She spoke to the tall, rather stately looking man who seemed to be the leader. The name Holland was mentioned several times, then she shook her head. 'He doesn't know. Only that they need you for something.' The spotlight had been switched off and I could make out the figure of a man moving along the wharf towards us. It proved to be Teopas, and when he reached us, he said, 'We wait here now.'

'Why?' Perenna demanded. 'Where's my brother? Is Captain Holland out looking for us?'

He shook his head, his eyes sullen. 'Your brother not well.'

'Not well? What's happened?' She tried to push past him, but he held her back. 'I must go on board — now.' Her voice sounded wild, tiredness and alarm combined as she tried to wrench her arm free.

'Mr Hans speak with me on the radio. You do not go to the

ship until he has talk with you.' He was looking at me now. 'So we wait here. Okay?'

I nodded and the two of us stood there waiting in an uneasy silence, the islanders talking quietly amongst themselves. Twice I asked Teopas why Holland wanted me, why the ship had been moved from the slip to the loading wharf, but he ignored my questions, standing with his back to me, his gaze fixed on the Anewa approach road.

About ten minutes later the loom of headlights showed beyond the fuel tanks. It was a car, driven fast, its headlights sweeping the bay as it came round the bend, then blazing straight at us. Perenna's face, picked out in the full glare, was white and very tense, her eyes closed, her lips moving wordlessly. I had no doubt who would be in that car, nor had she, and again I was conscious of the powerful effect he seemed to have on her.

The car stopped and he got out, the red hair limned by the lights, the same jaunty, commanding air as he stood for a moment talking to Teopas. Then he came towards us, glancing briefly at Perenna before turning to me, his face in shadow. 'Where the hell have you been?' There was anger in his voice, the anger of a man under considerable strain. 'I've had to waste an hour looking for you. Well, where were you?'

'Up at the mine.'

Something had clearly gone wrong and I thought that might provoke him. But all he said was, 'I see.' He was silent a moment, looking at the two of us. 'You walked out then. How?'

'By the old tote road.'

'Why not the highway?'

'You've blown that and there were guards there.'

He stared at me hard. 'So you know what's going on?' And then, his tone suddenly changed: 'Well, that makes it easier.' He was forcing himself to relax. 'I said I might be able to give you command of a ship. You can have command of one right now.'

'Is that why you've been looking for me?'

'Yes.' He nodded towards the wharf with the LCT lying

alongside. 'I want you to take her out right away, a run up the coast to Buka.'

I heard Perenna give a little gasp. Then she had moved between us. 'Where's Jona? What's happened to him?'

'He's drunk.' His voice came in a whiplash, full of contempt. 'He's no good, Perenna. No guts.' Her shoulders sagged and he stepped past her, facing me. 'Well, now's your chance. If you want a job with the Holland Line . . .' He stood there, staring at me.

No point in asking him why he needed the ship taken to Buka so urgently, I'd find that out soon enough. And if I refused . . . I could see his face now, tired and edgy, full of nervous tension, and his eyes lit by an inner glow, excitement overriding exhaustion, the adrenalin still running. 'Well?' His hand reached out impatiently, gripping my arm, propelling me towards his car.

'Why not Luke?' I asked. 'Or Mac?'

'Don't trust them,' he snapped.

It was no moment to obstruct the man, the whole island in his grasp and only a skipper needed to take the ship up to Buka. 'What's it worth to you?'

He laughed then, a sudden explosion of nervous relief. 'A future. That's what I'm offering you.'

'Cash,' I said quietly, and I saw Perenna's mouth open, anger chasing disbelief.

'No cash,' he snapped. 'Just a stake in something big. Bigger than you'll ever be offered again.'

'And the cargo?' It was the cargo that would dictate my terms.

He jerked me round, his face thrust close to mine, and suddenly that description of his father flashed into my mind again. 'Yes or no? Make up your mind.' He saw my hesitation, his eyes suddenly smiling as he released my arm. 'You'll know about the cargo soon enough, so let's go.' He nodded to the car. Behind me I heard Perenna say, 'It's Jona's ship.'

'Is it?' He laughed, pulling open the rear door and jerking his head for the two of us to get in. Teopas sat in the front with him and as he drove off, he said, 'What's happened here tonight has been brewing a long time. You'd have to have lived with these people to understand. It's their whole future. Just remember that. Also that I'm a business man. I'm involved only to the extent that – ' His words were cut short by the sound of a shot. Even above the noise of the car I heard the clang of the bullet on steel, the whine of its ricochet, followed by shouts and then the sudden staccato rattle of automatic fire, a noise like calico ripping. A single scream was followed by an appalling silence.

'Shit!' Hans Holland thrust his foot down, swinging the car fast round the end of the slipway and out on to the open area of the loading wharf. No sound now, no movement, the ship still and silent except for the hum of its generator as we drew up at the gangway and tumbled out. Teopas was first on board, talking to one of the crew who was holding a machine pistol pointed down into the tank deck. A thin wisp of blue smoke curled up from the short barrel. 'Some polis,' Teopas reported. 'They try to climb out.'

By then I was across the gangway and looking down at the cargo held captive in the tank deck. There must have been upwards of a hundred men down there, police and officials, all of them black, no whites. The loading lights were on and they were standing very still, well clear of the ladders, most of them facing aft so that the whites of their eyes flickered in the glare. At the foot of one of the starboard ladders three men lay in a pool of blood, one of them with his face smashed in, still kicking out with his feet, his back arching. Nobody took any notice. Half the crew seemed gathered on the catwalks, all armed and chattering away like sparrows. Death meant nothing to them. It seemed to mean nothing to me either, not for that moment, the whole scene strangely unreal. Even the human cargo on the tank deck seemed determined to ignore it, a space left round the bodies as though the cause of death could be contagious, their minds, all their attention, focused on the after part of the ship as Hans Holland stepped forward into the gleam of the deck lights.

He moved fast, almost dancing forward on the balls of his

feet, like a ballet dancer, or an actor making his entrance, then standing, suddenly quite still, staring down at the mass of men below him, his silence, and his stillness, increasing the effect. He spoke to them briefly, in their own tongue, his voice high and harsh, then silence again, staring down at them, allowing time for the words to sink in. Finally he turned abruptly, moving out of the glare back to where I was standing. 'I've told them – the next man trying to escape they will all be shot.' He nodded to the guards posted on the catwalks. 'They'll see to it you have no trouble. They've been well trained.'

'Who trained them for you?' The question was a prevarication, an avoidance of the one I knew I had to ask.

He shrugged, gave a little bark of laughter. 'Vietnam left a useful legacy of unemployed deserters floating around in the Pacific.'

'And the rest of those men down there . . .' my voice trembled. 'What are you going to do with them?'

'That's your problem.' He was already climbing the ladder to the wheelhouse, Teopas close behind him. He paused, looking down at me over the handrail. 'Till you reach Queen Carola. There you land them on Hetau and the Co-operative take over. Got it? And you return here with whatever cargo they give you.' He went on up to the wheelhouse, still issuing instructions to Teopas. I followed, pausing on the bridge wing. Perenna had gone in search of her brother. I was alone for a moment, looking down at my cargo and the guards with their pistols, the same Japanese machine pistols we had uncovered in those crates. God! it had been neatly organized, and Jona Holland just about the only hitch.

I was still standing there when they brought him out, drunk and barely conscious, his eyes glazed as I tried to speak to him. They carried him down to the car and Perenna went with them. Hans Holland was suddenly back at my side. 'Just remember this,' he said, his vitality brimming over. 'A few days and Bougainville will be Independent. Then we can expand, raise money, buy ships, get moving.' And he wasn't talking like that to bolster his courage.

'You really believe you'll get away with it?'

He laughed, clapping me on the shoulder, his mood infectious. 'Think about it on the run up to Carola. The whites employed at the mine, the redskins from PNG, all of them locked in on this island, hostages for the reasonable behaviour of the other parties to the Independence negotiations. And, when it's all settled, I'll have the contracts for the shipping out of the concentrates. Think about that, too. You could do very well out of this night's work.' And he added, 'But just in case you don't see it that way, Teopas will be sailing with you.' He stared at me a moment, a hard, calculating look, then turned abruptly and went down to the car.

The ship's engines had already started up, the deck vibrating under my feet, and there were men up for'ard standing by the warps. Teopas came out of the wheelhouse. 'Let go now, Kepten?' His broad face grinned at me from under the beetling brow and the mop of fuzzy hair.

I nodded and went into the wheelhouse. Luke was already there, looking sullen. 'You take her out,' I said to give him something to keep him occupied. One of the Buka crewmen was standing beside the helmsman with a machine pistol gripped in both hands, the same man who had let loose that shattering deadly burst of fire. There would be another in the engine-room; even the men hauling in the warps were armed.

The time was 03.21 as we steamed out of Anewa Bay, the stars still bright, the sea calm with a light breeze from the north-east. We cleared Bara shoal on a backbearing, passed the Takanupe light close to port and, quarter of an hour later, we were out through the gap between the Kuruki and Banaru reefs and had turned on to our course of 325° to pick up Cape L'Averdy at the north-eastern end of Bougainville. The black outline of the mountainous spine of the island was clear against the stars and in less than an hour we could identify the volcanic mass of Bagana and the higher peak of Balbi beyond it.

In ordinary circumstances it would have been a night to dream about, the sea so quiet and the ship ploughing serenely through the diamond-bright velvet of the darkness under the

Southern Cross. But the armed crewman in the wheelhouse, the others on the catwalks, the mob of captives huddled like slaves on the tank deck . . . everywhere I looked there was something to remind me of the situation we had left behind. The simplicity of it, the speed, the organization! In just a few hours it had all been over, the copper mine unprepared and held in pawn, the Administration, all the services, taken over, the airport out of action. An armed landing at Kieta or Anewa, anywhere along the coast, would be met now by a warning that the lives of Australian and other expatriates would be at risk. And Perenna and her brother, would they be at risk, too? Were they now hostages for the safe delivery of my human cargo to that island off the Queen Carola anchorage?

I learned a lot about myself that night, my mood introspective, which is something quite unnatural to me. Normally I act without too much thought, taking things as they come. But now there was Perenna. For the first time in my life I was emotionally involved with another human being and it made a difference – made me think.

In the darkened silence of the wheelhouse, the course set and nothing else to do but let thoughts chase one another through my mind, I found myself in a state of uncertainty. I knew I ought to do something, try to gain control of the ship, free the human cargo. It was Perenna's ship as much as her brother's, her name on the stern, her capital locked up in it. But then there were moments when I was able to persuade myself that the whole thing was a political matter where the divisions between right and wrong are blurred and principles depend upon circumstances. When a man like Hans Holland takes the plunge, risking all on one wild attempt to alter the balance of forces to his personal advantage, then I suppose there are always people like me who will throw overboard any principle they ever had in the hope of bettering themselves.

Oh yes, I learned a lot about myself in the small hours of that calm, quiet night.

But then Teopas had the three bodies thrown over the side, an action that altered my perspective, so that as the night wore on, sleepily steaming along the coast of that high-backed Pacific island, my mind dwelt more and more on the heroics of action, weaving fantasies that had no basis of reality. I knew damn well I wasn't going to do anything heroic. I was going to drift along with events, deliver those poor devils to Hetau and steam back again, hoping there'd be something in it for myself, and without too much risk.

I tried to pretend that it was because I didn't care who ruled Bougainville, that I was just a visitor caught up in something that didn't concern me. Why should I stick my neck out when for all I knew the Buka people, and those Bougainvilleans who supported them, had right on their side? But deep in my guts I knew it wasn't that. There was a side of my nature that said, make the most of it, seize the opportunity. I could just see myself captain of a big ore carrier making the run up to Japan or across the Pacific to California with a shipload of concentrates. That side of me admired what Hans Holland was doing, admired his determination, his ruthlessness, his efficiency. And in a few years I could be Marine Superintendent, in charge of a whole fleet of ships. Why not?

Dreams, all dreams, fantasies woven by a tired brain. I was just a pawn, useful to replace a man who had drunk himself into a stupor rather than do what I was doing. *I could use a landing craft man*. He hadn't said anything about ore carriers, only that it was a chance to become part of something big. So why build castles? My eyes were closed and I was rocking on my feet, thinking suddenly of Perenna, the flash of anger and despair as I had asked the price of co-operation. If I did what I was told and stayed with Hans Holland, would she stay, too? Would she accept it? For the sake of the Holland Line, her brother – me? And there was Hans. Hans with his boundless vitality, his essential male dominance. I thought of that wretched little house and shuddered. The first masterful man she had met in ages and she had fallen flat on her back with her brother lying desperately ill in the next room. I pictured that scene, that bed, the mask hanging over them.

A hand was tugging at my arm and I opened my eyes. It was

Luke. 'Cape L'Averdy,' he said.

I went to the porthole, my eyes wide, peering into the night ahead. The stars were paling over the mountains. Dawn was approaching. 'There!' A flash low down on the horizon. I counted six and it came again, almost dead ahead and the ship's bows swinging across it. I checked the course and then handed over to him, telling him to wake me when we were abreast of the Cape, which would be about 08.00. There would just be time for both of us to get a couple of hours' sleep before we started the run through the Buka Passage.

In the alleyway a guard sat with his machine pistol resting on his knees, his back propped against my cabin door. He was a young man, his eyes closed, sleeping peacefully, and I hesitated, suddenly alert as I considered whether I could get the pistol from him. But his hand was on the butt and as I moved softly towards him some animal instinct seemed to trigger off the mechanism of his body, his dark eyelids flicking open. In one quick, flowing movement he was on his feet, wild-eyed and the gun pointing, his finger on the trigger.

I smiled at him, holding my hands wide, and went through into my cabin. It was hot and I was tired, but sleep didn't come easily, my mind active. I was thinking of the Buka Passage, all that had happened there during the war, and the Hollands, that house of theirs on the island of Madehas, wishing Perenna were with me, that this was a different sort of voyage and we could stop for her to show it to me. But then, of course, the memories of her grandfather, and of the yearly visits made when she was a child, were now overlaid by the tragedy of her mother's death. The Passage, Madehas, Kuamegu in Papua New Guinea – all the past of the Hollands. And that house in Aldeburgh, The Passage – was that nostalgia or had the name some deeper significance? Four hours and I would be in the Passage. There, somewhere, I felt, must lie the key to the chequered past of this strange family.

An hour later the cook woke me. What was he supposed to do about feeding the men on the tank deck? He hadn't enough bread and to give them all something would just about clean him out. Could we purchase food for the voyage back at Chinaman's Quay? I told him to check with Shelvankar, then remembered Hans Holland had taken the little Indian off the ship. 'Do the best you can,' I said, adding, 'Use the lot if you have to. The crew can go short.' He was from the Mortlocks and he nodded, smiling. Though black as the Buka men he was not in sympathy with them.

There was a different guard on duty in the alleyway outside, an older man who watched me suspiciously as I went to the heads. Sun streamed in through the porthole. I had a leisurely shower, shaved and relieved Luke. We were about two miles off Cape L'Averdy. To port was the little harbour of Teop and for a moment I toyed with the idea of turning into it and running the ship aground. But a glance for'ard at the tank deck, with its huddle of humanity sprawled listlessly on the steel plating and the four guards lounging on the catwalks above them, showed the impracticability of such a move. Even the slight alteration of course for the entrance to the Passage brought Teopas swaggering into the wheelhouse, wearing nothing but a pair of shorts, a machine pistol slung over his bare shoulder, demanding why we changed direction. And when I told him to send men to the galley to give the cook a hand, he tried to argue that it would do 'them dam' polis' good to be without food for a day.

He stood there, grinning, confident that it was he who was in command of the ship. I was short of sleep, my eyes tired, but the shower had freshened me. I was in no mood to be challenged on the bridge. 'Very well,' I said, picking up the chart I had been studying and walking with it to the open door of the bridge wing. 'You see this?' I held it fluttering in the breeze of our passage. 'You either feed those men or it goes overboard.' The chart was Aus.683 with large-scale plans of the Solomon Island ports. 'Without it we can't navigate the Buka Passage.'

The grin faded, his confidence ebbing. 'Then we go round the north of Buka.'

'It also gives the plan for the passage through the islands into Queen Carola Harbour.'

'Luke been there many times.'

'Does he remember all the bearings, all the shoal patches? Do you know them? You must have been there as often as Luke.'

The entrance was easy, but he wasn't to know that. He couldn't read a chart, had never navigated. His eyes dropped. 'Okay. I give them some food.'

'And water,' I said as he turned sullenly away. 'It will be hot as hell on that tank deck when the sun gets into it.'

He nodded and went out. I put the chart back on the table, feeling pleased. A small victory perhaps, but an important one. I now knew I could bluff him on navigation. I watched as the tank deck came to life, buckets full of chunks of bread, cheese and cold meat being lowered to them from the catwalk. Time passed, the heat increasing and my mood changing. I had got them fed and watered, but that was all. Samson brought me my breakfast on a tray. It was a rough meal and I wasn't hungry, but the coffee was good. And then Holtz came up to say he was having trouble with one of the generators and we would be without electricity for two or three hours. 'You going to do anything?' he asked in a whisper. 'I could arrange an engine breakdown.'

I had already thought of that. 'Teopas would open the sea cocks and drown the lot of us, and they'd get away in the boat.'

He pushed his cap back, rubbing at his hair with oily fingers. 'So, there is nothing to be done.' He nodded slowly. 'I've been thinking about this. I don't believe it is intended anyone should be killed. Why else should Mr Holland go to such trouble to have them transported to Hetau? It has palm trees for shade and they will be as secure there as if they are in prison. No, they will simply be held there until the future of Bougainville is decided.' He stared at me, waiting for me to say something. 'So, you agree with me.'

'Yes,' I said.

He seemed relieved. 'Three hours at most, then you have electricity again.' He straightened his cap, nodded and went out.

We were closing the coast all the time now, low cliffs and the tip of Bougainville merging with Buka, no indication of a passage through. If Luke hadn't joined me I would have stood further off until we had opened up the gap. Through the glasses I could see the first of the Buka villages on the clifftops, thatched wooden huts, some of them quite large, half hidden in the shade of dense plantations of palms. We were barely a mile off, the shoreline beginning to separate; suddenly, there it was, a narrow gut about three cables wide running south-westerly, straight as a die, with open water at the far end of it.

'You turn now,' Luke said. He was at the chart table and as our bows swung towards the opening he added, 'The tide is with us, and it is near maximum, so we must have plenty steerage way till we are through.'

A flat-bottomed vessel and the south-west going stream building up to six knots. I hadn't been in anything like that since my early days on the west coast of Scotland. But there was no wind here, and as the coast of first Bougainville, then Buka, closed around us, the surface of the water took on a flat, oily look disturbed here and there by the swirl and ripples of the tide. I could feel the grip of the current under the ship now, the shoreline slipping past faster and faster, the tension in me mounting. Palm trees lined the Passage. Ahead, on the Buka side, there was a quay with a small coaster lying alongside, beyond it a row of wooden buildings with signs over them. 'Chinaman's Quay', a voice said behind me, but I barely took it in, my glasses fixed on an old-fashioned, high-sided vessel coming out from the shore, its tall funnel packed round with fuzzy-haired blacks all dressed in the brightest colours. It was in the narrowest part, crabbing across the current to the Buka shore and right in our path. 'Just hold your course.'

I turned to find Mac standing right behind me, cold sober and looking ghastly, his eyes staring. 'Johnny Ferryboat will gi' way.' His voice was slow, a little slurred, but not by drink. This, and the staring eyes, made me wonder if he was ill. 'You all right?' I asked him.

He eyed me as though I had no right to ask him such a question. 'Stole my gun,' he hissed. 'Right from under my nose.' He turned his head, glancing obliquely towards the guard standing impassive with one of those Japanese machine pistols cradled across his chest. 'Bastards! I was asleep.' He leaned forward. 'Don't do anything,' he hissed in my ear. 'Whatever happens don't move.' He pushed me aside, lurching forward past the helmsman to grab the ledge below the porthole. He hung there, his yellow-skinned, liver-blotched hands clinging to the ledge like a prisoner peering out. 'Mechanics, the Old Man called them. Mechanics, not skippers. Coming through the Passage under engine, that's easy. But under sail ... I tell you, if there wasn't enough wind, then we'd wait for the tide and drift through like the East Coasters with their barges. Aye, and I've beat through against the tide with my little schooner so loaded with copra, and such a mass of humanity clinging to her deck, that there wasn't one of them didn't look as though they was swimming.'

The ferryboat hooted, a puff of steam at her funnel as she swung bows-on to the current to let us pass. To starboard was a jetty bright with the colour of waiting passengers, and behind the jetty a row of shops along a stretch of pot-holed tarmac, names like Yu Wong and one of them split down the middle, Mac said, because the two members of the family that owned it couldn't agree. Another, narrower passage, a rocky gut, opening up to port. It ran due south between Buka and the little island of Sohano on top of which stood a big verandahed house. 'One time DC live up there,' Luke said. And Mac muttered. 'One time Japanese Officer Commanding. We got him two nights after we raided Madehas.' His mind seemed rooted in the past.

The ferryboat hooted again as we swept past her, the people on her all waving. I wondered whether their excitement had anything to do with the night's events. Did they know their Co-operative had taken over Bougainville? The guards on the catwalks, I noticed, made no attempt to conceal their guns.

Past Sohano, with its shallow reef topped by wooden toilet huts built out on stilts over the water, the tide slackened. Here the water became muddy, the channel marked by iron beacon posts set on the edge of reed-covered shallows, Minon Island so low that the thicket of bushes covering it seemed to be growing out of the water. Mangrove swamps fringed the Buka shore. 'I seen crocodile here,' Luke grinned.

It was no place for a stranger to navigate and I left it to him, following the course he took with the chart folded in my hand. Any moment now we should sight the island of Madehas. 'Shall we be able to see the house?' I asked Mac. But he didn't answer, his eyes blank, seeing only what was in his mind.

'You want to see Colonel Holland's house?' Luke was leaning with his bare elbows on the back of the captain's chair, quite relaxed and only occasionally checking our course. 'You see that beacon?' He pointed ahead to a lop-sided post topped by a triangle with its point upwards that marked the limit of the shoal area on the Buka side of the channel. 'When we are there, we are clear of Minon and I show you Holland house.'

'That's No. 7 beacon.' Mac suddenly turned, his eyes wide, a fleck of froth at the corner of his mouth. 'That night we raided Madehas, we were waiting in our canoes right here on Minon. The Jap guard boat was late, and the mosquitoes – the bloody bastard mozzies . . . there were six of them and we got every one, over there by No. 7.' His words came slowly, his voice strange as though it was somebody else speaking through his mouth, and he wasn't looking at me or Luke, or even at the helmsman. He was looking straight at the guard, who was standing at the back of the wheelhouse between the Decca and the echo-sounder. 'Yu,' he said suddenly, his hand outstretched, pointing. 'Yu savvy olpela armi Kiap? Yu savvy Colonel Lawrence?'

The man nodded, his eyes widening, his face going pale as Mac moved slowly towards him, talking, talking, his voice getting wilder, the froth gathering on his lips. He was speaking in a voice that was quite strange to me and in a language I didn't understand, and yet I got the drift of it. And the man's eyes grew wide with fear. This was the older man who had been on guard outside my cabin after dawn. He would have been a teenage youth when the Japs ruled in Buka and Colonel Holland and his men raided from the mountains. He would have grown up in fear of him, a legendary figure, and now this madman frothing at the mouth was claiming he spoke with the tongue of

Colonel Holland, moving steadily closer, imposing his will and impressing his words by angry stabs of his left hand, the fingers spread. I watched, mesmerized. So did Luke. So did the 'ard, a growing horror in his eyes. And then, with a quick, p erful thrust of his right hand, Mac lunged forward.

The guard's mouth opened, a scream – but it never came. Mac's left hand clamped over the lips, blocking the sound in, thrusting at the man's body so that it was forced back against the bulkhead, and all the time the nerves jerking it in the violence of death, the heavy galley meat knife buried the full length of its blade inside his stomach. The jerks subsided, the eyes glazing. Mac held the body there a moment, then put his knee against it, tugging at the knife. It pulled out suddenly, thick with gore, and some guts and a thin trickle of liquid spilled out with it. He let the dead man drop then, taking the pistol carefully from the limp hands, the body hitting the deck with a thud. He was smiling. 'Oldest trick in the world. Pretend to be a man back from the dead . . .' He gave a cackling laugh. He knew I hadn't the stomach for it and was sickened by his callousness. 'What did you expect?' he growled. 'Mutiny and bloodshed go together, don't they?'

I stared down at the body lying on the steel deck, a man of about forty, with a wife no doubt and a thatched hut full of kids. And now the black face gone grey, the eyes staring, no life there, and Mac standing over him with his gun in one hand and the other red with half-congealed blood, holding a butcher's knife. The Passage had suddenly become an evil, haunted place. 'You'll get used to it.' He pushed past me, spitting a piece of soap out of his frothing mouth and dropping the knife as he reached for the mike of the ship's broadcast system, his eyes all the time on the helmsman who stared back at him like a petrified rabbit. 'Call Teopas to the bridge.' He thrust the mike into my hands.

I did as he said, unable to keep my voice steady and wondering what he was going to do now. Holding the mike to my lips I could feel the stickiness of half-congealed blood on the handgrip. 'Coxs'n to the wheelhouse, please. Coxs'n Teopas.

To the wheelhouse please.' I put the mike back in its cradle and we waited. Nobody spoke. Mac had withdrawn to the chart table, putting Luke between himself and the sliding door to the bridge wing. I saw him checking the safety catch, to see that it was on, I thought. A minute, maybe a little more, passed before Teopas's bare feet sounded on the ladder to the starboard bridge wing. A moment later he came in, swinging his rifle loosely by the breach, relaxed, smiling, confident. 'What yu want, Kept ...'

The short burst of fire caught him in the stomach first, then the chest. It flung him backwards, yet his feet were still making forward-pacing movements so that his big torso, the jet black skin stitched with small holes, was forced over to lie on its back twitching with death-throe reflexes. That burst of fire had sounded shattering in the confines of the wheelhouse. 'Why did you do that?' The words burst from my lips. It was killing for the sake of killing.

Mac looked at me. 'He's their leader.' He said it flatly, and still in the same flat voice he added, 'You should've done it yourself if you wanted it done different.' He turned to Luke, telling him to get Teopas's body out on to the bridge wing. And when he didn't move, standing frozen into immobility as he peered down at the man's chest with the holes leaking blood, Mac grabbed hold of him and shook him. 'You want to get killed?' He reached for the telegraph handle, slammed it to Stop Engines and picked up the broadcast microphone again, this time speaking into it himself, using the Buka language, not Pidgin. 'Get that body out of here, on to the bridge wing where they can see it,' he shouted to Luke. 'Go on, move! Yu tu.' He motioned to the helmsman with the machine pistol. 'Mekim.' Then he was speaking into the mike again. The ship's engines had stopped, everything very still as we lost way, the reeds and mangrove trees almost stationary, the bows swinging.

For'ard the guards on the catwalks, all four of them, were facing aft, eyes showing white and the dark faces puzzled and uneasy. Suddenly one of them fell prone, wriggling behind a ventilation cowl, his gun thrust forward. The others followed his example. 'Sitting targets,' Mac said, still with the mike to his mouth so that his words boomed round the ship. He caught my eye, nodding towards the dead coxs'n. 'Get him to the bridge wing and pitch his body down on to the deck. Go on – move! Show the bastards he's dead. If they don't throw their guns down into the tank deck then, we'll have to kill them.' It was the threat to kill them that got me moving. Luke, too, I think. We got hold of the body, half carrying, half dragging it to the doorway. 'Now stand him upright,' Mac said. 'Let them see how he's been shot to pieces. Then pitch him down the ladder.' And as we pushed Teopas into an upright position, holding him there on the bridge wing so that guards and prisoners alike could see, Mac's voice boomed again from the loudspeakers. 'Push him over,' he called, and we pitched the body down the ladder. It fell with a sickening thud, the round black head rammed against the metal grating, blood staining the woolly halo of hair.

Silence! Then Mac's voice again and movement on the tank deck. Luke and I dived for the shelter of the wheelhouse. The rifle Teopas had been carrying so casually, with such total confidence, lay abandoned on the deck. I picked it up. It was the first conscious independent action I had taken. Mac nodded approvingly. 'You take the door. I'll cover the deck.' But there was no need. Men were swarming up the ladders from the tank deck, spilling on to the catwalks, and the Buka guards were rising sheepishly to their feet, their hands in the air, their guns on the deck.

It was over without a fight. Armed now with machine pistols that they knew how to use better than our Buka crew, the police moved in on the bridge housing in a quick crouching run. Two of them came direct up to the wheelhouse, one of them with sergeant's stripes on his shirt. The other, short and broad and smiling, announced that he was Inspector Steve Mbalu. He went straight through into the alleyway, shouting for the Buka crew to surrender as his men began moving down the ladders from deck to deck towards the engine-room. For'ard all was chaos as the mass of captives struggled to escape the oven heat of the tank deck, climbing the ladders on to the catwalk, crowding the foredeck, spilling over into the shade of the bow door housing, anywhere to get a breath of air to relieve the humid, suffocating heat. The sun was half obscured, the air thickening all the time, the heat impossible. A shot sounded from down in the bowels of the ship. It turned out to be no more than a warning shot, and a minute later the Inspector came back to report that he was now in complete control of the ship.

Mac had hung his pistol by its strap on the back of the captain's chair and was leaning heavily against it, his screwed-up features the colour of mud, his eyes staring out through the open starboard door of the wheelhouse. No breath of air now, the ship drifting slowly sideways with the current and a view back down the Buka Passage framed in the doorway, the scene darkening as heavy cu-nim clouds obscured the sun. 'Always was a tricky place.' He was muttering to himself, wiping the sweat from his face, the hand holding the dirty handkerchief shaking uncontrollably.

I moved out to the port bridge wing. Released prisoners crowded the deck below, clung to the ladder leading up to where I stood. Our bows had already drifted past No. 7 marker post, the current carrying us out towards another pole beacon with a flat top marking the last of the Minon Island shallows, and beyond that beacon, in line with our stern, the island of Madehas was coming into view with a small hill covered with palms and a house just visible on North Madehas Point.

I went back into the wheelhouse and got the glasses. It was a wooden building with a verandah, rather taller than the old DC's house on Sohano and with storage sheds. There was a track leading down to a reef-enclosed creek. Something that looked like a light was stuck up on a pole. 'Is there a jetty there?' I asked Mac.

I got no reply. He was staring past me, straight towards the house, his eyes quite vacant, seeing only something that was in his mind. The body of the dead crewman was being carried out, but he didn't notice. The Inspector was talking to Luke, the ship drifting, everything in a hush of suspended animation, nobody – least of all myself – knowing what to do next. Luke

221

kept glancing at Mac, hesitating. Finally he turned to me. 'Inspector Mbalu say we must get under way. We cannot stay here.'

'Of course not.' If we didn't get moving soon even a shallow draft vessel like this would be aground. 'But where does he want us to go – continue on or turn back into the Passage?'

There was a long pause, and then the Inspector said, 'On. We go on.' It was obvious he hadn't thought what he was going to do next and needed time to consider. Rain began to fall, large drops as big as coins. Thunder rumbled in the distance. Mac turned his head, jerked suddenly out of his trance. 'Holland House Cove,' he said quietly. 'There's five fathoms close off the jetty. You can anchor there.' He peered out through the bridge wing door. 'Aye, and you'd better do it quick or you won't be seeing a bloody thing.' And he climbed into the captain's chair and just sat there, staring moodily ahead.

I rang for engines and with a little backing and filling got the ship's head round. We were already past the flat-topped marker post, another fine on our port bow and not much more than half a mile to go. The Buka Passage vanished behind us, engulfed in a thundering, inky blackness. The raindrops bounced on the flat brown surface of the water, leaping to meet the next drop falling, lightning ripped the indigo heavens, a crack of thunder and a distant hissing growing closer.

We were just off the eastern reef of the cove when the storm hit, everything suddenly wiped out in the torrent of water pouring down. Luke was aft seeing to the stern anchor, the Buka crew working under police guard, and I was left to con her in, nothing visible – only the echo-sounder recording seven fathoms and the vague impression of the reef-edge yards away to port. I could see nothing, absolutely nothing. I took her in on the echo-sounder, dropped the stern anchor by guesswork and then ordered Luke to the bows to supervise the letting go of the main anchor.

About ten minutes later the wind hit us. It came from the north at first, tugging at our stern anchor. The rain, lessening now, drove horizontally past the ship and there was nothing else to see – just the wind-driven rain and the water round us lashed to such a frenzy that at moments the surface of it took off and became airborne. It was like that for perhaps a quarter of an hour. It seemed much longer, the wind backing and the noise so violent it was impossible to speak, even to think. Gradually the wind shifted to south so that we were under the lee of Madehas, gusts alternating with lulls, and then for a moment there was no wind at all, the rain much heavier now and falling vertically in a steady, persistent downpour. That's how I arrived at the Hollands' house on Madehas, looking up at it through a curtain of tropical rain with the sun's faint glimmer coming and going.

PART FOUR

THE BUKA PASSAGE

—

1

It was Mac who took me up to the house, hiding himself under a large black umbrella so that he looked like a two-legged beetle walking its carapace up the hill. It was just after midday. The rain had eased to little more than a drizzle and the sun, striking vertically down on us through what was now only a very thin cloud layer, gave off such a glaring, humid heat that every movement had become an effort. I wouldn't have gone up there if it hadn't been for something he told me, something that switched my mind back to that half breed Lewis up at Cooktown and his story of the Dog Weary mine.

It must have been about an hour after we had anchored. The wind had dropped considerably and I had just completed a tour of the ship with Luke and the police inspector. When we got back to the wheelhouse, we were still discussing whether to put in to Chinaman's Quay and land everybody there, or wait in an attempt to make a night landing close to the airfield. Mac was alone, still sitting in the captain's chair, his body hunched and looking shrunken so that I had the impression he had suddenly aged. The large-scale chart with the plan of the Buka Passage gave no indication of depth along the shore in the vicinity of the airfield. Luke couldn't help, he had never been in there. I turned to Mac and asked him if he could pilot us in.

He didn't seem to hear me. I repeated the question and he turned slowly, staring at me blankly. 'The airfield?' He shook his head. 'That wasn't why we killed the Japs. He'd never go for that. It was too well guarded.' He was still back in the past. 'No, that was our target . . .' and he pointed straight ahead, beyond the bows and the straining anchor chain, to the house which was just emerging from the rain, a grey, dripping shadow among thrashing palms. 'A boatload of Japs killed, half a dozen Buka men, and two of our own injured. All because he wanted to have it out with that cousin of his.' He turned to face me again, fastening me with those pale watery eyes, so bright and birdlike I was reminded of the Ancient Mariner. 'Something had got into him,' he breathed, seeing nothing but what was in his mind. 'Something . . . I don't know what. Been there a long time, I reck'n. And that night . . .' His head swung round to stare at the house again. 'I'll never forget how he looked that night. We were in that little office he'd had built, the two books laid out on the floor beside the open safe and himself crouched there and staring down at a letter in his hand. Dear Red, it began; it was a letter to Red Holland, you see.' A long pause, and then . . . 'Pity the bastard wasn't there . . . that was the house we should have burned over his head . . .' And he added, 'It wasn't as big then. Not much bigger than the native hut young Carlos built on the self-same site when he ruled the Buka Passage.' Another longer pause and then he said, so quietly I only just heard him, 'It was accursed then. Reck'n it's been cursed ever since. Still is,' he muttered to himself, relapsing suddenly into silence.

'Why was Colonel Holland so determined to make a raid on the house?' I asked.

I thought at first he hadn't heard, or else he wasn't going to answer. But after a while his brain seemed to catch up with the question and he said, 'How the hell do I know what was in his mind? From the time I joined him, he was always the same as regards Red Holland – very reticent. An Australian cousin, you see, a distant one, and that young brother of his, Carlos – the one that went down with the *Holland Trader* — leaving him everything. I am told the two were so alike the islanders thought it was Carlos come back from the dead, and that didn't help either. And then, after the 1929 crash, when trade just about came to a standstill, the Old Man had to come across from PNG and bail him out. Sold practically everything he had to keep the Line going and virtually took over the running of it, living up there with Red Holland and building a small extension, just an office and a bedroom, out on the west side.'

I asked if he'd still been living there when the war started, and he said, No, the Old Man had been at Kuamegu then. It was early 1940 before he was back at Madehas helping to organize the coast watchers in case the Japanese came into the war. 'But if you ask me, he had another reason, too. He wanted to keep an eye on Red Holland and the schooners. Didn't trust him. Don't believe he ever trusted the man from the moment he first set eyes on him.'

He went rambling on about the war then and it took me some time to get him back to the night they'd landed in the cove below the house after ambushing the guard boat. I wanted to know more about the letter that had so upset Colonel Holland, but he said the Old Man hadn't commented on it, either then or later. No, he didn't know who it was from, only that it was written to Red Holland and addressed to him. He had seen the envelope lying on the floor beside the books. It was addressed care of the Holland Line at a P.O. Box number in Kieta. He'd been hoping to find Japanese code books in that safe, operational plans, secret documents of some sort. He had thought that was what the raid was all about until he had seen the Colonel sitting back on his heels there with that letter in his hand. 'All the blood seemed to have gone from his face and he was shaking like a man in a fever. Anger, hatred – I don't know what it was . . .' He hesitated, shaking his head slowly. 'I never seen a man's eyes like that, so horror-struck, so appalled – and tears . . . if he'd seen someone he loved blasted to hell by a land mine it couldn't have affected him more deeply.'

'What happened to the letter?'

'I never saw it again. Never. Only the books. He showed me those, after the war. Long after. But it was the letter,' he

muttered, shaking his head. 'It must have been the letter.' And
he went on, 'I tell you, man . . .' his voice rambling . . .'I tell
you, from that moment he became obsessed with the urge to
destroy Red Holland. An' it wasn't because he was a collaborator. It was personal. Did I tell you we caught up with him
eventually near Queen Carola?'

'Yes.'

'He had a house there. A native house. All wood and a
palm-thatched roof. Went up like a hayrick. He was inside. The
Old Man knew that. Told him so myself. There was Red
Holland and one of his skippers, some women, too, but he still
gave the order. Petrol-soaked arrows, that's what we used. Fired
the first one himself, and when the whole place was a roaring
furnace with screaming figures running out of it and the sound
of a single shot coming from inside, from the centre of the
flames, he suddenly turned away, tears streaming down his
cheeks.'

The memory of that night raid on the Queen Carola
anchorage seemed as vivid and disturbing to Mac as the night it
had happened. I couldn't get anything more out of him, except
that maybe we'd go up to the house together, later. Now, as we
walked carefully up the mud-slimed, slippery track, I asked him
about the books, wondering why Colonel Holland had brought
them out of the house. It was a casual question, made for no
particular reason except that I was puzzled by his behaviour and
felt they must have some bearing on what had happened
afterwards. 'Diaries,' Mac said. 'That's what I thought they'd
be. Old logs, journals of voyages, something like that. They
were a special sort of book, you see, with brass hinges and metal
clasps. But all they contained was stamps. Nothing else – no
writing, nothing. Just stamps.'

I stopped abruptly, standing there bareheaded, oblivious of
the drizzling rain, staring at him. 'Did they have green leather
covers? Dark green, rather worn?'

'Aye, green.' He nodded, frowning.

'And one of them with die proofs at the end – parts of the
stamp printed in black?'

Again he nodded, his eyes alert now and questioning. 'That's what the Old Man showed me. Sent his launch over for me when I'd just got in from Choiseul and opened up the safe just to show me that. Said it could have been something to do with the Holland Line and had I ever seen a stamp like it.'

'And had you?'

'No, never.' He shook his head, peering up at me under his umbrella. 'But you have, is that it?'

'No, only the albums.' And I told him about the collection Perenna had asked me to sell for her.

A man appeared suddenly out of nowhere, a blanket round his shoulders and a red flower stuck in his hair. He accompanied us up to the house, a disconcerting shadow, smiling all the time, his rather protruberant eyes watchful and curious. 'Houseboy,' Mac said and went on to tell me the safe was now under the stairs, the first four treads of which folded back. 'It was the Old Man's idea. Did you ever see one hidden like that before?' It had been put there in 1949 after the house had been rebuilt and he didn't think Hans would know about it. 'He was too young. In fact, I think there's only two of us has any idea it's there. And I'm the only one alive now that can open it.'

'After Colonel Holland's death, what happened to those stamp albums? Did they remain in the safe?'

'Yes, I think so, along with the deeds of Madehas, ship registration papers, medals, all the things he valued.'

'And Hans Holland didn't know about it?'

'No. Nor the combination. It's a combination lock, you see.'

'So it was you who gave Timothy Holland the albums?'

'No, not me. He must have opened the safe himself.'

'Who told him about it? Colonel Holland?'

He shook his head, moving on up the track. 'Mr Tim wasn't there when the Old Man took off. He was still at school in Australia. None of the family were there. The Old Man's son, Captain Philip, he came across from Kuamegu, but that was after he'd gone. He must have known about the safe or I don't reckon he'd have been able to settle the Old Man's affairs. Aye –' He nodded his head under the umbrella. 'He must have known

228

about it, and also the combination, because the deeds of Kuamegu were in that safe and he would have needed them when he sold up and went to England. He died there, what was it . . .?' He screwed up his face in an effort to remember. 'Almost three years ago it must be. It was only a few months before Tim was sent here to look into the activities of the new co-operative everybody was talking about. My guess is his father had written him about the safe before he died, he may even have told him what to look for. Captain Philip thought a lot more of Tim, you see, than he did of Jonathan.'

'And what about the letter that so upset Colonel Holland? Did Tim take that, too, or is it still there?'

'We'll see.'

'Is that why you suggested we put into the cove here?'

'There was a storm coming up.'

'But you wanted to go up to the house and have a look at that safe again.'

He didn't answer. We reached a little wooden summerhouse half-hidden under a tangle of vines. Our black shadow pointed to it. 'Mi bring Coca Cola, coffee, tea, anything yu want?'

Mac shook his head. We were on grass now, recently mown, the house looming over us, its verandah bearing the rot scars of damp and neglect. Beside the entrance steps was a green-painted drum overflowing with blackish water scummed with drowned insects. An unswept pile of them lay under the naked light bulb by the front door. The place looked like bachelors' quarters run by servants, and when we were inside there was no doubt about it, everything worn, dusty and uncared for, windows open to the rain, broken panes and curtains only half pulled back. No woman had been mistress of the house for a long time. 'Doesn't anybody live here now?' I asked.

Mac shook his head.

'What about Hans?'

'His home is at Queen Carola. He's lived up there ever since he was a laddie.'

We had moved from the entrance hall into a big central room that reached up to the roof. God knows what design the house

229

was based on, vague memories of baronial halls perhaps. There was a grand staircase opposite the door, dividing at a landing and then climbing to a gallery that ran round the four walls with doors leading off, presumably to the bedrooms. The room in which we stood was panelled in some darkish wood that looked like teak and the panels were hung with pictures. There were some water colours of schooners and Pacific islands that reminded me of those in the Aldeburgh house, but most of the pictures were prints of well-known London buildings, the sort you can pick up in English country house sales. They looked quite incongruous in this setting. There was also a stuffed crocodile hanging above the landing halfway up the stairs. Two tattered tiger skins faced each other either side of the hearth, which was built of stone to pseudo-baronial proportions. 'Who perpetrated this?' I asked, my gaze lifting to the heavy carving of the gallery balustrade.

'The Old Man.'

'Yes, but what mad architect?'

'No architect. He designed it himself. Saw to the building of it, too.'

'After the war?'

'Aye, there was a bit of a boom out here then, and ships were cheap. Old MFVs, a few schooners, hundred-baggers mainly – that's bags of copra, you understand. Business was very good.'

'And he put the safe under the stairs.'

'Yes.' He turned to the houseboy hovering in the entrance. 'Yu go.' He pushed him out and locked the door, also the door to the servants' quarters. Then he crossed to the staircase, feeling under the carved base of the balusters on the right hand side, while I stood staring up at the open-plan interior of the house Colonel Holland had built. It told me something about the man himself – his need of material recognition for what he was and what he had achieved out here in Bougainville-Buka, his nostalgia for home and his pride in the City where he had learned the shipping business. His interest in wood and carving seemed to reflect a fundamental simplicity that must have been at odds with the paranoiac desire for grandeur. 'Give me a hand, will you?' Mac pointed to a hairline crack along each edge of the lower treads. 'Made it himself.' There was deep admiration in his voice. 'He was always a perfectionist, and very good with his hands.'

He bent down then, motioning me to put my fingers under the lip of the bottom tread. There was a groove there and together we lifted. I think one man could have done it, but the treads were heavy, the wood at least an inch thick, and the hinges were stiff with dirt or corrosion. Four and a half treads folded back like the boot of a car to fit snugly against the treads above, revealing a 3-ft high compartment thick with dust and cobwebs. The safe stood at the back against a wooden partition, the steel of it clean and glowing in the half dark. Mac wiped his fingers across the metal surface and sucked in his breath.

'How long since you last opened it?' I asked.

'Me? I haven't been to it since the Old Man was alive.'

'Then who?'

He shrugged, bending down with one knee on the floor. 'Hans most likely.' He reached to the combination dial, his fingers turning the knob.

'I thought you said he lived up at Caroia.'

'So he does. But this place is handy for him when he's got ships in the Buka Passage.'

'So you think he knows about the safe?'

'Either that or Jonathan has been here. I didn't tell him the combination, but I did tell him about the safe and where it was hidden. I had to do that. It was a few months back. I knew I was drinking myself to death and he'd a right to know.' He looked up at me. 'Something I don't like, now I come to think about it. It was just after Mr Tim's accident that Hans began using the place.' He bent again to the safe, his eyes on the knurled dial as he turned it deliberately. 'I had to tell someone,' he murmured. There was a click and he straightened up, giving the door a good strong pull. It came slowly open to show the inside of the safe crammed with stuff. There were dollars, tens and fives in packets, ships' papers, two small gold bars, deeds covering the various properties, including Madehas, and right at the back, tucked in behind some ledgers, a large manilla envelope. He pulled it out with all the rest and the name LEWIS stared up at me.

I reached down across his shoulders, picking it up from where it had fallen amongst the dirt and the cobwebs of the floor-boards and the first thing I pulled out of it was an envelope bearing the Solomons Seal stamp. It was addressed to Mrs Florrie Lewis of Dog Weary, Cooktown, Queensland, Australia, and it carried the Seal-on-Icefloe stamp in deep blue with SOLOMONS at the top and HOLLAND SHIPPING on the two sides, just as Pegley had drawn it for me, and PAID at the bottom. This was cancelled by a smudged postmark as though the Post Office clerk at Port Moresby had not only been in too much of a hurry to notice that the letter was incorrectly stamped, but had failed to make a clear cancellation. The clerk at Cooktown, on the other hand, had obviously been on his toes, for the Australian Postage Due 2d. stamp, though slapped on at an angle in the bottom left hand corner, had been clearly postmarked 28.JY.11

No doubt about it, this was the cover Berners had bought at the Robson Lowe auction two years back. The catalogue description fitted exactly. So he had bought it for Hans Holland, and now it was here, in this safe, confirming that Hans not only knew about the safe, but also the combination, and that he was in the habit of using it. And that wasn't all the envelope contained. It was a bulky packet, the main contents a tightly folded, badly stuck together wadge of gummed paper, blotched by damp. I managed to separate one of the innermost sheets and open it out. I couldn't help thinking of Tubby Sawyer then, how excited he would have been, for what I held in my hands was a complete sheet of sixty of the Solomons Seal ship labels. In the mass like that they looked really beautiful, all recess-printed and of a wonderful deep blue. *Bright* blue, Pegley had called it, but it looked to me in the dull light of that big room more a rich Royal Navy blue.

'You collect stamps?' Mac had stopped turning out the safe and was peering down at the sheet spread out on my knee. I nodded, wondering what they'd fetch at auction – wondering whether he'd let me take them away, or at least a sample sheet. And then, as I examined the whole wadge to see how many there were and the extent of the damage caused by damp, I came across the letter. It was an old letter, written with a steel nibbed pen on quite superior pale blue notepaper that was faded at the edges, the ink gone brown with age. And the writing was the same as the writing on the cover addressed to Florrie Lewis in Cooktown. *Dear Red*, it began, *This will come as a shock to you I am sure thinking me dead. . . .*

Mac seized hold of it. 'That's the letter I was telling you about. The one that upset the Old Man so much the night we raided this place.' His lips began forming the words, reading slowly . . . 'Who wrote this?' He opened out the folded sheet. It was signed *Merlyn Lewis* and when he turned back to the beginning again I saw the date – *Fifth June 1910.*

If it had been addressed to Carlos Holland I could have understood, but a letter to Red Holland back in 1910 . . . that was a full year before Lewis had posted the letter to his wife from Port Moresby and stamped it with the Solomons Seal ship label. That was what I couldn't understand. It was Carlos, not Red Holland, who had had those sheets printed. And if Merlyn Lewis was the father of Minya Lewis from Cooktown, then he hadn't been heard of since the year the *Holland Trader* had disappeared.

Mac finished reading the letter through, then handed it back to me. 'Didn't you mention the Dog Weary mine, some crazy story told by a half-breed also named Lewis? Well, you read that letter.' He was frowning, his eyes screwed up in concentration, the hand holding out the letter to me trembling. 'Something there that don't make sense.'

Fifth June 1910.

Dear Red,

    This will come as a shock to you I am sure thinking me dead. But I got out thanks to some abos who took me walkabout across by Alice and down as far as the Nullabor. I was there two years working at Gt Boulder then at Ora Banda to earn enough to come after you now I know where you are.

I'm back east now, in Queensland, panning up round the headwaters of the Palmer, and for summer I have a shack over at the coast by Cooktown. I call it Dog Weary, just so I don't forget you and what you did. You made a fortune, you bastard, taking all the water and leaving me to die. I nearly did too but not quite and now I'm coming for my share of the ships you got out of the Dog Weary money.

Merlyn Lewis.

'He calls him Red, you see.' Mac pointed his finger at the final lines. 'My share of the ships, he says, and he's writing it in 1910, remember, when it was Carlos running the schooners here. As I say, it doesn't add up, does it?'

'Unless, of course, it was the cousin who had staked Carlos. If Red Holland had financed the purchase of the first schooners, it would explain why Carlos left everything to him instead of his brother.'

Mac shook his head. 'That wouldn't have upset the Old Man the way the sight of that letter did. He was crouching there in that office, just as we are here, reading it by torchlight and the effect on him . . . shattering, that's what it was. And he was quite different after that, very morose and bitter, and he couldn't seem to settle, not until after we'd raided Queen Carola. After that he seemed suddenly himself again, as though burning Red Holland's house over his head had exorcised a ghost.'

It was Mac's use of the word *ghost* that started me thinking again about the disappearance of the *Holland Trader*. But then he said, 'Couldn't be Jonathan that showed him how to open the safe.' He was referring to Hans. Most of the things in the safe belonged to Hans Holland.

'Colonel Holland might have given him the combination,' I suggested.

'No, definitely not.'

'Tim Holland then?'

'He wouldn't have told him.'

'Maybe Hans Holland caught him here with the safe open and those albums in his hand.' But Mac wasn't listening. He was reading through Lewis's letter again, his hands trembling slightly and a shocked look on his face. When he finished, he folded it up slowly and sat quite still for a moment, squatting back on his heels and staring at nothing. Finally he passed the letter to me. 'You'd better keep it. Take it back with you to Australia, find out what happened to Merlyn Lewis.'

'I know what happened to Lewis,' I said. And I told him how he had shipped out of Sydney as a stoker.

'And why would he do that, do you think? A year later, a whole year after writing that letter. There's more mystery for you.' He was rummaging around in the safe again, and when he found there was nothing else of importance there, he began packing the money, the papers, everything back the way we had found it. But as well as the letter he let me keep that single sheet of the Solomons Seal blue stamp, and so that they wouldn't get wet, I tucked them between the pages of an old copy of *Playboy Magazine* I found lying on a table among a pile of faded newspapers.

After closing the door of the safe and replacing the lower stair treads, Mac unlocked the doors. The houseboy had been joined by an older man, also a woman, with two girls hovering in the background, one of them wide-mouthed and smiling. She had long bare black legs, their length and their shapeliness emphasized by the shortness of her dress, which was a brilliant red and too small for her so that her nubile breasts seemed bursting out of it. She was excited, the dark brown eyes staring straight at us, her hair standing up like a golliwog, and against the green of the lush growth outside, drab in the falling rain, she looked like some bright tropical fruit, the bloom on her jet black skin adding to the lusciousness of her youthful abandon. Her eyes caught mine, the smile widening, white teeth in a black face, and then she turned away, overcome with embarrassment, simpering and giggling with blatant sexuality. I heard Mac telling the houseboy to bring us some coffee and then he took me on a tour of the house.

I don't know whether he was looking for anything in particular, but if he was we didn't find it. The bedrooms upstairs were spartanly furnished with iron bedsteads and marble-topped washstands complete with china ewers and basins. The beds were unmade, the mattresses rolled up. Downstairs the rooms had a feeling of emptiness and decay. It was a sad, neglected place, unloved and uncared for, the big kitchen, where Perenna had fought off her mother's murderers, opening on to weedgrown flags of coral cement.

We had our coffee and left, the rain still falling steadily and the track even more slippery as we made our way down the hill to the cove, the two girls following us, but keeping a discreet distance and only betraying their presence by their giggling and the occasional flash of a red dress through the palm tree boles and the ferns. The rain didn't seem to worry them.

It wasn't until we were halfway down that the ship gradually emerged from out of the dripping miasma. Seen through the tropical green of island foliage, a rusty, battered relic of a long-dead war, there was a sense of unreality about her, a ghostly quality that matched the empty house behind us. I turned to Mac. 'What do we do now?' I asked.

He smiled up at me from under his umbrella. 'See if the outboard starts.' We had come ashore in the rubber dinghy. 'Afterwards . . . we wait till dark, I imagine.'

'Then go for the airfield?' I was thinking of Perenna, all the whites down in Arawa; they'd all be at risk if the police held an airfield and the PNG government were able to fly in troops.

He nodded. 'Either that or Queen Carola. It depends which the Inspector thinks he's a better chance of holding.'

'And suppose his men have had enough and don't want to risk their lives again?'

'Then he'll have a mutiny on his hands.' We had reached the floating wooden jetty where we had left the rubber dinghy. The oil drums were rusted away, the planks half-submerged, and he stood there on the rocks gazing out across the flat, rain-pocked water to the ship, lying grey in the rain against a background of reeds. 'And so will you,' he added. Then turning to me, he gripped my arm. 'A word of warning: these people – they look innocent enough, like children, smooth-skinned and smiling. Seeing them like that you'd think there was no more friendly people in the Pacific. But just remember this, they were cannibals only two or three generations back and they still eat people when they have a chance in the more remote parts of PNG. And like children, their mood can change very quickly. D'you understand what I'm trying to tell you?'

'I think so. You're explaining why you had to kill that man in the wheelhouse and then shoot Teopas down in cold blood.'

'Aye.' He nodded vehemently. 'They're a primitive people and no amount of missionary work is going to change their pagan hearts. Not in my lifetime, anyway,' he muttered, as he released the painter from the rock we had tied it to.

'And they practise sorcery, do they?'

He turned then, the painter in his hand. 'Perenna's been talking to you, has she?' He stepped cautiously on to the floating jetty, balancing carefully. 'Tim was a fool to come here knowing there was pay-back owed for Red Holland's death. And taking those albums. It would have been dangerous enough just doing the job he had to do with the Co-operative becoming more powerful every day. But taking those albums . . . maybe they're not of any great significance, but he was asking questions . . . the man was a tactless fool.'

'Perenna thinks he's had a death wish put on him.'

'Aye, she told me. She wanted to know if it was Hans who had done it.'

'What did you tell her?'

'That I didn't know.' He shrugged. 'Sapuru, more like. Or one of the elders of the Co-operative anyway.'

'But you believe in that sort of thing? It could happen?'

'Oh, aye, it happens all right. Tim would have known that. He must have had a lot to do with it in PNG, which is why I say he was a bloody fool, meddling around here. And if you believe in that sort of thing, then you're vulnerable, eh? But not me.' He gave a quick little laugh. 'I never believed in it, not really.

Though, mind you, living out here it's difficult – ' He was interrupted by a shout, somebody hailing us from the LCT. I couldn't hear what the man was shouting, but he kept waving to us so I grabbed the painter and waded out to the dinghy, the water warm as I pushed it clear of the rocks, swinging it stern-on and climbing in. The engine started first pull and as soon as Mac was settled under his umbrella in the bows, I swung the outboard round and took her fast back to the ship.

An excited murmur of voices greeted us as we climbed on board, but nothing I could understand. The excitement seemed tinged with fear as we pushed our way up the ladder to the bridge, where Luke stood waiting for me, and with him the senior administration officer, Mr Treloa. Apparently one of the District HQ personnel had attended a radio course and with Luke's permission he had been given the run of the signals office. He had not attempted to make contact with the outside world, but while familiarizing himself with the equipment, he had tuned in to Sydney and picked up an ABC newscast announcing that Bougainville was in the hands of insurgents. The rebel leader, Sapuru, was reported to have declared Bougainville-Buka an independent sovereign state affiliated to the Solomon Islands group and the newscast had ended with a statement from the Australian government that it was in consultation with the Government of Papua New Guinea.

So the mining people had been able to get a message out, or had the news come from Hans Holland and the Buka Co-operative? Whichever it was, the news was out, a fact that had encouraged Inspector Mbalu to make up his mind. They would go for the airfield in the early hours of the morning and would I kindly arrange to put them ashore shortly after midnight as near to the target as possible. The time was then just after noon. Ten hours to wait and nothing left to eat. We still had fresh water for another day, perhaps two days if everybody was careful. I had already had the supply to all taps cut off, the men on board divided into groups of twenty and each group rationed to one bucket every eight hours.

It was a depressing, wretched day, the rain never letting up and nothing to do but sit around in the steaming heat thinking about what was going to happen. I tried looking at that Solomons Seal sheet. Having somehow survived the loss of the *Holland Trader*, I was more and more convinced they were in some way connected with what had happened. And the letter. I tried reading that, too. I must have read it through half a dozen times, visualizing the scene out there in the waterless wastes of Central Australia where Merlyn Lewis and his partner had struck gold and been so tired they had called the place Dog Weary. Had they had a row? Had they fought over it? Or had Red Holland murderously and cold-bloodedly walked out on his partner in the middle of the night? And Lewis, waking up to find him gone, alone there in the desert, nothing left to drink and only death for company.

But did that justify the violence of Colonel Holland's reaction? *Dear Red* . . . as Mac said, it didn't add up, for if it had been Carlos then Colonel Holland's reaction at finding a letter reminding him of his young brother would have been one of sadness, not anger against the man who had inherited after the *Holland Trader* had gone down. And the stamps . . . Lying naked on my bunk, except for a towel round my loins, I stared at that sheet of sixty damp-blotched Solomons Seal labels. If they could only tell their story, explain how they had survived, how one of them had been aquired by Lewis anf used on the letter he'd sent to his wife in Cooktown. The Port Moresby postmark had been just decipherable, the date 17 July 1911 indicating he had posted it just before the *Holland Trader* sailed out into the Coral Sea and oblivion.

Mac had offered to take the first Dog watch and when I relieved him at 18.00 I asked him whether he had ever heard of a part-white, part-indigene called Black Holland.

'Black Holland. What do you know about Black Holland?' he asked.

'He was killed in a bar brawl up near Cooktown, and I'm pretty certain it was Merlyn Lewis's son who killed him.'

'When did it happen?'

I told him what little I knew and he nodded. 'Killed him in

1952, eh? Black Holland would have been about fifty then . . .
no, older – nearer sixty. He was Red Holland's son by the
daughter of a chieftain down near Kieta. He and his father were
very close, birds of a feather you might say, and when the Japs
occupied the islands he became one of the leaders of the Black
Dogs. But that wasn't how he got his name. He was called Black
Holland down at Kieta to differentiate him from his father up
here in Buka.' And he added, 'The war must have seemed pretty
good to those two bastards, for a year or two anyway.' He looked
at me thoughtfully. 'Merlyn Lewis's son, you say – and he killed
him because of that Dog Weary mine.' He spread his lips as
though smiling and sucked in air through his teeth. 'He's your
man then, isn't he? He'd know what happened to his father.'
And with his lips spreading and contracting, and that peculiar
hissing intake of breath, he pushed his way down the crowded
alleyway to his cabin.

Apart from the functional parts of the ship and the officers'
cabins, every nook and corner that gave prospect of shelter was
crammed with bodies. And when the rain finally stopped most
of the men stayed where they were as though, huddled together
like that, they were protected against the dark uncertain world
outside. Mbalu came to see me shortly after the clouds had
rolled back and the night sky had cleared. He and his three
sergeants had decided to make their attempt on the airfield at
02.00; with that timing in mind, when and where would it be
best for them to be put ashore? I got hold of Luke and the three
of us pored over the chart. I couldn't see anywhere I could run
the ship in without grounding and, in any case, I wasn't at all
certain I wanted to be involved. A lot of people could die as a
result of the airfield being opened up, and if the police didn't
succeed, or took it and failed to hold it . . .

I think Mbalu must have sensed that I was hesitating, for he
suddenly went aft and routed Mac out. He came into the
wheelhouse smelling of whisky again and with a belligerent look
in his eyes. He was in no doubt at all, either about the need for
the operation to go ahead or the way it should be launched. We
should put back into the Passage itself and land the police force

at the usual LCT landing place. There would then be no danger of anything going wrong in the landing and they would have the airport road for their approach march with no chance of anybody getting lost in the darkness or in the thick growth of the plantations.

And that was what we finally did, fetching our anchors shortly after midnight and steaming slowly north-east out of the cove. Navigating by echo–sounder, we back–tracked past the marker posts, which were just visible in the starlight, until we had the Buka Passage open on radar. After that it was quite straightforward. But though Luke knew exactly how to run the ship in to the landing place, it was almost 01.15 before we were finally squared off to the shore with a kedge out to hold us against the current, the bow doors open and the ramp down. Of the twenty-seven strong police force waiting to go ashore, Mbalu had only been able to arm eight with the weapons he had seized from the Buka guards.

The ship seemed suddenly very empty as they moved down the ramp, vanishing one by one up the road into the darkness of the palms. In case things went wrong I had the ramp winched up and the bow doors closed, with the Chief and one of his officers on stand-by in the engine-room and the bos'n waiting by the stern anchor winch. Luke and I moved to the upper bridge, where it was cooler and we had a clear view in every direction, and I invited Mr Treloa and some of his more senior administration officers to join us.

There was nothing to do but wait after that, the hot night air very oppressive, the stillness exaggerating the sound of the current running past our stern. It was running fast, a gurgling sound which seemed to grow as the whisper of hidden voices died away and the bodies strewn about the ship lay sleepless, wondering what the dawn would bring. We had only just enough fuel to get back to Anewa and if the police failed . . . The tension in the ship was very strong, the uncertainty and the strain of waiting communicating itself to all on board.

I tried to lessen my own reaction to it by doing the rounds with a Mortlock helmsman I had come to trust. Below decks the ship seemed deserted, the day's heat trapped and hardly a soul to be seen. Topside there were bodies everywhere, but none of them asleep, the white glint of eyes following me, sometimes the white of teeth as well as mouths opened in a nervous grin. Back on the upper bridge, I paced to and fro, glancing surreptitiously at my watch, trying to conceal the nervous tension inside me, wondering about Perenna and Jona Holland, all the other whites, picturing in my mind those men moving on to the airfield in the darkness and only eight of them armed. And all the time the gurgling menace of the tide running past our stern and the dark straight line of the Buka Passage like a smooth black tarmac road under the stars. Not a light anywhere, just the shape of the land black in outline, the feeling of something hanging over the place, a brooding, overpowering, tropical presence.

At last the luminous hands of my watch pointed to 02.00 hours. No sound – nothing. Only the tide to break the stillness. A minute, two minutes – and still no sound of any shots. An anticlimax tinged with fear, the minutes ticking by and nothing happening; only voices murmuring through the ship as men gave utterance to thoughts that we on the upper bridge kept strictly to ourselves, fearing now that the police had either lost their way or been taken in ambush without a shot being fired.

I went down to the signals office, where Simon Saroa, a native of one of the fishing villages near Port Moresby, was sitting with earphones on and an expectant look on his face. He had briefed one of the police on the equipment at the airfield and was listening out for him. He shook his head. Nothing had come through so far. I went back to the bridge, very conscious now of the six Buka men imprisoned behind the locked door of the old sergeants' mess. I rang down for the engines to be started up and then began to haul off on the stern anchor while at the same time transferring the kedge hawser from stern to bow. I was taking no chances, intending to lie off, bows-on to the current, until I knew definitely what had happened.

We were halfway through this operation when, above the throb of the engines and the sound of the big drum winch aft, I heard a man shouting. Then more shouts, the shouting relayed along the length of the ship until all the blacks on board seemed to have gone out of their minds. Even the senior administrators, gathered in a huddle at the rear of the upper bridge, were leaning over the rail yelling themselves hoarse. A hand touched my arm. 'Kepten.' It was Luke. 'They have taken the airfield.'

I stared at him. 'Without a shot?'

'Yes, without a shot. There is only a small guard and they take them by surprise. It has just been reported by radio.'

I should have realized that in the islands of the Solomon Sea, and all through the South West Pacific, radio was the equivalent of the telephone in more densely populated areas. It was the main means of communication and Simon Saroa had instructed the police officer to tune to the channel commonly used for communication throughout the Bougainville District. The result was that within minutes of the announcement that the airfield had been taken I was called to the signals office where Simon Saroa thrust the mike into my hands without a word as though glad to get rid of it. The voice that answered me from the loudspeaker wasn't the soft voice of Inspector Mbalu; it was a harsh, abrasive voice with a strong Australian accent. 'What's happened, you bastard? What's happened up there? You tell me. Over.'

'Who's that?' My voice sounded taut in the hot little cabin.

'Hans Holland, you fool. Who else? Now just you tell me what's happened. The airfield is in the hands of the police, right? . . . How did they get free? Where did they get the arms? And where's Teopas? I asked to speak to Teopas, where is he? Over.'

I told him briefly what had happened. I didn't tell him who had killed Teopas, but he guessed. 'It was Mac, was it? He's the only man . . . that drink-sodden bastard! I should have got him off the ship. Where did he get hold of the gun?' I started to tell him, but when he realized that Mac had been armed with nothing more than a knife, he shouted at me, 'And what were you doing? Looking on and applauding? An old drunk with nothing but a knife – '

'He was sober,' I said. 'And he knew what he was doing. He

had the guard mesmerized and nothing I or anyone else could do. It all happened too quickly. And once the man was dead and he had his gun . . .' I didn't enjoy making excuses, knowing I'd been in two minds what to do and had let events take control. And when he told me I'd have to move a lot faster if I wanted to skipper one of his ships, my temper suddenly flared. 'If you think you can handle the situation here any better, why don't you come up and do it.'

'I will,' he snapped back at me. 'I'll do just that. Meanwhile you pull out into the stream and stay anchored there. Don't let anybody ashore.'

I told him we should have to go ashore for food, but he ignored that. 'Haul out into the Passage and stay there. Tell your operator to remain tuned to this channel. I'll see if I can raise Queen Carola, get them to send a truckful of boys down to Chinaman's Quay. The airfield isn't all that important. PNG won't dare fly in troops, not after the warning we've given them. But still . . .' He was thinking aloud. 'Open like that it's a temptation. Some silly sod of a politician might be tempted . . . You still there? . . . Good. Keep your operator tuned on this channel, and it's VHF only. No communication with the outside world. Understand? We keep this to ourselves till the airfield's retaken. Okay? Over.'

'I'm not exactly my own master,' I said. But all he replied was, 'Tell whoever is on that radio of yours I'll string him up in the Buka Passage if it's reported to me that he's been operating key. One word in morse about that airfield being open and he's a dead man. You tell him. And don't you fool around with me. Just think of Perenna, your own future, where you stand in all this. Over and out.'

That was the end of it and I looked down at Simon Saroa, his face pale in the glare of the overhead light bulb, his hand not quite steady as he put the mike back on its bracket. 'Three trucks were blocking the runway.' His deep voice shook slightly. 'They are clearing them now.' His eyes lifted to mine, a frightened stare as he asked, 'What do I do about Port Moresby? Inspector Mbalu asks me to try and contact somebody right away.'

I didn't know what to say and before I could reach any decision Hans Holland's voice came out of the loudspeaker again wanting to know the strength of the force now holding the airfield. 'Here we reckon there were some twenty-five to thirty police captive on your ship. With six guards, plus Teopas, only seven of them can be armed. That correct? Over.' I hesitated, wondering whether to say there were more, but it didn't seem to matter very much. I told him his information was about right, but of course the effectiveness of the force now in control of the airfield would depend on the weapons they had captured. He didn't like that, but since I had nothing more to add, he signed off. I was back with Simon Saroa then and his question, which I couldn't answer. In the end I told him it was nothing to do with me. It was between him and his superiors to decide whether he should risk his neck or not, and to the inevitable question, Did I think Mr Holland would carry out his threat, I told him, 'Yes.'

What else could I tell him? I left him and went to my cabin. Let the government officials sort this one out. I lay down on my bunk and tried to think, but apart from organizing enough food to keep us going, there didn't seem much I could do but stay here and wait upon events. If the operator decided to send and troops were flown into Buka, then it could be a messy business. And where did that leave me? I couldn't help smiling to myself, remembering how I'd let my imagination build a future on the strength of Hans Holland's offer. Captain of an ore carrier . . . Bloody hell! I'd be lucky to come out of this alive the way things were at the moment.

I fell asleep shortly after that. At least, I suppose I was asleep. My eyes were closed, I know that because I remember opening them as the light flashed on my face. And I was dreaming, my mind chaotic, with a picture of Tim Holland as I had seen him in that photograph, but sitting in the sea with the circular huts all belching smoke through their thatch and one of them in flames with pigs like little balls of fire running out of it. He was sitting propped against a pillow in the water, whittling away at a piece of wood. Suddenly he looked up at me, his eyes empty sockets, his hands proffering me the piece of wood, and at that moment a booming voice – 'Kill them now . . .' A gun stammering, and it wasn't Teopas who was slammed off balance, falling backwards; it was Hans. Hans Holland with his red hair, dancing on the balls of his feet, and Perenna holding the gun, a chattering stream of staccato bullets building to a cry I could not understand, the gun swinging, the barrel pointing, pointing at me and blasting light, and I woke suddenly, in a sweat, my eyes blinded, my mouth open.

The torch shifted and I heard a voice say, 'On your feet now.' A hard voice, and the face in the torchlight bending over me, hard with red hair flaring. His hand shook me roughly, 'Come on now. I want the engines started and the anchor up.'

I lay there, staring up at him, wondering how the hell he'd got here, 'What time is it?'

'Coming up to six. Soon be dawn.'

I swung my feet out of the bunk and sat up. 'How did you get here?'

But all he said was, 'Malulu here will be watching you. Get some clothes on. You're going up to Queen Carola.' He turned abruptly and left the cabin. 'Mi lukluk.' Malulu jabbed the hard steel muzzle of his machine pistol into my ribs. I pulled on my shorts and a shirt, slipped into my canvas deck shoes and went on to the bridge. The ship seemed full of men being herded at gunpoint down into the tank deck, and lying alongside was the tug I had last seen in Anewa.

'Yu get engines started,' Malulu said, waving his gun at me.

I put the engine-room telegraph to Standby and to my surprise got an instant response, a gentle vibration under my feet. I wished I could have had a cold shower. I was sticky with sweat and my brain still sluggish. Even a tug couldn't have got him up here in under four hours. I cursed myself then for not remembering that VHF has a range of only thirty-forty miles. When the news that the airport had been taken was broadcast, he must have been more than halfway up the coast already. Which meant, of course, that he'd had some sort of radio contact set up between Anewa and Queen Carola so that by midday, at the latest, he would have known I hadn't arrived and that something had gone wrong. I ought to have anticipated that. Instead, I had turned in, and now, under cover of darkness, he had boarded the ship and regained control of her so quietly that it was only his torch on my face that had woken me.

The anchor was coming up, a helmsman took his place at the wheel. Luke came into the wheelhouse, his jet-black skin shining with sweat, his heavy lips jutting, his eyes sullen. He went through on to the bridge wing, stood for a moment staring for'ard, then came back and reported, 'Anchor upan'down now.' He came and stood beside me. 'Kepten Holland, he is on the tug. Also Miss P'renna.'

I went to the bridge wing, Malulu at my heels. Down on the tug Jona was standing at the open entrance to the caboose staring up at our slab side, watching one of the Buka men fooling around with his gun. He didn't see me. But Perenna did. She was sitting on the tug's bulwarks, close up near the bows, and for a moment our eyes met. Then, very deliberately, she turned away to stare fixedly at the bos'n who was coming down off the foredeck after checking that the anchor was properly stowed.

Back in the wheelhouse I found Mac had been brought in. His wrists were tightly bound, his lips swollen, one eye half-closed. He was so beaten up, or else he was so drunk, he could hardly stand, the skin of his face like paper turned yellow with age. 'What've you done with it?' he mumbled through his bruised lips.

'Done with what?' I asked.

'The letter, of course.' His eyes creased up so that I think he was attempting a grin. 'I told him how we went up to the house on Madehas and opened the bloody safe. It got him mad as hell. Said he'd have that letter back if he had to kill me for it. You've hidden it, I hope.'

I shook my head, trying to remember what I had done with it.

'That's right,' he mumbled. 'Keep your mouth shut. Don't admit to anything.' His eyes switched apprehensively to the door, then back to me, and again that mockery of a grin. 'I havena got the guts, you see. Not any longer. Need another bottle at least. One more bottle'd put me right out.' He shook his head. 'No more bottles now. Not a drop left.' There were tears in his eyes.

We had started to drift. Dawn was breaking fast, a beautiful, rain-fresh cloudless dawn, and I could see the shore trees sliding past. The tug hooted, a sudden blast of steam at the funnel, and the stern warp tightened, the propeller churning a wake as she began to stem the current, holding both ships steady. Hans Holland appeared on the catwalk below, moving with a rolling gait, his head down, his hands clenched. He climbed to the bridge wing, stopped just inside the doorway, staring round the wheelhouse, then came across to me. 'McAvoy tells me you've got a letter of mine.' I didn't know how to answer him so I kept my mouth shut. 'From a man named Lewis.'

'The letter to your father?'

'Yes, to my father. Where is it?'

'Up at the house, I think.' And I added quickly, 'I'm not sure. I know I read it. But afterwards I can't remember what I did with it.' But now I did remember. Just before I had fallen asleep I had slipped it back between the pages of *Playboy* and put the magazine on the shelf above my bunk. And the sheet of stamps, they were in it too. 'I'm sorry,' I said. 'It was written so long ago I didn't think it of any importance.'

He eyed me coldly and I watched him trying to make up his mind whether I had told him the truth. 'All right,' he said. 'As soon as this ship has got under way we'll go over to the house and find it.' He pushed past me on to the port bridge wing and called down to Jona Holland, telling him to take command of his ship again. 'And you,' he said, turning back to me. 'You come with me. McAvoy, too.' He started down towards the tug, and when I insisted on getting my things, he merely shrugged. 'Give you five minutes.'

It was less than that when I clambered down on to the tug with my bag. I had purposely left it only half zipped up, the copy of *Playboy* visible on top of my clothes. Walking out through the wheelhouse I found Jona sitting on the captain's chair, his long fingers nervously scooping baccy from a battered pigskin case into his pipe. He seemed more or less himself again, but his hands trembled and his eyes had a strangely vacant stare as he gazed straight down the length of the ship. It was almost as if they were made of glass, no life in them, and his lips moving as he muttered to himself under his breath. He made no reply when I wished him a good trip. I don't think he even saw me.

The tug's warps were let go and the rusty box shape of the LCT was instantly swept clear of us by the current. We hung in the tideway until she had manoeuvred herself round with her bows to the west, then we headed for the wooden pier. By the time we were tied up, leaving just enough room for the ferry, the LCT was abreast of Minon Island and already turning to go out past Madehas by the North Channel. Watching her fade into the morning haze, I wondered what Hans Holland had said to Jona, what he had done to make him go back to his ship again. Had he convinced him that the independence of Buka and Bougainville was now so assured that the future of the Holland Line was in his hands? Or was it something else, something more sinister? Hans was ashore now, talking to a group of Buka men gathered in a bright huddle round an aged truck. But Perenna was still there, in the bows, her hair stirring gently in the breeze that was beginning to ripple the surface of the water. I moved up the deck to join her. 'Good morning.'

She turned her head, a quick sideways glance, but she didn't say anything.

'What's happened to your brother? When I left him on the bridge there he was like a zombie.'

'If you'd lived here – ' Her shoulders lifted in a shrug which seemed to suggest I was a child and impossible to communicate with.

'He looked as though he had been hypnotized.'

She turned on me angrily. 'Brainwashed. That's the modern term, isn't it? But out here . . . Oh, you'll never understand. You've got to be born here.' She was staring into the distance again. 'It's . . . it's in the genes. It's psychological. Tim, Jona,

249

me, Hans – we kick against it – not Hans, of course, he's different – but we can't avoid it, none of us. Not here. Particularly not here.' Her voice was so subdued I could barely catch the words. 'If you'd lived at Madehas ...'

'Mac said the house was cursed.'

'Perhaps.' And she suddenly turned her head and looked at me. 'What've they done to Mac? He's been beaten up. Why?'

I told her about Teopas's death, and then about the safe and the letter.

'So you've been to the house?'

'Yes.'

There was a sudden awkward silence. Finally I said, 'Hans told Mac he'd kill him if he didn't get that letter back. Do you think he would?'

'Why, do you have it?' She was staring at me dully. 'Can I see it please?'

I glanced up the road. Hans was still there and another truck had arrived. I got the copy of *Playboy* from my bag and gave her the letter. She read it through slowly, then read it again. And when I produced the sheet of Solomons Seal ship labels she sighed. 'So that's what it's all about, why he wanted those stamp albums. He was prepared to do anything – to me, to Tim – to get his hands on them.'

'Why?' I asked.

'It's his father, isn't it? His reputation. That's what's at stake.' She gave a little humourless laugh. 'His closest ancestor, his godhead if you like. And that man Lewis – he left Lewis to die. That's the same as murder.'

'Was Hans that fond of his father?'

'Oh God!' she said in an exasperated tone. 'Ancestor worship. Don't you understand? He worships him.'

'But that's paganism.'

'Yes, paganism. Cry to one ancestor for disease and relief of pain, to another for wealth, which is the same as Cargo. Hans isn't a man unless he has Cargo.'

'Do you mean power?'

She shook her head. 'No, I don't mean power. Among all

these blacks, he's the dominant one. He has power already. What he needs is success and everything that goes with it. Money is what drives him. Greed. And Mac says it's greed that drove his father.' She handed the letter back to me. 'And what about you? Is it greed that's driving you? Is that why you took over Jona's ship without a thought about what your action meant to him, or to me?'

I shook my head. I couldn't answer her, not in any way that would make sense in her present mood. 'Where's Mac?'

'Below somewhere, locked up I think.' She was silent then and I returned the copy of *Playboy* to my bag. The skipper of the tug, a young Australian with close-set eyes and a small sun-bleached beard, was in the caboose drinking coffee. I joined him and he poured me a mug, handing it to me with a sly grin. 'You always get the girls hotted up with *Playboy*, mate?'

I was back in a world I understood. Afterwards I went ashore. The sun had gone, the sky clouded over. There was a heaviness in the air as I stood under the solitary banyan tree looking across the road to the line of Chinese shops with their worn wooden steps and exotic signs. They were already open and youngsters in from the villages were gathered in chattering huddles sucking ice cream and drinking lolly water, which is their name for a soft drink. Beyond the shops, just before the turning down to the Government wharf where the coaster lay, was an open concrete building something like a pagoda. This was where the trucks had stopped and as I walked towards it, I realized it was a market, the throng of people gathered there mostly stallholders setting out their produce.

It began to rain, warm, heavy drops. Umbrellas and plastics sprouted like mushrooms. Hans crossed the road to a prefabricated wooden building that looked quite new. It had a sign like the Chinese shopfronts that read *Buka Trading Co-operative*. I reached the market just as the atmosphere became so heavy that the rain poured out of it, the noise of water drumming on the market's tin roof drowning the chatter of people crowding in. There was one white woman amongst them, a blonde with a thin, bony face, her white cotton dress immaculately ironed. She squeezed through between the piles of fruit and vegetables to ask me whether I knew what was happening over in Bougainville. She was a Mission School teacher and she had friends in Arawa. An aerial mast, just visible through the rain across the road, caught my eye and I suggested she ask at the Buka Co-operative for news, but she seemed to freeze at the suggestion as though I had advised her to consult with the Devil. A moment later I saw her talking to a young nun who had just stepped out of a mud-bespattered Toyota four-wheel drive looking calm, collected and very Catholic in her habit.

The rain stopped as suddenly as it had begun, a tap turned off, and in an instant bare black feet had churned the area round the market into a quagmire. The sun's heat was filtering through, burning up the thin veil of cloud that was now so low that the further shore of the Passage was hidden from my sight. The dirt road, running straight as a sword through endless plantations, was a brown slash of steaming mud out of which strange shapes emerged as villagers bringing woven mat baskets of produce in to market. I bought some bananas and ate them, wandering round the concrete display counters – so much colour, so much ripe fruit, so many bare breasts – and then the nun came and spoke to me. They had heard on the radio that a Ruling Council had been formed in Kieta and Daniel Sapuru had been elected first President of the Republic of Bougainville-Buka. Was I off the tug? Did I know Mr Holland? Could I give her any more detailed information?

I shook my head, wondering what Hans Holland's role really was, just how much he was in control. The nun knew him, of course, but only to greet, she said. She was Italian from the big Catholic Mission halfway up the island, and when I questioned her about Hans and his relations with the Co-operative, she said very coolly, 'I have nothing to do with him. He is bisnis. Always bisnis.' She changed the subject then, very firmly, asking me about myself and telling me about the produce on the counters as she made her purchases. There were paw-paw, of course, and yams and mangoes, real bananas, small and perfectly ripe, as well as big coarse plantains for cooking, green oranges and a large pink grapefruit she called *pomolo*. There were also things I had never seen before: betelnut, *pit-pit*, *lou-lou* like a big crunchy apple, snake bean, Chinese cabbage, taro and casava and the sweet potato they call *kau-kau*.

It was when she was leaving, having by then in her quiet way discovered how I had come to Buka, that she told me something about the Hollands that surprised me, and not in answer to any question from me, but of her own volition. There was talk, she said, among the expatriate inmates of the Mission that long ago, before World War II, Mr Hans Holland's father had been a convert to the Catholic faith and that he had done it to make his peace with God because of some terrible transgression. 'A man with red hair like that – ' she smiled up at me, a gleam of amusement in her eyes as she shook my hand – 'they always have evil tempers, no? We have them in Sicily. They are descendants of the Vikings and do terrible things.' She hesitated. 'This Hans Holland, he also has red hair. Has he done something bad? I'm told he has some island blood, but he still comes to us regularly to confess.'

'He's a Catholic then?'

She nodded. 'Since last year.' And she added, very quietly, 'There is good in all people, don't you know, my friend, so God be with you.' And she smiled as she got into the Toyota and was driven off, her head bowed, her hands on the beads of her rosary, and only the satisfaction of a quick sidelong glance to assure me of her femininity.

I ate another banana, watching the Buka Co-operative and chatting about the weather to a big-breasted sultry-looking woman selling fruit. She spoke Pidgin mixed with Mission English and assured me the sun would shine. 'Bik fella rain tru finis'im. No rain. Sun nau.' She chuckled, her mountainous bosom heaving under the coloured cotton that did little to conceal it. 'Bik fella rain tru, yu savvy? It mean rain all time. Not rain all time nau.' She gave me a huge betelnut smile and almost instantly the daylight faded and the rain poured down again.

The door of the Co-operative opened and Hans Holland

peered out. He called to one of the truck drivers, then he saw me and shouted, 'You. Slingsby.' He hesitated, glancing up the road, then made a dash for it through raindrops bouncing knee-high. 'Where's Perenna? Still on board?' He licked the rainwater from his lips, staring at me, his red hair plastered to his skull. 'I saw you talking to her. Did she say anything about Highland workers up at the mine? Well, did she?'

I shook my head, wondering what it was all about. He seemed to have been thrown off balance. 'Something wrong?' I asked, but he had turned, signalling to the truck driver who now had his engine going. The truck drew up close to where we stood, the door swinging open. 'I'm going up to the ADC's office. They've got a direct line to the radio station over on Sohano. You'd better come too, unless you want to get soaked.' He climbed in and I followed him. 'Kiap's office,' he told the driver. Then, as we drove off into the thundering grey wall of the teeming rain, he turned to me. 'It's Arawa,' he said. 'They're down into Arawa, a great crowd of redskins, I'm told, all raising hell.'

'You mean Chimbu Highlanders?'

'Yeah. Highlanders from Papua New Guinea.'

'What are they raising hell about?'

'That's what I want to know. They've no weapons. Not firearms anyway, so they can't do anything. They're just making a bloody nuisance of themselves, and they won't talk to anybody but Perenna. That's what they say. I don't know what the hell they want.' He had been yelling in my ear to make himself heard above the tom-tom beat of the rain on the cabin's tin roof. Now he relapsed into silence, not saying anything till we drew up at the Sub-District HQ. A truck and two Toyota short-wheelbase land-cruisers were parked outside, and sheltering in the corrugated iron garage was a bunch of Buka men armed with old, rust-worn rifles. 'You wait here.' There was a guard on the door, an elderly man with close-cropped hair holding what looked like a Japanese rifle, and he had two very old grenades fastened to the waistband of his shorts. It was a wet soggy world, the rain a steady downpour now and the light so dim it was a steaming sepia colour. Hans Holland was only gone about five minutes He came back in a hurry. 'Tugboat.' He jumped in and slammed the door, his tanned leathery face tight-shut and frowning.

'What's happened? What's the news?'

The empty truck bumped and skidded its way down the track and for a moment he didn't answer me. Then suddenly he said, 'If I'm not there they make a balls of it. If I am there they say I'm trying to run things myself. I told them to put a guard on that tote road when I found you'd come out that way. They didn't, of course, so now they've got these redskins in Arawa and they don't know what to do about them.'

'How many of them?' I asked.

'I don't know. Sapuru said several hundred, but he's probably exaggerating. Why do you think they insist on talking to Perenna? All their leader keeps saying is *Yu send Miss Perenna, we speak with her*. That's what Sapuru says.'

I was remembering Perenna in conversation with that thick-set Chimbu Councillor outside the Immigration Office. 'Did he say what the man looked like?'

He shook his head. 'Just one of those PNG people they employ for the hard manual work up at Paguna. If it were only a few of them, it wouldn't matter. But the riot squad was always having trouble with those people. They get on the beer – they're not used to beer – and now if they go on the rampage, like they did a few years back . . .' He turned and looked at me, a hard stare. 'You asked me what their leader looked like. Why? Do you think you've met him?'

I hesitated, but there was no point in not telling him what Perenna had said, and when I had finished, he nodded. 'Chimbu,' he said. 'They're most of them Chimbu. But a fight leader. I never heard of a fight leader coming over to work at Paguna.' I was still trying to explain what she had told me about that when we drew up at the ferryboat jetty.

I thought he would have forgotten the letter by now, but as we walked along the wooden boards to the tug he started asking about it again. 'Who's read it? Yourself, McAvoy – anybody else?'

255

'What's it matter?' I was wet and irritable, my shirt sodden. 'It happened seventy years ago, maybe more.'

'Perenna.' He stopped there, staring at me hard, his face so close to mine I could see every pale line of the crease marks in his skin, exaggerated by the water streaming off his bare head. 'What about Perenna, has she read it?'

I shook my head slowly, something in the expression of his eyes warning me. 'No;' I said.

'You didn't show it to Jonathan? No, you couldn't, of course. But anybody on the LCT? Who else has seen it?'

'I've told you, nobody. Just myself and Mac, that's all.'

'You're lying.' He stood there in the rain staring at me, and suddenly, for a moment, he was a different man. There was something in his eyes, a sort of madness – or was that my imagination? I seemed for a second to be looking into his soul, into pools of unfathomable darkness. A trickle of water reached my crotch and I shivered.

'Okay,' he said, his voice and manner suddenly normal again. 'As soon as I get back from Sohano, we'll go over to Madehas – you, me, Perenna, McAvoy too. I want that letter, understand? Meanwhile, you stay on board.'

2

Hans took the ferry, the *Barreto Chebu*, across to Sohano, one of his Buka guards going with him, and while he was away a truckload of armed men came in from Queen Carola. Their weapons were World War II rifles, and they sat nursing them in the back of the truck, staring out at the rain, none of them doing anything except relieve themselves against the banyan tree. The *Barreto* stayed moored to the Sohano jetty, which was only just visible through the rain.

The rest of the morning passed slowly. The tug was primarily a harbour tug and the quarters, entered by a companionway at the back of the little caboose of a wheelhouse, were cramped and pretty basic. Perenna and her brother, as well as Hans, had spent the night dozing with their clothes on in the tiny saloon. Now she was lying curled up on the bench beside the small mess table. I don't think she was asleep, but she didn't speak to me. The incessant rain and lack of sleep had affected us all, the rain particularly.

About 10.30 we moved to the bunkering wharf close by the market and took on fuel. With no truckload of armed men to stop me, I thought it an opportunity to slip ashore, but I was stopped by the fair-bearded Australian skipper. 'Much as my job's worth to let you go wandering in the bush, mate.' He wasn't armed, but there were armed men at the Co-operative he could call upon, so I stayed with him in the caboose. He was aiming to make his fortune backing the new Sapuru regime, and Holland he regarded as a guy who was going places. 'Got it all planned, finance for ships, everything. Stick with him, mate, and you won't go wrong.' Half an hour later we were back at the jetty.

At midday we picked up a news bulletin on the radio. The Australian Government had ordered the frigate *Dampier*, on fishery protection duty off the Barrier Reef, to proceed at once to Bougainville to stand by to evacuate Australian civilians. Papua New Guinea was reported to have sent an ultimatum to the rebel Council of the Sapuru regime giving them until noon to release all prisoners and hand over power to the legitimate administration; if not the forces at present standing by would be ordered to take the necessary action to restore the legal government. Since the time was now four minutes past midday and no reply had been received from the rebel regime, it was presumed that military action would be taken. Preparations for such an eventuality had already been made. There followed an eye-witness account from Port Moresby of troops embarking in the harbour, also an announcement that Air Niugini Fokker Friendships were being requisitioned to act as air transports.

Then, right at the end of the news, there was a news flash: *A report has just come in that security forces of the PNG administration in Bougainville recaptured Buka airfield in the early hours of this morning. The time limit for surrender of power by the rebel regime having expired, we understand that the airlift of troops to Buka, the island to the north of Bougainville that is virtually a part of the mainland, has already begun. We will keep listeners informed as soon as we have further news.*

Within minutes of that announcement the little *Barreto* had cast off and was sidling across the tideway towards us. Somewhere in the distance a shot was fired. I thought it came from the direction of the airfield, but then there were more shots, a sporadic outburst of firing that clearly emanated from the rising ground in the vicinity of the administration buildings.

Hans Holland had already seen the truckload of men waiting and he was shouting somebody's name as the ferryboat bumped alongside and he jumped on to the jetty and went running towards the truck. A stocky jet-black man, bare-chested and with a great shock of hair, climbed out of the cab. They stood there for a moment, the two of them in the rain, Hans's voice loud and angry, the other's soft and sullen. Finally the man from Queen Carola got back into the cab and the truck drove off. 'They should've moved on the airfield an hour ago,' the tug skipper said. 'Looks like they've lost the initiative now.'

Hans was walking back towards the tug, his head bent, oblivious of the rain. He was walking slowly, pausing every now and then to turn his head and listen to the sound of firing which continued very sporadically. He reached the bulwarks and climbed on board, then stood there a moment as though undecided. The skipper stuck his head out of the caboose window. 'You heard the newscast, did you, boss?'

Hans nodded. 'Yes. And the stupid bastards have got themselves cut off – ' He seemed to take a grip on himself, his mouth shut, his lips a hard line. Water poured off him as he came slowly down the deck. The firing had ceased now, everything quiet except for the sound of the rain and the faint hubbub of voices from the shops across the road. He stood listening for a moment outside the caboose door. 'That firing, from the Sub-District office, wasn't it?'

'Reck'n so.' The Australian pushed open the door for him. 'Sounds like the police have captured it now.'

He nodded, still listening intently, his shirt and trousers clinging to him, his head lifted and his eyes staring at nothing with great intensity. Then he looked at his watch. 'Still plenty of time. If those aircraft really did take off . . . What is it – five, six hundred miles? They'll be nearly two hours yet.' He looked at the pair of us and suddenly that cocky jauntiness was back. 'Come on. We'll grab a truck and some arms and get out to the airfield. Three trucks. That should do it. Three trucks parked on the runway should stop them, and in this rain . . .'

He was already heading back along the jetty and such was the magnetism of the man that we were both out of the caboose and actually running after him when we heard it. At first we didn't stop. It was coming from behind us, out of the west, a soft whisper like a line squall whipping up the sea. It grew steadily, swelling to a solid, high-toned cacophony of sound that we must have identified at the same instant for we stopped in our tracks, all three of us, standing there listening, our eyes searching the leaden overcast beyond Sohano, beyond Minon. And suddenly, there it was, coming in low over Madehas, the roar of its engines getting louder and louder.

It was the first of four and already it had its wheels down. It was so low they seemed to brush the marker posts. It came straight down the Buka Passage, sweeping close over our heads, the Air Niugini bird of paradise insignia bright against the low-hanging cloud, and by then the others were in sight, coming in like dragonflies low over the water.

'The bastards! The bloody, cheating, sodding bastards!' Hans's voice was strangely shrill. 'They were in the air,' he cried. 'They must have had them in the air . . .' His voice was drowned in the scream of the engines close over our heads as they peeled off to circle the airfield, and we stood there, rooted to the spot, as all four of them were lost to sight beyond the plantations.

The market was in turmoil, people standing staring up at the

259

sky, others running. And down at the Government wharf the crew of the freighter were throwing off her warps, pausing every now and then to glance up at the overcast, as though expecting bombs to fall, for the sound of engines was growing again. Then one by one the aircraft reappeared to make the approach run. We watched them descend in quick succession, the sound of their engines dying to a gentle murmur as they completed their landings and began to taxi.

The Australian was the first to speak. 'Well, mate, I guess that's it.' He was looking at Hans. We both were, and in that moment I was sorry for him. He had taken one hell of a gamble, and now . . . 'Looks like those bastards in Port Moresby have called your bluff.' The skipper's face was sour with disappointment.

Hans turned and stared at him, anger in his eyes, and something else – 'I wasn't bluffing,' he said, his voice a hard whisper of sound that was more implacable than if he had shouted.

'You mean . . .' The Australian gazed at him, open-mouthed. 'Christ! I believe you would, too.'

I didn't know what they were talking about, but the words had a curious effect, the Australian with a shocked look on his face and Hans actually smiling. 'We lose Buka, it doesn't matter. So long as they can't land at Kieta – ' He began walking back to the tug.

The last of the aircraft had cut its engines and in the sudden silence the sound of human voices from the shops and from the market seemed very loud. The freighter had pulled out into the stream. She was very high out of the water and the slowly revolving prop was making a steady thumping sound as it flailed the surface.

Hans reached the end of the jetty and turned to the skipper. 'We'll go across to Sohano now. They're arranging radio contact with Sapuru for me. President Sapuru! He likes the sound of that. And now that he's in a fix I guess he'll do it.' He nodded. 'Yes, I think so. He's no alternative now. And you,' he added as he climbed on board. 'While you're waiting for me at Sohano see if you can raise the LCT on VHF, tell Captain Holland to dump the prisoners anywhere he can and return here immediately. Madehas. We'll meet him at Madehas. By then we should've stopped those bastards in their tracks.'

The tug was manned by one Mortlock and two Shortland islanders. The engineer was from Buin in the extreme south-west of Bougainville. They knew their job, all of them, so that a shout from the Australian skipper and we were cast off with the engine turning over almost before our feet touched the deck. And on the other side we didn't stay at the Sohano jetty after Hans had leapt on to it, but backed off and anchored out past the first of the water loos that stood like little wooden bathing machines with their legs in the water. 'Nobody's going to rush me, I tell ya.' And then he was looking at me closely as he said, 'You think they'll do it? You think Sapuru's got the guts? Or will they just lay down their arms?'

'Do what?' I asked.

'Start killing them. Do you think he'll do it?' And when I asked who Sapuru was expected to kill, he stared at me as though he thought I was trying to be funny. 'Why, the whites, of course. The expats. And don't pretend you didn't know. You heard what the boss said. I thought he was bluffing, that's true, mate. I really did think it was a bluff. But it isn't, is it? He's gone to get Sapuru on the air, tell him to go ahead, to start killing. And that frigate, the *Dampier*, hasn't a hope of getting here in time to stop it. Do you think Sapuru will do it?' He was staring at me, nervous and excited at the same time.

'How the hell should I know?' I was appalled, aghast at the thought that I had got myself into a position where I could be accused of complicity. 'I've never met the man.'

'Never met him?'

'No.'

'Well, he's not much to look at, I can tell ya. A dried-up little mummy of a man, a sort of elder-cum-wizard, and very much feared by his people. 'Fact, they're dead scared of him, so if he tells them to start killing the odds are they'll do it.'

Murder! What else could you call it? It wasn't even

indiscriminate bombing as in Northern Ireland. True, the motive was political and almost anything it seems can be justified these days if that's the motive. But to hold people hostage and then shoot them down in cold blood . . . Or was a revolution the same as war? Did the writ to kill cover innocent civilians? We were still arguing about it when the distant whine of aircraft engines started up again.

By then the sky had lightened and the rain had eased up, a breeze blowing down the narrow tideway, wind against current so that the surface of the Passage was ruffled with little breaking waves. The noise of aircraft engines was steady for several minutes so that I guessed they were taxi-ing out to the runway. Then, suddenly, the noise increased as, one after the other, they took off and rose above the palms like insects on a string. I thought they'd taken off to fly back to Port Moresby for reinforcements, but instead of heading out to the west, they banked and came straight across Chinaman's Quay and the Buka Passage heading south-east. 'Kieta,' the Australian murmured unbelievingly. 'They're headed for Kieta.' He turned and stared across the water at the Sohano jetty which was deserted. 'Something's wrong,' he muttered. 'Kieta should be blocked.' He reached for the radio, switched on and began fiddling with the tuning as he slipped the headphones on. 'I'll try the normal air channel. See if they're talking.' His fingers checked, his face concentrated as he listened intently. Then he nodded and switched the loudspeaker on: '. . . Just hear you. Over . . . That's better. ETA over Arawa 13.25. Have your helicopter in position 1000 feet above the downwind end of the chosen section. Okay?. . . Yes, as a marker. We'll come in below him. If the road is not clear he's to switch his nav lights on and fire red warning flares. Okay? Over . . . Yes as soon as the boys are out we'll turn straight round and take off downwind . . . Thanks, Paguna. If the rain stops the road surface shouldn't be too bad. We'll contact you again as we approach Arawa. It's important about the vehicles, remember. They don't want to footslog it in the heat. Over and out.'

He switched off. 'Something Holland never thought of, them

using a road.' He shook his head. 'He should've. A road surface would be a damned sight better than some of the fields I've seen those Friendships land on in Australia.' He got up and peered out of the window. The time was 12.52. There was nobody on the jetty, apart from two kids playing tag in the light drizzle, and the path down to it from the radio station and the hospital was deserted. 'Well, he'd better hurry up or I'm off back to Anewa. Think they'll give me a medal for bringing their tug back safe and sound?' He grinned at me, running his fingers through his blond beard. 'Pity. We might've finished up driving ships as big as tankers, with nice cosy quarters, a bar on board and women. Oh, well . . .' He gave a little shrug, reaching for the packet of cigarettes lying on the window ledge. 'No sweat as far as I'm concerned, but Hans Holland now – wonder what he'll do? Finished here, ennee? Be lucky if they don't stand him up against a wall and shoot the . . .' Footsteps sounded on the companionway and he turned. It was Perenna.

'Shoot what?' she asked. 'What's happened?' And when we told her she stood staring out at Sohano, her face pale and dark shadows under her eyes. 'So it's all over. He's lost. Lost everything. He'll be sent to prison.' She turned, groping for the helmsman's chair, and sat down. 'Oh, my God! It's no place for a man like Hans.'

It struck me as odd at the time, and it still does, but in that moment her thoughts were not for the men who had been killed to no purpose, or the expatriates in Bougainville whose lives were threatened if Sapuru didn't capitulate, or even for her brother. They were for Hans Holland, as though he were some sort of exotic butterfly that couldn't exist in the strict confines of a prison cell.

I can't remember what we talked about, the three of us huddled together in the wheelhouse waiting for the arrival time of the planes over Arawa. I don't think we said very much, the time passing slowly as the rain finally stopped and the sun began to burn through the thinning cloud layer. At 13.15 we were tuned to the same VHF channel, but hearing nothing except static, the skipper switched to the shortwave frequency used locally. On this we caught disconnected snatches of talk. The reception was very bad, but a scattering of words came through: 'Opposition', was one of them, also 'good landing' and 'cars at the bridge thank God . . .' And then at 13.34, very clearly, came the words, ' . . . four of us airborne now, course two-four-five and climbing to sixteen thousand. Our ETA . . .' The rest was lost, fading into a crackle of static. The Australian switched off. 'Course 245, that means they're headed back to Port Moresby, don't it?'

I nodded. 'Papua New Guinea anyway.'

'And just time to get back to Kieta again before nightfall with another eighty or so soldiers.' He was on his feet, calling to his crew to get the anchor up. 'I'm not hanging around here any longer. I'm on my way.' He winked at me, his teeth showing brown nicotine stains against the bleached hairs of his beard. 'A good law-abiding citizen, that's me, bringing the Company's property back where it belongs. And don't you say anything different, mate, or I'll shop you for a gun-runner.'

The engines were throbbing away, the anchor coming up and Perenna was on her feet saying, 'You can't just leave him.'

'Can't I?' He laughed. 'Look, miss. He had it all sewn up, the future, everything. But now it's all fallen apart and he's in the shit, ennee? Right in it up to his neck, so I aim to put as much space between him and me –'

'He's coming down to the jetty now,' I said.

He turned, staring at the shore.

'So what are you going to do?'

'Oh, hell!' he said. 'I dunno. Take him to Madehas, I guess. That's where he said.' And he swung the wheel over, turning the tug's bows towards the Sohano jetty. 'Can't leave him on Sohano to be picked up by the army. They're bound to commandeer the ferry and send a section over to grab the radio station.'

'Where's Mac?' Perenna asked.

'That little monkey-faced man with a bladder full of liquor? He's coiled up in the big hawser aft sleeping it off. You coming back to Anewa with us, miss?'

264

Her head jerked up, her expression suddenly changed. 'Yes,' she said sharply. 'Yes, of course.' Then she was silent, looking straight ahead, watching as the bows sidled towards the jetty where Hans stood facing us, very still and watchful as though events had made him suddenly suspicious of everyone and everything. The Australian slid the tug alongside so that its bulwarks barely touched the wood and almost before Hans had stepped on board he had the prop in reverse and we were backing out into the Passage, the bows already swinging so that when he went ahead they were still turning towards Minon. 'You still want to go to Madehas?' he asked.

Hans didn't answer immediately, standing just outside the open door to the caboose, his eyes not seeing anything, only his thoughts. At length he turned his head and said, 'Did you manage to raise the LCT?'

'Yep. Passed on your message.'

Hans nodded. He had his shirt outside his trousers. It was almost dry now and like that it was only when he moved I could see the shape of a gun stuck into his waistband. 'Another hour then and Jonathan should be back.'

'Thank God for that,' Perenna breathed and the Australian said, 'Depends what he decides when he's heard the news, doesn't it? He might head straight back to Anewa like I'm going to do soon as I've dropped you.'

Hans looked at him, his silence and the contempt in his eyes saying more than words. 'Put me ashore at Madehas,' he said finally. 'The north of the island, below the house.' He turned to me. 'And you'll come ashore with me. I want that letter.'

' That he should have remembered it, with all that had happened – that really did strike me as very strange. Then, as we passed through the narrows between the Minon and Buka Island markers, I forgot all about it, Perenna pulling me to one side and saying, 'Have you seen his eyes? He's desperate. I'm afraid he'll do something terrible.'

'Nonsense,' I whispered.

'You just look at his face. That shut look. And he's got something under his shirt. A grenade?'

'It's a gun.'

'You can't be sure. It could be a grenade – '

Her voice had risen slightly and he turned, quick as a cat. 'What's that you say?'

'Nothing.' The freckles on her face showed very clear against the pallor of her skin, her eyes wide as she stared straight into his face.

He smiled, but it was more of a grimace, reminding me of ancient gargoyles. 'Who put the curse on us, Perenna? Eh? Who was it? My father, your grandfather – or somebody further back, some devilish Holland we don't know about? And Red Holland – my father – murdered by your grandfather. Nothing went right for them, did it?' His voice had risen, the words spat out between clenched teeth. 'And now, ten years' work, ten years' preparation, coaxing, organizing, building for a big future, and what happens? It goes sour on me, a ghastly failure, and just because a gorilla from the Highlands of Papua New Guinea, a man who should be back in the dark ages living in a goddam cave, comes down from Paguna with two or three hundred followers armed with pangas telling Sapuru he's magicked their jobs away and for that he's going to put a bigger magic on him. That's what he said, a bigger magic – because he's more than a fight leader, he's a sorcerer and capable of bigger magic than Sapuru. And you know what?' He thrust his face close to Perenna's, staring at her, his eyes gone wild. 'It was you they wanted. Yes, you. If I didn't bring you back to speak for them they'd tear every Buka man in Arawa limb from limb and eat them at the biggest sing-sing since before the first missionary came.'

He had been talking so fast spittle had formed on his mouth. He wiped it away with the back of his hand and turned to me. 'You think you're going to marry this little bitch and make the Holland Line your own, eh? Oh, I heard all about you and what happened on the trip over. But you'll never do it, not if you've any sense. Let the ships, the name, everything, sink into oblivion – like the old *Holland Trader*.' His voice had quietened as though he was beginning to come to terms with what had happened. 'Maybe that's the answer.' He had turned away and was staring for'ard towards the house, which was just coming into sight on the high ground at the north end of Madehas.

Nobody spoke after that, the only sound the swirl of water at the bows and the background hum of the engines. Perenna looked very shaken, almost cowed, and suddenly I was seeing her in quite a different light, not as a highly attractive, sensual woman, but as somebody with very real problems that made her vulnerable. The broadened nose, the fullness of the lips, the thrusting breasts, the way she walked even and the way her hair fitted her head like a cap – it was all there, traces of a mixed blood, the people I had seen in the market and at the quayside shops.

She saw me staring at her and half-reached out her hand, a timid gesture that was retracted almost before it was begun. I felt a sudden surge of emotion – pity, love, compassion, I don't know what it was. She lowered her head as though in embarrassment, and for that moment the sensuality of her body, its ability to arouse me, all my previous feelings for her were quite lacking. And then she lifted her head again, her eyelids too, so that our eyes met, and something passed between us, something deep and personal. She lowered her eyes again, but squared her shoulders as though strengthened by some resolve. 'Are you going up to the house with him?' she asked.

'Perhaps. I don't know.'

Hans heard me and said, 'You haven't any choice. I want that letter.'

'I'll come with you then,' she said.

He turned on her. 'You'll do as you're told and stay on board till your brother arrives.' We had left the last marker astern and were approaching North Madehas. 'You wait here for the LCT,' he told the Australian. 'As soon as you've put Miss Holland aboard, then you're free to head for Anewa.'

'You'll remain at Madehas, will you?'

Hans nodded.

'So what do I tell them down at Anewa?'

Hans gave a quick, humourless bark of a laugh. 'Don't reck'n you need me to coach you. You were coerced. I brought you up here against your will. At gunpoint, was it?' He smiled. 'You're a two-timing sodding bastard, aren't you?'

'Just impressionable.' The Australian's teeth showed brown in his beard as he reached for the engine controls. I never did discover the man's name. A relief driver, that's how he described himself. The revs dropped and we slipped through between the shallows to the north and the reef arm reaching out from Madehas.

I didn't see them anchor. I was down below, getting the letter from my bag and slipping it in with the dollars in my hip pocket. If Perenna hadn't been there I could have said I'd made a mistake and handed it straight over to him. I didn't want to go back to that house, and certainly not with Hans Holland. There *was* something evil about it. I had felt it when I was there with Mac, a brooding menace hanging over it. And to go there now with a man whose world had collapsed . . . but I had no alternative. I had said the letter was still in the house and if I produced it now he would know I had shown it to Perenna. *Pagan bad*. Mac's words came back to me as the chain rattled out and I climbed the ladder to the wheelhouse.

The dinghy was already over the side. Perenna looked at me, a wide-eyed stare. But she didn't say anything. No last minute appeal to me not to go, and I knew then she was scared – scared of what he would do if he discovered she knew the contents of that letter. And neither of us understood why it mattered so much to him. 'You ready, Slingsby?' He was waiting for me out on the flat rounded stern where the Mortlock man with the jet-black skin was holding the painter. As I went to join him, seeing the bulge of the gun under his shirt and myself unarmed, I wasn't feeling all that confident. And what made it worse, the sun was coming out, everything fresh and sparkling after the rain. For the first time since I had arrived in the Buka Passage I was glad to be alive and in such a place.

Never having fought in a war, or seen a man in total defeat before, I had no yardstick with which to gauge Hans Holland's state of mind. The fact that he had mixed blood, some of it, like

Perenna's, of Melanesian origin, did that make him more, or less, fatalistic? And to be worrying about a letter written in 1910 when the Papua New Guinea Government would almost certainly blame him for what had happened and seek some form of retribution, a public trial, an execution even . . . I watched him as the Mortlock islander rowed us ashore. He was bareheaded, his red hair gleaming in the sun. Even his bare arms had a reddish glow. He didn't talk, sitting silent in the bows, a small canvas grip at his feet and his eyes staring into space. What was he thinking, I wondered?

What the hell was he thinking?

The bows touched the landing pontoon where the oil drums on which it floated were still intact and he stepped out of the boat, the painter in one hand, his canvas holdall in the other. It was then that I got the letter out of my hip pocket and slipped it into a side pocket where I could get at it easily. He held the boat for me and as soon as I had joined him on the pontoon, he tossed the painter back on board and the boat headed for the tug. I should have called the man back, told him to wait, but I was afraid that might be taken as provocation. I was treading warily, as though dealing with a psychopath, and I was very conscious that Hans was aware of my unease. He seemed to be smiling to himself as we reached the shore and started up the path together.

The houseboy appeared as mysteriously as before. Hans said something to him and he fell in behind us, a silent shadow. I saw no sign of the woman. 'Have you remembered where it is?' Hans asked abruptly.

'In the safe probably.'

'That isn't what McAvoy said. He seemed to think you'd taken it with you.'

It was very hot, the air humid despite the sparkle. 'It'll be there somewhere,' I said. And then I asked him what he was planning to do now. 'Where will you go?'

He turned his head, a hard, angry stare. 'D'you think I'd tell you even if I knew?' His tone was hostile as though he thought I was gloating. It was a sharp reminder of the delicateness of my position, alone with an armed man whose mind might well be unhinged, and only his own houseboy, a native of Buka, witness to anything that happened. We walked in silence the rest of the way to the house, passing the little flyblown summer house, the houseboy drawing level and plucking at Hans Holland's shirt. But before he could make his ritual offer of coffee or Coke he had been silenced by the coldness of his master's gaze.

We reached the entrance porch with its unswept pile of winged insects. Hans trod them underfoot, not apparently noticing, pushed open the door and then stood back, motioning me to enter. From that moment he contrived always to have me in sight as though he were afraid I'd try to rush him. The sun was streaming in through the cobwebbed windows high above the halfway landing of the double staircase, dust motes shimmering in the air, and there was a lazy buzz of trapped insects. Where it had been gloomy before, it was now positively macabre, the stuffed crocodile, the carving, the panelling, everything brilliantly illuminated like a stage set. Hans closed the door. Then, watchful now and still keeping behind me, he pointed to one of the chairs against the wall at the foot of the staircase. 'You sit there,' he said.

Now that we were alone in this dreadful room his voice had an edge to it that I didn't like. 'You'll need some help – ' I began.

'Sit down.'

'If you don't mind – '

'Sit down, damn you – where I can see you. I told you you were lying, remember? Go on, pull that chair out and sit down.' His voice was calmer now. The chair he had indicated was by the table with the old newspapers. I dropped the letter on top of them as I picked up the chair. He was already standing at the bottom of the stairs. 'Sit down.' He watched me until I was seated, then he bent down, felt for the catch and with both hands under the outer edge of the bottom tread, gave a quick heave and raised all four treads, folding them back in one easy movement. 'Did you take anything else?' He was already bending over the safe, his fingers turning the combination lock.

'Nothing,' I said. 'Everything was put back just – '

'What about McAvoy?' He glanced up at me. 'Are you saying he put it all back, neither of you took anything?'

'Yes, it was all put back, money, gold, everything.'

'Except that letter.' He straightened up. The door of the safe was opening slowly to the leverage of his body. Quickly he checked the contents, finally pulling out the envelope marked Lewis, taking a quick look at the Solomons Seal sheets, then putting it back and turning to me. 'All except the letter,' he said, the sunlight glinting off a cracked wall mirror making patterns on his face. 'Where is it? What've you done with it?' And when I started to tell him I couldn't remember, he laughed a little wildly and said, 'Don't give me that crap. You took it with you and showed it to Perenna. I told you you were lying. I saw you on the tug this morning. But why did you take it? What made you think it so bloody important that you had to show it to Perenna?'

'I don't know,' I said, conscious of my tongue on my lips, moistening them nervously. And then I thought, no point in not telling him what puzzled me. 'It started off *Dear Red*, so I took it to be addressed to your father and it's dated July 1910. In it Lewis says he's coming to get his share of the ships that were purchased with the gold from the Dog Weary mine. That's what I didn't understand.'

'Because Red Holland didn't inherit the Line until over a year later?'

'Yes.'

'Did Perenna know what it meant?'

'No, she didn't understand it either.' Looking at him, so tense, so wary, a thought suddenly occurred to me. 'Did Timothy Holland know?'

He didn't answer.

I got to my feet. 'Well, did he?'

'Sit down,' he shouted, his voice suddenly out of control and the gun in his hand, a heavy revolver, the muzzle pointed straight at my stomach.

'So it wasn't an accident. And at Aldeburgh, after months of nursing . . .' I had said too much. At that moment I expected him to fire, and every muscle in my body was tensed in expectation of the bullet's slam. But then he said in a quieter, more reasonable voice. 'And McAvoy. What did McAvoy think?'

'About the letter?'

'Of course, yes. The letter. What else?'

I hesitated, wondering what he was after. 'He was just as puzzled as I was,' I said carefully.

'But you told me he came ashore here yesterday for the specific purpose of opening the safe and reading the letter. Why? What made him think it that important?' And when I told him about the wartime raid on Madehas and how Mac had described Colonel Holland as being shattered when he had opened the safe and found the letter, he said in a slow, almost unbelieving voice, 'So that's why he attacked Carola and murdered my father. He burned him alive. Did you know that?'

I nodded. 'But it wasn't quite like that, not according to Mac.' I wanted to mitigate the horror of it for a man already under great mental strain. 'There was a shot, from inside the house. He killed himself before the flames reached him.'

'Shot himself? My father shot himself.' He said it reflectively as though the idea was new to him. 'Yes, of course. He would have had a gun, and outside they would have been waiting for him, like a bunch of hunters round a foxhole.' He was silent for a moment, thinking about it, his head bent slightly, staring at the gun in his hand. And then slowly he seemed to relax, a conscious, deliberate unwinding of nervous tension. 'So he doesn't know. That little drunken bastard doesn't know. And now . . .' He hesitated, seeming to give the matter careful thought. 'Now nobody knows.'

'Knows what?' I asked, wondering if this was a form of madness, his mind wandering.

He shrugged, the gun forgotten, staring into space. I think I could have rushed him then, but I didn't; I was held in my chair by the look on his face, the way his whole body seemed frozen into immobility. 'Doesn't matter now, does it?' he said slowly. 'Doesn't matter how it all started, or what happened to the

Holland Trader. Tim knew. Old Colonel Holland knew. Now nobody knows but me and – ' He gave a little laugh. 'This morning it mattered. Now it doesn't.'

There was a rattling sound from beyond the windows leading to the verandah and he crossed the room, standing, staring out towards the cove. 'That's the LCT just arrived.' He looked at me, slowly putting the gun back into the waistband of his trousers, his mood altered. Suddenly he seemed in need of companionship. 'I don't remember my father, you know. Not really. I was only three when that old bastard moved on Queen Carola and fired burning arrows into the palm thatch of his house. His death didn't mean anything to me, not then.'

'But it does now?' He had fallen silent, pacing slowly.

He stopped and looked straight at me. 'You thought about death, about what it really means, or've you been too busy trying to make something of your life?'

'You sound like Mac,' I said. 'He started thinking about death.'

'So he should. But I'm not talking about drink and cirrhosis of the liver. That's something you bring on yourself. I'm talking about external forces, things you can't control and what it's like when it all blows up in your face.' He shook his head, muttering to himself, and then stood quite still, staring at nothing. 'We destroy people, like Red Holland going off and leaving that poor bugger to die of thirst, without giving a thought to what it means. Bombings, famines, executions – it's other people, isn't it? Never ourselves. And life – the fight to exist, the struggle for power – and then suddenly you've had it. That's what I mean by it all blowing up in your face. That's when you suddenly start wondering what the hell it's all in aid of. A mine collapses, a ship goes down, somebody shoots somebody, they're all expendable, all except oneself. That's right, isn't it? We form alliances, live in groups, get married, anything to conceal from ourselves the one terrible truth – that we're alone in this life.'

I got to my feet. 'You're being morbid,' I said, alarmed that in this sort of mood he might be capable of anything. 'You'd better start thinking about how you're going to get yourself out

of the mess you're in.' I couldn't make up my mind whether his
mood was suicidal or if he was now intent on destroying others.
'Are you staying here or coming back to the ship with me?' I
couldn't imagine anybody wanting to stay in this empty,
abandoned house.

He didn't answer, pacing slowly.

'I'll go back then.' I picked up the letter. 'You wanted this.'

He stared at it, frowning, as I held it out to him. He seemed
to have forgotten its existence. Then he suddenly laughed. 'He's
dead, too, isn't he? They're all dead now, just Perenna and
Jonathan left.' He nodded. 'Okay. You go back. The LCT is
right there, waiting to take you to Anewa where you'll make long
statements to satisfy government officials. But I tell you this,
Slingsby.' He was suddenly leaning forward, the red hair blazing
in the slanting sunlight, his eyes staring into mine. 'You marry
Perenna, you marry the Holland Line.' He came towards me,
smiling. 'You do that and you marry a curse. It was built on
hate and fear and disaster and it's done for every one of us –
every man that has tried to make his fortune out of it. My father
started it and he died an unnatural death. So did the old Colonel
and Perenna's mother, now Tim's dying, he's given up and he'll
die hating me, hating his sister, hating everyone, the whole
world.' He pointed his finger at me. 'You, too. You try and
succeed where I failed and you'll never know a minute's peace.
I'll haunt you, Slingsby. Even as my father has haunted me, I'll
haunt you.'

He was silent a moment, breathing heavily, his eyes staring
at me, unblinking. 'Okay,' he said. 'Get out now. Go back
to the world of trucks and ships and transistors. I'm taking a
different road.' He walked with me to the door almost in the
manner of a host in his own home. 'But just remember what I
said. There's enough evil in the world without you go looking
for it.'

He didn't say goodbye. He didn't offer me his hand or say
anything more. He just stared at me, his face set in harsh lines,
the hair no more than a dull reddish brown in the gloom of the
passageway, but the freckles visible against the dark leather of

his skin.

The last I saw of him was when I reached the summerhouse and some compulsion made me turn my head. The house was in shadow and he was standing in the main entrance, just his face lit by a shaft of sunlight striking through one of the tall palms so that I saw it as a disembodied face staring after me, the bones picked out in sharp crease shadows so that he looked suddenly older, the skin stretched taut like parchment, a death's-head almost, except for the hair which shone bright red as though it had been dyed.

The tug was already fetching her anchor as I started down the slope to the cove. The Mortlock islander was leaning over the blunt bows and framed in the open window of the caboose was the bearded face of the Australian. There was no sign of Perenna. Beyond the tug, looking unnaturally large by comparison, was the rusty box-like hulk of the LCT. The sun was already falling towards the west so that the two ships and their shadows seemed to fill the tiny cove. The water lay placid between the reefs and everything wilted in the hot humidity that lay like a haze over the Buka shore. It was enervating, but nevertheless comfortingly real after the house with its strange atmosphere, its sense of being entirely remote from the world outside Madehas.

Walking slowly, I tried to recall exactly what he had said. But though I can remember the words, it is not so easy to convey the impression they made on me. It wasn't only that I was surprised at his need to unburden himself, also I was conscious of a deep sense of uneasiness, and this uneasiness remained with me all the way down to the half-submerged pontoon. By then the tug was under way, steaming carefully past the LCT's stern out round the end of the reef. I watched her till she was lost in the haze of the Buka Passage beyond Minon, still thinking about Hans Holland, remembering the words he had used and wondering at their meaning, wondering whether Perenna would be able to make more sense of them than I did.

The silence of the cove was shattered by the busy roar of an outboard and the rubber dinghy came away from the LCT's side, swinging in a tight arc, heading for the pontoon. Five minutes later I was climbing the rope ladder and Perenna was standing there saying, 'What happened? I was afraid you weren't coming back.'

'Would it have mattered?'

'Yes, of course.' She said it without any trace of feeling. 'But why did you go?' She was frowning, and in that moment I was oddly reminded of Hans, the same vertical crease between eyes that had narrowed.

'I had to. I thought it was important. But apparently not.'

'You're being very mysterious. What has he told you? What did he say?'

'Nothing.' But that didn't satisfy her, so I said, 'He talked about his father's death . . . I don't know, a lot of things.' She was still frowning and though her eyes were looking straight at me, they had a strangely faraway look. At that moment she didn't seem conscious of me at all, so that I was reminded of what Hans had said about her, about all of them, wondering whether it was true that there was a dark, primitive side to her nature.

She walked with me up to the bridge in a sort of daze. Jona was there. 'Hans is staying on, is he?'

'Yes,' I said.

He nodded. 'Then there's nothing to keep us here.' And he started giving orders to man the foredeck and get the anchor up. They had picked up a brief exchange between one of the Fokker Friendships and Port Moresby. All four had landed safely on the roadway just beyond the Bovo River bridge. Cars had been waiting for them the other side of the bridge and the first troops were already moving on their objective by the time the planes were airborne again. 'Hans will have a lot of questions to answer.'

I thought he would, too, but all I said was, 'What made you come out to Buka with him in the tug?' He was looking more himself now, which was doubtless the effect of being in command of his own ship again. But he took a long time considering my question, and just as he seemed about to answer it, he was called out to the bridge wing. Luke, on the foredeck to see to the anchor, was pointing to the shore where the houseboy stood calling for the boat to come in. He was waving what appeared to be a letter in his hand.

So we stayed there in the heavy afternoon heat and Luke took the inflatable in. Clouds were building up over Bougainville, the sun hazy now, the glare from the water very trying. I was sleepy, too, physically and mentally exhausted. Luke reached the pontoon and I saw him talking to the houseboy. I was out on the bridge wing with Jona, trying to imagine there was a little breeze and thinking about a cold shower, when there was a sudden shout up for'ard, and then, as heads turned shoreward, a prolonged a-ah. 'Lukluk, Kepten!' Somebody was pointing, up beyond the palms and tree ferns, up to the house. For a moment I didn't see it, my mind just didn't register. I thought it was haze.

But then Luke yelled from the pontoon. 'Fire!'

I saw it then for what it was, smoke drifting lazily above the sloping roof. Suddenly there was flame added to the smoke, flames flickering yellow tongues out of an upstairs window. The ship was still and very silent, everybody staring. We could hear the crackle of the flames now. 'Why?' Perenna whispered. 'It's such a pointless thing to do.'

And then, as though to answer her question, came a shot. It was just one crack of sound, muffled, but very distinct, as though trapped and magnified by the sultriness of the atmosphere. 'Oh, my God!' Perenna reached out her hand, gripping mine so hard I could feel her nails biting into my palm. 'Did he have to do that?'

I didn't answer, merely put my arm round her shoulders. It was one way out and I understood now his need of companionship in those last minutes when I had been alone with him in the house, understood the drift of his talk, too, his concern about death. I was just sorry I had told him how his father had really died. But though that might have influenced the method, it wouldn't have affected the intention. 'I'm sorry,' I said, feeling Perenna's hand trembling. 'Such a waste. A man with such big ideas ...' What else was there to say except that he had been responsible for a number of deaths, including now his own.

The ship had erupted into violent activity, full of shouts and movement, so that I barely caught Perenna's words as she said, 'Are we all going to die – violently?' Her eyes were wide and staring, full of fear – a fear that was inside her, part of her being. 'Did he say anything about a curse?' she asked. And then, more urgently – 'Well, did he?'

'He wanted the letter, that was all.' And it was there in my trouser pocket, a crumpled piece of paper that was of no importance to him now he was dead.

Luke came back with the dinghy, loaded men and ferried them ashore. But even in this humid climate a few hours' sun was enough to bake wood dry as tinder. The house burned with an unnatural fury and nothing we could do about it with only fire buckets from the LCT and water from a rain cistern. And when the roof and the internal gallery collapsed in a roaring inferno of sparks and flame, that was the end, great billowing clouds of yellow smoke hanging over the north of the island like an enormous bonfire. In less than an hour there was nothing left of the main house but a great heap of grey ash from which a few smouldering beams and bits of buckled iron protruded. All we saved was some of the outhouses. We dampened everything down with countless buckets of water, then searched the debris. The safe was there, standing like a low tide rock in the ash, marking the position where the staircase had once been. The door was still open, everything inside it destroyed by the heat. No sign even of the little gold ingots. We found the gun, a blackened revolver, its barrel and chambers buckled by the heat. But no trace of Hans's body, which was really what we were looking for, to give him burial.

I don't think any of us were surprised not to find even a single bone, the heat had been so intense, the fire so furious. In the end, Jona scooped up two or three handfuls of the damp ash from the tangle of charred beams where we had found the gun and these he took on board with him carefully wrapped in his handkerchief and there transferred them to a round chromium plated cigarette box with rope and anchor decoration that was part of the wardroom furnishings. Then we went out with him into the middle of the cove in the rubber dinghy – just Perenna and myself with Luke at the outboard – and he read the burial service, then dropped the cigarette box into the water.

I remember thinking, as I watched the bright round metal of the box disappearing slowly from sight in the warm plant-green water of the cove, surely that's the end of it, the finish of what had begun so long ago with a man abandoning his partner at a place they had called Dog Weary in Central Australia? I was looking at Jona then, and at Perenna. Surely the malevolent effect of it couldn't go on for ever?

Luke had restarted the outboard. By the time we were back on board it was almost six, the sun set and the light fading. The Buka islanders were demanding to be put ashore. A gentle rain began to fall as we weighed and steamed out of the cove, out through the narrows between the Minon and Buka marker posts, past Sohano, past the jetty and the shops of Chinaman's Quay, past the market to the Government wharf where we lay alongside just long enough for Hans Holland's men, still armed, to scramble ashore. Then into the channel again, with the *Barreto* ferry sidling over from the mainland, and down the whole length of the Buka Passage until at last we were into the Pacific. It was only then, when we had turned south eastward toward Cape L'Averdy, seeing the dark green slopes of the Emperor Range rising into a thick mist of cloud, only then, with the old ship rolling slowly to the long ocean swell and the open sea ahead of us, that I felt myself free at last of the strange, haunting, and at times, it had seemed, positively evil atmosphere of Buka and the Buka Passage.

But then I remembered the note the houseboy had handed to Luke. The envelope, addressed to Perenna, was still in his pocket. He had forgotten all about it. But when I took it to her, she refused to read it, insisting that I read it for her. And when I had done so I didn't know whether to tell her or not. Hans had scribbled it moments before setting fire to the house. He had known what he was going to do, and he had done his best to ensure that the person most vulnerable should feel the weight of

the past hanging over her. She was looking up at me, very tense;
she must have seen my reaction for she suddenly changed her
mind. 'What's it say? Read it to me.' And when I had done so
she said hotly, 'It's a lie, a stinking, bloody lie.' And she added
quickly, 'I've heard it before. Tim mumbled it in delirium. But
it's a lie. My grandfather would never had done a thing like that
– his own daughter-in-law. It's unthinkable.' And she told me to
tear it up and throw the pieces overboard and not to say a word
about it to Jona. But I doubt whether it would have mattered
very much to him, not then. He had other problems on his
mind, for Simon Saroa, back in the signals office behind the
wheeelhouse, had picked up a message from Port Moresby
instructing the LCT to proceed with all speed to Kieta to
embark government troops being airlifted in the following
morning.

The situation, however, had changed by the time we had
rounded Cape L'Averdy. Kieta airport was unserviceable.
Before retreating the insurgents had blown the runway.
Moreover, there had been heavy rain during the late afternoon
and visibility had been so bad that the second airlift, which
would have had to use the road again, had been postponed until
the weather improved. We ourselves were then steaming
through a drizzle of rain that was so thick and humid it was
virtually cloud.

Dawn broke grey and miserable, the humidity thick and the
rain still falling. We had been ordered to Anewa, Kieta town still
being held by the Sapuru regime, and we were coming in on
radar with the tug just ahead of us as we steamed through the
northern channel between Takanupe Island and Bougainville. It
was almost nine before we were alongside the loading wharf,
where we were met by the captain in command of the PNG
airborne force. He was pale black, almost coffee-coloured,
dressed in jungle combat gear with a parachute flash on his arm
and he was asking for Perenna. Apparently his men had virtually
no ammunition left. Most of it had been handed over to the
police at Buka airfield and the rest had been expended in driving
the insurgents out of Kieta airport. With no further airlift from

Port Moresby to re-supply them they were now very vulnerable, the mining people having no weapons and being under orders not to become involved. But what Hans had said about the Chimbu mineworkers was true. There were several hundred of them in Arawa. They had already mounted a massive demonstration against the illegal regime which had already cut the insurgents off, so that they were now sealed into the Kieta Peninsula, except for a few key buildings they still held. However, the situation was still precarious, since the Highlanders refused to support the government forces without some guarantee for the future. This had been the situation for the past twenty-four hours, Tagup, their leader, insisting on speaking with Miss Holland before his people took any further action.

It was a strange situation. For that moment, it seemed, the fate of Bougainville lay in Perenna's hands. 'I think it is because the name Holland still means something, both here and in the Highlands of Papua New Guinea,' the captain said to her as we drove out of Anewa in a requisitioned Company car. 'I refer, of course, to your grandfather, Colonel Holland. The Chimbu mine workers need to be reassured that support of the legitimate government will secure their jobs at Paguna.'

Tagup was waiting for us at the sports centre where the Chimbu were camped in the stand and the changing rooms. On their way down from the mine they had found a red clay and with this they had decorated their bodies so that now they no longer looked like a labour corps but like the warriors they really were, and they were armed with whatever they had been able to lay their hands on at the mine – pangas, steel bars, giant spanners that they held like battle axes, some had even made bows and arrows from wood cut from the rain forest.

The captain took Perenna alone to meet Tagup, then left the two of them talking together in the Chimbu tongue. The tribesmen were gathered round, but still leaving a space, so that they remained a little apart, and everyone waited.

Finally Tagup raised his hand in parting, smiling now. Then he turned abruptly and went towards his men, his face set and determined, his eyes flashing as he gave the order to march.

281

Perenna, rejoining us, said, 'I told him what had happened at Madehas and in the Buka Passage. He realized the driving force had gone out of the insurrection, the organization too. Now he'll settle it in his own way.'

The battle that followed was a most extraordinary affair, a very noisy, blood-curdling, colourful non-event. The insurgents were concentrated in the new District Office building and in the Police Station. Cut off from Arawa, they had only been able to grab some half dozen expatriate whites whom they were holding as hostages on the top floor of the District Police offices. No attempt was made to storm either this building or the District HQ. The Chimbu labourers advanced in serried ranks, their bodies half naked and freshly daubed with paint, crayons, cosmetics, anything they had been able to get hold of, but each advance was no more than a mock attack to be followed by withdrawal and a wild yelling of taunts. Advance, retreat, advance, retreat, the noise increasing, the distance lessening. Half Arawa, expatriate whites included, came out to cheer them on. Occasionally a shot was fired from District HQ, but more in warning than in anger. Nobody was hurt.

The rain had lessened to a light drizzle, the clouds were lifting and it was hot when Tagup, dressed in nothing but a few broad green leaves, his body painted with an intricate pattern in red and wielding a brand new fire axe, came out to stand a dozen yards or more ahead of his Chimbu battle groups, all drawn up in line. Here he called upon Daniel Sapuru to come out and fight, challenging him to single combat.

They were two men of uncertain age, but both of them elders and certainly not young; this was politics, not mortal combat. At first there was no reaction from the other side, the white concrete walls of the District Offices standing blank and silent in the hot glimmer of misty humidity that lay like a blanket over the scene, Tagup standing there shouting taunts that were echoed by the black glistening lines of bodies behind him. Perenna, translating for me, suddenly said in a quite different voice: 'He's changed it. He's challenging Sapuru, not as a fighter – as . . . he's challenged his power – '

'What power?' I asked.

'They're not just political leaders, they both have – ' But a door had opened and a small, very dark man in a light blue suit came out. He stood there for a moment, his head held high, the black halo of his hair framed in the arch of the entrance. The ranks of the Chimbu swept forward, a tide of glistening bodies uttering a low menacing roar. Tagup raised his hand. The ranks of his men halted, the roar fell to a murmur, then a sudden silence and Tagup walked forward, moving very slowly, very deliberately. Sapuru, too, was moving forward. A shot was fired. It came from one of the ground floor windows, sounding very loud in the stillness. A howl of fury swept the Highlanders' ranks. Sapuru half turned, his face clouded with anger, his hand raised.

Silence again and the two men walking towards each other. Sapuru was unarmed. The Chimbu leader discarded his axe. They met halfway between the black ranks of the Chimbu and the white blank face of the District Offices. They talked, and while they talked the glimmer of sun heat in the mist increased. Tagup turned, shouted something to his followers and they answered with a roar, fanning out on either flank and moving forward, stopping suddenly when he raised his hand. This movement was repeated three times, each time the black mass of men spreading out to encircle the offices, moving steadily nearer. And then, suddenly, it was over, Sapuru turning and walking back into the building, Tagup calling to the PNG captain who came marching forward at the head of his men to take up a position facing District HQ.

There was a moment's hiatus then when time seemed to stand still, no sound, no movement, everybody waiting, tense and expectant. And the glimmer turned to sunlight, the mist burning away to reveal the high green interior of the island still wrapped in cloud, pinnacles of grey rock appearing and disappearing. Then Sapuru reappeared. A great *a-ah* of released tension went up from the crowd as the hostages came out behind him. They hurried to the safety of the jungle-green uniforms, and then the Buka insurgents were coming out of the building, some of them men I recognized as having been part of the crew of the LCT coming across from Australia, all of them carrying their weapons and laying them down in front of the captain.

There had been no fight, no last ditch stand. The insurrection was over and the defeat of the insurgents had been achieved by bluff, by a show of strength. And something else, too – some inner power. He's more than a politician, Perenna had said, and I could only guess at the secret trial of strength that had gone on between those two men. And now suddenly it was over, no bloodshed, not a single hostage harmed. By evening more troops had arrived and the LCT was under charter to the PNG Government to take the insurgents back to Buka, all except Daniel Sapuru and a dozen or so leaders of the Buka Trading Co-operative. ·

That night I lay between fresh-laundered sheets in a bed that was rock steady and did not move with the motion of the ship. I was tired, but I couldn't sleep, thinking of Perenna just a few doors down the cement walkway of the motel where we had found accommodation, wondering what she would do now, whether she would accept Hans Holland's advice or whether she would ignore it and try to run her brother's life and the Holland Line, the two in harness. The torn pieces of that last letter of his were drifting soggily somewhere in the dark depths of the Pacific, and though it was that first line of his to which she had reacted so violently – *My father and yours were brothers, each destroying what the other built* – I could remember every line. It had gone on – *Take my advice. Let the Holland Line founder. It has cost too many lives. Or else burn the stamps so that nobody else can ever know.* And he had added, *Goodbye, Perenna. I was cursed before ever I was born.*

It was that last line, in conjunction with his opening – *My father and yours were brothers* – that my mind fastened on, and Perenna's reaction, her statement that it had been blurted out by Tim. She had leapt to the instant conclusion that he was saying her grandfather, Colonel Lawrence Holland, had been her natural father. *His own daughter-in-law . . . It's unthinkable*. But unthinkable or not, if it was Colonel Holland, then the only

284

brother he had ever had was Carlos of the *Holland Trader* and the wooden masks and stamps. Carlos Holland! If it was Carlos Holland who was Hans's father, then he must have survived the loss of the *Holland Trader*, must have known what had happened to it, and had then spent the last thirty years of his life masquerading as a distant cousin. It would explain Colonel Lawrence Holland's reaction on finding that letter from Lewis in the safe at Madehas. No wonder he had been filled suddenly with such demoniac anger that fratricide became the only answer. A man who could leave his partner waterless . . . I was thinking of the *Holland Trader* then. Christ! Lewis, that letter, the stamps . . . The thought that had leapt into my mind was enough to bring curses upon any family.

There was a gentle tap on the door and Perenna came in. 'Roy.' She was a dim shape in the darkness, feeling her way towards me. 'I couldn't sleep. I think I'm too tired to sleep. I keep thinking . . .'

'About what?'

I pulled back the sheet and she reached down to me. 'About Hans — that letter chiefly and what happened to him.' I could smell the warmth of her as our bodies met and I held her close. 'Do you think he's really dead?' she breathed. 'Or was the letter, the shot, the fire . . . was it all a stupid game?'

'He's dead,' I said, but with more conviction than I felt. 'He won't trouble you again.'

'No?' She lay very still. 'Then that's the end of Carlos Holland. Hans was the last of his blood.' She was trembling slightly as she said that. 'Where's Mac? Is he all right?'

'He's sober again, if that's what you mean. He's gone north with your brother.'

'I'm glad. But I ought to have gone with them. As long as I'm with Mac . . . He's getting old now.'

'You think you can keep him off the drink?'

'I could try. But not now.' She pressed her body close against me.

'What about the stamps?' I asked. 'Are you going to take Hans's advice — burn them, forget all about the past and — '

'No. I want to know the truth now. If I know the truth, then I can face it and that's the end of the curse, isn't it? If only Tim . . .' She stopped there, burying her head in my shoulder. She stayed like that, very still for a moment, then she whispered, 'But that's for tomorrow. Let's forget now.'

So we forgot, leaving the truth for the morrow.

PART FIVE

SOLOMONS SEAL

—

The next few days became increasingly difficult for us as the
PNG Government moved quickly to restore its grip on the
island. Two airlifts of troops were followed by police reinforcements and the civil administration was strengthened with the
arrival of a senior Government official and extra staff, together
with a judge and two political officers to enquire into the cause
of the insurrection. Screening of personnel began immediately
and all whites, other than mining company employees, had their
passports confiscated. In our case, we not only became for the
time being prisoners-at-large in Bougainville, but were subjected
to endless questioning as a result of a statement made by
Shelvankar.

It was from this statement, passages from which were read out
at various times when I appeared before the Court of Enquiry,
that I learned the full seriousness of Jona's position. In no sense
was he Hans's partner, he had simply borrowed money from
him. As managing director of the Holland Line, a private
limited company of which he and Perenna were the sole
shareholders, he was responsible for the fact that it had been
operating so consistently at a loss over recent years that its sole
asset, the LCT, had become totally committed as security for
loans the company could not repay. As a result, he had been
forced to agree to the cargoes Hans had arranged through
Shelvankar, and in the case of the voyage from Sydney to Anewa

and the lifting off the Queensland beach of the two truckloads of automatic weapons that had made the establishment of the Bougainville-Buka Republic possible, he had known very well that he was becoming involved in something highly illegal.

All this came out in the first two days of the Enquiry, so that on his return from transporting troops and police reinforcements to Buka, Jona was arrested and the LCT impounded. Later he was released on his undertaking not to leave the Bougainville District. I thought at the time stronger action might have been taken against him if it had not been for his sister's part in persuading the Chimbu workers to parade their strength and so save the lives of the hostages. Also, something quite unexpected occurred the day after his return. This was the death of Sapuru.

He wasn't executed. Nobody had arranged his assassination. His body was quite unmarked. And I can vouch for that as I saw it in hospital when I visited Perry, who had been roughly handled trying to escape back to Paguna. And it wasn't a heart attack, or cancer, or any identifiable disease; it was sorcery. Witness after witness swore to the fact that he had just lain down and died. And the doctors found nothing wrong with any of the organs. Rumour had it that it was a case of pay-back, that Tagup was a great sorcerer and could call upon spirits more powerful than Sapuru's island ancestors. Logic, on the other hand, suggested that it was probably a case of extreme dejection following the failure of his coup, a complete moral and physical disintegration resulting in total lack of the will to live.

But if that is the explanation something occurred immediately afterwards that is totally beyond rational explanation. However, I didn't know about it at the time. All I knew was that Sapuru had died suddenly and mysteriously, and that Eddie Wurep, the Senior Government official, had ordered a post-mortem to be carried out in the presence of Joseph Nasogo and one or two other Buka islanders who had worked at District HQ. This was to forestall any rumours that he had been eliminated for political reasons. The pathologists were from the hospital in Arawa, a black doctor and a white surgeon assisted by two black nurses. A Government medical officer was also present.

By then I was told it was generally accepted, even on Buka, that responsibility for his death did not lie with the police or with any government agency, that nobody had physically assaulted him. But what he had died of neither of the medical experts were prepared to say. I made a point of talking to them afterwards and both of them admitted they had experienced cases like this before, cases where a man – it was men, rather than women – had just lain down and died for no apparent reason. Sorcery? They agreed it was a distinct possibility, though the word sorcery was mentioned with reluctance as something that by their training and profession they should have outlawed completely from their minds.

The white surgeon was a New Zealander and he took me to his home in Arawa, where he gave me a drink and to make his point clear produced an encyclopaedia. This bracketed sorcery with witchcraft, and under *Witchcraft in Australia and Melanesia* it said that, as in Africa, death or illness was seldom thought to be due to natural causes, adding that the chief function of sorcery was to discover the person who had caused the illness or the death. *Vengeance must then be taken on the enemy*. This it referred to as pay-back and said it could be done by pointing a stick or bone. Pointed at the victim, and saturated with the sorcerer's curses, *belief in its potency does the rest*. And of Melanesia, in particular, it said, *Belief in the possession of supernatural powers by certain men is universal and these powers are feared and sought by all*.

That evening Tagup came to the motel to say goodbye to Perenna. He was flying to Port Moresby and on to Goroka in the morning. Dressed again in his white shirt and shorts, the silver Councillor shield glinting over the breast pocket, he looked very different to the near-naked fight leader who had pranced and taunted and brandished his axe at the head of the black howling ranks of his Highland people. In twenty-four hours he would be over 5,000 feet up in his grass-thatched house, with his wives and his many grandchildren, wearing nothing but a few broad blades of grass. No, he said, smiling in self-derogation, he was not really responsible for Sapuru's death. But he had warned him that a death wish had been put upon him by a man he had tried to harm, a man who was injured and was a kiap. 'He knew at once,' he said, looking directly at Perenna. And he added that an old curse, one that had not been powerful enough to destroy a man like Sapuru, who was himself a sorcerer, until after he had been defeated, could well have brought about his death when his vitality was at a low ebb and the will to live so reduced that he had become vulnerable.

That I think is the nearest anybody will ever come to a solution of the mysterious death of Daniel Sapuru, the two-day president of Bougainville-Buka. Shortly after that Perenna and I had our passports handed back to us and we were told we were free to leave whenever we wished. By then we were into the second week of August. The LCT was still in Kieta Bay, empty except for a police guard. The three RPLs were anchored nearby and up for sale. The Government had confiscated all Hans's property, together with that of the Buka Trading Co-operative. Everything, land, trucks, ships, was being sold to provide compensation for the cost incurred by Government in re-establishing their authority in the island. Jona and Perenna had been informed that the LCT was being held as the property of Hans Holland and would be sold under the terms of the compensation decree already issued unless they could repay all loans made to the Holland Line by Hans Holland before the end of the month. And it was made very clear that this concession, and the leniency shown to her brother, was in recognition of the part she had played in saving the lives of the hostages and bringing the insurrection to a speedy and bloodless end. Unfortunately, the concession as it applied to the LCT was of little help to us. The amount outstanding now totalled 38,000 *Kina*, which was the equivalent of just on A$47,000. This was almost exactly what enquiries through the kind offices of the mine management indicated the ship might fetch for scrap in the open market.

It was the end of any hope I might have had of taking over the running of the ship and trying to make the Holland Line profitable. And it had been profitable until Hans had started undercutting the two coasters Jona had originally operated with his more economical, more practical Ramp Propelled Lighters.

It was the end of the Holland Line and for Perenna a bitter blow. She felt it much more than Jona for whom the Line meant very little. It was only the ship that mattered to him, and even that wasn't very important since he didn't anticipate any great difficulty in getting command of a vessel belonging to one of the major shipping companies, which would have the advantage that he would no longer have to worry about the business side.

The day I left for Australia we drove down to Kieta early in the morning, just before sunrise when the world was still fresh, and walked along the beach hand-in-hand under the palm trees. All the eastern horizon was a blaze of red, and against this flaming dawn sky the slab-sided, box-like shape of the LCT rose black in shadow, a cut-out silhouette of a ship, the sea so still and red it might have been molten lava.

She was an ugly vessel. At least I suppose she was, being totally functional, with no concessions to anything other than the purpose for which she had been designed. But to me she had the beauty of an unattainable dream. I don't know whether it was the dream or the ship I had come down to say goodbye to, but there it all was – a ship of my own and a line to run . . . and I was taking the flight to Port Moresby later that day.

For Perenna it was much more than the end of a dream, and she was in tears as we stood looking at the familiar shape of the little vessel standing so clearcut against that translucent sunrise sky. And then the red eliptical curve of the sun's rim inched up over the horizon right behind her, so that the shape of her became framed in the thrusting orb and Perenna gasped in astonishment, for it appeared as though she was being consumed in fire. I could feel her fingers digging into my hand, sensed her feelings that the ship represented something that had been a part of her all her life. That was all that remained of the trading schooners, the old post-war coasters and MFVs, the long line of vessels stretching back three-quarters of a century to the *Holland Trader*, and in a few weeks' time it would go for scrap . . . 'Carlos, my grandfather, Jona, us – ' Her grip on my hand had tightened, her voice more husky than usual – 'Red Holland, too, I suppose – Carlos in a new guise – and Hans.' She paused, thinking back to her childhood. 'Mac, all those skippers – I can't remember their names now – there must have been half a dozen of them – and the crews. So many people, all involved in keeping the islands supplied and taking their crops to market. And now it's finished – up for sale. Scrap.' There was a catch in her voice as she said that final word and she let go of my hand, turning abruptly away.

Halfway to the car, in command of herself again, she said in a small, tight voice, 'When I came on board, that first day, in the evening, standing in the wheelhouse – I watched you at the chart table working out our position – I thought then, knowing something of your background, conscious of the way you had dealt with those stamps and got money out to me when I needed it, I thought – this is the man to get the Holland Line on its feet again.'

'Is that why you fell into my bunk?' I said it lightly, an attempt to lift her out of her mood, though deep down I was hurt, knowing there was a calculating streak in most women.

She stopped, turning on me quickly. 'Don't be silly, Roy. It's just that I never thought to fall in love with a man who could match my own background – my own needs if you like. Not physical, I don't mean that – ' Her voice trailed away. 'I'm not putting it very well.'

'You're putting it very clearly.' Suddenly I wanted to hurt her, test her reaction, and I couldn't stop myself – 'You wanted a man with certain business and technical expertise to put the Holland Line back in business. You think I'm the man, so you fall in love with me – to order.'

She looked at me, her lips trembling, the scar over her left ear white in the sun's blaze. I thought she was going to burst into tears. Instead, she suddenly gave that explosive little laugh. 'If that's what you want to believe – maybe it's true. Maybe women do fall in love – to order, as you put it – when they meet a man they think can turn their hopes into reality.' And she added, 'It's as good a basis for mating as any, very practical.' She turned and walked quickly back to the car.

But later, when she drove me to the airport, her mood had softened again and it was I who was thinking about the future. All morning I hadn't been able to get the sight of those ships out of my mind, and now, standing in the shade of the airport building, waiting to board the Fokker Friendship shimmering out there in the hot sun, I told her about my arrangement with Chips Rowlinson. 'As soon as the sale is over I'll have some idea what my ten per cent of the increased value of the property will amount to. It won't be enough, but I should be able to borrow the rest of it on the scrap value of the ship.'

She stared at me unbelievingly. 'Are you serious? You're ready to throw everything you hope to get . . .' She was suddenly laughing, almost crying, her arms round my neck, her lips on mine. 'Darling! You're incredible. I love you.' Everybody was staring at us, passengers, ground crew, everybody, white teeth bright in the dark faces. They looked as though they were about to cheer as I took hold of her arms rather self-consciously and said, 'There are conditions.'

She leaned her head back, her hair in the sun now and shining like fire, her eyes narrowing against the glare. 'What conditions?'

'First, that I take over the business management of the company. And get paid for it. I'm looking for a job, remember. Second, that the company is reorganized and only those who put new money into it hold shares. Third, you contribute anything more you get from the sale of the Carlos Holland stamp collection.' I didn't tell her about the single sheet of the Solomons Seal labels in my briefcase and I warned her that I might make nothing out of the Munnobungle sale, and even if I did get something out of it it might not be enough and I might not be able to raise the rest of the money. 'So just keep your fingers crossed. Oh, and there's another condition,' I told her as the boarding announcement was made and I kissed her goodbye. 'You and the LCT go together. Is that understood?'

'What's that supposed to mean?' she called after me.

'That we get married,' I said, waving to her as I joined the passengers moving out to board the aircraft. And as we turned at the runway end I could just see the brightness of her hair moving through a crowd of islanders to the parking lot.

Next day I was in Brisbane and Cooper was facing me with a decision I didn't want to take. He had received two offers for Munnobungle. The first, from a neighbouring station owner on the Burdekin, had been made shortly after I had sailed for Bougainville. The second was from an agricultural company and was the result of his having advertised the sale. Both offers were close to the figure he had thought the property should fetch. The private buyer had now matched the company's offer so that I had the choice of two certain buyers at a price that would put almost nine thousand dollars in my pocket. Just enough, I thought, to make up the difference between the amount the Holland Line owed and the loan I could expect to raise on the scrap value of the ship.

'Two birds in the hand,' Cooper said. 'Better than I'd have expected on the figures.' He advised acceptance. The policy of the company was to buy privately, never at auction, and with the present state of the market he thought the best we could hope for at auction would be something around the present offers and it might well be lower.

I said I would have to cable Rowlinson, but he had already done that and handed me the reply. It was terse and addressed to me personally: *Decide for yourself its what your there for – Rowlinson*.

Auction or private treaty, it made little difference to the agents' commission, so I accepted Cooper's advice as being impartial and left for Munnobungle the next day. I felt McIver had a right to some say in the choice of purchasers and both he and his wife seemed quite touched that I should have thought of consulting them. I had expected them to prefer the local station owner, but as soon as they knew who it was they opted for the company, one of whose directors had already visited Munnobungle and had indicated that if the company offer was accepted the McIvers could stay on.

I phoned Cooper in Brisbane, told him to close with the

company, and with that settled, I was free to take a trip north to Cooktown to locate Minya Lewis. I wanted to find out what had happened to his father, if he really was the Merlyn Dai Lewis who had shipped as stoker aboard the *Holland Trader* in July 1911. Also, I had a feeling I might discover the reason Hans had been so determined to get his hands on anything connected with those Solomons Seal ship labels. It was almost as though they were some damning piece of evidence that had to be acquired at any cost.

Cooktown from the air was a straggle of neatly laid out clapboard buildings facing on to the muddy estuary of the Endeavour River and its mangrove swamps. The memorial to Cook was clearly visible as we came in over Grassy Hill and there were wallabies bounding through the long grass at the edge of the airfield where we landed. We were met by a minibus and as soon as I mentioned the name Lewis the driver said, 'You want the Old Timers' Hotel. They'll get Dog Weary Lewis for you.'

We passed the gold rush cemetery and shortly afterwards he dropped me off at an old wooden hotel building. The big bar room that occupied most of the ground floor was almost empty, only a few old men propping up one end of the counter and the barman talking to them. Silence fell as I dumped my things and enquired for Lewis. 'Old bastard's usually here by now,' the barman said, coming over to me. 'Want to buy him a beer and hear his story, do you?'

'Something like that.'

'Okay, mate.' He looked across at the little huddle of habitués. 'Go fetch him, Les.' He came and joined me, leaning hairy arms on the counter, the pale dome of his head with its few hairs carefully slicked down outlined against one of the gold rush murals that decorated the walls. He had a beer with me while we waited and when I asked him where the Dog Weary mine was, he said it was on the edge of the Simpson, way over beyond the Georgina. 'Helluva long way from here, and what's so bloody silly, he can't get it into his thick woolly head that it was worked out years ago, before he was even born, I reck'n.'

He wouldn't tell me anything about Black Holland, only that Lewis had killed him because of an argument over the mine. 'Ain't fair to spoil his racket for him. That's how he pays for his drinks, telling Pommies and others like you about the Dog Weary and how he killed a man over it. Except for one time when he got some sort of a legacy, or maybe he stole something. Anyways, he was flush with money for the better part of six months.' I asked how long ago that would be, and when he said about three years, I knew it must have been the cash from the sale of the Solomons Seal cover.

Frosted glass windows, and mirrors advertising plug tobacco I had never heard of, gave the place an Edwardian appearance. 'Custom-built for the gold miners,' the barman said over his shoulder as he dealt out beers to the old men at the far end. 'All red plush. You wouldn't believe it, looking at the town now, but there were sixty-five saloons and a score of eating houses then, that's what they say. And the cemetery full of kids dead within months of being born. You have a gander at the gravestones. There's men there that were brought in by ship at the turn of the century dying of blackwater fever.'

We were on to our second beer when Lewis finally arrived. God knows what age he was, his hands gnarled and trembling, his shoulders stooped, the muscles of his neck standing out like cords, wiry hair turned grey. He was small and tough-looking, his face so creased and wrinkled it looked like the face of a mummy dried and preserved in the hot Queensland sun. 'Heard you're gonna buy me a beer.' His voice was deep and husky, barely intelligible. 'Then I tell you about Dog Weary mine.' He wore a dark serge suit that hung loosely on his thin frame and the bulging eyes that stared at me greedily were blue like sapphires in a bloodshot yellow setting.

I bought him a beer and straight away he began talking. It was a long, rambling tale about his father being left to die in the desert by his partner. In essence, it was what I had already read in that letter.

'What was your father's name?' I asked.

'Him Lewis.'

'I want his Christian names.' The blue eyes stared uncomprehendingly. 'Was his name Merlyn Dai Lewis?'

He nodded, the black wizened face without expression.

'And the partner, what was his name?'

'Him take water, gun, everything. Come back after, dig gold.'

'Who? Who was his partner?'

'Holland.'

'The man you killed?'

He looked puzzled. 'Him Black Holland. This man his father. Red Holland.' And he went on to tell me how his father had been rescued by some aborigines on walkabout, how he had travelled with them back across all the deserts of Australia. He had married an aborigine girl and had worked in the gold fields around Kalgoorlie. 'Me born in the desert and some time we live in Ora Banda.' Then they had come east, to Cooktown where he had been brought up, and his father had gone off to find the man who had left him to die in the desert and get his share of the gold.

'What happened then?' I asked.

'Him never come back.' And he added, 'Mama spik me. She very sad papa no come back, she very poor so me go look white fellow. But white fellow him dead too.' There was something I couldn't follow then, about being shot and put in a hospital. The name Black Holland was mentioned. And then suddenly with a sweeping gesture of his hand: 'Sometime me hear him working Queensland, find him and he laugh at me. Him very drunk, say many things – say Dog Weary bilong him. So me kill him an' now Dog Weary bilong me. Savvy?'

The barman laughed, coming towards us and leaning his elbows on the counter again. 'Same old story, is it? Can't get that bloody mine out of his head. Talks of going there, but never has. Lazy bastard.' He looked across at Lewis, smiling and tapping his forehead. 'Yu *longlong*. That's Pidgin for crazy. Reck'n it was the war.' And without my asking he got another can of beer out of the fridge.

'You mean he was wounded in the war?' I asked him.

'That's right. Something I reck'n he didn't bargain for since he was in the Pioneer Corps. Got sent to Bougainville an' the Black Dogs put a bullet through his neck. Got it through there, didn't you, mate?' And he pointed a dirty finger at the old man's neck. 'Well, never mind. Drink that.' And he put the can down in front of him.

Lewis filled his glass and drank half of it in a single swallow. Then, wiping his mouth on the back of his hand, he began telling me how he had found Black Holland working on a sugar plantation near the coast. His voice was already a little slurred and it was difficult to follow, but I thought what he was saying was that this was the man who had shot him during the war. There was an argument over his father and who owned the Dog Weary mine and Black Holland had suddenly drawn a knife. Then, quite clearly, he said there had been a fight and in the struggle he had seized the knife and ripped the man's belly open with it.

'When did this happen?' I asked.

It was the barman who answered. 'A long time back. In 1952, and this murdering old bastard gets away with manslaughter.' The barman's face cracked in a grin that showed sharp, brown-stained teeth. 'The way he tells it you'd think the other fella started it. But I've heard it said it wasn't like that at all, and the old-timers here, they say it was pay-back, that after the war he went looking for Holland. That's right, ennit?' And he glanced along the counter to the old men drinking and listening, and they all nodded.

'Because he was wounded in Kieta?' I asked.

'No. Because of the mine and what happened to his father.'

It seemed incredible that this shrunken, wizened little black should have gone looking for the man and killed him because of what happened out there on the edge of the Simpson so many years before. 'What happened to your father?' I asked him. 'He's dead, isn't he? When did he die?'

The old man stared at me, and when I repeated the question, he buried his face in his beer and didn't answer.

'Always the same,' the barman said. 'Tells his story the way he wants, but start slinging a few questions at him and he shuts up.'

'In July 1911,' I told him, 'your father was in Sydney and signed on as a stoker on the *Holland Trader*. That's right, isn't it?' The old man nodded almost imperceptibly, but when I asked him what had happened to the *Holland Trader*, he just stood there staring at me out of eyes that had suddenly become frightened, his black face puckered and worried. He knew I wasn't a tourist, and when I asked him about the letter his mother had received, at almost the very moment the *Holland Trader* had disappeared, he seemed to confuse it with the envelope, those blue eyes of his darting this way and that as he said, 'Bilong me. Yu speak Father Matthew. He get stamp money and take forty dollar for the Mission.'

I tried again, explaining that I knew about the stamps and the money he had been paid, but what I wanted was the letter that had been inside the envelope. But all he said was, 'Yu polis?' And he gulped down the rest of his beer like a man about to flee.

'I told you,' the barman said with a grin. 'Start asking him questions and he clams up.'

But I got it out of him in the end. I took him by the arm and more or less frog-marched him to a table, then I bought him another beer, sat him down opposite me and began talking to him, asking him the same questions over and over again. I wasn't police, but he must have thought I was giving a pretty good imitation. How did he know it was Red Holland who had been his father's partner? Had his mother told him or was it in the letter? But hadn't she shown him the letter?

It was a silly question. He'd had to go to Father Matthew to have the letter about the stamps written, so it was obvious he couldn't read or write. 'Were there any other letters from your father?'

He shook his head. 'No. No more letters.'

'So why did you kill Black Holland? He wasn't your father's partner. He had nothing to do with it. Why did you kill him?'

'Him say things against my papa.'

'What sort of things?'

'Bad things.'

'Accusations, lies, taunts – what? What sort of things?'

Those sapphire blue eyes were wide and staring. He was drunk now. He didn't care and suddenly it all came out, the whole terrible story. It was pay-back and the avenger blown to pieces, obliterated, sunk by his own weapon of vengeance. And he hadn't got it from a letter or from his mother. He had got it direct from the drunken mouthings of Red Holland's illegitimate half-caste island son, the man who had become notorious during the war as one of the chief leaders of the Black Dogs of Kieta.

The way he told it I found great difficulty in piecing it together into a coherent story, but the first thing to emerge clearly confirmed that Carlos Holland and Red Holland were the same person. It was Carlos Holland who had left his partner to die on the edge of the Simpson desert. It was Carlos who had formed a mining company and developed the Dog Weary mine, and with the money from that he had founded the Holland Line of schooners and made himself the uncrowned king of the islands around the Buka Passage. And in Sydney, in July 1911, the past had caught up with him, his one-time partner shipping as stoker on his newly acquired vessel. Lewis was an experienced miner. He had time fuses and explosives concealed in his personal belongings, and with these he had mined the ship.

But it hadn't been his intention to blow it up. It was merely a threat, his son assured me, the means by which he hoped to force Carlos Holland to give him the compensation he had so far refused. Instead, Carlos Holland had drugged him and had him carried on board the *Holland Trader* as a drunk. He had put him in his own bunk, where he had smothered him with a pillow. He had then gone ashore again – 'Him spik Kepten big bisnis in Port Moresby. After, ship sail and finish downbilow sea when bombs explode. All men die.'

When he said that I knew it was true. It explained something that had been worrying me since Mac had described Colonel Holland's reaction to that letter we had found in the safe. If Carlos and Red Holland were one and the same person, Colonel Holland would have known it at once. After all, Carlos was his younger brother. He might pass himself off to the islanders as a

distant cousin who bore a close family resemblance and who had
inherited the Holland Line, but he couldn't possibly have fooled
his brother Lawrence. Presumably he had been able to produce
some specious and very convincing reason for his behaviour –
debts, for instance, something as impersonal as financial
difficulties that would explain his leaving the *Holland Trader* at
Port Moresby and assuming another identity. Colonel Holland
may have had his suspicions, but if he had, doubtless he had put
them aside, making allowance for his brother and giving him the
benefit of the doubt. But that night, when he had raided
Madehas and opened the safe, reading the letter that had begun
Dear Red and discovering for the first time that Carlos's wealth
was built on the abandonment of his partner to a slow death,
that he had lied and lied again, that he was a pitiless monster –
that sudden opening of his eyes to what his brother was capable
of doing had come as a great and appalling shock – shattering,
Mac had called it. Not only had Carlos Holland killed Merlyn
Lewis, his one-time partner, but he had sent the captain and his
entire crew to their deaths, and he had done it without pity,
without a thought for their families. This was what his son,
Hans, had had to live with ever since he opened the safe and
found that letter, those sheets of stamps. Ever since then he had
known his father was a pitiless murderer. And he had known,
too, that the money he had inherited, the basis of his little fleet
of RPLs, was blood money, stemming from those murderous
actions.

It was then that an idea came to me – if I could show in a
court of law that Hans Holland's assets were based on money his
father had obtained from the sinking of the *Holland Trader*, then
the insurance company, not the PNG Government, would have
the prior claim. At least it might delay things until after the
stamps had been sold. Even if I could raise a loan, interest rates
were high and an extra two or three thousand pounds would
make all the difference to our ability to keep the ship
operational.

I wrote out a statement for Lewis to sign right there in the
hotel, then took him along to a solicitor and had it typed, signed

and witnessed as a statutory declaration. I think he was so frightened and confused that he barely knew what he was doing.

Next day, in Sydney, I checked with the newspaper offices, but to turn up any story they might have run on the amount of the insurance paid out on the *Holland Trader* meant searching page by page through the file copies for the last months of 1911 and probably most of 1912 as well. They suggested I contact Lloyd's agents. This I did and within the hour they phoned me back to confirm that the *Holland Trader* had been insured with a Lloyd's syndicate. The claim was for £8,900 and it had been met in full. Payment, however, had been delayed due to the owner having been on board and the need to wait for his will to be proved. Settlement had finally been made on January 4, 1913. And they added that, since the ship was a total loss, the Lutine Bell had been rung for her.

I got the name of the Lloyd's syndicate from them and turned the whole thing over to the solicitors who were looking after the Munnobungle sale for me. The information was sufficient for them to get an injunction in the High Court in Port Moresby restraining the Government from impounding any of Hans Holland's assets pending proof of ownership. That was on 18 August and two days later the LCT was loading copra off a beach in the north of Bougainville for delivery to Rabaul. She sailed with Mac as master and Perenna on board to keep an eye on him.

It was, in fact, most fortunate that we were successful in freeing the vessel without immediate payment, for as foreigners, I had by then discovered that it was impossible for us to obtain a loan in Australia. A few days later I had another piece of luck – quite by accident I was able to arrange a cargo for the ship at Rabaul, a consignment of road building equipment urgently needed in Guadalcanal. If I hadn't been invited to the City Club sauna I wouldn't have heard about that cargo and it occurred to me then that Sydney was probably the key to the successful operation of an LCT in the South West Pacific. I rented a room in Strathfield, between the Paramatta and Hume highways, installed a telephone and within a week I was in business, booking cargoes forward.

Booking them was one thing, however, getting paid for them quite another and it didn't take me long to realize we had a cash flow problem. Fuel bills and running costs had to be met and by the end of September the ship was in Lae and unable to proceed to Madang for her next cargo due to an unpaid fuel bill. By reducing the freight charge I was able to get payment in advance, but with legal charges to meet and the bank insisting we clear our overdraft, there was only one thing to do if the Holland Line was to survive. That was to return to England and sell everything we had. For Perenna it meant the woodcarvings as well as the stamps, also a few other mementoes she had kept out of the Aldeburgh sale; for me it was my boat, my car, my own collection of stamps and the Solomons Seal sheet I had taken from the safe at Madehas.

I had already been notified that Josh Keegan's big autumn stamp auction was fixed for the two days commencing 24 October and when I phoned him to say I now had a full sheet of sixty of the Solomons Seal ship labels, he said he would decide whether to include them in the auction when he had seen them; he advised me to bring them in my hand luggage, packed flat and in cellophane, and to take great care of them. He had sounded sufficiently interested for me to think we might just scrape together enough to give us the working capital we needed.

Perenna arrived in Sydney on 20 October, the day before we were due to fly to England. Those few hours we had together should have been a carefree, happy interlude. The LCT was at sea, Mac was still sober and I had booked sufficient cargoes to keep the vessel going for three months. Also Perenna had at last got some good news about Tim. The nursing home had written to say that he was much improved, had quite suddenly thrown off his lethargy and was now getting about with the aid of a frame support. But, though we did our best, a sense of happy abandon was difficult to achieve, our mood overshadowed all the time by the knowledge that we were both of us putting everything into pawn for the sake of a single aged and rusting ship. We discussed it endlessly. We couldn't help ourselves.

To my surprise we were met at Heathrow by Tubby Sawyer. I didn't need to ask him why he was there. Almost the first thing he asked me, after I had introduced him to Perenna and she had gone to phone the nursing home, was whether there were any more sheets of the Solomons Seal, and when I told him all the rest were burned, he said, 'Marvellous! That's marvellous! You can tell me all about it as we drive down to the country. But first Josh wants to see you. He's made the sheet a separate lot and included it in the catalogue.'

Perenna came back radiant. 'I spoke to him. He even came to the phone himself. He's so much better.' Tubby was leading us out to the car park. 'I'm to ring up again this evening. They say I can see him tomorrow. And to think at one time I despaired of ever seeing him alive again!'

At his office in the Strand, Josh Keegan greeted Perenna as though she were some sort of princess. 'I have to tell you, dear lady, you've made my first big auction. I've had acceptances from just about every dealer of importance. I don't know what it's going to fetch, that little collection – your great-uncle's, isn't it? – but there's no doubt about the interest it has aroused. I'm serving champagne. There! I'm a business man, Miss Holland, and I don't do a silly, show-off thing like that unless I'm on to a winner. And we will have a bottle right now. It's the best thing after a long flight.' And as one of the girls came in with a bottle and four glasses on a plastic tray decorated with Penny Blacks under perspex, he turned to me and in quite a different voice said, 'Now, where is the sheet? I want to see it.'

While I was getting it out of my briefcase, he picked up a copy of the catalogue, which was lying on his desk, and held it up for us to see. 'There you are. I've taken a chance on what you told me on the phone from Sydney.' And there it was, on the cover – a reproduction of the two Solomons Seal proofs under the heading: THE INCREDIBLE HAS FINALLY HAPPENED, and then, below the facsimile of the proofs: *The only remaining sheet (sixty) of the blue Solomons Seal Ship Label is being delivered to the J. S. H. Keegan offices from Sydney in time for this unique auction offering – design collection, proofs, and resulting sheet of the*

most startling transplant ever perpetrated. 'There!' he exclaimed
again. 'You can't say I haven't done you proud, eh?'

It was Perenna who asked him what it was all about, but he
laughed and shook his head, looking like a learned professor in a
relaxed moment as he toasted her, raising his glass and smiling.
'Commander Sawyer – Tubby – he's driving you down to
Essex, I gather. He'll explain it.' And he added hastily, 'But I
think I must say this; the fact that it has aroused a great deal of
interest doesn't mean they'll bid the price up to a ridiculous
figure. They're business men, all of them, and a glass of
champagne or two won't stop them keeping their feet firmly on
the ground. We've got them to the auction. What happens then
. . .' He shrugged. 'Now, that sheet please.'

By then I had got it out of my briefcase and he stood looking
at it in silence for a long time, the magnifying glass screwed in
his eye. Then he shook his head. 'Pity! All those blotches, and
only part original gum. Pity it isn't mint. If it were in mint
condition . . .' He hesitated. 'But then, I don't know. Maybe
it's better like this. It's so obviously been in the heat and
humidity of the Solomons. Yes, better perhaps, more real
looking, more genuine. And a nice shade of blue, a genuine
Perkins Bacon blue.' And he winked at Tubby, laughing quietly
to himself. 'It really is quite humorous. He'll tell you. Very
funny indeed. Perkins Bacon, of all people. Such a stuffy,
banknote sort of outfit. Theft, forgery . . . you tell 'em, Tubby.
That's what I said to Mr Slingsby here when he came to see me
months ago, I said I wouldn't spoil it for you, so you tell 'em –
later.' He refilled Perenna's glass and said, 'You'll be attending
the auction, I hope, Miss Holland? It could make quite a bit,
that sheet.'

She glanced at me and I nodded. Nothing would stop me
being there after what he had said. £5,000 . . . if that sheet
made £5,000 I thought we could manage. That would about
double the total capital we could raise. It should just be enough.
'Yes,' she said. 'Thank you, Mr Keegan – I'll be there, listening
with bated breath.'

Tubby, with a proper sense of the dramatic, held off from

305

telling us until we had reached his house. He needed his books, he said, to explain it all properly, but that was just an excuse to get the story of the Solomons sheet out of me first. Once we were in his comfortable, black-beamed living room with a drink in our hands, and Perenna had phoned the nursing home again to arrange a time to visit her brother next day, he took down from his bookshelves the larger of the two blue-covered volumes of the *Perkins Bacon Records*. Standing there, holding it out to me and saying, 'Ever browsed through these books?', I knew we were in for one of his lectures. But this time, with so much at stake, he had my full attention.

'You should,' he said. 'To anybody interested in printing, any British collector, they're fascinating. They don't cover the GB printings – that was dealt with by Sir Edward Bacon himself in his *Line-Engraved Postage Stamps of Great Britain*. I've got a copy of the 1920 first edition here somewhere. But all the other printings . . . This first volume deals with British Colonial issues, the other one deals mainly with printings for foreign countries.' He put it down on his desk, turning to the end where he had marked it with a slip of paper. 'Here it is, page 509 – the last chapter. That'll give you the background.' And he turned it round so that we could read it. It was headed THE BEGINNING OF THE END:

The Home Government exercised the strictest supervision over the production of the postage stamps of Great Britain, but the Agents General of the Colonial Office, first George Baillie and then Edward Barnard, as also the Agents for the various Colonial Governments, in no way controlled the production of the stamps ordered. The quantity was merely checked on arrival in the Colony. Perkins, Bacon classed postage stamps in the same category as needle, soap and tobacco labels, and although the firm usually produced only the supply of stamps ordered, in some cases the quantity printed was greatly in excess of the number immediately required.

This method continued until Penrose G. Julyan was

appointed Agent General for Crown Colonies towards the end of 1858. The following documents make it clear that he considered that the dies, plates, paper and other material for the production of stamps ordered and paid for by his department should be under his control.

'It was back in 1851,' Tubby went on as we both looked up to indicate we had finished reading, 'that Perkins Bacon were invited to tender for New Brunswick and Nova Scotia labels. Up to then the only stamps they had printed were the GB Penny Blacks and Reds and the Twopenny Blues. During the next seven years they printed stamps for some twenty-five or thirty of our colonies, including Western Australia, and since they were really banknote printers, regarding stamps as much the same as tobacco labels, they probably were a little slack. On Julyan's appointment as Agent General a running battle began, de Worms recording pages of correspondence interspersed with his comments. What the Agent General was complaining about initially was late delivery, colour discrepancies and other technicalities. Then in April 1861 he discovered the printers had been approached by Ormond Hill on behalf of two or three stamp collecting friends of his and had released specimens of everything they had printed, six of each stamp. Julyan blew his top over that, switching his attack to security.'

He began refilling our glasses. 'Well, there you are, Roy. That's the background. But you'll never guess what it led to.' He was smiling, enjoying himself. 'Ormond Hill, you see, was Superintendent of Stamping at the Inland Revenue. He was also Rowland Hill's brother. In the circumstances Perkins Bacon's protest that they'd seen nothing wrong in sending him cancelled specimens seems reasonable enough. But Julyan took a different view. In the end, he demanded that all dies, plates, stocks of watermarked paper and stamps printed in excess of orders, everything in fact relating to each colony should be delivered to the Agent General's offices.' He put down the decanter and came back to the desk. 'Now turn to the end of the book, the last page but one. Perkins Bacon had argued that, if not stored by experts, the plates would rust or otherwise deteriorate. And they'd been fairly dilatory in meeting Julyan's demands.' He leaned forward, pointing halfway down page 525. 'Now read those two letters. Then you'll begin to understand why I wanted that collection, why the auctioning of the Solomons Seal die proofs is attracting so much attention.'

The letters read:-

Office of The Agents-General
for Crown Colonies,
6, Adelphi Terrace, London, W.C.
2nd June, 1862.

Gentn.

I beg to draw your attention to my letter of 12th ultimo requesting you to forward to this Office the Postage Stamps, Paper Moulds, and facsimiles in your possession, and shall be obliged by receiving a reply to that communication.

I am, Gentn,
Your obedient Servant.
P. G. Julyan.

Messrs Perkins, Bacon & Co.

This was the end of the struggle, but up to the last Perkins Bacon were able to produce an excuse, a strange admission for a firm of Security Printers.

69 Fleet Street, E.C.
June 3, 1862.

Dear Sir

We beg to apologize for the delay which has arisen in sending you the P Stamps, Envelopes & Moulds in our possession, but the loss of time on other matters forced upon us by the discovery of a thief in our employ, has occasioned the apparent neglect. We hope to be able to send all by the beginning of next week.

We are Dear Sir

yr obdt serts
   Per Proc. Perkins Bacon & Co.
    J. P. Bacon.

P. G. Julyan Esq.
Agent General.

I looked up at him, not entirely sure what it meant.

'That's all we know about it,' he said. 'We don't know who this thief was or what he stole. Maybe it was banknotes. Perkins Bacon were banknote and bond printers long before they started printing the Penny Blacks in 1840. If you look at the top of that page you'll see a letter from the Agent General referring to delivery of fifty facsimiles for preparing Natal Bonds. It could have been notes the thief stole or bonds or some of the excess sheets of printed stamps. As you will have gathered Perkins Bacon were in the habit of running off extra sheets. At their best they were very meticulous printers, always concerned about colour, which was sometimes liable to fading, and they found it difficult to get paper with the right depth of watermarking.' He glanced at Perenna. 'The watermark is achieved simply by a slight thinning of the paper. And gum – gum was a problem, too, particularly when the order was for the tropics.'

He hesitated, a significant pause as he turned back to me. 'On the other hand, it could be that the thief had been borrowing material for a friend of his, a would-be forger, say. He could have borrowed dies, plates even. Copies could have been made of them and then the borrowed dies or plates returned. It might have been going on for some time.'

I realized what he was suggesting then, that the use of Perkins Bacon dies and plates need not have been confined to just this one label.

'A nasty thought,' he murmured. 'It would raise doubts about the authenticity of some of the rarer mint condition stamps. After all, the mania for stamp collecting goes back even further than the Ormond Hill controversy.'

'But it would surely have been easier to steal printed stamps.'

'I don't think so. Perkins Bacon's security wouldn't have been that bad. Any stamps the thief could have got his hands on would have been from cancelled sheets. They would have been overprinted with the word SPECIMEN. But it's very doubtful whether they would have regarded Colonial stamp dies as objects liable to be stolen. Josh says security at Perkins Bacon was very strict for GB dies, but probably quite negligible as regards the dies for foreign and Colonial issues, and a print shop like theirs would have been full of stored plates and dies.'

But by then I had remembered something he had said to me here in this room, so long ago it seemed now. 'Hold on,' I said. 'The seal – that's from an early Newfoundland stamp. Didn't you say those stamps were printed in America?'

He nodded. 'That's quite correct. The 1865-70 set was a completely new issue printed by the American Bank Note Company of New York. The Seal-on-Icefloe die was used for the five cent brown, also for the two later issues, first in black, then in blue. After that the seal was re-designed and the printing switched to Montreal.'

'You're surely not suggesting there was a thief at the American printing house, too?'

'No, of course not.' He sounded quite shocked. 'The seal was designed by Jeens on the instructions of Perkins Bacon and the die was made by them here in London and sent across to New York. In addition to the seal, Perkins Bacon engraved and cast a die of the Jeens Codfish design. But that design was used for banknotes only. The Jeens codfish has a straight tail, the codfish on the two cent stamp a curled-up tail . The seal, on the other hand, was used for both banknotes and stamps.' He picked up the *Records* book, turned back the pages, and having found what he wanted, pushed it across to me again. 'There's de Worms' account of what happened.'

It was a long note headed SEAL AND CODFISH at the end of the chapter on Newfoundland, and a few pages back there were illustrations of both the seal and the codfish designs. It confirmed that the die for the Jeens seal had been engraved in London by Perkins Bacon, probably for the banknotes first, and this die was presumably stored there in 1862 when the thief was discovered.

I was still reading when Tubby went on, 'Well, there you are, Roy. That's the mystery that has puzzled all the experts ever since the results of Percy de Worms' painstaking research into the Perkins Bacon files and letter books was published. On the face of it these two volumes appear quite straightforward, a fascinating, but very mundane day-to-day record of correspondence, meticulously copied and filed away by the Perkins Bacon clerks. We know how many stamps they printed of every colonial issue, how many they dispatched, every detail of the advice they gave on design, paper, ink, gum, perforation, how the sheets were to be preserved in transit, all their costings. And then, in the midst of a protracted battle with the Crown Agents, that laconic statement that there was a thief in the print shop. No details, nothing – just the bald declaration to excuse a delay. As de Worms says, a strange admission for a firm of security printers to make.' And he added, raising his glass to us with a slightly wry smile, 'Here's to you and the Solomons Seal collection. We'll have some idea of what other experts think when the bidding starts on Thursday for Lots 96 and 97.'

The auction was still a full day away so that Perenna and I had two nights together at Great Park Hall before driving across country to Birmingham. Keegan had given us copies of the catalogue and I looked through it that evening. The first 72 lots were GBs, including some very good Seahorse issues and of course the block of four £5 orange. Lots 73-95 were collections of GB and Commonwealth stamps, then came the Carlos Holland ship label design collection followed by the Solomons Seal sheet. There were estimates of what each lot was expected to fetch, but not against ours, the blank at the right of the page making them very conspicuous. Presuming the lots were disposed of at about the same rate as at Harmers or other London auction houses, Lots 96 and 97 would come up sometime around 3-3.30 p.m. It was sensible timing since the wealthier dealers, who might have come down specially for those two lots, would have plenty of time for lunch, and if the Carlos

Holland collection fetched about £5,000, which is what he had originally suggested, how much, I wondered, would the full sheet fetch?

We talked it over during the evening meal, finally settling for a figure of £10,000 for the two lots. Afterwards I showed Perenna my own collection. Keegan, knowing roughly its contents and quality, had said it could fetch somewhere between £2,500 and £3,000 in view of the high prices now being paid at auction for second rate material. But sending it to auction meant a delay of three months at least, and the same was true probably of Perenna's woodcarvings. What we needed was cash, now.

Wednesday I spent a miserable day arranging the termination of my lease of the Hall and the sale of my boat, having first delivered Perenna to the nursing home near Colchester. When I picked her up in the evening our moods were very different – where I was depressed, she was buoyant, bubbling over with the extraordinary progress Tim had made. 'It's unbelievable. And not at all gradual. It happened just like that, quite suddenly he was a different man. They can't understand it. The Matron even phoned the doctor so that I could have a word with him. He couldn't explain it either.'

It had been one of those glorious, still October days and I still had the hood down, so that we had to shout at each other to make ourselves heard. 'So what do you think? That the curse was lifted?'

'Yes, of course. But I couldn't tell them that.'

'When did he snap out of it?'

'August 5. You're thinking of Hans, are you?'

I nodded, glancing at her quickly sitting there beside me with the red-orange hair blowing in the wind. I was remembering the log book and Jona's neat entry recording his death and the burial of his ashes in the cove to the north of Madehas. The date had been July 30.

'It wasn't Hans who put that curse on Tim,' she shouted into the wind. 'It was Sapuru. Sapuru died on August 5. Remember? And Tagup, remember what Tagup said that evening he came to say goodbye to us at the motel? He said

Sapuru could have been killed by an old curse, one that his weakened vitality was no longer able to resist. Tim spent weeks fashioning things out of driftwood and all sorts of bits and pieces I scavenged for him off the seashore. He'd sit for hours staring at them, his lips moving. He knows all about sorcery.' And she added, 'Funny, isn't it? Sapuru puts a curse on Tim after he'd discovered what the Co-operative was planning. But it wasn't strong enough and in the end it's Tim's curse that kills Sapuru.' She laughed, not humorously, but a little wildly. 'You don't believe me, do you? But it's true, I tell you. It fits. It must be true. The only possible explanation. Oh, my God – how little this civilized world remembers or understands.' She put her hand on my arm, a quick, urgent gesture. 'Forget it, will you. Please. You don't have to believe it. I see you don't, so forget it. And when you meet Tim, don't ever let him know what I said. Please.'

That night we fell into bed still arguing about the future and whether we shouldn't just give up, forget about the Holland Line and that battered old LCT. No point in destroying ourselves and losing everything we had for the sake of a ship. It was pride, too, of course. But I think both of us had by then come back down to earth and knew bloody well we couldn't make a go of it on the sort of capital we could hope to raise. The cost of ship repairs alone was such that the first major breakdown would see us broke.

We fell asleep in the end through sheer exhaustion. The next morning we were up with the dawn and on our way by eight. The auction was being held in what appeared to be an old corn exchange. Two doves, left over from a Fur and Feather Exhibition, fluttered noisily through the ornamental iron roof girders. I was tired, I had had no lunch and had lost my way on the outskirts of Birmingham. We were asked whether we would be bidding and when I said No we were ushered to the stairs leading to a sort of gallery. But then Keegan saw us and waved us over to seats on the right of the auctioneer's dais. 'Reserved specially for you, dear lady,' he said, taking Perenna by the arm. 'You see, hardly a seat left except those we have reserved.' He

313

seized two glasses of champagne from a loaded tray on a nearby table and thrust them into our hands. 'Drink that and don't worry. We'll be starting any minute now.'

There must have been about 150 to 200 seats in this partitioned-off section of the hall. All those who were bidding had been issued with a large numbered card and a drink. The murmur of conversation was already loud. We had only a few minutes to absorb the atmosphere of the place before the auction started, prompt on one-thirty. Keegan was sitting a few feet from us. The auctioneer, a smiling, slightly florid man with a habit of pushing his glasses up into his thick greying hair, was seated on a tall chair with a desk in front of him on the dais. 'Lot 1, gentlemen please – *ladies* and gentlemen.' He had a strong Midlands accent. 'Lot number one. I am bid eighty pounds – a hundred, a hundred and twenty, forty, sixty, two hundred – two twenty? Going for two hundred.'

I began timing the bids; just over a minute for each lot. Prices seemed high, but then I hadn't attended an auction for more than two years. By two o'clock every seat was taken and we had reached Lot 22. I was beginning to identify the more active dealers and the different nationalities – German, Japanese, French, Italian. Berners was there, sitting very still, not bidding. 'I can't follow it,' Perenna whispered. 'It's so fast. And I can't see who's bidding half the time. A nod or a slight lift of the pen – '

'Just concentrate on the final bid figure given by the auctioneer,' I said, showing her my catalogue with the final bid entered on the right. In almost every case it was way above the estimate, in the case of a perfect block of six 1870 Three Halfpence over twice the estimate.

'Why didn't he put an estimate against our lots?'

'He couldn't. It wouldn't have meant anything.'

One of Keegan's staff, an elderly woman, was standing close beside the auctioneer. For most of the lots it was she who started the bidding. Keegan had a big mail order business. So probably had the Birmingham firm he had taken over. These were the postal bids. We reached the first of the Wyon embossed of

1847-54, an assistant displaying a single Die 2 of the 1s. deep green in mint condition. 'Starting at four-fifty – five, five-fifty, six, six-fifty, seven – seven I'm bid, seven hundred, seven-twenty, thirty, forty, fifty, sixty – seven-sixty. At seven-sixty.' The little ivory knocker fell. I was waiting now for the £5 block. The estimate was £3,800. It made £5,500. 'Lot 73 – '. We had reached the collections. They went equally fast. At 3.27 the auctioneer announced, 'Now we come to the Lot many of you have been waiting for – Lot 96 . . .' And he glanced across at Keegan who jumped to his feet.

'I think I must say a word about this Lot and also the next Lot.' He was speaking quickly, a little nervously. 'We offer them both as seen, of course, with no guarantee that they are what we all think they probably are. I don't have to tell you – but I will – ' A ripple of laughter that was more a release of tension ran round the enclosed area – 'how Perkins Bacon excused their dilatoriness in delivering stamps and moulds to the Crown Agents. There was a thief in their print shop, and as Percy de Worms said, that's a strange admission for a firm of security printers accustomed to holding banknotes and bonds. They didn't say what he stole. It was an age when property was sacrosanct, so they probably felt they had said too much already. And now – ' He waved his hand to the assistant who was holding up the two albums, the vital one open at one of the die proof pages. 'Now, you have this Solomons Seal ship label. You have examined it and taken the same view that I have, that this is the Jeens engraving for the five cent Newfoundland popped into the 1854 Western Australia Penny Black frame – otherwise you wouldn't be here. May I simply add this, the Holland Line, for which that label was printed, is still in existence, and Miss Holland herself–is here today. The two albums, originally the property of her great-uncle, Carlos Holland, are now her property and she is selling them to provide additional finance for the Holland Line, which she now runs with her brother and Mr Slingsby here.'

He looked so distinguished, such a born showman as he asked us both to rise that I half expected them to applaud. And then he called for Lot 97 to be displayed, adding, 'And this is the finished label, printed from a plate cast from those borrowed dies – I say borrowed because we can't be sure the thief stole them. Also, we do not know what happened to the plate, whether it was thrown away or melted down, or even whether it is still in existence somewhere. I can, however, assure you that this is the only surviving sheet, the others having been destroyed in a fire at a house on the island of Madehas in the Solomons. Both Miss Holland and Mr Slingsby witnessed the fire and it was Mr Slingsby who managed to preserve this – the one and only sheet. And as regards the fire, its cause and what it destroyed, he has made a sworn statement before a judicial enquiry set up by the Papua New Guinea Government to probe the cause of an insurrection on the island of Bougainville. So, here you have it, something quite unique in the history of stamp collecting, something that can never be repeated, with a background story of extraordinary fascination and excitement, and all of it supported by sworn testimony, which is in itself most unusual. I now leave it to you to decide what these two valuable items are really worth. Thank you.' And he sat down abruptly, the silence suddenly electric.

'Lot 96.' The quiet monotone of the auctioneer's voice seemed very ordinary and matter-of-fact after Keegan's flamboyant piece of tub-thumping. 'The Carlos Holland design collection, including the die proofs at five thousand pounds I'm bid. Six anybody? Thank you, seven, eight, nine, ten – ten thousand – eleven, twelve.' The auction area was very still. One of the doves flew over with a noisy clapping of wings. 'Twelve thousand.'

'And a hundred.' It was Berners' voice and the bidding started again, going up first by hundreds, then by fifties. At thirteen thousand seven hundred there was a sudden silence in the hall, no movement anywhere. 'At thirteen seven hundred then . . .' The hand holding the knocker was poised for a moment, then fell. Carlos Holland's albums – the proof of his murder of a whole ship's company including his one-time partner – had gone to a German dealer.

'Lot 97. The only remaining sheet of the Solomons Seal blue ship label. Starting at five thousand pounds again – six, thank you, seven, eight, nine, ten . . .' And it didn't even pause there, it went straight on up to fifteen thousand in a matter of seconds. It was as though everybody there had been seized with a feverish determination to out-bid everyone else for this second item in the Holland collection. 'And five hundred? Thank you – sixteen, and five, seventeen – ' Suddenly there was a silence, a wary stillness where they all waited, wondering whether it was too much, the bidding too wild.

A card was raised. It was Berners. 'And two fifty,' he said in his sharp, rather acid voice.

'Seventeen two-fifty, seventeen thousand two fifty I'm bid . . .' The knocker was poised. 'Five hundred, seven-fifty, eighteen thousand – and a hundred? Thank you . . .' The bidding crawled upwards, then came to an abrupt halt with Berners jumping several hundreds to nineteen thousand. The auctioneer waited, his eyes searching the room. 'At nineteen thousand pounds – to Mr Berners.' The knocker fell, the sound of it sharp in the stillness.

Perenna and I looked at each other, smiling. In less than ten minutes, allowing for commission, everything, we had raised some £30,000. It was fantastic. Keegan was suddenly standing in front of Perenna congratulating her and she was so excited she leapt to her feet and threw her arms round his neck. We went out then to the little office at the back where Keegan produced a bottle of champagne. And after that we drove slowly back through the late afternoon sunshine, stopping at an hotel near Cambridge to linger over dinner, discussing all the various possibilities now that we had the capital we needed. It didn't matter now whether it was the PNG Government or a Lloyd's syndicate that finally established prior claim on the LCT, we could afford to buy it, and with the ship as security we could raise the loan as and when we needed it.

That evening, back at the Hall, we walked beside the moat hand-in-hand in the moonlight, still talking it over, dreaming dreams of ships and islands, a world I think we both knew in our hearts would take a deal of sweat and blood to translate into reality. And then Perenna suddenly stopped and turned and faced me, holding my hand tight as she said, 'That day you left Bougainville – remember what you said as you walked out to the plane?'

'What?' I asked, teasingly.

'You know bloody well.'

I nodded, laughing and lifting her off her feet, carrying her in my arms. 'For tonight,' I said, 'you'll just have to be content with this.' I was kissing her as I carried her across the threshold. 'Tomorrow I'll think about making an honest woman of you.' We were both of us laughing as we went up to bed. The moon was very bright that night and there were owls hooting – Bougainville and the Pacific seemed a million miles away, and so did reality. What fun life is! What a glorious everlasting struggle to survive and to build something worthwhile! And as I fell asleep I was thinking of that indomitable old man, her grandfather, sailing out in his canoe towards the horizon and infinity.

AUTHOR'S NOTE

I have written of Bougainville, and of the Highlands of Papua New Guinea, as I found them on the journeys my wife and I made in 1975. At that time the islands of Bougainville and Buka, though geographically a northern extension of the Solomon Islands group, were administratively a part of Papua New Guinea. This situation has not changed as a result of Independence, which came later that same year. But the form of the internal government has changed. Where, before Independence, the country was divided into thirteen administrative districts, there are now nineteen provincial governments, each with an elected chamber and a small staff. Port Moresby, the capital, also has provincial government status.

This change is political, intended to meet the needs of a people isolated by a very mountainous terrain and as a result speaking a multiplicity of languages and patois.

In the case of Bougainville District, the new title of North Solomons Provincial Government gives recognition to the anomalous geographical situation, but the islands have a record of civic disruption, on occasions quite serious, and whether this administrative change will be sufficient to satisfy the political aspirations of the people only time will tell. The training and educational facilities provided by the copper mine, the generally progressive policy of the management, will inevitably over the years have a profound effect upon an island people who, until World War II, had very little contact with the outside world. This, and the wealth generated locally, will make for a changing political climate, something the central government in Port Moresby, 600 miles away, will increasingly need to take into account.

Apart from the very considerable assistance I had in Bougainville and Buka, I was fortunate in the guidance I received with regard to the Solomons Seal ship label, and in particular the cancellations at Port Moresby and Cooktown. It was reasonable that I should turn to Tony Rigo de Righi, the Curator of the National Postal Museum, for expert vetting of the very strange idea I had conceived based on one of the letters in the Perkins Bacon Records, but then to find that he was a collector of Australian postal history – this was totally unexpected. There can be very few people in the world who could have given me, not only details of the date stamps used at Port Moresby and Cooktown, but also the mail boat routes and sailing schedules. I am deeply grateful for his help and for his kindness in checking the stamp references and putting me right on certain points. Also for the information that, quite fortuitously, a man named Solomon happened to be Postmaster in Newfoundland in the period immediately prior to the issue of the Seal-on-Icefloe stamp.

KERSEY, 1980